The Paris Understudy

The Paris Understudy

A Novel

Aurélie Thiele

alcove
press

Copyright © 2024 by Aurélie Thiele

Published in the United States by Alcove Press, an imprint of The Quick Brown Fox & Company LLC.

Alcove Press and its logo are trademarks of The Quick Brown Fox & Company LLC.

Library of Congress Catalog-in-Publication data available upon request.

ISBN (hardcover): 978–1–63910–861–9
ISBN (ebook): 978–1–63910–862–6

Cover design by Lynn Andreozzi

Printed in the United States.

www.alcovepress.com

Alcove Press
34 West 27th St., 10th Floor
New York, NY 10001

First Edition: September 2024

10 9 8 7 6 5 4 3 2 1

To my mother

Part One

One

Yvonne Chevallier stepped onto the stage of the National Conservatory of Music as if she weren't afraid. The audience, composed mostly of her competitors' relatives, greeted her with indifferent applause. Soon they were fanning themselves with the program again, slumped in threadbare seats. The one burst of clapping surely came from Yvonne's husband and son. She took her place at the edge of the wooden planks, chin high, shoulders back, and turned toward the first row, where the judges sat. Beads of sweat ran down her neck. For a moment, she forgot to breathe. At last, she nodded to Madeleine Moreau, the most famous soprano in Paris, who'd won the same contest two decades earlier and served as that year's judge of honor. Madeleine met Yvonne's gaze but didn't nod back.

Yvonne pressed her hands against the sequins of her sleeveless dress. She'd bought the Elsa Schiaparelli gown in a consignment store on the rue Vieille du Temple. Cut low in front and glittering under the spotlights, the blue dress had raised eyebrows among the other female contestants. They would've ruined their reputation in that dress, but at thirty-two Yvonne was older, more respectable too, because she was married, and she could wear clothes they couldn't. The gown matched the color of her eyes and brought out the golden shade of her hair. She wasn't above trying to impress the judges by every means.

Madeleine tapped the lead of her pencil onto her notebook. She was more heavyset than Yvonne, always had been, even before the trips to sing all over Europe—London, Milan, Vienna—had taken their toll.

3

She claimed to have turned forty-eight that spring, but it was an open secret that she was fifty-four and dyed her hair raven black every other week. Her Vionnet dress in red silk chiffon stretched awkwardly across the bulge of her hips. Her jawline sagged. She enjoyed enough fame, though, that opera singers who believed she could help them claimed to see remnants of great beauty in her. Her most striking feature was her eyes, piercing like those of a falcon.

Yvonne searched for Paul and Jules in the few seconds she had before the crowd became impatient. She found them on tattered armchairs eight rows behind the judges, at the exact spot Yvonne had told them to sit, where her voice would best merge with the music. Paul, a mop of hair falling over his face, wore a wrinkled linen suit that hung loosely over his shoulders. He looked anxious about Yvonne's performance. Both Yvonne and he knew much depended on it. Jules, seemingly older than fifteen in the Sunday clothes Yvonne had ironed for him, chewed the tip of a pencil. It relieved Yvonne to find him. Locating her son in the room would bring her good luck, she was certain of it. She dabbed a handkerchief on the back of her neck and gave her signal to the accompanist.

Yvonne had chosen the "Vissi d'arte" aria in *Tosca*. She loved picturing herself as a famous singer who anguishes about the fate of her beloved after a dictator's henchmen has captured him and wails that God has abandoned her. Opera wasn't known for minor story lines, which suited Yvonne perfectly. Her life had been insignificant enough. She enjoyed imagining herself in someone else's skin. Audience members, sitting up after her first bar of music, leaned forward in their seats. Yvonne's voice rose in the hall and wrapped itself around them like a spell. She lived for moments like these: for the way the energy in a room shifted when she shared her gift with the world, the feeling she was doing what she'd been put on earth to accomplish, and the certainty no one could replace her if she remained silent. While the other contestants had only sung, she acted too—shook her head in sorrow, paced the floor, conjured a memory with a sweep of her arm. Most opera singers demonstrated little acting skill, but Yvonne became Tosca in that instant. She hoped—no, she was sure—spectators who'd come only to support their relatives forgot they sat in a hot, dreary room near the Gare Saint-Lazare and found themselves transported into other worlds thanks to her artistry.

The applause thrilled Yvonne when she finished singing. She'd expected her competitors' relatives to keep their acclaim for their family member, and Paul and Jules couldn't make that much noise on their own. Yvonne bowed left and right, grateful the crowd had appreciated her aria, and struggled not to lose her balance in the emotion of the moment.

What a pity the little ladies of Dijon didn't attend—those women who'd ostracized Yvonne's parents after they'd counted the months between her wedding and the birth of her son. Seven months. God help us, the end of civilization is coming nigh. But once Yvonne became a famous opera singer, the mayor would host a luncheon for her at the Grand Hôtel La Cloche and the notables' wives would have to sing her praises twenty different ways before she sat down next to them.

At last, Yvonne saluted the judges. She searched Madeleine's face for a hint of approval but didn't find any. Her smile vanished. She stared at Madeleine, almost imploring. Madeleine waved the back of her hand at Yvonne with the nonchalance of a queen dismissing a subject.

❦

The judges gathered in the reading room on the second floor, around a large mahogany table so polished they could see their faces in it. One floor down, winners from previous years entertained the crowd while the jury deliberated. Madeleine looked around and decided that nothing had changed since she had been a student.

The jury president, Ferdinand, a potbellied man who chaired the Conservatory's voice department, tapped his pen against the sheet of paper where he had scribbled down notes. "Among the female contestants, Yvonne Chevallier stood out."

Madeleine, at the other end of the shiny table, gave him a long, cold stare. She had hoped he would notice anyone but that woman.

"Yvonne shone," Charles-Antoine agreed. He was seated between the two of them, exactly in the middle. "I can't remember a more promising student since our dear Madeleine herself graduated."

Madeleine snapped her fan open. "Yvonne Chevallier? That's out of the question." She refused to give the prize to someone who had sung her own signature piece. It would be too obvious a passing of the baton. "I found her singing quite ordinary for a Conservatory student."

"Her high notes were breathtaking," Charles-Antoine said.

Madeleine fanned herself harder. The red fan showed drawings of roses in black-and-white ink, their thorns as lifelike as their petals. An admirer had bought it for her in Ceylon, years earlier, when men still professed their undying love for her. They knew she was married to Henri Moreau, the conductor of the Paris Opera Orchestra, but bought her gifts nonetheless.

"We don't give out the award based on effort or potential," Madeleine said. She agreed with Charles-Antoine about Yvonne's high notes but would never admit it. Soon Madeleine would no longer reach these notes, and it bothered her that an unknown performer would sing her signature role better. How rude of Yvonne to hint that Madeleine's reign over the Paris Opera would shortly be over. How presumptuous too.

Madeleine leaned back into the armchair at one end of the table, as if she presided over the jury. Ferdinand was reading over his notes, perhaps looking for the name of another competitor, but Charles-Antoine looked disappointed by Madeleine's antics. His cane rested against the armrest of his chair. His rimless glasses and imperial beard, reminiscent of Napoléon III, gave him a distinguished air. He had taught Madeleine at the Conservatory, and his teaching had made her career possible, although she did not like to admit she owed him her fame. But she was fond of him. He had been kind to her when no one else was, before she had amounted to anything.

Bookshelves around the judges overflowed with symphonic scores and musicians' biographies, most of which Madeleine had read when she was a student. She liked to tease her husband Henri, who conducted the orchestra, with her knowledge of obscure operas and long-forgotten composers, daring him to prove himself more learned than she was.

"Yvonne shows the biggest talent," Charles-Antoine said.

If the little striver had sung a different aria, one that was not part of Madeleine's repertory, Madeleine would have given her the prize without a second thought. But she could not let go of the slight—a perfect unknown, in that tawdry dress, demonstrating that she could sing Madeleine's aria better than the star.

"Catherine Desmarets impressed me most," she said. She didn't care for Catherine either, but she had guessed from her attire, especially the hat with an ostrich feather, that she came from a wealthy family, and people who had money quickly renounced any career in the theater, scalded by the rejections and the long hours.

"Opera is only a pastime for her," Charles-Antoine said—Madeleine's point exactly. "Yvonne has more hunger for it."

"I wish I could be more positive about her," Madeleine said. "I can tell she put her heart into it. But the aria proved too difficult for her. The Paris Opera has standards I care to uphold. I can't send that woman over and cover myself with ridicule in front of Emile and the rest of the management." She folded her hands. That settled the debate, didn't it?

"She drew the best reaction from the crowd," Ferdinand said in a small voice. "People would come to hear her sing."

"You mean she would sell tickets," Madeleine said, her voice so high-pitched that Ferdinand visibly shrank in his seat. "Is that what you teach the girls these days? Forget about craft, forget about art, if you can please people who don't even know what E-flat sounds like?"

"Whatever little extra something brings success to a singer, Yvonne has it," Charles-Antoine said.

"This is the silliest comment I've ever heard, and I've had admirers tell me I should sing Donizetti," Madeleine said. She pointed her fan at Charles-Antoine like a blade. "Yvonne Chevallier doesn't belong in the opera world to begin with. She's too old to make a debut, and not half as glamorous as she thinks she is. I refuse to waste the award on her."

Today, at least, the last word was still hers.

The contestants lined up along the edge of the pit. Male and female students stood shoulder to shoulder in their best clothes, their faces tense with the desire to win. A young man who'd sung Rossini clicked his tongue. His neighbor tapped on the planks with the tip of his shoes. Hadn't he chosen Bellini? Yvonne had already forgotten his performance. She picked a good spot, toward the center of the stage, although her neighbor, a bass-baritone twice as large as she was, kept trying to stand in front of her. She tugged on the sequins of her dress, glittering under the lights. Was she imagining things, or were spectators' gazes lingering on her? She must be their favorite to win.

Ferdinand adjusted his monocle. "I will now let our esteemed graduate, respected colleague, and grande dame of the Paris Opera, Madeleine Moreau, read the results."

Madeleine marked a beat under the spotlight, enjoying the audience's applause before she opened the envelope. Yvonne's stomach clenched. *Make it be me*, she thought. *Please make it be me.*

"In the women's category, after extensive deliberations, the jury reached a unanimous verdict," Madeleine said.

Yvonne struggled to keep her composure. Surely, Charles-Antoine had voted for her. He always praised her singing. A unanimous verdict, then, meant she'd won over Ferdinand and, most importantly, Madeleine Moreau herself. She leaned forward, ready to step out of the line to shake Madeleine's hand. Her mother's disappointment when Jules had been born so soon after the wedding, the drudgery of Yvonne's work as a secretary in Dijon, the struggle to practice arias in her scant free time, the fear she'd never gain a foothold in the opera world—all that receded in the distance. The gamble to study at the Conservatory had paid off. She'd wrestle respect from anyone who'd ever doubted she belonged. She'd sing at the Paris Opera, on the biggest stage in France.

"And the winner this year is"—Madeleine graced the audience with her most engaging smile—"for her extraordinary performance as Gilda in *Rigoletto*, Catherine Desmarets."

Yvonne put a foot forward and then stepped back as if the boards were on fire. In the row of contestants, Catherine covered her mouth with her hands. The ostrich feather on her hat bobbled up and down. A dozen audience members clapped heartily, seated next to each other in Lucien Lelong afternoon dresses and Cristóbal Balenciaga business suits. The Desmarets clan, apparently. The rest of the spectators hesitated and then followed suit. They'd been quick to cheer for Yvonne but turned their back on her just as fast. She'd languish among the other contestants: the leftovers, the not-good-enoughs. Maybe she didn't deserve to become an opera singer after all.

☙❧

Crouched on the hardwood floor of the empty rehearsal room, Yvonne pressed her back against a wall in need of a new coat of paint. Her son Jules was hunched next to her, thumbs pulling down the pockets of his Sunday suit. It was already getting too short for him, but she had no money to buy him a new one, no money to buy him anything.

"I bet her old man bought off the jury," Jules said of Catherine. "Her folks looked like they're dripping with cash."

Yvonne wanted to believe him. It would hurt a lot less than thinking she wasn't good enough.

"That's the high society for you," Paul said from the bench in front of the baby grand.

Yvonne wished he'd looked more upset on her behalf. He was saying all the right words, but he sounded like he was commenting on one of those movies they liked to go and watch at the Grand Rex when their landlord had yet again cut off the heat for nonpayment. Paul seemed almost relieved, though, perhaps because the outcome of the voice contest gave him permission not to aim high.

Paul pressed the palm of his hands over the keyboard. "Thieves and rascals. All of them."

Yvonne pushed a strand of hair away from her eyes. It'd be much harder for her to get cast without that win.

"We need to make a plan," Paul said. "I got a call from the bank again."

He'd lost his job as a bookstore clerk at the end of April. The economy was worsening by the week and the manager couldn't keep him.

Now Yvonne had no prospect for work either. Oh, they made the perfect couple, the two of them together.

Yvonne wrapped her arms around her knees. The sequins rubbed against her chin and the undersides of her arms. How dumb not to bring a change of clothes.

"We could go back to Dijon," Paul said.

Dijon, like the mustard. Dijon, like the provinces that didn't understand the first thing about good music or real talent.

"Or we could stay here," Yvonne said.

"I'll find a job there more easily," Paul said.

He no longer spoke of publishing another collection of poems. The critics had praised him when the Gallimard publishing house released his first book, but the next one had sold few copies. Most critics hadn't even reviewed it. Paul stopped writing. Why bother if his poems couldn't find a public? Perhaps that was why he so disliked Paris, despite the cafés of Montparnasse chock-full of like-minded artists. Dijon reminded Yvonne of the small-mindedness of her parents' neighbors and customers, but the city had witnessed Paul's former glory. He'd succeeded as a poet there, not in Paris.

"We should wait another year," Yvonne said.

"Even if I find a job tutoring for the baccalaureate exam, Jules takes a paper route, and you give music lessons, Paris is far too expensive," Paul said.

Embers of rage flared in Yvonne's heart. "I'm not talking about music lessons. I'm talking about auditions, small parts, any opportunity for me to be onstage. I only need one aria. I'll convince a director in eight bars, if he doesn't have more time."

The rectangle of light from the window had dimmed at her feet. Soon the sun would disappear behind the rooftops on the rue de Madrid. Paris was where successful people lived.

"You can sing in Dijon," Paul said. "I'll study for the teaching certificate. We'll start over."

Jules pulled on the button of his jacket until the thread broke. Paul rose from the piano bench and wrapped his arm around the boy's shoulders.

"I can't leave. That'd mark me as finished." Yvonne dug her compact out of her purse and freshened her makeup. "Let's go to the reception. There's nothing at home for dinner."

☙❧

On the Conservatory's first floor, in the main gallery decorated with portraits of well-known graduates, contestants swarmed around Madeleine while she struck a pose next to a large photograph of herself. It showed her with a shield, spear, and horned helmet, singing Brünnhilde in a 1928 production of *Die Walküre* by Richard Wagner. Her voice now wasn't the same as it had been in her prime, but she hoped most audience members couldn't tell the difference, nor Conservatory students. They vied for her attention, eager to receive a word of wisdom from the star. Catherine wedged herself by her side while Madeleine waved a flute of Veuve Durand at her—bad champagne, but champagne nonetheless—and regaled her audience with stories about rehearsals and performances, embroidering as she went.

The woman who had sung Tosca in that tawdry blue dress swallowed amuse-gueules by the buffet. Yvonne. She ate at frightening speed. Next to her, a silly-looking man with a big mop of hair and a gangly teenage boy stuffed themselves with cheese and salami, the exact same forlorn expression on their faces. It surprised Madeleine that Yvonne had a son that old. She sensed a story there, a weakness, but mostly it bothered her that Yvonne had a child when she did not. What Madeleine had instead was a succession of miscarriages and a stillbirth at twenty-five weeks. The doctor had said the baby was a boy. Her husband, Henri, had hoped for one.

The young tenor and baritone who had tied as winners among the men now argued about their favorite role of Madeleine's. Norma or Maria Stuarda? Each rattled off arias that Madeleine had impressed them in. The tenor, Guillaume, had sung Faust brilliantly, but really Madeleine had favored him because his curly brown hair and square jaw gave him the air of a leading man. She was determined to sing opposite him. Younger singers always forgave the flaws in her technique because her fame impressed them so. Charles-Antoine, contradicting her again, had insisted that the baritone—Édouard—deserved the prize more. He looked like he would not side with her twice. Madeleine had offered to have two male winners to make sure Guillaume won.

Madeleine took a sip of champagne. "My favorite role is Isolde, naturally."

Both Guillaume and Édouard appeared stricken that the idea hadn't occurred to them. *Tristan und Isolde*. Of course she would excel in that.

Charles-Antoine ambled from group to group. Students' faces lit up when he exchanged words with them. He must be praising their performance. Would he relay what had happened in the meeting room on the second floor—that Madeleine alone deserved the blame for Yvonne losing the contest? He had changed his vote only after she threatened to block the casting of his students at the Paris Opera. But he had changed his vote, after all, and would not want Yvonne to know that.

More students elbowed each other to grab a spot near Madeleine: a boy who had belted out Eugene Onegin, a girl who had ridiculed herself as Mimi in *La bohème*. Catherine stuck to her place on Madeleine's right, as if she were her designated heir. Madeleine hoped that Catherine would get married soon and renounce the stage to care for her children.

The ostrich feather on Catherine's hat bounced up and down when she spoke. "Richard Wagner? Wouldn't you prefer a composer who is"—she hesitated—"not German?"

Madeleine took another sip of champagne. Naturally, she wished Wagner had not been German. What a silly question, after the Great War. But he used leitmotivs, orchestration, harmonies, chromaticism in revolutionary ways, and he had been dead since 1883.

"His music speaks to the soul," Madeleine said.

The students had drawn too close to her. Madeleine inched backward. She disliked it when admirers touched her, unless they were handsome or powerful men. "And he writes the most difficult roles. I'm not in this business to bother with the easy parts." She tapped her fan against the foot of Catherine's glass and widened her smile. "Only a handful of us can sing Isolde without ruining our voice. Don't try until much later, if you try at all."

Catherine's eyes narrowed. Madeleine made a wider smile.

"But the Germans have runaway inflation and homeless men at every corner now," Édouard said. "War veterans, I've heard. Besides, that Hitler sounds like a madman."

Madeleine glared at him over the rim of her glass. "I didn't say I felt any enthusiasm for Germany—only Wagner. Whatever has happened to the country since his passing, he can hardly be held responsible for it."

An awkward silence fell over the group.

Madeleine raised her flute higher. "My brother fought in the Great War. Died in it too. When he was alive, Wagner was his favorite composer."

At Alexandre's funeral back in 1916, their parents had played the opening of *Parsifal* in the church. He was now buried in the cemetery outside Verdun. Henri, once drafted, had never left Paris. A friend of the Moreau family had discovered an urgent need for him to push papers at the War Ministry.

Madeleine slapped a smile on her face. "Thankfully, we won the war."

A short man waded through the crowd, pulling on a moustache trimmed like a circus ringmaster's. That was Alphonse, the school director. "My dear Madeleine! I just got off the phone with Hector. You were right, the role of Don Ottavio hasn't been cast. Hector is thrilled to take Guillaume on." Alphonse pumped Guillaume's arm up and down. "Welcome to the Paris Opera house, son! How exciting for you to make your debut with Madeleine."

Guillaume smiled with the content air of someone sure that life would go his way.

Alphonse dropped Guillaume's hand as fast as he had seized it and pulled Madeleine aside. "I still can't believe what happened with the women. It's such a shame Yvonne lost. The only one worthy of you! I hope you're not upset. Teachers can be so detached from the professional world."

Madeleine freed her arm. "I'm fuming indeed, but not for that reason. You could've asked me to sing. What party doesn't have any music?"

Catherine's voice rose behind their backs. "Sing, please, sing."

Madeleine liked her more now.

Alphonse made a little bow. "I hadn't dared to hope you'd agree, Madeleine dear, but of course we'd be delighted."

Madeleine strode toward the grand piano and snapped her fingers at Charles-Antoine. He gave her a tired look from across the room. Perhaps he guessed what she was planning to do. After a moment he placed his empty plate on a tray and shuffled toward the piano bench. His cane smacked the stone tiles like a wordless rebuke.

The contestants and their relatives gathered around the Érard piano. Yvonne followed them, arms folded across her chest.

"Tosca," Madeleine told Charles-Antoine, her eyes cold. "'Vissi d'arte.'"

⌒～⌒

The room erupted into applause after Madeleine hit the last note. She searched for Yvonne in the crowd, keen to check that she had made her point, but the little striver was gone.

Madeleine had received all the acclaim she could hope for and drunk enough bad champagne for the day; she saw no reason to linger. Alphonse cleared a path for her to the stairwell, waving students away and babbling into her ear about a master class that he would love to organize for her. The two of them strode down the stairs, through the corridor, out of the Conservatory. It was a warm evening. Across the rue de Madrid, a sign in a window advertised rooms for rent. Storefronts were covered in grime. A black Peugeot idled near a no-parking sign. Madeleine's chauffeur, Gustave, always showed up early.

Yvonne was waiting by the lamppost next to the car, wrapped in a man's jacket. Madeleine would have picked the same spot if it had been up to her. She had never seen a circle of light she did not yearn to stand in. The man with the shabby suit sat at the bus stop in his shirtsleeves, legs outstretched, while the gangly boy looked at a billboard on the side

of the shelter. Its advertisement for the Grandes Fêtes de Paris promised rowing races on the Seine, marching bands playing military airs,
and even an aerial demonstration by the national flying squadron, the
Patrouille Acrobatique. Envy tugged at Madeleine's heart. She would
have brought her boy to all those fairs. She would have purchased a
plane for him if he had shown any interest.

Yvonne had noticed her, and ventured closer. "I wonder if you have
any advice for me."

Wonder *whether*, Madeleine thought.

"Your singing is so inspiring," Yvonne said. "I've attended every production of yours since I arrived in Paris."

"Everyone needs to develop their own style," Madeleine said. "You
have to rely on yourself."

Alphonse opened the door to the Peugeot. In front of the steering
wheel, Gustave adjusted his cap.

Yvonne stepped in front of Madeleine. "But what can I do to get
cast?"

Madeleine hesitated. In two or three years, maybe four, opera connoisseurs would lament her declining voice. She didn't need to hasten
her own demise by training her replacement. But she could get ahead
of this and keep Yvonne below her, where she belonged. After all, it
might be her last opportunity to surround herself with younger, admiring musicians who put her on a pedestal and made her forget she stood
at the twilight of her career. "You could understudy me, if you'd like.
I'll be singing Pénélope at the Opéra-Comique in the spring."

Yvonne's eyes glimmered with delight. She squeezed Madeleine's
hand. Madeleine squirmed.

"It'd be an honor," Yvonne said. "I'd make you proud, if the need
came."

Madeleine slid onto the back seat of the car. She had the health of
a workhorse and would never allow Yvonne to upstage her. But worse
things happened than being adored by the next generation of singers.

She tapped her fan against Yvonne's arm. "What a shame you didn't
win."

Two

Two years later
September 1938

Yvonne dashed toward the Palais Garnier with a box of macarons topped by a pretty bow. The back of the opera house faced the Galeries Lafayette department store—away from the opulence of the square in front of the building, the gilded statues on top of it, the nearby four-star Royal Opéra hotel and the art-deco Grand Café Capucines. Yvonne had been working at the opera house for two years now, but the sight still amazed her when she approached the building. She'd come a long way from being a seventeen-year-old mother in Dijon. All around her, Parisians trudged, head down, along the boulevard Haussmann. Dark clouds filled the sky. How easy to ruminate on the direction the country was taking on a day like this.

Like everyone else, Yvonne worried about the instability of the government and the general strikes protesting the rollback of social laws passed by the Popular Front, on the grounds that the country had to get ready for war, but the pride of entering the opera house through the artists' door overshadowed her fears for France. She'd felt shy around her teachers at the Conservatory, all so knowledgeable, and awkward around her fellow students, who were much younger than she was, but she'd finally found the place where she belonged, and the politicians would handle the turmoil that'd befallen the country. It couldn't last long.

Charles-Antoine already stood by the door, leaning on his cane. Yvonne had hoped he'd be late. She felt sorry she hadn't written or called him more—she'd sent him a card the first Christmas after she'd gradu-ated from the Conservatory, and she'd meant to invite him to lunch so she could ask for his advice about her stalled career, but then it'd embar-rassed her she hadn't made her debut yet and she'd let their correspon-dence dwindle. Yvonne remained grateful for what Charles-Antoine had taught her, but these days she rarely thought of him. Her future belonged with Madeleine.

"I went to fetch macarons for our star," Yvonne said. "She loves eat-ing them on her breaks."

Charles-Antoine examined Yvonne from her hat to her shoes. She glanced down but couldn't see a stain on her salmon-colored dress. She would've picked a different color for her clothing—pink didn't go with her hair—but nothing else had been available at the consignment store, and Yvonne liked how smooth the fabric felt on her skin. It did irritate her that at age thirty-four she still had to buy clothes secondhand to wear what she liked best, but hopefully she wouldn't have to wait much longer to purchase them new.

Jules often said that in that pink dress with the matching scarf, she reminded him of a bonbon from the Maison Pécou, and she knew him well enough to know it wasn't a compliment, but that was all her finances could buy her. What a blessing that he'd stayed with her after the divorce. Paul had decided to return to Dijon, with or without her, and as it'd turned out, it'd been without. Yvonne had worked too hard on her singing to leave Paris now. Paul had requested full custody of Jules because he earned a higher income as a high school teacher than Yvonne as an understudy at the opera house, but the judge had sided with her: children belonged with their mother. Yvonne didn't know how she would've coped if she'd been left alone in Paris without her son. But now that Jules had stayed with her, the thought of not being a good example for him terrified her. Any failure on her part would make Jules conclude he didn't have much talent either. He'd give up on his dreams of becoming a pianist. This had to be avoided at all costs.

"You shouldn't be running errands for Madeleine," Charles-Antoine said.

As if Yvonne didn't know that.

"She's come to rely on me." Yvonne pretended to be flattered, although it only meant Madeleine found her to be a good personal assistant. "Sometimes she gives me extra advice to return the favor." The advice Madeleine provided seemed rather unimportant, but maybe Yvonne didn't understand the gems she had in front of her.

She didn't add she only felt a genuine part of the Paris Opera family when she stood at Madeleine's side. Madeleine was the matriarch of the clan, and a lot of artists approached her whom Yvonne would never have met otherwise. She liked riding on Madeleine's coattails.

Charles-Antoine's cane beat the black-and-white tiles inside the opera house. "What can I hope to see you in this year?"

"A recital in Tours in November, if you don't mind taking the train," Yvonne said. She wasn't looking forward to leaving Paris for even one day, but she needed the experience. "They invited me back after my performance in *Pelléas et Mélisande* last year."

"You must have dazzled them."

"The local critics praised me to the skies, but they don't have much to compare." Yvonne tried not to wrinkle her nose. "With the bad habits I learned before I moved to Paris, I've had more of a slow start than most."

Charles-Antoine paused in the lobby to admire the gilded mirrors, elaborate lamp holders, and touches of gold over the doorframes. Yvonne waited until he'd caught up with her. Two stagehands bounded out of the stairwell, arguing about the set change before *Tosca*'s third act. Yvonne hoped they'd nod at her in front of Charles-Antoine, but they ignored her. She wasn't completely sure they'd noticed she worked there.

"You sang beautifully at the Conservatory," Charles-Antoine said.

"Everyone here graduated at the top of their class," Yvonne said.

"Don't stay an understudy too long."

As if she'd chosen that fate.

"It's like a game of dominoes," Yvonne said. "I must align them well so that they all fall after I knock out the first one. Once I debut in

Paris, I'll need a lot of leading roles in a row. Word of mouth. Praise from the critics. And in the end, full houses and, for my son, the best of everything."

"So you still have your ambition," Charles-Antoine said.

Yvonne avoided looking at her reflection in the full-length mirror near the staircase. Of course she still had her ambition, but she had dreadfully little to show for it.

"I'm blessed that Madeleine took me under her wing," she said.

That wasn't a complete lie. They shared many happy moments together. Madeleine loved it when Yvonne shared the gossip swirling about backstage: the tenor singing Rigoletto caught in the company of a choir girl, his pants around his ankles, or the bass singing Don Bartolo, who'd slept through a dress rehearsal, found snoring and cradling a bottle of vermouth. Those anecdotes entertained Madeleine, although Yvonne wished she'd show more interest in her as a singer. But she took plenty of notes about the star's singing. That'd pay off when Yvonne finally became a principal, whether Madeleine wanted to help her or not.

"I'll be ready for the limelight soon. And"—Yvonne beamed—"she makes sure Emile treats me like royalty. No other understudy gets more money."

Charles-Antoine pinched his lips tightly together. Yvonne tugged on her scarf. Of course she should have kept her sight on the principal roles. Didn't he think she knew that? Getting crumbs as an understudy should've been beneath her, yet she needed to pay her bills.

Yvonne strode alongside him through narrow hallways, past closed doors and peeling wallpaper, under light fixtures from the nineteenth century that lent the maze of corridors an air of faded grandeur. A lady wearing a large hat and a blouse with flounced sleeves glided toward them from the opposite direction. The best mezzo-soprano in the house, journalists agreed. Yvonne nodded a greeting at her, but the mezzo-soprano kept staring ahead. Principals never acknowledged understudies, although they expected understudies to acknowledge them.

The schedule for the rehearsal rooms was tacked on a bulletin board. A name, written in red, popped up again and again: Madeleine's.

"Do the rest of you rehearse at night?" Charles-Antoine asked.

"She doesn't take her success for granted," Yvonne said. She liked that about Madeleine, and not much else.

"I thought of you when I heard she was preparing Tosca," Charles-Antoine said. "I would have predicted you would be Tosca by now."

Yvonne tapped her pink shoes against the tiles. "The crowds come for Madeleine. If she doesn't sing, people won't splurge for tickets. And her health's been very robust all the time I've worked with her."

The box of macarons dangled from the tips of her fingers, dangerously close to being dropped to the floor. Yvonne refused to talk about the hours she'd spent learning the notes, everything memorized before the first rehearsal. She wouldn't talk about the phone calls she'd made home to tell Jules he might hurry to the theater for her debut—*Madeleine says she's falling ill*—until she'd caught the sadness in his voice as he tried to moderate her enthusiasm. She refused to talk about the night following the last performance of each opera, when the cast gathered at Le Lapin Mangeur to celebrate the end of a good run and Yvonne, before joining them, rubbed her hand against Madeleine's dresses in the costume shop, dresses that would soon be packed away to storage and Yvonne would never wear.

"Maybe you can create other opportunities for yourself," Charles-Antoine said.

"The world isn't exactly knocking on my door."

Once, Yvonne had asked Madeleine to recommend her for the role of Olympia in *Tales of Hoffmann*. Madeleine had shaken her head in dismay: she'd never tell casting directors whom to hire, even to help someone she was fond of. Yvonne agonized that directors would reject her, one after the other—the second best among hundreds of applicants but never the best, just like at the Conservatory—and then she'd be left out on the street because Madeleine wouldn't hire her back.

"It would be a mistake for you to give up just now," Charles-Antoine said. But what made him so sure? He didn't know her much.

Yvonne reached a metal door. Behind it stretched the largest stage in all of Europe, with enough space to fit four hundred and fifty artists on the planks and two thousand spectators in the seats. Her stomach tied itself in knots every time she placed her hand on the doorknob.

"Let me bring her the macarons," Yvonne said to Charles-Antoine. "Would you like to listen to her? She's rehearsing 'Qual occhio.'"

Charles-Antoine didn't move.

"You should hear the way she sings it," Yvonne said, because she wanted him to follow her backstage. She couldn't do anything else for him, but she could give him that access.

She disappeared in the wings, holding the box with both hands in front of her, as if she were about to make an offering at the feet of a goddess. It was overly theatrical, but Madeleine liked it when she behaved that way. Charles-Antoine traipsed behind her. Yvonne could hear his cane smacking the tiles. Visitors weren't normally allowed backstage during rehearsals, but Yvonne had quickly figured out she'd never get punished for bringing Madeleine more spectators.

After she handed off the pastries, she and Charles-Antoine wedged themselves between wooden panels on the side next to pipes and electrical cables. Madeleine, standing onstage in a burgundy dress, chewed one of the coconut macarons Yvonne had bought. At the front of the parterre, the director—a short, wiry man with round glasses— shared words of advice that Yvonne couldn't decipher. Madeleine's husband, Henri, waved his wand out of the orchestra pit while he made his point. He cultivated a resemblance to Clark Gable, his hair slicked back, his moustache trim. For a while, Madeleine only ate and listened. But as soon as she spoke, both the director and Henri nodded their assent. She was still the uncontested queen of the opera house, for now.

"No one dares contradict her," Yvonne said quietly. She was tempted to ask Charles-Antoine what Madeleine had been like as a student, when she'd sung Tosca's "Vissi d'arte" at the voice competition, but she decided not to. Madeleine wouldn't stay much longer at the Paris Opera. Henri could conduct for twenty more years, but before long,

Madeleine would have to stay at home and reminisce over her glory days. Then Yvonne would get cast in her roles, and more.

Madeleine and the tenor who sang Cavaradossi returned to their spots. Yvonne disliked seeing Guillaume next to Madeleine. She'd studied with him at the Conservatory. Now he was onstage, and she wasn't.

The musicians played again.

Madeleine's voice filled the hall, her Tosca so fiery and passionate that her high Cs resonated straight into Yvonne's heart, until she interrupted herself midsentence. The violins and cellos screeched to a halt in a heap of dissonant notes.

"The score calls for *andante sostenuto*," Madeleine said. "That is not what I am hearing."

The musicians slid to the edge of their seats, ready to make any modification requested by the star. The director mumbled a comment from his seat. Madeleine exchanged an exasperated glance with Henri, then looked at the director again.

"Enough with that idea of being Tosca while I sing," Madeleine said. "If people wanted to see more acting, they'd go to the theater."

Yvonne wrapped her arms around her chest. When she practiced, she was doing exactly what irritated Madeleine the most. But Madeleine had never raised the matter with her.

The director said something Yvonne didn't catch.

"I've been singing this role for twenty-five years," Madeleine said. "If you don't like the way I do it, you can go and direct opera at Thonon-les-Bains." She took another macaron from the box.

Charles-Antoine clicked his tongue.

"She becomes insufferable when she's anxious about a performance," Yvonne said.

Guillaume whispered in Madeleine's ear. His career had soared since she'd taken an interest in him: *La bohème* in Lyon, *La traviata* in Brussels, and now *Tosca* in Paris. Madeleine had taken an interest in Yvonne too—Yvonne didn't dispute that—but Yvonne's and Guillaume's careers had diverged quickly.

Guillaume kissed Madeleine's hand. She held his fingers a second too long after he released his grip.

"She thinks he's madly in love with her, despite the difference in age," Yvonne said. "She encourages him, even. He lives in fear she'll find out he's engaged to the director's daughter."

Madeleine pressed her palm against her forehead and, her elbows high in a pose that begged for photographs, gave Henri her most exhausted look. "Let's go over 'Vissi d'arte' again. At least we all agreed on that piece yesterday."

Yvonne prodded Charles-Antoine toward the exit. The pair slid into the corridor as the first notes of Tosca's aria rose into the auditorium. Yvonne closed the door hard behind her. It embarrassed her to think maybe Charles-Antoine understood why. She should've won that contest.

"You have to audition," Charles-Antoine said.

Yvonne smoothed her dress with the palm of her hand. At night, when the rest of the staff had gone home, she sneaked onto the stage of the opera house and sang to the rows of empty seats, imagining them filled with her rapturous public. But she'd never admit it.

"You can find roles in Paris," Charles-Antoine said. "You are more than good enough."

"My manager says it's too early. I only have one opportunity to make a strong first impression."

"You need time onstage. What experience does he have, to give you such advice?"

"He's Madeleine's manager," Yvonne said. She was proud of it.

"Hire someone who doesn't work with her."

The stage door opened, and Guillaume stepped out before Yvonne could ask why.

"What a splendid rendition of Cavaradossi," Charles-Antoine said.

Guillaume looked at him blankly before a hint of recognition flickered in his eyes. He didn't shake Charles-Antoine's hand. "You didn't expect me to succeed, did you? You thought Édouard would outshine me and I'd become an also-ran."

Édouard, who'd shared the men's prize, was now garnering praise in Geneva. Yvonne, though, didn't browse through the newspapers to read about him. Catherine had received positive reviews in *Werther* and *Ariadne auf Naxos*. It pained Yvonne to find that woman's name in *Paris-soir* where she dreamt to see hers.

"Madeleine told me I almost lost the contest because of you," Guillaume said. "I wouldn't have a career today if she hadn't fought for me."

"Deliberations are confidential," Charles-Antoine said. He cared about such details.

"Confidential or not, she told me who voted for me."

Charles-Antoine tapped his cane against the tiles, one, two, three, four times, until Yvonne placed her hand on its pommel.

Guillaume kept his eyes on Charles-Antoine. "I don't give a dead rat. Every opera house in Europe is begging for me." He pulled on the lapels of his jacket. "Anyway, I was going to get a drink of water. Not that I don't enjoy telling you how wrong you were, but I'm short on time. The ransom of success, I'm sure you understand."

He left without glancing at Yvonne.

Charles-Antoine touched her elbow. "Is there a place we could talk?"

Yvonne showed him a corner with a sofa and two armchairs. She waited there every performance night until the second intermission, as required in her contract, in case Madeleine fell ill and she had to go on in her place.

"A place we won't be overheard," Charles-Antoine said.

Yvonne led him to the stairwell and, one floor up, to the first dressing room in the corridor. It bore the name MADELEINE MOREAU on a golden plaque. No one except Madeleine was allowed to use that room, even for opera productions that Madeleine didn't star in. On either side were doors without names—on the left, the dressing rooms for tenors and bass-baritones, and on the right, those for mezzos and sopranos. A placard hid a walled-up door where another dressing room had been, right next to Madeleine's, until Madeleine had ordered the wall separating them knocked down.

Yvonne sneaked inside Madeleine's dressing room, Charles-Antoine behind her.

The score of *Tosca* lay on the coffee table in front of the sofa, next to a collection of shawls wrapped on a mannequin. Reviews of Madeleine's performances were tucked in the mirror. A photograph of Henri wearing a white carnation in his lapel was propped on the dresser near pots of makeup. Next to it, a black frame showed a very young man in military uniform, a boy really, looking like an extra for *La fille du régiment* rather than a second-class infantryman. It was all very proper, as if Madeleine had decided to show her visitors exactly what they expected. Even the setup in her dressing room was part of the performance she gave to her admirers.

Charles-Antoine turned toward Yvonne. "You would've won the contest at the Conservatory if Madeleine hadn't opposed it. We didn't dare go against her. None of our students would've been hired at the opera house again if we had."

Yvonne clutched the edge of the dresser. How could she have been so naïve? Just because there was room for two sopranos in Paris, she'd been certain that Madeleine, secure in her fame and the adoration of her public, wouldn't undermine a little unknown like her.

"She says I have a golden future ahead of me, if I play my cards well," Yvonne said. She'd been so proud of the compliment, but now she understood it'd been a honey trap, venom in the disguise of a gift. There were only shame and consternation left now when she recounted Madeleine's compliments. "She says I shouldn't pay any heed to folks who want me to sing before I'm ready. They're just trying to make money off my talent. She says I might even sing in Strasbourg next year, if she can spare me."

"You should've sung in Strasbourg last spring."

Yvonne thought the same thing, but she wouldn't admit it. She hated to recognize pity in Charles-Antoine's eyes—she'd pitied him herself when she'd recognized him in front of the opera house, an old professor whose performing career had never soared past modest fame among connoisseurs. She was certain she'd arouse the admiration of thousands of spectators once she finally stood in the spotlight.

"I was hoping you'd make your debut anyway so I wouldn't have to tell you this," Charles-Antoine said. "But don't give up on getting cast. You have a very good voice."

Yvonne opened one of the pots of makeup and slowly daubed her eyelids with Madeleine's favorite color of eyeshadow. She felt cheated— of Charlotte in *Werther*, of Ariadne in *Ariadne auf Naxos*, of Olympia and Antonia in *Tales of Hoffmann*, but also of the acknowledgment that she deserved to sing onstage, the applause of the crowds, the praise in the newspapers.

Yvonne's chest rose and fell, rose and fell. She plucked the review of Madeleine's Elisabeth from the mirror and dropped it on the floor, as if a draft had pulled it away.

Charles-Antoine touched her elbow. "You walked yourself into a dead end. It is time to try something else."

Three

October 1938

Madeleine's manager, Raymond, leaned over his mahogany desk and aimed a jubilant smile at her. "You'll never get a better opportunity to leave your mark."

They sat in his office on the boulevard des Capucines in the shadow of the Intercontinental Hotel. Outside, the leaves of the chestnut trees had barely begun to change colors, and Madeleine dreaded another birthday coming near.

Her portrait hung on the wall behind Raymond, slightly above his head. The photographs of the other singers in Raymond's stable were propped on the shelves by the door. He rewarded the more famous singers with bigger frames higher up, while those floundering in their careers saw their likeness sink far down below eye level. Yvonne's picture, the size of a postcard, remained at the bottom of the display.

"Does Covent Garden want me again?" Madeleine asked. "I'd rather go to the Met." How dazzled her mother would look when she told her, her mother who had never really believed she deserved fame. The matriarch had expected the biggest accomplishments from Alexandre but not from Madeleine. Perhaps that was why Madeleine spent so much money on her mother's medications and expensive gifts, from Chinese silk scarves to felt hats, and was now letting her mother live in her and Henri's country house in Normandy.

"Not New York just now, but you'll be a pioneer all the same," Raymond said.

His conspiratorial air annoyed Madeleine. People weren't supposed to know things she did not, and when they did, they shouldn't lord their knowledge over her.

"The first Frenchwoman to sing Isolde at Bayreuth," Raymond said in a stage whisper.

Madeleine became still. She had dreamt of singing at Bayreuth ever since she was a young woman. The composer Richard Wagner, now dead for fifty-five years, had launched it to showcase his works. They counted among the most difficult operas in the repertoire. For a singer who felt up to the task, no greater honor existed than being invited to the Festspielhaus. After she had triumphed on that stage, no one would disagree that Madeleine was the best singer in the past fifty years. She already heard the applause ringing in her ears.

But the festival was held in Germany, in a small town nestled in the hills two hours north of Munich. Bavaria: a Nazi stronghold, while the relations between France and Germany worsened by the week. Hitler had annexed Austria in March and the Sudetenland in Czechoslovakia in September. Why would he stop there? No one so far had stood up to him. Whatever he did next, Madeleine did not wish to be associated with it.

"Why are they inviting me now when they ignored me for years?" Madeleine asked.

The timing was dreadful.

Raymond pointed his Montblanc pen at her. "Winifred Wagner herself decided this was the perfect moment." Winifred was Richard Wagner's daughter-in-law. She had ruled over the festival since her husband had passed away eight years earlier. "I foresee record-breaking coverage in the press."

Raymond made a grateful smile at the engraving of the Virgin Mary propped up on his desk, which he kept there to suggest Jesus's mother was watching over his business deals. "You've just defeated all the German singers on their own turf. Wagner in Bayreuth—what a consecration for your career! And no one deserves the role of Isolde more."

Car brakes squealed in the street. A long honk cut through the air, breaking the spell of Raymond's words on Madeleine.

"What's the hitch?" she asked. "There's got to be a hitch. You're talking faster than the French cavalry storming the field at Ratisbon." She had worked with him long enough to know his tricks.

"The situation in Germany may bother some," Raymond said. "Of course, they are wrong not to see that art and politics are two separate things."

Raymond telling Madeleine not to pay attention to politics? That was an ominous sign. He only ever focused on the monetary amount at the bottom of the contract. But then, he'd never had a looming war to deal with.

"Someone has to be the first Frenchwoman to sing Isolde," he said. "It's going to be you or a rival of yours. If you say no, they won't invite you again. Why damage your career?" He was talking fast again. "You'll show the power of art in fostering friendship between our two countries. Frankly, Madeleine dear, you'll do more to preserve peace than the bigwigs who trade insults in the press."

"I thought it was Hitler who was causing trouble," Madeleine said. "Not our side."

Neville Chamberlain had brought disgrace to Great Britain when he signed the Munich Agreement, allowing Hitler to claim Czechoslovakia's Sudetenland on the pretext of avoiding war—Madeleine could recognize a doormat when she saw one. But Henri insisted that Chamberlain had saved the peace.

Raymond plucked his silk handkerchief out of his breast pocket and dabbed it on his forehead. That handkerchief too, like the Montblanc pen, he owed to Madeleine's fame. "You might have to spread the blame more evenly when you get there. Just so that the good folks of Bayreuth don't feel the need to pick an argument with you. Let's be honest. The Fritzes who clamor for war aren't going to be the ones who come and listen to *Tristan und Isolde* for four hours."

"You really want me to go," Madeleine said. She would have wanted to go, too, if Hitler hadn't been in power. Now, after the turmoil of the past few months, she wasn't sure she cared whether the Germans applauded her or not.

"It's not Winifred's fault that Hitler's threatening more bloodshed. What's she going to do? Tell him to stop scaring the living daylights out of her season subscribers?" Raymond shoved his handkerchief back into his pocket. "Sometimes in life you have to hold your nose and remember what you're working for."

The phone rang in the antechamber. Raymond's secretary picked up. The tone of her voice, mellow at first, turned curt and unpleasant. She was talking to an artist down on his luck: someone begging Raymond to take him on but in no position to bargain. She hung up the phone.

Madeleine drummed her fingers against the armrest. She would certainly enchant Bayreuth's operagoers if she traveled to Germany. That Winifred Wagner had picked Madeleine, of all people, at this moment in time, was an enormous surprise.

Muffled by the thunderous applause in Madeleine's mind, an alarm bell.

"I need a couple of days to think it over," she said.

On the other side of the door, the secretary's phone rang again.

Raymond's stomach touched the desk when he leaned toward Madeleine. "You'll nab your place in the history books. Others can sing Mozart."

Madeleine allowed herself a smile.

Raymond pounced. "And you'd avenge your brother."

Madeleine's eyes stayed on him, her face still as ice.

"Taking the place of a German singer"—Raymond jabbed his thick finger at her—"showing the world you sing Wagner better than any of them. Isn't that why you specialized in his works in the first place? Go and settle the score."

Oh, he had been promised a good fee for her, all right. Madeleine stood up to leave.

Raymond scrambled around the desk. "The festival has nothing to do with the Third Reich. Nazi officers will stay away. Why would they come? Wagner is over their head." He grabbed a piece of paper, opened the contract at the last page, and held out his Montblanc pen again. "Trust me, the festival might as well be held in Denmark, for that matter."

The blank space at the bottom of the page was normally a magnet for Madeleine's signature, but she did not pick up Raymond's pen. "They're persecuting the Jews all over Germany, in Bayreuth like everywhere else," she said.

"The press is playing the situation up," Raymond said. "They all need to sell copies."

Madeleine strode to the door. Raymond's lack of concern troubled her. He would increase his own reputation if she went to Bayreuth: the manager who had engineered a historic deal. She needed honest advice. But Henri chased fame rather than money. He would advise her to take part in the festival out of self-interest. Madeleine could consult no one for a second opinion.

"Expect my answer by the end of the week," Madeleine said.

"They'll resent you if you make them wait."

"I've been making people wait my whole career," Madeleine said.

Raymond escorted her out of his office. His secretary, Hélène, handed him a piece of paper when they strolled past her desk. With her oversized glasses, she reminded Madeleine of a frog. "Two more calls from that man," she said. "The one who keeps saying that he was a respected tenor in Vienna until he left."

Raymond dumped the piece of paper into the wastebasket.

"I told him you're not taking new clients and hung up, but he called right back," Hélène added. "He said to tell you he sang the title role in *Otello* at the State Opera three seasons ago."

The ground moved under Madeleine's feet. "Stefan Kreismann is in Paris?"

Raymond nudged Madeleine toward the exit. "He and many others just like him."

"He's one of the best tenors in Europe," Madeleine said. "In the world." She had known he was Jewish, but she'd believed his fame would protect him. When she heard about the Anschluss, in the middle of her rehearsals for Tchaikovsky's *Iolanta*, she had not worried about him.

"I can't save everyone," Raymond said, as if he had saved anyone.

"We sold a lot of tickets when we worked with each other," Madeleine said, more insistently. "Vienna adored us. London too. You should bring us back together." She kept her voice even, despite the memories flooding her mind. She always looked down at singers who had had affairs with their fellow cast members.

"I can't give the job of a French singer to a foreigner these days," Raymond said. "Especially a German one."

"Austrian," Madeleine said.

Raymond shrugged, as if Austria had not been annexed by the Nazis. "You sell out any performance hall with your name alone."

He opened the door and waited for Madeleine to step out into the hallway. Madeleine tried to think, but her mind wouldn't function. Stefan in Paris! She would have helped him if he had contacted her.

But she knew why he hadn't reached out. Back at Covent Garden, he had decided not to leave his wife for Madeleine, and now that he'd fallen on hard times, he didn't dare call on her. He feared that she held his rejection against him. And he wasn't too wrong.

Raymond opened the door wider.

"If he left Austria to escape Hitler, I can't justify going to a place that glorifies that lunatic," Madeleine said.

"If he thought that his actions should influence you, he would've let you know he's here. In Bayreuth, Max Lorenz will make a great Tristan, and"—Raymond's eyes twinkled—"Wilhelm Furtwängler will conduct, just like last year. Since the leading conductor of his generation is returning to the festival, surely you can go as well."

Lorenz and Furtwängler in Bayreuth with Madeleine: surely they would set the standard for all the productions of *Tristan und Isolde* to come. She desperately wanted to sing at the Festspielhaus before her voice declined. The acoustics were said to be spectacular, even unique in the world, because of the recessed orchestra pit and the continental seating that allowed spectators similar unobstructed views of the stage. Yet Madeleine was also aware that she was trying to rationalize her decision, when her gut told her not to go. The Hitler matter concerned her.

"Did Stefan leave a phone number?" she asked Hélène.

"He's staying at Hôtel Stanislas in the fifth arrondissement," Hélène said.

"He's strapped for cash," Raymond said. "That's a seedy boarding-house behind the Luxembourg Gardens."

Madeleine felt sorry that Stefan had ended up there. "I would've lent him money if he'd asked me."

"He might be under the impression that Henri would refuse to give him a centime," Raymond said.

What had Raymond learned behind Madeleine's back? He took pride in the size of his network, in Germany and Austria as much as in France. Maybe someone had seen Madeleine and Stefan together in those few months when they had thrown caution to the wind.

"Anyway, Madeleine dear," Raymond said, "we all need you to dazzle the Germans. Be an ambassador for world peace. Only you can pull it off." He took her hands in his. "Now that I think of it, Stefan has such a riveting personal story, I should be able to secure a role at the Paris Opera for him, if that makes you happy. Maybe Arturo in *Lucia*?"

"Edgardo," Madeleine said. The leading male role. Madeleine and Stefan had never sung in *Lucia di Lammermoor* together. They would spellbind the crowds.

"You had me cast Guillaume in that, but I promise you he'll be paid his worth as Arturo," Raymond said. "Isn't it what matters? It'll put my reputation at risk to aid someone with a name that sounds German, but you know I'd walk through fire for you." He paused as if he expected Madeleine to break into applause.

Maybe she could convince Emile to swap the casting. Guillaume as Arturo, Stefan as Edgardo. If Stefan was desperate for money, he would accept any small role, but she could not let him humiliate himself.

"Let me give him the news," Madeleine said.

Raymond bowed over her hand. "You'll shine in Bayreuth, I can tell."

Against her better judgment, Madeleine wondered how Stefan would react if she told him she might travel to Germany that summer.

Yvonne ran around groups of students in the corridors of the Music Conservatory. She'd hoped to return to her past school famous, but aspiring singers had no idea who she was as she hurried past them. She'd picked more elegant clothes than what an audition would deserve—a hat with a veil, a black dress with white trim—to give the illusion of success. Hopefully, that'd impress the guest, especially if he didn't notice the signs of wear.

At last, Yvonne reached the room that Charles-Antoine had reserved for them. He was already there, chatting with a man in a business suit, fifteen or twenty years older than Yvonne: the casting director of the Marseilles Opera, who'd studied under Charles-Antoine as a young man. His tiny rimless glasses surprised her. She hadn't expected people outside Paris to wear such fashionable glasses.

A lone music stand stood at the center of the room. The small window in the back opened onto the inner courtyard. An Érard piano was pushed to the side, in front of a floor-to-ceiling mirror. Yvonne had taken refuge in that very rehearsal room after she'd learned she hadn't won the voice competition in 1936. Maybe it'd see her luck turn.

"The subway stopped half an hour in a tunnel," Yvonne said. "Someone jumped onto the tracks a few stations ahead."

Despair among refugees had been mounting. But who knew if the victim had not been a student upset about his grades, or a jilted secretary?

Charles-Antoine made the introductions. "Yvonne, Gérard. Gérard, Yvonne."

"No one but Madeleine can outshine her," Charles-Antoine said to Gérard, "and Madeleine isn't leaving Paris."

Yvonne dropped the folder where she kept her scores. The loose sheets scattered all over the floor. What a klutz. After such praise, Charles-Antoine would ridicule himself if she failed. But it was kind of him to push for her success. He had to hear something in her voice that she wasn't even sure was there.

"Let's listen," Gérard said.

Charles-Antoine sat down at the piano. Yvonne wanted to tell him to walk more slowly, to give her time to collect herself. The room was too hot, probably because she had run all the way from the subway station. Yvonne dabbed her forehead with her handkerchief. Charles-Antoine was already looking at her, waiting for her signal. She gathered her papers and imagined she'd put on a long, sleeveless dress and sandals like the Antiquity statues in the Louvre museum. She took a deep breath. It was time to become someone else.

Yvonne sang "Es gibt ein Reich" from *Ariadne auf Naxos*. It was a good role for her, burdened with fewer expectations than Brünnhilde or Isolde. She could act while avoiding the comparison to sopranos cast before her, and she sounded like a native German speaker. She imagined herself as Ariadne, desperate after her lover, Theseus, had abandoned her, looking forward to traveling down the land of death, where she'd find relief from her pain. Her diction was clear, her timbre light, her notes precise. Gérard listened with his mouth half open, so entranced he didn't even blink.

Yvonne could've sung until the next morning. She was disappointed when the aria came to an end and she had to return to being herself.

Gérard tapped his pencil against the page and turned to Charles-Antoine. "You weren't joking. It's incredible she's not famous yet." And to Yvonne: "All hiring is subject to the general manager's approval, but I'd recommend you highly."

"A wise choice," Charles-Antoine said.

Marseilles! It wasn't Paris and it wasn't Lyons, but it was the third-best option. The opera house was well regarded. Provence had better weather than Paris. Yvonne would live by the Old Port and the Mediterranean Sea. Marseilles had excellent high schools for Jules to finish his studies, and renowned piano teachers. It'd be a good life indeed.

"Now, we already have several dramatic sopranos, and they've been in the company a long time," Gérard said. "They have many powerful friends. We can't ask them to step aside. You could sing small roles for now, though, or lyric soprano parts."

How foolish of Yvonne that she hadn't seen the bad news coming, that she'd believed her luck had turned at last.

"The Marschallin in *Der Rosenkavalier*," Gérard said. "Or Tatyana in *Eugene Onegin*. The letter scene! Audience members would faint."

"And you don't have star singers for that?" Charles-Antoine asked from the piano bench.

"We have one," Gérard said, "but she is likely to retire within a few years. Her voice isn't what it once was. We'll make room for your former student on the calendar."

Yvonne couldn't imagine that the lyric soprano at the Marseilles Opera would step down any more willingly than Madeleine. She must've made a face, because Gérard said, "Wherever you go, you'll find established singers in those roles. Your position is always going to be thorny at first. You can't let that frighten you."

"I hadn't pictured myself in those parts," Yvonne said. They made different demands on a singer's voice.

"They're excellent roles," Gérard said. "Then your career will probably lead you elsewhere anyway, and we'll be delighted to have contributed to your success." He uttered these last words with a magnanimous smile, as if Yvonne had always had the upper hand.

If the leading lady didn't retire for five years, though, and the casting director only kept Yvonne twelve months, it'd look like she didn't know which repertoire she was good at. Her career would sputter even further, maybe even stall. She'd have no other choice than to become a voice teacher. But who would take advice from her?

"You can also stay in Paris if you prefer, although I'm not hearing that things have been going swimmingly for you here," Gérard said.

If he withdrew the offer, she'd again be left with no prospect to sing.

"Many singers change their signature roles throughout their career," Charles-Antoine said after a long silence. "That is the sign of true professionals. They adapt to their evolving voices."

But Yvonne's voice hadn't evolved, and they both knew that. Yvonne couldn't tell if he was trying to convince himself she should change her repertoire or was attempting to persuade her. He had organized the meeting, after all. He wouldn't encourage her to decline Gérard's offer.

"I might have erred when I told you to focus on dramatic soprano parts," Charles-Antoine said. "Do not say no out of pride." It didn't matter that Yvonne's voice could convey the anguish of the fiercest Wagnerian heroines if she was never asked.

Gérard rummaged through his satchel. Just when it seemed that he wouldn't find what he was looking for, he brandished a score with a sweep of his arm. "Here, take a stab at it."

He handed Yvonne the part for Tatyana's aria in the letter scene. *Eugene Onegin.*

Yvonne pulled herself together and sight-read the score. Who was Tatyana again? She wished she understood the role. When she sang Tatyana, she felt sheathed in a tight dress, but she'd had no time to practice. Maybe she'd become good at it, eventually.

"That was remarkable," Charles-Antoine said at the end.

Didn't he always praise her, though?

"See, you'd shine as a lyric soprano too," Gérard said. He seemed pleased by his idea of making her change her repertoire.

"How many performances would I get?" she asked in a small voice.

"It's hard to say just now," Gérard said. "We haven't finished scheduling the season. But our singers also deliver concerts at the homes of our benefactors—patrons who rent the loge boxes, society ladies who host members' tea, and on occasion, friends and politicians. You'll have plenty of opportunities to sing, even if our leading lady doesn't retire anytime soon." He pushed his glasses up on his nose. "You have a much more pleasing physique. Surely, you'll be in high demand."

Yvonne didn't like the glint in his eye.

"At least it starts your career," Charles-Antoine said, apparently oblivious to the drift in Gérard's voice. "And once you are there, you can advocate for yourself." He looked at her expectantly.

Yvonne's hands shook when she gave the score of *Eugene Onegin* back to Gérard.

Four

Men in cotton business suits and women in sleeveless evening gowns chatted amiably over the soft ding of silverware in the Tour d'Argent restaurant. Heads turned when the maître d' led Madeleine and Henri through the dining room, over the blue-and-gold rug, past the chairs upholstered in azure velvet and the cream-colored silk tablecloths. Someone whispered the Moreaus' name to his table companions. This pleased Madeleine, although she pretended not to hear and applied herself not to look at the dinner guests. The high society consisted of two tiers: those who were recognized and those who did the recognizing when their lives intersected in the most fashionable establishments of the city. Madeleine had long ago decided that she and Henri belonged in the upper tier and made sure to act like it.

Henri had reserved their favorite table for four by the window. The light of the streetlamps along the Pont de la Tournelle reflected in the water, in soft blurs made jagged by the waves. On the side, the towers of Notre-Dame loomed over Paris. The dining room, on the top floor of a six-story building at the intersection between the quay de la Tournelle and the rue du Cardinal Lemoine, gave the impression that it was floating in the sky. The view would fill Stefan with awe. Madeleine knew how to impress her guests.

The maître d' handed them menus and placed two more on the edge of the table.

"We'll get a bottle of Château Margaux while we wait," Henri said. If it had been up to him, Madeleine would have accepted the invitation to sing at Bayreuth weeks ago. But he had chosen one of the most expensive wines on the list, so Madeleine could tell he wanted to impress Stefan too, even if he didn't care to admit it. "And foie gras as an appetizer."

Madeleine had told Henri that the situation in Germany worried their manager Raymond and that he had asked her to contact that famous Austrian tenor she had shared accolades with, because her accepting the invitation to Bayreuth could affect her future fees in France. They needed the advice of someone who had witnessed the situation firsthand. The idea hadn't enthralled Henri, but he had not opposed inviting Stefan and his wife to an establishment rated three stars in the Michelin guide. Madeleine had taken that as a good omen.

"I can't believe they're late," Henri said.

"We're early," Madeleine said.

This would have aroused Henri's suspicions if her refusal to say yes to Bayreuth on the spot hadn't irked him so. It was the perfect day for him to forget that Madeleine made everyone wait—except, it turned out, a former lover she might remain smitten with.

A waiter popped open a bottle of champagne. Two men and two women laughed amiably while the waiter filled their glasses, the men almost as dashing as Henri, the women thinner than Madeleine. But they could not sing.

Madeleine drummed her fingers against the tablecloth while she monitored the front door. She had not seen Stefan in four years, since he had admitted after their last performance of *Tristan und Isolde* at Covent Garden that he would not leave Ilse for her. She wanted to feel all the time how she felt when he was around. With him, she never regretted not having had children. But his arguments had been very rational and a little bit heartless. Two famous opera singers could not create a happy life together. Instead, they would compete for the limelight until the career of one overtook that of the other. Whoever got forced into a supporting role would become bitter. Wasn't it obvious neither of them had the temperament to play second fiddle?

Madeleine saw Stefan's point. She had tried to convince herself it was for the best. She had loved Stefan because of the chemistry they had onstage, but she could not stand the idea of staying in the shadows to help his career, and she was sure he felt the same about her. Yet she missed him every time she looked at the tenor singing opposite her. It was to forget her old beau that she sang only with much younger men now.

The waiter returned with the bottle of Château Margaux. He made a show of uncorking it in front of Henri and giving him a sip. Henri swiveled the wine in his glass, sniffed it, frowned while he ostensibly debated whether to send the wine back.

"That'll do," Henri finally said, looking his most discerning self, although the wine cost twenty times the price of an average bottle.

The waiter poured the Château Margaux into crystal stemware and left.

Madeleine smiled. "Do you actually notice the difference, or are you putting on a show? For me all Bordeaux taste the same."

"That's because I only buy you the best," Henri said, and took another sip. His eyes twinkled.

Madeleine chuckled and reached for her glass just as Stefan and Ilse stepped into the dining room. She lowered her hand, worried that she would spill the wine if she brought the glass to her lips. She had not expected the mere sight of Stefan to move her. The familiar tenderness was now mixed with pity. Stefan had aged ten years since they had parted. His hair, which used to be pitch-black, had turned entirely gray. His face had become bloated. His eyes seemed bleary behind his round glasses. Yet he stood erect on the threshold of the dining room in a crisp dark suit and white dress shirt, as if he should command every guest's attention. She had loved that man, and perhaps she still did.

By his side, Ilse fidgeted in a shapeless burgundy velvet dress. She slid out of a sable fur coat that did not go with the gown but at least looked worthy of the restaurant. What a happy finding, that Ilse lacked taste.

The maître d' reached for Ilse's coat. She wrapped her arms around it, refusing to give it up. Madeleine could tell from her grip that she worried it would get misplaced or stolen. For a second the maître d' just stared at her, and then he dismissed her as if she were a tourist who had wandered into the dining room by mistake.

A waiter led Stefan and Ilse toward the table where Madeleine and Henri were waiting for them. They didn't even glance at the view, and they certainly did not look impressed by their surroundings. Instead, they looked tired and numb. Madeleine wondered how it felt, to suddenly lose everything.

Henri clicked his tongue. "They look like fish out of water, and we look like idiots for bringing them here."

"At least pretend to be keen on dining with them," Madeleine whispered back. "They're in enough trouble. I feel terrible for them."

"It's nice of you to want to help them out," Henri said, rather coolly.

Madeleine stood up when Stefan neared her table. In her sparkling Lucien Lelong dress, she knew she must look like a movie heroine— Danielle Darrieux, perhaps, to match Henri's handsome airs.

"Stefan, I can't believe you were in Paris and didn't tell me." Madeleine kept a neutral voice, polite yet not especially kind.

Stefan shook Henri's hand first, then kissed Madeleine's. Old feelings stirred when his lips touched her skin. To her dismay, Stefan was already letting go of her fingers. "We have been busy trying to obtain exit papers. When would we have had a chance to visit with you?"

He still spoke French with a thick accent and perfect grammar, although his pronunciation was rather pedantic. Madeleine had found his halting, careful pattern of speech so attractive back in Vienna. Yet his words stung. She'd hoped he had not reached out to her because he did not dare, after he had rejected her, but perhaps he was telling the truth: he couldn't find time for her. To him she was just a distant memory, while she was constantly reminded of him.

"You did not have to do this," Stefan said.

He sounded neither amused nor resentful. As the favorite tenor at the Vienna State Opera, feted and dined by throngs of powerful people in the most rarefied society circles, he had enjoyed more fine restaurants than many of the Parisians seated at that same minute on the quay de la Tournelle—more than Madeleine herself, even. But he could no longer afford them. Singers were engaged over a year in advance, and no one in Paris would care to make room for him, Guillaume least of all—Guillaume, whom Madeleine herself had anointed the ruling tenor at the opera house.

"It seems fitting for the occasion—my treat," Madeleine said. "We haven't seen each other since Covent Garden, have we? We should celebrate properly."

They sat down, Ilse next to Madeleine and Stefan by Henri. Ilse's presence on her right grated on Madeleine. She wished that this woman whom Stefan preferred to her had sat on the other side of the table, away from her.

Stefan poured a glass of Château Margaux for Ilse and then one for himself. The label was affixed on the side of the bottle away from him, and he didn't bother looking at it. "We certainly could use an occasion to celebrate."

A waiter brought two plates of pressed duck to the next table. Stefan followed the dish with his gaze. Even Madeleine allowed herself a moment to enjoy the smell drifting toward them. Ilse steadied herself against her chair. Was it her stomach growling, or Stefan's?

"We should sing in *Lucia* together next season," Madeleine said, sipping her wine as if she had all the time in the world. "Lucia and Edgardo. Are you available? We'd triumph."

Henri did not betray her, did not say that the role of Edgardo had already been cast. Besides, castings could change, couldn't they? So it wasn't a complete lie.

Stefan almost put down his glass on the edge of his plate. "I did not expect that from you." He did not add *given how we parted*, but Madeleine was sure he thought as much. His face brightened. "Where do I sign?"

"I'll have Raymond draw up the papers. Let's drink to that." She was thrilled.

They dutifully raised their glasses, although Henri did not raise his glass as high as the others. "We should order soon," he said. "The kitchen is often slow in preparing the food."

Madeleine suspected he did not want the dinner to last any longer than necessary. Soon they were all poring over the menus.

Madeleine could tell when Stefan was reading the dishes' prices, because he blinked and returned to that line again. The women's menu did not bear that information, and Ilse happily tapped her fingers next to the most expensive items. They all talked about vegetables they favored and what a specific sauce would taste like. Henri asked about Stefan's favorite dish. It was sauerbraten, but only from a certain restaurant. The conversation was excruciatingly boring. Madeleine remembered her long, animated chats with Stefan in Austria. In a discussion about Mozart or Strauss, Stefan would have won handily over Henri. And antagonized him. Perhaps that was what he was trying to avoid.

They ate the foie gras. Madeleine and Henri took their time appreciating every bite, but Stefan and Ilse chewed fast and took second servings. Henri blinked hard at them, yet he asked for another breadbasket on their behalf. His tone was detached, as if they had sat down at his table by mistake and he was just trying to be polite. Madeleine was tempted to kick him under the table so he wouldn't make faces.

"By the way, I have some news to share," Madeleine said a bit too hurriedly, although she had rehearsed her question at home in front of her mirror. "I was invited to sing at Bayreuth."

Ilse cocked her head so far to the side that her ear almost touched her shoulder. Stefan became as still as a statue.

Madeleine rearranged the silverware around her plate. "Who could've imagined, in this lifetime, that they'd pick a French singer?"

She wished that the silence had not been dragging on so long.

"I hadn't pegged you as the type to go to Germany in times like these," Stefan said.

Ilse's fingers wrapped themselves around his. Madeleine itched to pry their hands apart but restrained herself. In the back of the room, a redhead with two rows of pearls around her neck laughed her heart out.

"Daladier negotiated peace," Henri said. "France has nothing to fear."

"You cannot seriously believe that Daladier's big words will stop Hitler." Stefan raised the tip of his knife at Madeleine while looking at Henri. "She hopes to travel to Germany when everyone who can tell right from wrong is attempting to exit. It will look like she supports him."

Another moment of silence, even more awkward than the previous one.

"Winifred chose me," Madeleine said. "It's not her fault that politicians have lost their minds." But her voice lacked confidence. It was too easy to blame it all on a few politicians—they did what would bring them votes. The entire country of Germany had gone mad.

"You know you should say no," Stefan said.

At the next table, a man seated in front of a steak au poivre fulminated about Maurice Thorez, the leader of the French Communist Party, who was apoplectic about the Munich Agreement. Had Thorez lost his mind? That agreement had saved Europe from war. The patron's wife, tugging on the feather boa around her neck, glanced at Madeleine's table between bites of *lotte à l'américaine*. Whatever was happening on her left interested her far more than her husband's rant.

"Hitler is an elected head of state," Madeleine said. "It's not my place to meddle in another country's affairs." It sounded thoughtful and measured when she said it, but a second later it seemed weak and expedient. She was ashamed of herself, although she still yearned to go to Bayreuth. She needed to sing. She needed spectators. And if she said no, she would not be asked again.

"He annexed Austria and the Sudetenland," Stefan said coldly, without even raising his voice. "He has his eye on Poland. He passed laws that deprive us of citizenship." Stefan meant Jews like him and Ilse.

The lady with the feather boa wrinkled her nose. She was clearly eavesdropping and disapproved of his mentioning the Jews' fate aloud. Her husband was still praising the Munich Agreement, unaware that she had stopped listening to him.

"You can look the other way if you choose, but do not hope I will admire you for it," Stefan said to Madeleine.

Madeleine held his gaze for an instant, then looked away to munch on a toast of foie gras. Crumbs scattered on her dress. She had felt so assured a moment ago, and now she struggled to find words that would change Stefan's mind. "Art and politics are two separate things," she said, remembering Raymond's phrase.

"You are not that naïve," Stefan said.

"The whole situation has been wearing you down," Henri said, almost kindly, to Stefan. Madeleine had not expected him to jump in. For a moment she felt relieved that he would take her side. "Once you get back on your feet, you'll have a different perspective," he said. "It's good for her career if she goes."

Stefan planted his elbows on the table. He kept his eyes on Madeleine. "So you want my blessing. My absolution, even." His tone was so harsh Madeleine was tempted to say no, even if his absolution was exactly what she wanted.

"Perhaps this can wait until dessert," Ilse said. Her accent in French was even thicker than Stefan's.

Stefan looked at Madeleine. "Is that what your brother fought for?"

Henri banged his wineglass on the table.

For a moment, Madeleine could not breathe. "I wish people would stop talking to me about my brother," she finally said, her voice barely above a whisper.

Stefan pretended not to hear. "I doubt he thought, when he was lying in the trenches at Verdun, *I hope that my sister will travel to Germany to advance her career when Hitler threatens to make war against France again.*"

Madeleine's face burned. She wiped the corner of her mouth with her napkin to hide the redness that must be creeping across her cheeks. "My brother would be overjoyed for me, if he were still alive. He would know how much this would matter to me."

She held Stefan's gaze.

"No politician will allow another catastrophe so soon after the Great War," Henri said. "In five years, we'll have forgotten all about these tensions. But Madeleine is at the peak of her powers now. Of course, it's inconvenient that the invitation came this year. Yet the opportunity is too good to pass on."

"Everyone who can stay out of Germany should," Stefan said, "even those who cannot get enough of the limelight. The publicity will not be worth it, no matter how much certain prima donnas long to see their name in the papers."

He had never called her names before, and the fact that he was doing so for the first time now hurt Madeleine more than hearing the insult itself.

"You have some gall, insulting my wife after we invite you here," Henri said.

"Our opinion is not for sale," Stefan said.

"You can pay for your own dinner then, if you'd like," Henri said.

"He doesn't mean that," Madeleine said to Stefan.

"I mean every single word of it," Henri said.

Stefan wasn't paying attention to Henri, only to Madeleine. "Where is the hope for victims of the Reich if you associate with evil—you of all people, who do not need the work?" he asked her. "You cannot play heroines in front of thousands and then compromise yourself when you walk off the stage. Take a stand."

"You're putting a lot of weight on my shoulders," Madeleine said. She turned toward her neighbor with the feather boa. "Darling, you're going to fall off that chair if you lean in any closer."

The lady, looking away, stabbed her *lotte à l'américaine* with her fork.

"I cannot believe you are considering it," Stefan said. "You singing for that madman."

"He won't be there," Madeleine said. "He'll be busy fearmongering in Berlin."

Stefan pushed back his chair. "I had never realized that you were only an opportunist ready to make a pact with the devil."

Madeleine dropped her fork. The lady with the feather boa let out a little shriek, like a teapot whistling off-key.

Henri jumped up. His chair tumbled behind him. "You will apologize," he said to Stefan.

The room grew quiet.

Stefan was already striding toward the exit, his coattails fluttering in his wake. Ilse grabbed her sable fur coat and a slice of toasted bread and ran behind Stefan. Diners watched them go by, silverware frozen in the air.

Henri would have run after them, but Madeleine held him back. "Let's enjoy our dinner." She was humiliated enough already.

The maître d' put Henri's chair back upright.

Henri plopped down on the cushion of blue velvet. "What a silly idea from Raymond to ask this man for counsel."

"He had good points," Madeleine said, hoping Henri would never bring it up with Raymond. Stefan's contempt pained her. She could handle envy, greed, pettiness. But scorn from a man she had loved, that she could not accept. "I should say no."

"And then what?" Henri said. "They will still put on *Tristan und Isolde* this summer, and the role of Isolde will go to someone else. Winifred Wagner will never invite you again. No one will even know you turned her down." He poured her another glass of wine.

"Maybe it doesn't matter if I never sing at Bayreuth," Madeleine said.

Henri eyed her over the rim of his glass. "Why does Stefan have you under his thumb? You don't normally let people talk you into making colossal mistakes."

"Few talk to me honestly in this business."

"He's not being honest," Henri said, his face tense with anger. "He's ruining your career. What happened at Covent Garden that you two haven't sung together since then?"

Madeleine gave him a long look. "I prefer singing opposite younger singers now. They sound better."

❧

Yvonne interrupted herself midconversation with her manager's secretary, Hélène, when her manager finally trudged into his office from the street. Did he even remember he was Yvonne's manager? Some days, Yvonne wasn't so sure. But Hélène, who peered over all his contracts, was convinced he did. It didn't hurt that Hélène was Yvonne's best friend. She'd told Yvonne over coffee the previous day that the big man usually appeared at work around eleven and shuffled papers before heading out to lunch with power brokers he didn't name, but it was half past one o'clock now, and Yvonne had been waiting for three hours with the score of *Tristan und Isolde* on her lap.

She'd spent most of that time listening to Hélène tell her in apologetic tones that Raymond hadn't been himself lately but he'd show up, he always did, and Yvonne shouldn't take his delay as a sign she should give up on her singing career once and for all, and how did Yvonne prepare for a role like Isolde again? Her method to get into character seemed truly groundbreaking to Hélène. Among all of Raymond's singers, Yvonne was the one she'd become friends with, because Yvonne asked her questions about her life and her children and topics that had nothing to do with advancing her own career. And then she even remembered Hélène's answers without writing them down. Hélène would've signed up for a nomadic life in the circus after all that, so pleased she was that Yvonne had treated her well.

Yvonne's hat sagged around the rim; her scarf, though, was genuine silk. The woman who'd brought it to the consignment store had told the clerk it was a gift and she'd never even used it, whether that was true or not. Yvonne hoped if she wore one expensive item, that piece of clothing would impress Raymond enough he wouldn't pay attention to the rest. Then maybe he'd treat her like someone who could make him richer than he already was.

Raymond exchanged a look with Hélène when he recognized his guest. To her credit, she didn't wince.

"You're not returning my calls," Yvonne said. She tried to sound sweet, so he wouldn't take umbrage at her comment. But the message was clear. She couldn't get paid without him, and she had no savings.

Raymond hung his felt hat and his Burberry coat. "I don't have time for you just now, doll."

He unlocked his door and headed straight to the liquor cabinet. This was unlike him. He hadn't won so many deals for Madeleine by being a drunk.

Yvonne lingered near the threshold. She couldn't stand begging Raymond for roles. When she'd first signed with him, she'd convinced herself she was done begging—Raymond would take care of the more annoying facets of the job from now on. But stars like Madeleine kept him too busy for newcomers. A lesser-known manager would've tried harder to get her cast. She resented herself for this error in judgment.

"How am I ever going to earn you money if you don't talk to me?" Yvonne tried to sound flirtatious, although he'd wasted too much of her time that morning for her to put much effort into it.

Raymond poured himself a shot from the bottle of Courvoisier. "Doll, don't make me spell it out for you."

"I'd love to become enlightened about it. So would my electricity company."

"You're earning me money. Just not the amount you were hoping for." Bastard.

"I want principal roles," Yvonne said.

Raymond coughed on his liquor. "Who doesn't?"

Hélène pressed herself against the back of her chair and kept looking at Yvonne. Yvonne couldn't face her. She looked out the window and fanned herself as if the air were too hot and nothing else mattered. That plot was unlikely to succeed. Raymond topped off his drink.

Yvonne's own manager was losing interest in her. She would've looked for a new one on the spot if she'd believed she had a chance to find someone else willing to represent her. But others would assume that Raymond had put some effort in finding her roles and failed, and if Raymond had failed, surely they would too. She was stuck with him.

Raymond threw down the shot and smacked his lips together. That was quite uncouth of him. Yvonne was used to him displaying impeccable manners, a little too smoothly, because he was playing a role, but at least he always stayed in character. She sensed an opportunity. Maybe he'd help her if he wasn't his normal self. She didn't have any other options left.

"I could've been rehearsing Tatyana right now if I'd said yes to Marseilles," Yvonne said. It was her biggest achievement that she could've.

At times, she worried she'd become one of those starlets past their prime who kept rehashing their one moment of glory, except that hers wouldn't involve glory at all, just an opportunity she'd turned down in hope of something better. How pitiable to cling to a minor event so tightly.

"And you didn't, and that settles that," Raymond said. "It boggles my mind that you refused to do it."

Yvonne was still second-guessing herself after she'd rejected Gérard's offer. Charles-Antoine insisted she'd made a monumental error. She could hardly expect him to help her again, and where did that leave her? But it'd been about more than getting cast. The roles hadn't been right, and the glint in Gérard's eye had made her look for the exit.

"I am a dramatic soprano, like Madeleine," Yvonne said.

"Let's not talk about our star just now." Raymond poured himself another shot. He placed the bottle of Courvoisier on his desk instead of locking it back in the cabinet but didn't invite Yvonne to join in.

Yvonne's gaze drifted to her portrait on the edge of the bottom shelf, pushed to the side and back, the least noticeable spot, so that Raymond could still claim he put pictures of all his singers on the shelves. Madeleine's photograph hung high over Raymond's head, her face bigger than life. She resembled a madonna.

"When will you find me work?" Yvonne asked.

Raymond uncapped his Montblanc and leafed through his notebook, pretending to work on contracts for more established singers.

"There's room for both Madeleine and me in Paris," Yvonne said.

Raymond placed his hand on his left lung. "You're piercing my heart every time you pronounce that name, *chérie*."

"What did she do, decide to sing cabaret?"

"She turned down an invitation to sing at Bayreuth. Isolde, if you can believe it."

Raymond confiding in her: a first. But Yvonne could see why. "Germany," she said. The news from across the border worried her. In two years, Jules would be eligible for the draft.

"That would've increased her fee by a third in all the opera houses in Europe, and she's already the best-paid singer by a kilometer," Raymond said. "We would've secured our places in the history books. But no, that wasn't enough."

He sounded genuinely sad when he said it, oblivious to Yvonne's meager salary and the Jews' plight across the border.

Yvonne inched her way to the leather armchair in front of Raymond's desk. Madeleine's refusal to sing at Bayreuth surprised her. She hadn't expected the diva to show any morals. "You can't force her to sing if she doesn't want to," she said.

Raymond rotated his Montblanc over his index finger, again and again, as if he wasn't listening to Yvonne but reading contracts instead.

"I can sing Wagner as well as she does," Yvonne said. She didn't mean in Bayreuth—they'd never invite her. "You could put in a good word in Lille or Montpellier."

Raymond's eyes glazed over. "I haven't come across any good role for you, but I'll keep looking."

Yvonne pressed her palms hard against the desk, making sure to leave fingerprints on the mahogany table. "Why do you only help Madeleine?"

"I don't want to hear her name today," Raymond said without looking up. "It's not that hard for you to understand, is it?"

That answer stopped Yvonne cold. Raymond never raised his voice at her or the lesser-known singers in his stable. Yvonne suspected he did not deem them worthy of the effort, on a normal day.

"So how did you break the news to Winifred Wagner?" Yvonne asked.

Raymond crumpled on his seat like a sock puppet after the puppeteer removed his hand. "I haven't told her yet. I'll insist the doctor has recommended vocal rest, but she'll see right through it."

Indeed. Anyone would.

"You could tell Madeleine the Germans want me to understudy Isolde," Yvonne said. If she helped Raymond, maybe he'd find roles to thank her.

Raymond rubbed his temples. They both knew the Germans weren't aware Yvonne even existed, but that wasn't her point.

"She'll sign the contract on the spot if she thinks I'm going to Bayreuth," Yvonne said, starting to believe her own plan. "Tell her Winifred Wagner summoned me over and you don't understand why, something about my being French, but I'm on my way to Germany. Madeleine will never let me anywhere close to Winifred by myself."

Raymond stared at her in disbelief and, after a long moment, nodded slowly. This could work.

"And then you can find me roles in the provinces, not too far from Paris," Yvonne said, in case she needed to spell out his part in the bargain.

"As soon as you're back from Germany," Raymond said. "If I tell Madeleine you're headed for Bayreuth, you can't stay behind when she goes."

"They'll never hire me," Yvonne said. "They only select established singers, even as understudies." She felt no desire to go to Germany. War was looming. Now was not the time to cross borders.

"But they do need someone to cover the role of Isolde, and Madeleine likes having people she knows around when she travels to foreign countries."

"What if war breaks out while I'm there?" Yvonne asked.

Raymond waved his glass of Courvoisier in the air. Color had returned to his cheeks. Yvonne's plan seemed to please him. "The government will pull us from the brink; that's politics. They don't mean a word of the big threats either side hurls at each other. You needn't worry."

"I'm not comfortable—" Yvonne started.

Raymond swatted her comment away as if a fly were buzzing around in the afternoon sun. "Think of it as some well-deserved weeks of leisure, Yvonne dear. The fresh air of Bavaria in the summer!"

Yvonne watched him gesticulate in front of her. He was putting on a show for her benefit. Just the idea of traveling to Bayreuth alarmed her. No one should be going to Germany now.

"Do you want roles in Paris or not?" Raymond said.

Roles, plural. He knew she would pick up on that.

"Good roles too," Raymond said. "Roles that'll make the critics rave about you, and all in the same season."

How Yvonne yearned to believe him. But he was a hustler: he only said what he needed to say to get people to do what he wanted.

"Put it in writing," she said. "And add that you'll pay me six months of my salary if you don't keep your word."

Was that a hint of admiration in Raymond's eyes? Although Yvonne wasn't paid much, six months would dent his bank account. He seemed to see her for the first time. She held his stare, a smile etched on her face.

After a while, Raymond burst out laughing. "You're a tougher broad than I thought. We're going to get along. But remember: no Bayreuth, no Paris. You bet I'll put that in writing too."

❦

Night had already fallen when Yvonne stepped out of the Louis Blanc metro station in the tenth arrondissement. Hélène had insisted on inviting her to a tea house to celebrate the good news. Yvonne hadn't dared say no, in case fate found her ungrateful and snatched her one success away from her when she'd had barely any time to savor it. Hélène had told all the waiters that Yvonne was about to become a famous opera singer, so of course the waiters had kept the petits fours coming and refilled their cups of tea for free. It had been a good evening. Yvonne would've stayed even longer if Hélène hadn't had to return to her family—her children were much younger than Jules, and her husband would never prepare his own dinner. Yvonne had promised to pay for the whole family to attend a performance of hers in Paris, when the time came. It wouldn't take much longer now. She broke into a run. She hadn't felt happier since she'd received her acceptance letter from the Conservatory.

Workers' tenements threw long shadows behind the rail yards. She carried a box of éclairs from the bakery near Raymond's office, where everything cost twice as much as anywhere else. Yvonne tried not to compare her neighborhood with the part of Paris she was just coming from, but it was hard not to notice the difference. The houses in her street needed a coat of paint. Moss had crept over the shop awnings. The dresses in the storefronts looked like they'd been made straight from cutouts in *Marie-Claire*, and Yvonne herself might've made a better job of sewing them. Yvonne hadn't expected to remain in this neighborhood for long, but here she was. She couldn't afford anything else. Oh, why ruin this evening with such thoughts? She admired the name of the bakery shop on the cardboard box. She'd almost lost hope she'd ever have a reason to buy from them. Yet here she was! She felt—what was the word?—victorious.

She slipped on a broken cobblestone when she crossed the street. She caught herself, clutching her box of pastries. Saved, she said to herself, proud of her quick reaction time. When her building came into view, Yvonne counted the windows down from the roof, left from the edge. A lamp drew a circle of light in her living room: Jules was home. She ran faster.

Sure, the elevator hadn't worked since April, but she wasn't going to let that decrease her enthusiasm. Yvonne stepped over cigarette butts and crumpled paper in the stairwell as if she sauntered across a field full of daisies. On the fourth floor, a Chopin mazurka filled the empty hallway. Jules played as well as George Enescu, didn't he? It boggled Yvonne's mind that her neighbors didn't pull up chairs in the corridor to listen to him practicing.

Yvonne fumbled with her keys, pushed her front door open. Home at last! Time to start the celebration, even if it was small. Better to ignore the pile of letters by the phone, the bills from creditors. Yvonne felt like singing Beethoven's "Ode to Joy," but she didn't know it by heart. On the walls hung cheap drawings of Paris she'd bought from the bouquinistes on the quays for the price of a croissant, hoping to impress guests if anyone came around, except that she didn't have friends and whoever Jules knew from school didn't venture up here.

Jules nodded at her when she entered the living room, although he kept playing the mazurka. He was seventeen now, the age she'd been when she'd become pregnant with him, and the spitting image of Paul at that age. What would've her career looked like if she hadn't had to stop her training because of him? She was desperate to set a good example for her son, but her career was in a ditch. Maybe he'd conclude he should become a pharmacist. That thought terrified her. Jules remained quiet about his plans after high school, but Yvonne was certain he should study the piano at the Conservatory. He needed a good teacher, though, and good teachers cost money. Yvonne had none. So perhaps Jules would've indeed been better off with Paul.

Jules ended the mazurka with a flourish.

Yvonne clapped. "Bis!"

"C'mon," Jules said, as embarrassed as if there'd been witnesses.

"I could listen to you all night," Yvonne said.

"Just wait until I play Schoenberg," Jules said.

Yvonne laughed. Records were stacked in haphazard piles by the window near the Victrola, the result of both Yvonne's and Jules's casual approach to order. Yvonne had spread her music scores over the dining table, while Jules kept his on the floor around the piano. Recordings of Beethoven piano sonatas were piled in precarious towers.

"What did you bring?" Jules asked, pointing at the pastries.

"Spinach and lettuce from the market," Yvonne said, because the bakery's name was written in big letters Jules couldn't fail to read. She laughed at her own joke before Jules could roll his eyes. "My luck just made such a U-turn I'm getting whiplash. I'm going to sing in Paris."

Jules bounded away from the piano bench. "When?"

Yvonne cut the rope wrapped around the box. "That's not decided yet, but it's going to be a good role. A great role, even."

Jules whistled when he saw the éclairs. He adored éclairs, like Paul. She'd bought them for that reason. "Come on, give me a clue," he said. He fetched plates from the sideboard.

"I'd love something Italian, but I'll sing anything they send my way. It'll say in my contract Raymond will owe me a ton of money if he doesn't find me roles, so he'll keep his word. Don't those éclairs look delicious? Oh, we can't have a party without music!"

Yvonne picked up her recording of Brahms's Double Concerto, the one featuring Jacques Thibaud and Pablo Casals. She took pride in knowing those names, in selecting the best recordings at the music store, where she knew more than the clerk. The Victrola began to spin. How did Madeleine celebrate when she learned she'd star in yet another production? She'd had so many leading roles in Paris, she probably yawned and went straight to bed when she snatched another one. But maybe, if she'd been cast at La Scala or Covent Garden, she'd open a bottle of Veuve Clicquot to show the fates she remained grateful. One day, Yvonne would have enough money for such extravagance. Until then, she'd stick to more modest ways.

She listened to Pablo Casals, in awe, for a few bars. Only Madeleine had ever been able to impress her so.

"You should try your hand at composing," Yvonne said. "Something with a soprano part?"

"Right after I get the Nobel Prize in Medicine," Jules said, smiling.

"And if you do want to become a soloist—"

"Perhaps I want to become a banker."

"That's why you practice Chopin," Yvonne said. She placed the éclairs on a serving plate, all parallel to each other. Fancy people like Madeleine must arrange them so.

"That'd sure impress the customers," Jules said.

Yvonne and Jules clinked their glasses full of sparkling water. At least it wasn't from the tap.

Jules took a bite of éclair. "Why did Raymond change his mind, after all this time?"

"Don't hold it against him he finally saw the light," Yvonne said.

"But what's in it for him? If he'd cared to get you roles, he would've found them a long time ago."

Yvonne put down her fork.

"Sorry," Jules said.

She served him another éclair to change the conversation. On the recording, violinist Jacques Thibaud displayed astonishing dexterity in the *allegro*. Yvonne heard longing, wistfulness, the ache of dreams that weren't getting realized.

You're distracting yourself with that music, she thought out of the blue, *but the problem isn't going to go away.*

"If things work out, and I'm praying the saints they will, you'll have to spend time with friends of yours in late spring while I'm out of town," Yvonne said. "But I suppose you could stay by yourself, too, if you prefer. You're old enough now. I'd only ask a neighbor to check on you every so often." She made a bright smile. Surely that'd win him over.

"Where are you going?"

"It's not sure I'll go yet," Yvonne said. "And once Raymond delivers the roles he promised me, I'll find steady work here."

Jules didn't reply. The recording circled on the Victrola. After the long violin solo, the orchestra made an entrance full of panache, imbuing the score with a sense of hope and determination.

Don't let your mind wander now, Yvonne told herself. *You'll make a mistake otherwise.*

"You're being really mysterious," Jules said. "The only thing you ever do is understudy Madeleine. Why would this be different?"

"My last time as Madeleine's understudy," Yvonne said brightly.

"So you're going abroad," Jules said. "The magnificent Madeleine Moreau wouldn't bother with the provinces. What role is it for? Tosca in Milan?"

Yvonne cut her slice of éclair in two, and then in two again. She might as well tell him now. She would have to tell him eventually.

"Isolde's understudy at Bayreuth. I'll be back before you even notice I'm gone."

Jules swiveled the water in his glass. "Bayreuth sounds like a German name."

"It's just a small town in Bavaria, deep in the hills," Yvonne said. "They don't care for Hitler's politics. With luck, powerful folks will notice me, folks who can help my career, and they'll invite me to sing somewhere else." Her eyes shone with possibility. The stay in Germany might be distasteful, but it wouldn't last long.

"And with no luck," Jules said, "Madeleine will get sick and you'll sing for the Fritzes."

"Madeleine won't get sick. She never does. She'll sing even if she's sick for the very first time in her career. She wouldn't let an opportunity like Bayreuth pass her by."

"You'll be stuck across the border if war starts while you're there."

Jules furrowed his brow just like his father did when he was angry. Yvonne waved away the image of Paul, Paul who'd remarried and, she was told, become the most popular teacher at the high school where he taught. He'd even won an award at the end of the previous academic year. It was almost as if the divorce—filed by Yvonne—had allowed him to scale new heights now that she no longer weighed him down. He had a wife who made a modest but stable living as a schoolteacher like him and whose dreams didn't overshadow her husband's. Yvonne was still waiting to meet the conductor who'd sweep her off her feet and help her reach the top of the opera world.

"I refuse to hear any dark talk from you," she said. "There won't be a war. It's all a lot of posturing from politicians who bring their countries to the brink to finagle a better deal."

Jules pushed his plate away.

"Finish your éclairs," Yvonne said, the smile still firm on her face but her voice less assured. "I'm not going to eat all that by myself. Here, take the biggest."

On the other side of the wall, Yvonne's neighbors turned their radio on. Accordion notes filled the apartment, ruining the brilliance of the Brahms double concerto. Surely Madeleine could listen to all the music she wanted in her big house in Neuilly.

"You shouldn't go, Mother."

"I won't sing in Paris next year if I don't go to Bayreuth now. If I can't get cast next year, my career is finished. I graduated from the Conservatory years ago. Waves of new singers are looking for the same jobs. The only person who can help me is Raymond, and he won't help without Bayreuth." She plucked a slice of éclair off the serving plate, clinging to the hope she could salvage her little party. The celebration wasn't turning out the way she'd planned.

"If Raymond didn't want to give you roles before, he'll find a way not to give them to you now," Jules said.

Yvonne dropped her éclair. It splattered onto the table, cream bursting out of the side.

"You haven't heard me sing in a long time," Yvonne said. "I mean, really sing, in a performance hall, not the way I sing over Rosa Ponselle here. I deserve to be onstage."

"Some people have loads of talent but never make it big," Jules said. "Isn't that what happened to Father? He wrote great poems, and yet he couldn't find readers for them."

"Your father gave up on his dream," Yvonne said. Her voice was sharper now.

"At least he's not going to hobnob with enemies of France," Jules said.

Yvonne wiped the cream off the table. "I'm headed to Bayreuth to be an understudy again. Who do you think cares about hobnobbing with me?"

Jules would've understood if she had quit. It pained Yvonne, in fact, that he would've understood her quitting but didn't understand her stubbornness. Did he take more after Paul than her?

"I'll enlist if there is a war," Jules said coldly.

A sense of dread came over Yvonne. "You and your big words," she said. "What if you injure your hands?" She bit her bottom lip. Of course she worried there'd be a war, even if in front of Jules she pretended otherwise. All she hoped was that it wouldn't start before the end of summer.

"We all have to contribute for the important things," Jules said.

"Ruining your future—"

"At least I'm not ruining my present," Jules said.

Five

May 1939

Madeleine climbed down the train onto the platform at the Bayreuth station under the late spring sun. She gritted her teeth and lowered the rim of her hat to hide one more swastika from her sight, that one hanging above the ticket office. What a blight on the landscape. Why did public officials so far away from Berlin put up with Hitler's delusions? How bewildering that an entire country had fallen under that madman's spell.

A bright sun drenched the platform. It was a day to sing Nabucco's "Ben io t'invenni," a day that should have warmed Madeleine's heart. But Francisco Franco had claimed victory in the Spanish Civil War, and Slovakia had just deprived thirty thousand Jews of their citizenship. Italy and Germany had announced an alliance—officially to maintain peace in Europe. Madeleine could recognize it for what it was, though. That alliance was meant to scare other countries. The political situation was about to worsen, and yet the Bayreuth festival was going on as scheduled.

Madeleine plucked her fan out of her purse and watched herself stand on the platform, searing the memory in her mind, regardless of whether making the trip had been a good idea. Her bright-red taffeta travel suit stood out from a hundred meters away among the modest, light-colored garments of German housewives scurrying toward the exit. It was the same red as the swastika banners, and it occurred to Madeleine that she should have brought a white-and-blue scarf so she could wear the French colors instead.

Next to her, Yvonne hauled their suitcases to the platform before the train rumbled away. Her off-white dress, flaring at the hem below the knee and adorned with a matching thin belt at the waist, reminded Madeleine of her maid's mop after she had dusted off the floors. She could tell Yvonne had bought it used.

"Did you take the suitcase with my cocktail dresses off the train?" Madeleine asked without helping Yvonne. She expected Winifred Wagner to invite her to tea and was determined to look her best.

Yvonne grabbed her own beaten-up travel bag and threw it on top of Madeleine's suitcases.

"I think I did," Yvonne said, pointing at a suitcase with her foot. Madeleine shut up.

Perhaps she was tired of the leading lady. Madeleine knew she could get insufferable when she was upset, and she had been more than upset since the train had crossed the German border. She wouldn't have gone if the festival organizers hadn't picked Yvonne to understudy Isolde, and she was also upset at herself for letting such a development sway her decision. Hopefully, Stefan would forgive her impulse to sign her contract in front of Raymond when she had heard the news. And if Stefan did not, hopefully the history books wouldn't find her important enough to mention. Madeleine had never had that feeling before—the feeling of wanting to be small.

Yvonne dragged one last suitcase out of the train. Madeleine's eight leather suitcases of the latest fashion were piled on the platform and, next to them, Yvonne's two worn-out and shapeless travel bags. "Everything is accounted for."

It would have sounded like a victory if Yvonne had been hired as Madeleine's personal assistant and not a singer in her own right. But Yvonne let Madeleine treat her that way, didn't she? So Madeleine did not shoulder all the blame.

The conductor blew the train whistle in the high pitch of the G major sixth chord: G, B, D, E. The train picked up speed. Now Madeleine was stranded in Bayreuth. Although the prospect of making history filled her with pride, she dreaded singing at the festival. Once the French

Railways locomotive had pulled its eight wagons across the German border on the trip from Paris, swastikas had sprouted left and right, dangling from lamp poles, wrapped around officers' armbands, shining like third eyes above the visor on their caps. At the border checkpoint, a battalion of brownshirts had patrolled the land as if refugees from the five continents clamored to be let into Germany. A soldier who looked too young to have graduated high school had barked at Madeleine, his finger on the trigger of his Karabiner rifle, when she had not located her passport fast enough. She was still fuming about it. She had never been more afraid. But she had made it through the checkpoint and back onto the train, while the soldier had remained at the border.

Then, in the train that Yvonne and Madeleine had boarded in Hamburg, their fellow passengers—two salesmen and an elderly couple on their way to visit relatives—had argued about whether the war would break out in July or in September. Madeleine had kept her face expressionless, pretending not to understand German, but Yvonne had turned so white one would have thought Count Dracula had just exsanguinated her.

The elderly couple and the more heavyset of the two salesmen expected war in July. The thinner salesman, though, insisted that the Führer would not launch hostilities before the end of summer: he would not put his soldiers through the numbing heat of August. The others laughed him off. Henri had insisted there would be no war at all, but that was not the Germans' opinion. Madeleine wished he had gone on the trip with her—it would have been good to see how he reacted at that moment. Perhaps he would have found something witty to say. Instead, he was preparing to tour Belgium, Switzerland, and the eastern part of France with the Paris Opera Orchestra.

Madeleine had spent the rest of the trip in the restaurant car, leaving a sick-looking Yvonne to watch over their belongings while she drank bad wine and watched Holstein cows graze in lush fields along the train tracks. If there was a war, France would win it hands down. And hopefully the French ambassador would telegraph Madeleine to cross the border in time. Before leaving for Germany, she had made sure to remind him of her trip.

In Bayreuth, train passengers hastened toward the exit. The sun baked the platform. On the other side of the gate, a young man in a loose-fitting suit, his blond hair carefully combed to the side, held a humongous bouquet of Peruvian lilies that hid half his face. Madeleine strolled toward the young man, careful not to appear easily won over.

"I take it you're my welcoming committee," she said in German to the youngster after she plucked the flowers from his arms. The lilies smelled like they had been cut that morning. The symphony of colors buoyed Madeleine's spirits. Winifred Wagner bore no responsibility for an ignoramus in a brown shirt at the border waving a gun and yelling at her.

"Only the best for our great accomplished Madeleine Moreau," the boy finally said in hesitant French, in the tone of a schoolboy reciting a poem, "whom it is our great honor to welcome to Bayreuth today." His delivery could not have been more wooden, but at least Winifred had ordered that Madeleine be greeted in French. Madeleine nodded appreciatively. If she could have forgotten about the swastikas for a moment, her trip would have been going well.

But she could not. The swastikas were there, immense in size, flapping in the wind.

The young man—Ernst, according to the name tag on his lapel—opened the rear door of a black Mercedes for Madeleine. Yvonne trudged behind them with the bags on a cart.

Madeleine sat down on the back seat and placed her handbag next to her. "Sit in the front," she told Yvonne.

Ernst shoved six of the suitcases into the trunk and two by Yvonne's feet before wedging himself behind the steering wheel. Madeleine rubbed her hand against the leather upholstery. Winifred Wagner was treating her well.

"Let's stop by the Festspielhaus before going to the hotel," Madeleine said in halting German.

The bouquet on her lap almost blocked her view, but Madeleine still caught glimpses of the landscape between the red, yellow, and white flowers. Spruce trees and silver birches lined the streets. The two-story houses were painted in the same pastel colors as the dresses of the German housewives. It was a pretty town, maybe a little bland. Swastika banners hung along the promenade, but that didn't mean the Bayreuth residents approved of them. They were all opera lovers, kindred spirits, in the only town in the world where Madeleine could expect just about everyone to adore Wagnerian works. And since those works were her specialty, that also meant the locals were about to adore her as well. Madeleine cherished the prospect of becoming the idol of people who hadn't heard her sing yet. What a treat for them.

At an intersection in the historic part of town, a sign was tucked in a restaurant's window: NO JEWS OR DOGS ALLOWED.

Madeleine had known stores were forbidding Jews, but it was different to see the sign in person. She buried her face in the bouquet. What was that feeling rising inside her—shame? disgust? Bayreuth had enchanted her for all of two seconds, but she would not like it again. On the next block, the windowpane of a storefront of a bookstore was splintered like a cobweb. Madeleine was tempted to ignore it but realized that her reactions were bound to be reported to Winifred Wagner.

"What happened?" Madeleine asked in German, pointing at the store.

"Children playing, I assume," Ernst said.

But children at play would not have painted a Star of David high on the front door. Madeleine should have listened to Stefan. What a mistake to come here. Her ambition had clouded her judgment.

"Please stop kicking my seat," Yvonne said in French, glancing at Madeleine over her shoulder. She had become pale. Her eyes swept from one side of the street to the other. She was naïve, sure, but far from dumb. And now they found themselves deep in enemy territory.

After another turn, the Festspielhaus came into view, on top of the hill amid thick shrubbery. It was a squat redbrick building sporting a round terrace on the second floor. Predictably, a swastika hung from its roof. Madeleine looked away. A sign at the top marked the name of the street. Adolf-Hitler-Strasse. Madeleine dug her fingernails into the stems of the lilies. She felt like a pawn on a chessboard, scrambling for safety and yet so far away from the knight and the tower who could protect her.

"I wonder if there's a statue for him somewhere," Yvonne said coldly. She had seen the sign too. But she should not be more upset than Madeleine. Yvonne's name didn't appear in the festival promotion materials.

Ernst's face showed no reaction. He didn't seem to understand French beyond the few sentences he had learned by heart. Instead, he tapped against the windshield, in the direction of the Festspielhaus, and spoke in German: "Herr Hitler saved it when the Jews left the country."

That Hitler man needed no compliment. If Madeleine had not had all her suitcases in the car with her, she would have opened the door and walked away. But she was also keenly aware that she had been stupid in accepting the invitation, and whatever she decided to do now, she had to be twice as smart.

The car inched toward the Festspielhaus behind a truck that puffed up the hill. A family of five lounged around a picnic basket in the grass while a group of boys chased butterflies. On a bench, an elderly man read the newspaper next to a perfectly manicured flower bed. They all looked like civilized people. And yet.

"The Jews had been buying most of the tickets before the new laws came into effect," Ernst said in German. He probably meant the Nuremberg laws, which had deprived German Jews of their citizenship. "When the Jews fled, he ordered his officers to attend the performances," Ernst said. "That gave Frau Wagner the money she needed to keep the festival afloat. A remarkable man, our Führer."

Madeleine pretended to admire the scenery outside the car windows. She pinched off one of the lilies from the bouquet and crumpled it between her fingers.

Ernst pulled over near the entrance of the Festspielhaus. Around the box office, a row of billboards bearing the Bayreuth seal announced the operas to be produced that season. *Parsifal. Der Ring. Tristan und Isolde.* Madeleine's name was printed in large letters on that last one. She sat straighter on the back seat. Seeing her name on a billboard filled her with a joy that nothing else could match. Her gaze drifted up to the conductor's name. Franz von Hoesslin.

She blinked hard.

"I guess Wilhelm Furtwängler won't be coming this year," Yvonne said.

Madeleine opened the door of the Mercedes so fast she was already out before Yvonne could even reach for the handle and stormed into the building. A lone typewriter clicked in the distance. Small plaques by the doors listed their occupants' names. For the longest time it seemed that Madeleine would not find the person she was looking for. Finally, she located his office at the end of the corridor.

A short man with an oversized forehead pored through stacks of files at a large wooden desk. His temples were much grayer than the top of his hair. He wore round glasses, like Dmitri Shostakovich. A bust of Richard Wagner had been placed on the edge of the table. People so predictable could not be smart.

The general manager, Heinz Tietjen, looked up when Madeleine charged in.

"I was told Wilhelm Furtwängler would conduct *Tristan*," Madeleine said. It upended her calculations if he did not attend. She had believed she had the implicit blessing of one of the best conductors of the decade, if he took part in the festival with her. But if he had fled, she should not stay either.

For a moment, Heinz's face remained blank. Then a smile popped up. "My dear Madeleine! My warmest welcome." Heinz hurried around his desk and kissed her hand. "How was your trip? Please, have a seat. Would you like a cup of coffee? Tea? Sparkling water?"

Madeleine did not sit down. "Why isn't Furtwängler conducting *Tristan*?"

Heinz kept his smile firmly on his face. "He's occupied elsewhere."

Madeleine struggled to find the words in German and switched to French. "How could he have had no other commitments when I signed the contract, yet be unavailable now?"

Heinz stared blankly. After a moment, Yvonne translated. It annoyed Madeleine that Yvonne's German was far superior to hers.

Heinz crumpled a piece of paper and threw it in the wastebasket. "You are the understudy," he said without looking at Yvonne, his voice colder. He took Madeleine by the arm. "Here, let me give you a tour."

They strolled toward the performance hall. Madeleine wished that Yvonne had stayed far behind, but she could hear her high heels clicking at her back. The three of them pushed aside thick drapes hanging from stone columns and entered the auditorium with the reverence usually reserved for church. The sets of *Parsifal* had already been hoisted onstage, but those of *Tristan* were propped in the back. A tower in cardboard reached toward the spotlights. Tristan and Isolde would meet in its shadow in the second act. Madeleine's face softened: the stage designer, world-renowned Emil Preetorius, had outdone himself.

"Think of this as an island of peace during these troubled times," Heinz said in German. "A bubble that exists far from the turmoil surrounding us."

Madeleine remembered just in time not to roll her eyes.

Heinz nudged her toward the costume shop. Employees scuttled in and out of offices. Stagehands carrying ladders on their shoulders nodded at him when they strode by. Yvonne remained a few steps behind Madeleine and Heinz, but Heinz showed no interest in her. Clearly, he had played no part in imposing her on the cast. That pleased Madeleine, but it also meant only Winifred could have served as Yvonne's advocate. Why would she have bothered plucking a French understudy out of obscurity? It worried Madeleine that Winifred might have heard something magical in Yvonne's voice.

The group's footsteps echoed in the costume shop, which was full of the most expensive fabric and the prettiest ribbons. Seamstresses threaded their needles along the hems of evening gowns and army uniforms.

Heinz pushed a mannequin toward Madeleine. "Isolde's dress in the first act. You'll look stunning. Critics seem inclined to write you dithyrambic reviews praising your musicianship to the moon—far better reviews than what Marta Fuchs got when she sang Isolde last year. Are you ready to make history?"

Madeleine ran her fingers along the side of the long, white dress. The cloth felt like tulle and silk. She could not pull her hand away. What bug had bitten her that she had considered quitting the festival because of broken windows downtown and a conductor's name that failed to impress her? Winifred held no control over the thugs roaming through the city. The ticketholders wouldn't care who stood in the orchestra's pit once they heard Madeleine sing. She could not wait to leave her mark on the festival.

☙

Yvonne turned around a street corner in search of the dry cleaners. She'd gotten lost earlier, wandering in the small streets of Bayreuth under the sun. Thankfully, an elderly lady had shown her the way. The lady had seemed to believe that Yvonne was a maid, that she was doing a favor to an invisible, wealthy notable, and that the favor would be returned to her a thousandfold. Yvonne had been in no mood to correct her. The strap of the bag full of Madeleine's dresses hurt her shoulder.

Madeleine sure had chosen her moment to inconvenience Yvonne the most. By running yet another errand for her, Yvonne would miss the social hour with Emil Preetorius that she'd so looked forward to attending. That night, he'd address festival donors and longtime patrons and describe how he'd designed the set for *Tristan und Isolde*. Yvonne didn't care for set design, but supporting singers and understudies from the cast would sing musical excerpts. She hadn't been asked to participate. Yet, if she was already there, perhaps she'd be invited to.

The same thought must've crossed Madeleine's mind, because she'd suddenly found an urgent need for all her dresses to be sent to the dry cleaners. Yvonne couldn't disobey the star of the show. So here she was, hurrying through Bayreuth, carrying a load of Madeleine's dirty gowns instead of practicing "Liebestod."

She entered the small shop and pulled the gowns one by one out of her bag, wiping the sweat from her forehead, proud of herself for reaching the store before closing time. "It must be done by tomorrow," she said in German.

The woman beyond the counter looked her up and down and counted the garments. "Name?" she asked.

"Frau Madeleine Moreau," Yvonne said. "She's singing Isolde at the Festspielhaus."

"But we pick up principals' clothes directly from the hotel," the clerk said. "Didn't Frau Moreau read the note we left in her room?"

I bet she did, Yvonne thought, while she dabbed her handkerchief all over her face. According to the clock on the wall, the social hour with Emil Preetorius had started twenty minutes earlier. She wouldn't be back in time. Perhaps she should admit she was bound for obscurity.

Six

Madeleine listened in awe and not a small amount of envy as Max Lorenz, standing in a large, airy rehearsal room with big windows at the back of the Festspielhaus, sang Tristan's "Unsre Liebe." They had been rehearsing for six weeks now, through the controversy of the *M.S. St. Louis* full of Jewish refugees from Germany being denied permission to dock in Havana; through Nazi troops gathering at Danzig, a Baltic Sea port that had been German before the Great War; through the southern part of England being darkened for one night for an air raid test. Madeleine had never read more newspapers than she did these days, although they were all biased in support of the Third Reich. French newspapers did not reach Bayreuth, nor did British ones. Madeleine was glad that the premiere would be held in two days, in front of opera connoisseurs. She expected a triumph, complete with euphoric praise from the critics and adoring applause from the spectators. It should have been exciting—it was perhaps one of the last opportunities she had to shine before her voice eventually betrayed her—but the looming war worried her. She had stopped caring about the possibility that Max would upstage her at the end of June, when Winston Churchill had made a speech urging Hitler to reconsider the course he was putting his country in. This speech had been met with derision by Nazi officers of any rank.

Max's aria ended. "I needed just a bit more time to get to the high A." He was speaking to Franz von Hoesslin, who was sitting at the piano.

"I'm at a loss to find anything to improve about this," Franz said.

Even Madeleine, who distracted herself from European politics by listening to Max with more intensity than she had ever listened to anyone before, had not detected any flaw in his singing. Max, who had thrown his felt hat on top of a chair, picked it up and swatted the air with it. His brown eyes and brown hair made him look as un-Aryan as Hitler himself.

"Ready?" Franz asked Madeleine from behind the piano. His voice seemed reproachful, as if he had been waiting for her for several minutes, although her daydreaming had lasted seconds.

Madeleine's old companion, sweat-drenching fear, reared its head again. But she launched into "Doch unsre Liebe" the way Wagnerian heroines stepped onto a warpath. The air was hot and sticky. Madeleine dabbed her neck with a handkerchief while she sang. She upgraded one of her high notes on the fly to impress Max.

"Please follow the score," Franz said in German when Madeleine was done. "I place great value in respecting the composer's intention."

The words stung. Max himself, smoothing his hat, did not appear to have noticed Madeleine's prowess. Or perhaps he was determined to slight her?

Franz played the first notes of "So Stürben Wir, Um Ungetrennt." Max and Madeleine, who did not talk to each other outside rehearsals, sang together like two smitten lovers, Max's voice joining Madeleine's in a firework of high notes sure to make attendees gasp. In that small room tucked in the far hills of Bavaria, Max peered at Madeleine the way Henri had before he married her, the way Stefan had when he first shared the stage with her. As their voices soared, she regretted that French journalists could not witness how she and Max reached new heights of musicianship together.

Franz pulled his glasses up his nose and eyed Max. "I'm running out of superlatives to characterize your performance." To Madeleine he said nothing.

The door to the rehearsal room opened. A plump woman in a shirtwaist dress and a matching cardigan, her hair curled at the ends in a vague approximation of style, poked her head inside. As always,

Winifred Wagner looked like a secretary straight out of the typewriting pool. Although she could make or break careers with a snap of her fingers, she seemed to relish looking bland and modest. An elderly man in a military uniform, his chest lined with ribbons and medals, stood behind her.

"Here's the *Tristan* cast," Winifred said. Next to her, a white-haired man smoothed his walrus moustache.

"Let me introduce you to our famous Max Lorenz," Winifred told the man. "Last year he received eight curtain calls at *Tristan*'s premiere. Or was it ten? Max, here's General Ewald von Lochow."

Ewald nodded at him. "I heard you took Bayreuth by storm back in '33, son."

"The best Siegfried these walls have ever heard," Winifred said. "Our Führer's favorite heldentenor."

Max bowed to Ewald, a deep bow that revolted Madeleine. "Your campaigns during the Great War kept me spellbound, sir, especially your command of the Third Corps at Verdun."

Verdun, where her brother had been killed. The Third Corps, which had done the killing in 1916.

Madeleine's rage boiled so quickly it took even her by surprise.

"And here's Franz von Hoesslin, the pride of Germany," Winifred said. "Only the most talented conductors can tackle *Tristan*'s scores."

Everybody smiled to everybody else with content airs. Madeleine's stomach convulsed, and she hoped she wouldn't throw up.

Ewald tapped his cane against the ground. "Loyal, not like his predecessor, I hear. What a shame that one let us down. Treasonous, if you want to know what I think."

"We wish Wilhelm much luck," Winifred said. "Franz will replace him brilliantly."

Wilhelm—that was Furtwängler. Had he refused to appear at the Festspielhaus because of Hitler's policies? And if a German had reached that decision, what was Madeleine doing here?

"And this is Madeleine Moreau, who's visiting us from France," Winifred said.

"Brangäne?" Ewald asked.

"Isolde," Winifred said with an even smile.

Ewald, leaning on his cane, stretched his arm toward Madeleine, a little too far out of Madeleine's reach so that she had to cross the space between them to shake his hand. She stiffened when his skin touched hers.

"Hopefully you'll show yourself worthy of this honor," Ewald said in German, not even asking Winifred if Madeleine could understand him.

Winifred made a little smile, as if the situation could only turn out for the best for her: either Madeleine let down everyone at the premiere, in which case all the Germans would feel superior to the French, or she awed the audience, and the newspapers would report on Winifred's stroke of genius in focusing on art when war was near. "We'll let our dear cast practice now." Winifred made her way to the door and glanced at Madeleine over her shoulder. "We wouldn't forget if they disappointed us on opening day."

Max touched Madeleine's elbow after Winifred and Ewald had left. "Do you need to sit down?"

He had kind eyes when he was looking at her, but Madeleine pushed his hand away.

She tottered to the door, followed the corridor in the direction opposite the one Winifred and Ewald had taken, flung the exit door open, stumbled outside into the sun-drenched garden, and started walking around the building so she could go and sit on a bench near the front.

Gleaming Grosser Mercedes were parked in front of the Festspielhaus. Madeleine collapsed onto a bench on the side of the building, where she did not have to look at the sedans.

One last black Mercedes, this one open-top, rounded the curve at the top of the hill and pulled in front of the door. A retinue of brownshirts scattered out of the car when the driver stopped. Goebbels? Himmler? A short man in a yellow mustard uniform, his brown hair cropped short, bounded out of the front passenger seat. Bystanders on the lawn broke into the Nazi salute. The officer raised his arm at them. His elbow hid his face from Madeleine, but his toothbrush moustache left no doubt of who he was. Madeleine pressed her back against the bench so hard she felt the wooden slats imprinting themselves in her flesh. An aide scurried forward and held the entrance door to the Festspielhaus open for Adolf Hitler.

Madeleine slid onto her knees and retched in the bushes. Footsteps drew near. She recognized the Oxford shoes.

"It must be something I ate," Madeleine said.

"I don't like them any more than you do," Max said, "but you're going to shove us behind the eight ball if you don't pretend a little better."

He helped her sit back on the bench. "I was tried two years ago after I was found with a younger man." It took a second for Madeleine to realize what he meant, because he wore a wedding band. "I would've been banned from the stage if Winifred hadn't fought for me, and my career is the only reason authorities pretend not to know my wife is Jewish. Franz is in their crosshairs too. His wife is Jewish too, and he's a quarter Jewish himself. He was exiled not too long ago for refusing to conduct the Horst-Wessel-Lied, Hitler's anthem. It took Winifred all her influence over the Führer to get him back. We've got to remain in his good graces."

What could Madeleine say in her broken German that wouldn't sound trite? She was used to grand gestures onstage, pronouncements about music and her fellow singers that hammered in her superiority over her colleagues. She had no clue how to talk about politics to innocent people tormented by Hitler.

"I need us to make wonders onstage, even if you loathe who's in the audience." Max pulled out a blade of grass and rolled it between his fingers. "You're aware that Hitler will attend our performances, aren't you?"

Madeleine fixed on the one tiny cloud in the blue sky until the urge to retch had again faded. "I am now," she said after a while.

"He and Winifred are close friends. He stays at her house when he's in town. Their parties last till dawn. We're expected to be there. Surely your manager warned you."

Raymond would hear from Madeleine the first chance she got to call him.

"I'm trying to keep my wife and her family out of harm's way," Max said. "You're the one who had the choice to stay home but came here. Put on a good face."

Madeleine wiped sweat from her forehead with her handkerchief. She wished she hadn't left her fan inside. "What were they saying about Furtwängler?" she asked.

"After last season, he decided not to conduct in Germany as long as Hitler is chancellor. I'm not sure he'll be able to keep his word. The powers that be put a lot of pressure on him to pretend he supports the regime. They're mad he's helped so many Jewish musicians from the Berliner Philharmoniker go into exile. You look like you're going to faint."

"I'll go back to the inn and lie down. Tell Franz I'm not feeling well."

Madeleine hurried down the road, under the leafy poplar trees and the swastikas that hung from the streetlamps. Singing for Hitler! Was there still time to withdraw? She didn't even know if her contract included a penalty for leaving. And what about those in the audience who had not thrown in their lot with the Nazis? Wouldn't they be enchanted by her singing? Would she disappoint them if she fled?

At last, the inn came into view. A well-dressed woman with a big pouf of gray hair leafed through the *Völkischer Beobachter* under a painting of Richard Wagner. Madeleine dashed toward the elevator, which was manned by an attendant in leather pants and a Tyrolean hat. The one front desk employee who spoke French made a big smile at her.

"Did you see our Führer at the Festspielhaus?" he asked. "Some of our patrons mentioned his car was headed that way."

"I did not," Madeleine said.

The clerk looked sad for her. "It's only a matter of time. You'll see him at the premiere. I bet he'll come to your dressing room to congratulate you."

I will lock the door, Madeleine thought. She motioned toward the elevator.

"And you'll be seated next to him at dinner," the clerk said brightly in her back. "It's not too often that we have a French singer among us."

Madeleine decided on the spot that she had developed serious food allergies that prevented her from attending any formal dinner. She was relieved when the elevator doors closed between the two of them. The attendant pressed the button of her floor. *Breathe*, she kept telling herself. *Don't let your face show any expression. I bet employees here will report every word I say to Winifred.*

In the imperial suite, spacious and lavishly decorated, Madeleine rummaged through the cupboard until she retrieved the bottle of German wine she had ordered from the kitchen. The wine tumbled out into a water glass, one inch, two inches, three inches. Socializing with that madman! She took a long swig but did not feel better.

The suite had a sweeping view of the hills surrounding Bayreuth. Photographs of Madeleine in performance lined the desk, next to books the hotel management had gathered about Wagner in German and French—a volume about Wagner's life and legacy, one about Wagner's early works, the meaning of *Parsifal*, the years he had spent writing the *Ring*. Madeleine had thrown away the leaflet that contained the Führer's latest speeches at the Reichstag, printed on quality paper, when she had discovered it on her nightstand. She had placed pictures of Alexandre there instead. Her brother must be rolling in his grave now. Such stupidity on her part, obsessing over dazzling German audiences when the thunder of war rumbled near.

She lifted the phone receiver and asked the operator to connect her to France. But she did not plan to speak with Raymond—she gave the number of her home in Neuilly. She paced the floor and sipped her wine while she waited for the call back. Soon the bottle was half-empty. She looked at it, nostrils pinched, and then poured herself one more serving.

"Hitler's here," Madeleine said to Henri once the operator had rung her back. "He's going to attend *Tristan*."

The silence at the other end of the line dragged on. Madeleine wondered if the connection had been cut off.

"Worse things can happen than having a head of state at your performance," Henri said, although his voice sounded hesitant. He knew as well as she did that this was not a happy development.

Madeleine tugged hard on the phone cord. "He gets along swimmingly with Winifred Wagner. Stays at her house, even."

"So what? You came to sing Isolde. Do the job."

Who was this man, talking in her husband's voice? How could she have misjudged him so? Or had the signs been there all along while she had refused to see them? Madeleine felt alone in the world.

"The two of them host parties that last until the wee hours of the morning," Madeleine said. "They expect me to join them."

"Maybe you'll meet people who can get you invited to the Met. It'll be fine. Just sing the best you can."

Madeleine closed her eyes for a second, willing herself to remain calm, before cradling the receiver between her ear and neck. "I'm thinking about going home."

"Soon enough," Henri said.

"Now," Madeleine said.

"Are you out of your mind? You'll create a scandal if you leave them high and dry."

"A tempest in a glass of water."

"The situation between France and Germany is already fraught enough. You don't need a world war on your conscience."

"But—" Madeleine said. She rubbed her hand against the top of Alexandre's frame.

"You're singing," Henri said. "I'll see you at the end of the month. Astonish them!"

The line clicked on his good wishes, as if they would make a difference.

But Madeleine no longer had any interest in impressing this public. Enough was enough—she refused to be on the wrong side of history. In front of her, the bottle of wine was empty. It broke when she hurled it into the trash can. She did not need Henri's blessing. The illustrious Madeleine Moreau was headed back to Paris. She only had to figure out how to salvage what was left of her honor.

c ~ ๑

Madeleine, facing the rows of empty seats on the stage of the Festspiel-haus, sang the most poignant "Liebestod" that she was capable of. Franz waved his baton in the air for the orchestra's benefit, his sleeves rolled up in a futile attempt to fend off the heat. The premiere would take place the following day, and the air was electric. Madeleine finished singing.

"This was better, but the score calls for a slower tempo," she said in German.

Franz peered at her from over his glasses. "Spectators will get up and have a cup of coffee between notes if I slow it down further."

"Don't you take pride in respecting the score?" Madeleine smiled. "Let's try again."

Franz gave the musicians their signal. The orchestra played through another "Liebestod," and Madeleine delivered another masterful perfor-mance. Oh, they would miss her when she was gone, even if the tempo had become so slow that at every instant her voice risked falling from the precarious heights where it had perched itself.

"You have to correct the flutes," Madeleine said sweetly. "They're covering my voice."

"The flutes couldn't cover your voice even if they thought they were horns," Franz said.

"Are you suggesting I'm imagining things?" Madeleine took pains to sound astonished but not acrimonious. Perfectly polite. A professional.

Franz did not reply.

"Either the flutes are right or I am," Madeleine said. "Which one is it?"

"The flutes," Franz said.

This was exactly the reaction Madeleine had been hoping to draw from him over the previous hour. He had done her bidding at the speed of a tortoise, but he had done it at last.

"I will not work with people who have such poor understanding of Wagner that they denature his music," Madeleine said, gathering her papers. "I will not associate with a production where the staff displays such inferior musicianship." Her fingernails tore through the last page of the score. She hesitated one last moment before she took the jump, sweeping the air with her arm like Brünnhilde summoning the Valkyries around her. "I quit!"

Franz recoiled on the director's stand. In the pit, a violin bow dropped to the floor.

There was no turning back now. Madeleine felt awful that she'd had to criticize Franz in front of the musicians. He had, after all, proved a far better conductor than she had expected, and she didn't want to get him in trouble with the authorities. But she needed a reason to return to Paris. Otherwise, she would have to pay large indemnities to Winifred Wagner, a woman who supported the Nazis.

The flutists threw concerned glances at each other. "We could try again," the principal player said slowly, although he clearly did not understand what his group had done wrong, and with good reason.

"Our artistic differences cannot be bridged," Madeleine said. "I wish you good luck for the premiere."

Artistic differences—it meant that Madeleine had given the festival a try and it had sorely disappointed her. Not even the Festspielhaus measured up to her standards. Of course, there was no chance Winifred would let Yvonne step in—not another Frenchwoman, not after the scandal Madeleine was creating.

"This is such a detail," the concertmaster said, stumbling on his words, not believing what was happening.

Before she became tempted to agree with him, Madeleine grabbed her jacket, her hat, her purse, her shawl, her fan, the half-eaten bag of chocolates that Yvonne had procured for her that morning, and marched off the stage, careful not to rush, so that everyone could take a good look at her leaving. "And on top of it all, you can't even tell what's important from what's not in an aria," she said with contempt, so they would make it easy for her to go.

Once outside, she braced herself for footsteps behind her—they could not let her go without attempting to change her mind—but she was already outside and halfway down the hill when the festival's artistic director, Heinz Tietjen, caught up with her, panting like a tired old dog, struggling with the right words in French. "Now, Frau Moreau, what is it that I hear, you want to leave us?"

"I refuse to work with that conductor," Madeleine said, ashamed that she had to disparage Franz but knowing she had to save herself. "You'll get savaged in the reviews on opening day."

Heinz gave her a blank stare. She probably had talked too fast for him to understand.

"Emotions are running high because the premiere is upon us," he said in bad French. "But that's not a reason to give up."

"You should cable Marta Fuchs," Madeleine said, before she changed her mind. "I have a train to catch."

❦

The baritone understudying Melot stumbled into the small, windowless rehearsal room out of breath, his score of *Tristan* tucked under his arm. "Moreau is leaving Bayreuth!"

The other understudies gathered around him, eager for details, except Yvonne, who remained in the back. Did another Moreau besides Madeleine work at the festival, someone she hadn't heard of?

"She had an argument with the maestro," the understudy for Melot said. "Then she grabbed her things and left. Even Herr Tietjen couldn't make her reconsider. She must be on a train to Paris as we speak."

Yvonne's heart pounded. That man was talking about Madeleine all right, Madeleine who had never been sick in all the years Yvonne had worked with her.

"They cabled Marta Fuchs," Melot said.

Yvonne felt a wave of relief. She wouldn't have to sing for the Nazis.

"The problem is," Melot said, "Fuchs is vacationing in Greece, and even if she leaves for Bayreuth right away, she won't be here in time for the premiere."

Seven

Standing in the wings of the Festspielhaus in Isolde's white dress a day later, Yvonne rubbed her hand against the pulleys for good luck. Her words, her notes, her cues—everything had vanished from her mind. Had Madeleine ever suffered from such bad stage fright? What if the audience booed her off the stage? Now that the time had come for her to make her debut, she wished she were anywhere but in Nazi Germany.

In the auditorium, the spectators launched into a song.

Max tied Tristan's cape around his shoulders. "It's the Horst-Wessel-Lied." The Nazi anthem. "Hitler's here."

The evening was rapidly headed for disaster. How lucky, how convenient for Madeleine that she'd gotten into a disagreement with Franz von Hoesslin. How tragic for Yvonne that Madeleine hadn't taken Catherine with her to Bayreuth so Yvonne could've stayed away from this snake pit. But she was in Isolde's costume now, and she had to make the best of it.

Yvonne peeked between the side curtains. Stragglers who'd been trying to reach their seats—wooden so that the singers' voices wouldn't get absorbed by the cushions' fabric—had stopped and now sang along. They were dressed as for a ball among kings in Versailles: gentlemen in tuxedos or military uniforms adorned with ribbons, ladies in dazzling gowns embellished by necklaces of pearls or diamonds. Luckily, Yvonne couldn't lean far enough to see the Wagners' box in the back of the hall. She wiped her palms on her dress and hoped she hadn't brought bad luck on herself when she'd sent a cryptic telegram to Madeleine's home in Neuilly: SINGING TONIGHT. MUCH LOVE, YVONNE. Madeleine might not even have reached Paris yet, depending on which train she'd boarded out of Bayreuth. She could've traveled through Switzerland or Belgium or straight from Germany. But once she learned Hitler had sat among the spectators, she'd have a good laugh at Yvonne's expense. She'd gone out just in time and left Yvonne to deal with the aftermath. That shrew.

The Horst-Wessel-Lied ended.

"If I didn't know where we are, I'd say you're standing in the middle of a highway about to get run over by a truck," Max said.

Yvonne couldn't decide if she liked Max. He reminded her of Madeleine: someone who'd been blessed with a meteoric rise to the top and hadn't struggled to become famous. It didn't help her opinion of him that he was German, though she shouldn't be holding that against him. She simply didn't trust Germans, under the circumstances. Yet Max had gone out of his way to make her feel at ease in the past twenty-four hours, explaining the precise ways the director had wanted Madeleine to move across the stage in their scenes together while the director himself sat slumped on a seat and repeated that, with that unknown French-woman as Isolde, his beloved production was doomed.

Audience members groaned when Heinz Tietjen stepped onto the stage. He delivered the news without emotion: Madeleine Moreau had bowed out. Her colleague Yvonne Chevallier would serve as her replacement for the night. No one clapped.

Yvonne stumbled in the dark to take her spot and hit her knee against a crate. The set imitated the cargo hold of a ship. She'd forgotten where the props were. She hadn't even had a rehearsal in the performance hall. No one had expected her to replace Madeleine. She'd seen the set, and it'd been good enough.

Finally, she reached her mark. In front of her, in the dark mass of the parterre, row after row of spectators were about to witness the defining moment of her career. German spectators. Nazi spectators, some of them. And Hitler in the Wagners' box. Yvonne's anxiety exploded into dead calm, as if she'd stepped into the eye of a storm. It was too late to feel scared.

Franz popped up on the conductor's stand. The first bars of the overture rose into the hall. Then, one ominous note of music: the Tristan
chord. Bayreuth was forgotten now. Yvonne was Isolde, brought across
the sea by Tristan to marry King Mark. The headlights drew pale circles
onstage for the first act. In this place full of history where the best had
sung before her, Yvonne's voice soared high into the air.

Spectators banged their feet against the wooden floors when Yvonne
staggered back onstage for the final bows. Sweat ran through her hair.
Her dress, black this time, from the third act, stuck to her skin. The
audience roared. The stagehands grinned at her as she came back toward
them for a sip of water.

"You sure have German blood in your veins," one of them said. "It's
not possible otherwise, for you to sing the way you did."

That was an odd compliment, but Yvonne had never been praised
in public before, and she'd take whatever she could get. She stopped
counting the curtain calls, dabbed a towel on her neck in the wings,
and returned for the next round. She'd won them over: the crew, the
spectators. Mixed with her relief was the dread that many in the audience might support Hitler's policies—no, the awful knowledge that
they did, and the revulsion she felt at herself for being grateful that
such people were heaping praise at her. But here she was, bowing to the
warmongers and the anti-Semites, basking in the applause, happy she
hadn't embarrassed herself, appalled Nazis were clapping at her.

The assistant stage manager slowly turned the lights back on in the
auditorium. German officers with swastikas on their armband and their
female companions in glittering dresses beamed at Yvonne. She placed
a hand over her heart while she curtsied, in a gesture she'd practiced at
home, and forced herself to smile.

A short man in a sand-colored uniform raised his hands high above
his head while he clapped from the Wagners' box. A wave of disgust
froze Yvonne on the stage. This time she couldn't even make herself
bow.

Max pulled her back into the wings. "I told you Hitler was here."

⁓

In the staid brick house where Winifred Wagner lived, German dignitaries mingled with actresses and military officers. The party was already in full swing. Yvonne felt like she was looking at them from behind a pane of glass. No one acknowledged her. They were all engrossed in their conversations, and perhaps they didn't recognize her without her costume and her stage makeup.

A bald man in a crisp business suit snapped photographs of attendees in front of artworks in gilded frames. He was either a reporter or a photographer hired by Winifred. Yvonne tried her hardest to stay out of his sight. She didn't want to have a record of her presence in the Wagner house.

Guests exchanged pleasantries around a white leather sofa and a matching white armchair. Yvonne waded through the crowd in her blue Schiaparelli dress—what else was she going to wear? She didn't have anything better. The bathroom was probably located at the end of that corridor. If the party became too unpleasant, she'd lock herself in it for an hour before tiptoeing outside and hailing a cab. When she saw all those swastikas on the men's uniforms, she even felt ready to take off her high-heeled shoes and walk back to the hotel.

A buffet of gargantuan proportions was set up against the back windows. Yvonne had barely eaten in eight hours, besides apples at the first intermission and almonds at the second. Perhaps that was why she was feeling faint now. Guests emptied platters of jumbo shrimp and carpaccio beef almost as quickly as waiters arranged them on the table. Toasts of caviar were snatched before the waiters had a chance to take two steps out of the kitchen, Coupes of champagne stacked into pyramids sparkled under the chandeliers. Yvonne raised her hand toward them but froze: she was clumsy enough to make the entire display topple and cover Winifred's hardwood floors with shards of glass and puddles of sparkling wine. But heck, it was her debut and she deserved to celebrate, no matter how much she'd have preferred for it to happen in France.

She fetched a glass and, when she'd emptied that one, picked another one. How many should she drink to recover from seeing Hitler in the audience? Thankfully, she'd soon return to Paris, since Marta Fuchs was headed this way—to Paris but also to safety, to democracy, and to more roles, as Raymond had promised. The coupe shook slightly in Yvonne's hand as she drank. Seeing Hitler had unsettled her. And that awful Horst-Wessel-Lied, which the audience had sung as if there were no better melody in the world than the Nazi anthem!

In a corner, Max waved his hands up and down while he chatted with a German officer. Yvonne would've joined him to avoid standing by herself, but he might introduce her to the officer, who surely itched to wage war against France. She sipped her champagne, holding the coupe with both hands. How long did she have to stay? She could hardly leave before the people who mattered noticed she was there. Someone had told her that Richard and Cosima Wagner lay buried in the garden with their favorite dog. She'd take some air later and discover if that was true.

"What a disappointment tonight was," a male voice said in German next to her. "The singer playing Isolde ruined my evening." It took Yvonne a moment to realize the man was talking to her. She glanced at him: he was tall and blond, in uniform, only a few years older than her. An Iron Cross hung around his neck, proof of his valor in the previous war, although that didn't impress her. Maybe Yvonne would go and chat with Max after all.

Slight crow's feet appeared around the German officer's eyes when he grinned. "I'd planned to nod off within the first few bars, and you kept me on the edge of my seat. When am I going to catch up on sleep? This party will run till dawn. I'll get in trouble with my superior tomorrow. I blame it all on you, Frau Chevallier."

The swastika on his armband dampened Yvonne's instinct to find some witty reply. Yet she hadn't heard too many compliments from strangers before.

"You're the best thing that happened to the festival since I started coming here back in '36," the officer said. "What a treat for Bayreuth to have you this summer."

Yvonne hadn't expected such enthusiastic praise.

"I won't sing the rest of the run. Marta Fuchs will."

"They'll keep you on. It'd be criminal not to let you sing." He probably meant she looked Aryan but was polite enough not to spell it out. The officer stuck out his hand. "I'm Hans-Hermann von Moderling. You can call me Hans." The *von* in his name hinted at old money, a man of inherited wealth who'd enjoyed prosperity long before Hitler had wrestled power from Paul von Hindenburg. Could Hans-Hermann have signed up for the National Socialist Party out of necessity rather than conviction? In Yvonne's eyes, real Nazis were jealous, mediocre men determined to steal from their more accomplished compatriots what they hadn't been able to rightfully earn. But it occurred to her she was trying to find excuses for Hans-Hermann because he was handsome and appreciated her singing. She took another sip of champagne to numb her shame.

A murmur rippled through the crowd. Yvonne knew right away it was very bad news. Ladies in gowns stood on the tips of their toes; gentlemen in tuxedos elbowed each other, their faces turned toward the front door like sunflowers greeting the sun. Finally, attendees parted and mumbled greetings when Adolf Hitler and Winifred Wagner strode past them. Yvonne looked down at the carpet until she was certain she wouldn't show any disgust on her face, no matter what she felt. The officers raised their right arm in the Nazi salute, Hans-Hermann with them, all in unison. Hitler made the salute back. Yvonne bit the inside of her cheeks. She was finding in herself a steely demeanor she hadn't known she possessed. They could all compromise themselves if they wanted. She'd be out of here soon enough.

Hitler ambled through the room as if he'd already won the war. Yvonne abandoned her coupe of champagne on a table before it could slip between her fingers. She regretted not leaving the party earlier.

From up close, the man looked exactly like the pictures Yvonne had seen of him in *Paris-soir*—hair combed to the side, toothbrush moustache. He wore black pants, a jacket the color of sand with a swastika sewn on his sleeve, and a black cap with another swastika above the visor. He reminded Yvonne of a bank clerk dressed for a costume party on New Year's Eve. By his side, Winifred wore white like a bride: a white dress with a collar high on the neck, a white cardigan with long, flowing sleeves, and a white, wide-brimmed hat. Yvonne had held Winifred in high esteem, but she liked her a whole lot less now that she was resting her hand on Hitler's arm. The photographer aimed his camera at them, changed the angle, pressed the shutter.

Hitler's gaze glided over the crowd and stopped on Yvonne. "Frau Chevallier."

The room became quiet. Yvonne coaxed a smile out of her lips. She hadn't expected the short, crazy dictator to recognize her, let alone remember her name. Finding something to say was daunting. She stood tall but couldn't speak.

"You were an enchantress tonight," Hitler said.

He could've said that she was good, or that he had enjoyed her performance—something bland and noncommittal, an easy way to show politeness while lacking specifics—but he'd called her an enchantress instead. Yvonne struggled with how to react. She wished he hadn't acknowledged her but, even more so, that she didn't feel so much gratitude at the compliment.

"I've never heard Isolde sung better, and I've heard a lot of them," Hitler said.

Yvonne nodded politely. She was swaying on her feet. The performance had exhausted her. Hans-Hermann grabbed her arm before she could fall and propped her up.

"Maybe you can sing Irene in *Rienzi* next time the festival shows it," Hitler said.

Yvonne had no intention to return, but she realized Hitler was really talking to Winifred when he was addressing her, and he was telling that woman to put on *Rienzi*. Thankfully, in a few days when Yvonne crossed the border back into France, it'd no longer be her problem, if it'd ever been.

"Isn't it the opera that convinced you to go into politics?" Winifred asked Hitler. She perched herself on the armrest of the leather sofa.

"Tell us what it was like, the evening you saw it. Do you remember the singers? The costumes? I've always wondered what made you decide."

"I'd tell you, but it would take all night," Hitler said.

"Where else would we rather be?" Winifred said.

Attendees laughed. Hitler sat down on the sofa. Winifred adjusted her seat on the armrest like an equestrian riding sidesaddle. Guests crouched down onto the floor, one after the other. They all looked as if they'd done it before, as if it weren't awkward at all to sit down for a long story by the Führer. Yvonne despised them all. Who in the world sat on the floor for a dictator? Winifred gestured at Yvonne to take a place in the front, yet Yvonne didn't move. She wouldn't embarrass herself.

Winifred pointed at the spot right in front of Hitler, more insistently this time. Yvonne looked for the exit, but the door seemed so far away. What should she do? Hitler could throw anyone who inconvenienced him into prison. Sweat trickled down Yvonne's arms. Hans-Hermann nudged her forward, twice. There was no escaping now.

Yvonne hiked up her dress and sat down on the carpet by the white armchair, as far from the dictator as she could.

Hitler stood up from the sofa. "So, let me tell you all about that evening where I first saw *Rienzi*." He walked toward Yvonne and lowered himself into the armchair, his feet just inches from her knees. She was smart enough to know she shouldn't move, not even by an inch—to know Winifred was watching her and the Führer too. She cast a side glance at Hans-Hermann. He smiled at her, so she let her face soften.

The photographer snapped a picture.

⸻

At about eleven o'clock in the morning, Madeleine arrived at the Gare de l'Est on the train from Italy. She could have arrived earlier, but she had purchased the wrong tickets at the train station in Bayreuth, unused to buying them herself, and had ended up spending the night at the Bulgari Hotel in Milan. Butlers in pristine outfits and deferential housemaids had catered to her every whim until she could resume her travel, soothing her pride after the fiasco of her trip to Germany.

Her mood had soared as soon as she crossed the border into France. She would forgive herself for setting foot in Bayreuth. Even stars had lapses in judgment, and she had corrected hers as soon as she realized her error. She took great pride in that.

Madeleine sauntered down the platform in a long dress with lace and pearls more suitable for evening parties than train travel yet perfect to draw attention to herself. The station smelled of garbage and sweat, but it was French garbage and French sweat. Her chauffeur, Gustave, stood in his uniform by the locomotive.

"Henri didn't come?" Madeleine said.

Gustave gestured toward the coffee shop near the departures board. "Monsieur is reading the newspapers from Germany in front of a *café crème*."

Surely that could wait, Madeleine thought, although she was curious to learn how Marta Fuchs had acquitted herself of her task at *Tristan*'s premiere.

Gustave shifted his weight from one leg to the other but did not speak.

Madeleine padded toward the newsstand. Henri hunched at a table under the departure board in his business suit, next to a cup of coffee he had not touched. A newspaper lay open in front of him and another one, folded, by his elbow.

Madeleine tapped her fingernails against the coffee table to make him look up.

Henri's mouth twisted when he recognized her. "Now you couldn't just fake an illness after the premiere, could you? You had to make a scene."

Madeleine stepped back. "The military was there. All the officers. Some from the Great War too."

"Because you've only sung for altar boys here?"

"I've never sung for people who murdered my brother," Madeleine said.

"You've been using your brother as an excuse for twenty years," Henri said.

He seized his cup of coffee before Madeleine could throw it at his face.

"Yvonne sang," he said.

Yet that was not what Henri had said, because Yvonne could not possibly have sung. Marta Fuchs had.

Henri turned the *Völkischer Beobachter* around and held Madeleine's hand in his.

"Triumph," the headline read. A picture of Yvonne singing on the Festspielhaus stage was printed above the fold.

Blood drained from Madeleine's face: audiences had loved Yvonne instead of her. Consternation seized her. But maybe the journalist had only written niceties to please the Wagner clan.

Madeleine opened the *Neue Zürcher Zeitung* and flipped through the pages, eager to learn what the Swiss had to say about Yvonne's performance. She gasped when she reached the arts section. The picture on the first page showed Yvonne sitting at Hitler's feet.

"She knows how to make friends fast," Henri said.

Madeleine swung her purse across the table, sweeping Henri's cup to the floor. It broke into tiny pieces. Patrons cast her side-glances. Madeleine pretended not to notice. She scanned the article, looking for comments on Yvonne's singing. Enchantress, according to the Führer himself. Madeleine trembled with jealousy. No one had ever called her an enchantress, even when she was at the height of her powers.

"She won't find work in Paris after this," Madeleine said.

"People will be curious to know why Hitler found her bewitching," Henri said.

Madeleine tucked the newspaper under her arm. "I decide who gets cast in this city."

Part Two

Part Two

Eight

September 1939

A train's wheels squealed when it pulled into the Gare de l'Est. Yvonne covered her ears for a moment; singers needed good pitch and timbre. But she wouldn't let Jules go to the station alone. Newsboys shouted: "France mobilizes for war! The military calls up five million men!" The station bustled with soldiers in uniform and the friends and family members sending them off. Germany had invaded Poland? Clusters of relatives crowded the platforms while stragglers jostled through the hordes of well-wishers. A military band played under the departure boards with more fervor than talent. Hundreds of Parisians shouted and waved over the din, like at a carnival. Euphoria floated in the air: the time had come for the French army to rout the *Boches*. Yvonne didn't feel jubilant at all.

Jules wiped sweat off his forehead. Yvonne couldn't get used to his hair cropped short. It made no sense that a pianist of his talent would volunteer for military service when he'd escaped the mandatory draft age by over two years. He could've kept studying music and instead he'd decided to enlist, when he hadn't graduated high school yet. He still had one year to go before sitting through the baccalaureate exam. Yvonne didn't recognize her son in the young man in uniform standing in front of her.

"You're like me, you can't stand authority," Yvonne said. "You'll regret signing up before you're even sent to your first battle."

"Your moral support warms my heart," Jules said.

Yvonne fanned herself with the small French flag band members had been handing out to support the troops. Around her, entire families bantered as if their boys would fire blank bullets and smear each other with tomato sauce on the battlefield. How could they be so naïve? Yvonne wanted to rewind time and lock Jules in his room before he could go to the recruiter and sign the paperwork. He hadn't even needed to lie about his age. Seventeen-year-olds were welcome to volunteer. The more the merrier, the recruiter had said.

"Don't play the hero," she said. "Keep your head down. Follow orders, even if you think your superiors are dim."

"They won't have to tell me twice to charge against the enemy," Jules said.

Yvonne couldn't picture him fighting with eighty pounds of gear on his back, knee deep in mud, ducking the rapid fire of German rifles—her son, who interpreted Chopin and Liszt like a god and brought her to tears with Beethoven's *Hammerklavier* sonata.

"But if they tell you to retreat, you've got to do it too," Yvonne said.

"You're such a defeatist." Jules took in the spectacle of the mobilization around them. "No one else here shares your views."

"They haven't seen the Germans like I have," Yvonne said.

Jules stiffened, then pointed at someone in the crowd. "Is that Father?" He dropped his bag onto his feet.

"It can't be," Yvonne said without even looking. Of course Paul was in Dijon. It annoyed her that Jules missed his father enough to imagine him in a crowd of strangers.

But yes, Paul was wading through the crowd. Yvonne had called him two days earlier to share the news about Jules's enlisting. He'd been exempted from going to the war because of a bad knee, and now his son was headed to the war in his place. Did he feel it was his fault? Jules would never have reached the same decision if the army had conscripted his father. There was no other way to explain Jules's signing up. Yvonne hoped Paul was racked with guilt.

Yvonne hadn't seen him since the divorce. His hair was cut much shorter than when he'd lived with her, surely the influence of his second wife. The failed poet now looked like a petit bourgeois. Yvonne tried to remember the name of his new baby girl.

She must've looked stunned to see Paul there—the army had commandeered all the trains—because Paul said, "The buses are still running. I made it to the Bercy terminal half an hour ago." He embraced Jules. "You didn't think I was going to let you off to war without saying goodbye, now, did you? Although I would've welcomed more advance notice."

Yvonne hated how happy Jules looked that his father had made the trip.

"I'm lucky you found us in this crowd," Jules said. "You should've warned us. We would've set up a meeting point."

"I didn't want to get your hopes up, in case I didn't arrive in time." Paul dunked a paper bag speckled with butter stains into his son's hands. "I bought you a *brioche au sucre*, a croissant, and two *pains au chocolat*. We've got to fatten you up before basic training. Who knows what you'll eat next?" He still hadn't looked at Yvonne.

Jules bit into the chocolate croissant and grunted approvingly.

"Aren't you incensed at him?" Yvonne asked Paul. "Someone else can fight for Poland."

"I understand why he's doing this."

Jules's face brightened.

Paul plucked a folded newspaper article from his breast pocket. "We receive the Swiss newspapers in Dijon. That's the advantage of being near the border."

He flipped a corner open with his thumb, just enough to let Yvonne recognize the image of her sitting at Hitler's feet. She drew a quick breath in. How mortified she was about that picture. She should've followed her instincts and dashed out of the party. Hitler had purposefully sat down near her when she'd tried to avoid him. Yet she wasn't sorry she'd sung Isolde on the festival's planks.

Jules pushed the piece of paper away, as if the mere sight of it burned. "Why else would I be doing it?" he said.

Yvonne's legs felt weak. The morning after her debut at Bayreuth she'd run to the newsstand, eager to read the journalists' take on her performance. The photograph of her at Hitler's feet, splattered over the front page, had felt like a whip stinging her face. Worse still, the clerk had insisted on giving her the newspaper for free. Anything for our Führer's friends, he'd said. Now it was her fault Jules was leaving.

"You didn't tell me you'd seen that picture," Yvonne said to Jules.

"Didn't you think I'd find out how you did?" Jules asked. "I bought all the German newspapers as soon as they reached Paris."

Paul couldn't have grimaced at Yvonne harder if she'd been covered in vermin.

"He came to sit near me," Yvonne said. "I didn't know the photographer would snap a picture."

"So if there'd been no picture, you wouldn't have minded sitting at the man's feet?" Jules said.

"You're twisting my words," Yvonne said.

Jules rolled his eyes, and Paul shoved the newspaper cutting back into his breast pocket.

"I kick myself enough about it," Yvonne said. "You don't need to add to it."

Two weeks earlier, Emile had informed Yvonne he wouldn't need her services for the coming year. He'd admitted that Madeleine had shown him the photograph—had shown it to everyone working at the opera house, in fact. Yvonne hadn't been hallucinating when she'd heard "traitor" whispered behind her back.

She'd complained to Raymond, but he already knew about the picture. He'd said she was lucky he wasn't dropping her from his roster. He hadn't explained why, but Yvonne had guessed he was hedging his bets. That was the kind of person he was. What about the roles guaranteed in her contract, though? He'd laughed: she could take him to court if she wanted, but no judge in Paris would take her side once they were shown that photograph.

"You didn't have to enlist because of a picture," Paul said to Jules.

"Not any picture," Jules said.

He had a point. Yvonne couldn't deny it.

The train conductor blew his whistle. A matron who'd wrapped a square kerchief over her hair hugged a soldier barely older than Jules, thin to the point of looking frail, seemingly incapable of shooting a target even at close range. The boy laughed at his grandmother: he'd return before All Saints' Day and they'd celebrate France's victory together.

"Don't miss the train," Paul said to Jules.

The two of them rushed to the end of the platform, where fewer soldiers packed the cars. Yvonne trotted behind them, worried she'd lose them in the throng. She brushed someone's arm, rubbed against a soldier's elbow, pressed her hat on top of her head while she threaded through groups of soldiers. Thankfully, Jules and Paul stopped in front of a car before Yvonne fell too far behind. Jules hugged his father and hopped onto the step. Yvonne pulled him down, kissed him on both cheeks. Jules remained stiff against her embrace.

The locomotive whistled. Jules jumped in and waved at Paul over the heads of fellow soldiers. Yvonne waved back, though Jules ignored her. Slowly, the train rumbled forward. Only when it disappeared out of the rail yard did Yvonne allow herself to cry. She turned to Paul, but the space where he'd stood was empty. He was striding toward the exit. Around him, soldiers' relatives were waving miniature French flags at each other, certain that their boys would shut up the *Boches* at record speed.

Shoving bystanders left and right, Yvonne reached Paul as he was pushing through the revolving door to the rue de Rome. The street was drenched with sun. Parisians should've been lounging by the side of the municipal swimming pool or sunbathing in the Tuileries Gardens. It seemed incredible a war was going on.

"We could have a cup of coffee," Yvonne said. It scared her to find herself alone, with Jules on his way to the front.

Paul ignored her and continued his march toward the bus stop.

"That man sat down right in front of me. I could hardly get up and leave after Winifred Wagner let me sing," Yvonne said. Singing at Bayreuth, not once but twice before Marta Fuchs had taken her place—she still had shivers when she thought about it. She'd mesmerized spectators the second time too. Her success hadn't been a fluke; it hadn't been beginner's luck.

The city bus rounded the corner. Paul flagged down the driver.

"At least tell me goodbye," Yvonne said when the bus pulled over. "We may not see each other again for years."

Paul leapt inside the coach without a word, as if Yvonne weren't speaking at all.

Nine

May 1940

Madeleine slipped on the uneven cobblestones of the narrow, winding street behind the Luxembourg Gardens, which were slick after the rain. She scanned the names of the shops on top of the dirty awnings, dismissed any storefront that did not look like a hotel, examined through the glass doors the interiors of inns she never would have considered setting foot into had she not been dealing with an urgent matter. Young women and the few young men who had not been drafted into the war clutched their books on the way to the Sorbonne University. Slumped on a doorstep, a beggar chewed tobacco and laughed to himself. It took Madeleine a moment to realize that her burgundy dress in silk organza entertained him. Finally, she found the Hotel Stanislas.

The lettering had faded, and two of the three Ss in *Stanislas* were missing. A sign in the window claimed a lack of vacancies. Madeleine swung the front door open. The faded brown carpet was speckled with stains. An elderly man in a frayed jacket read the *Berliner Tageszeit*. Surely cockroaches frolicked in the kitchen. Madeleine rubbed her thumb against the rubies in her necklace for good luck. She hoped she wouldn't have to stay long.

At the front desk, a clerk of an uncertain age flipped through a magazine, his chin resting in the palm of his hand. He had combed his hair to the side of his moonlike face.

"Stefan Kreismann's room," Madeleine said, thoroughly uninterested in seeming polite in such an environment.

The clerk raised an eyebrow at her. After a moment, he picked up the receiver.

Stefan carried Ilse's fur coat over his arm when he stepped out of the antiquated elevator a few moments later. The ceiling light shone on the bags under his eyes. His suit was in dire need of pressing. At the Tour d'Argent restaurant he had shown his old self, proud and self-aware, but now he walked like a defeated monarch facing more heartbreak. Hitler was drawing near.

Madeleine did not doubt the French would regain the advantage, but she understood his worry. The Dutch had surrendered on May 14, after the bombing of Rotterdam destroyed twenty-five thousand homes and killed over eight hundred civilians. The Germans had also shelled the Paris suburbs near the Renault factory. The death toll there had reached two hundred fifty. The French prime minister had dismissed his top military commander. The Allied armies, split in two, wandered about in disarray.

"I was about to leave to run an errand," Stefan said. Madeleine wished he looked pleased to see her, but he seemed too tired to show any emotion. He must know why she had come, though, since he had sent her the letter.

"I know a good seamstress, if Ilse's coat needs to be mended," Madeleine said.

"I am going to pawn it," Stefan said.

In Madeleine's world, pawnshops stood only one step ahead of brothels. She didn't know what to say. Usually she stayed away from people so down on their luck. But it was Stefan standing in front of her.

Madeleine waved the crumpled note Stefan had sent to her home. "You can't possibly leave Paris. *Lucia* will open in three weeks. I pulled strings to get you cast."

"I didn't send you that note to have you try to change my mind. I just thought that you should know we're leaving Paris for Marseilles, and we'll head for America as soon as we get our papers." He tapped his umbrella against the moth-eaten carpet like a wizard conjuring a vision with his wand.

"But France can still win," Madeleine said.

Stefan looked at her with what seemed like pity.

"You have to keep hoping," Madeleine said.

"I'll be thrown in jail if the Germans catch me. And not a French jail either. Better to stay one step ahead of them."

A group of middle-aged men in rumpled clothes trudged out of the hotel, talking to each other in a language that might have been Czech. A couple pulled two young children into the lobby. All four wore long-sleeved winter clothes in thick wool despite the mild weather, likely the only garments they'd had the time to take with them when they fled Hamburg or Leipzig earlier in the year. Madeleine would call the Red Cross and organize a collection of clothes for the refugees.

"The *Boches* will never make it to Paris," Madeleine said, her voice too assured, because she was also trying to convince herself.

"Get a cabin on the first steamer for New York City," Stefan said, not even bothering to argue with her. "You will find plenty of work in America."

Madeleine's heart fluttered. Of course she would love to sing at the Met, but that engagement would last a couple of months at most. What would she do next? She couldn't imagine leaving everything behind and settling in the United States. Henri, who had at least two more decades of musicianship ahead of him, would never give up leadership of the Paris Opera Orchestra. Stefan had made it clear he would not leave Ilse. Why would Madeleine go to America alone, where she would struggle to rebuild her reputation and gain new admirers before she retired?

"A gardener was planting flowers in front of city hall this morning," Madeleine said. "The mayor wouldn't bother if defeat was near."

"He's blind if he doesn't see the direction the wind is blowing."

Madeleine didn't know how to answer that.

"A job is waiting for me at the Curtis Institute in Philadelphia," Stefan said.

He looked up at the small chandelier, where three of the lightbulbs had burned out. "It's unfortunate we've used up the little bit of money customs officials let us take out of Austria."

Now Madeleine understood why he'd written her. He wasn't just sharing the news. He needed her help, but he wouldn't ask for favors, even when he was running out of options. His old self still simmered in there somewhere.

"Let me walk to the shop with you." Madeleine wouldn't pronounce the word *pawnshop*. "You need someone who can haggle for prices in French."

❧

Outside, an air of gloom hovered over the city. Parisians trudged about, their hats drawn low over their eyes. Black umbrellas dangled from their elbows, ready to be popped open at a moment's notice, offering protection from the rain but not the Germans. The newspapers kept reporting on military battles a few days late, all defeats. If the French had been winning, every little victory would have been praised on the airwaves that same day.

Madeleine and Stefan strode past the iron gates of the Luxembourg Gardens. Back in Vienna during their affair, they had discussed all the sightseeing they would indulge in when Stefan visited Paris, but they would not admire paintings by Vermeer or Titian at the Louvre now. Puddles of water stretched across the gravel alleys. In the distance, the Luxembourg Palace peeked between the chestnut trees.

"Weygand will turn things around," Madeleine said. "Pétain is too old, but Henri trusts Weygand." Since Stefan had chosen Ilse over her, she wasn't against mentioning Henri any chance she had.

"You can stay in Paris with Henri and sing for the Nazis or go to New York alone and sing at the Met," Stefan said. Henri going to New York to flee the Germans wasn't even a possibility for him. He had told Madeleine before that Henri was a second-rate conductor and knew it.

But Medea could not be the last role Madeleine sang in France before the world collapsed around her. The audiences had not liked that role in the new opera by Darius Milhaud, perhaps because Medea killed her two young sons.

"I don't even speak English," Madeleine said, trying to find a better excuse.

Stefan tugged on the small watch clasped inside his jacket. He had played with it constantly whenever they'd walked out together in Vienna to drink at his favorite café, Café Central. Its marble floors and high ceilings, vaulted like a cathedral's, had awed Madeleine. Chess players spent hours engrossed in their game, indifferent to the watchful eye of bystanders. Patrons discussed Freud and Trotsky with the same ease that Madeleine's colleagues talked about Berlioz and Massenet. Over two cups of Viennese coffee—coffee with Chantilly cream sprinkled with chocolate powder—Stefan and Madeleine had debated leitmotivs in Wagner's scores like two intellectuals focused on matters of the mind, as if they had not spent the afternoon in bed at Madeleine's hotel.

Stefan bored into the gravel with the tip of his umbrella. "We must leave as soon as possible. We should have left weeks ago."

Let us stay in Paris for now, Madeleine was tempted to say.

"Ilse insists that our only hope is to give the employees at the consulate a large tip, so they will put our application on top of their pile," Stefan said.

He hadn't been talking about Madeleine at all. She walked faster. In the Luxembourg Gardens, an elderly man fed breadcrumbs to pigeons while a teenage boy drew sketches with a charcoal stick. Madeleine berated herself for wallowing in nostalgia. How fortunate that Stefan had picked Ilse over her. Henri was a much more suitable husband, devoted to letting her shine no matter what, second-rate conductor or not.

"I was wrong about Bayreuth," Stefan said. "Maybe you would have made important friends there. You are going to need all the allies you can find once the Nazis are in Paris."

Nazis in Paris—that still seemed impossible to Madeleine.

"If you stay here, you cannot complain of the company," Stefan said.

Young boys pushed model sailboats across the round fountain. Madeleine and Stefan wandered through clusters of metal chairs painted a dark green, all of them empty except for a nanny who watched three children wearing different sizes of the same navy-blue outfits.

They reached the exit gates of the gardens on the d'Assas street. The back of Stefan's hand brushed against Madeleine's. "I would pay you back as soon as I reach America."

It hurt Madeleine that he was only interested in her money. She could not refuse to help, though, given the circumstances. She opened her red leather wallet and handed Stefan all her cash, not even counting it. His face brightened for a second, but the hope in his eyes vanished as quickly as it had appeared. Madeleine was offering him only eighty francs—a large sum to buy macarons, a derisory one to fund a trip across the Atlantic.

"Henri controls our accounts," Madeleine said. "I don't walk around with wheelbarrows of money. I'll have to come up with a good story. It may take a few days."

"Let us hope I can obtain a good price for this coat, then," Stefan said, although he pocketed the bills.

They trudged awkwardly out of the Luxembourg Gardens and through the fifth arrondissement, not close enough to each other to look like husband and wife, not far enough to come across as strangers. What a relief to reach the pawnshop. Watches and earrings glittered in a narrow storefront next to a pharmacy. Two more pawnshops stood on the other side of the street, including one that displayed a Mendini violin.

"That one," Madeleine said. She didn't trust the hotel clerk who had provided Stefan with the first shop's address.

Stefan entered while Madeleine lingered on the threshold. Pawnshops disgusted her. She steered clear of such places, dark and plain but perfectly organized, every item displaying a price label, the secondhand clothes presented on metal hangers, the previously worn jewelry tucked away from prying hands.

The buildings on the other side of the street blocked the sun from shining through the window front. A man in a crisp white shirt was inscribing entries in a ledger at his desk. A small lamp shone a circle of light onto the top of his head, which was completely bald over a crown of gray hair, as if he served as a beacon of hope for the desperate people who ventured into the shop. This could have been a Vermeer painting. Madeleine disliked the clerk instinctively.

Stefan placed Ilse's fur coat on the table. The clerk kept writing. Madeleine walked inside. A musty smell lingered in the shop.

"How much can I get for this?" Stefan asked in French when the clerk failed to acknowledge him. His thick accent left no doubt that he was a refugee who had escaped Hitler.

The clerk put down his pen without haste and ran his hand over Ilse's coat. "Five hundred francs."

The coat was worth at least six times as much. That crook reminded Madeleine of the tenor who had sung Scarpia's henchman Spoletta in her last *Tosca*.

"You mean fifteen hundred," Madeleine said.

She would have quoted a higher number, but Spoletta would have laughed her off. Yet she wore an expensive dress. The man would conclude that she and Stefan were not yet in dire straits if they were pawning off the coat rather than the dress.

"Eight hundred," Spoletta said.

"Wouldn't you like us to recommend you to our friends?" Madeleine asked.

"I've been doing a brisk business without your help."

"Twelve hundred or you can admire this coat in someone else's window." Madeleine pointed at the storefront that the hotel clerk had recommended.

"Someone else would've offered four hundred for that coat and not a franc more," Spoletta said.

"We will find out for ourselves." Madeleine moved to grab Ilse's coat.

The man pushed it out of her reach. Perhaps it had occurred to him that Madeleine wasn't Stefan's wife, that she was only helping a friend, that the husbands of women like her—French women with French husbands who had done well enough for themselves that they could afford organza silk and haute couture—knew people who could cause trouble for pawnshop owners. He opened the register and made a show of counting ten hundred-franc bills.

Spoletta slapped the money and the receipt into Stefan's hand. "I'd tell you not to lose it, but folks like you never come back to pick up their things." He pointed at Stefan's wedding band. "I buy gold too."

Stefan blinked, looking tempted.

Madeleine unclasped her ruby necklace, a present from Henri's for her fiftieth birthday. "And how much for this?" She would insist that the chain must have broken and search for the necklace in the corners of the sofa in Neuilly until Henri believed her.

"Madeleine," Stefan said, but he didn't tell her not to do it.

Spoletta examined the rubies under a magnifying glass. His eyes glimmered. "Nine thousand francs."

The tag in the Cartier window in Place Vendôme had indicated forty-five thousand francs. This time, Madeleine did not argue for a better price. She needed to leave. The atmosphere in the shop was too seedy.

Spoletta handed her the bills. She gestured at Stefan to take them. Her necklace sparkled under the lamp.

"Happy to take more of that anytime," Spoletta said, and placed the necklace in the display case.

Stefan nudged Madeleine toward the door. "I'll wire you my first paycheck," he said once they were outside. "My second and third too."

"First settle in America, and then we can discuss how you'll pay me back," Madeleine said.

Stefan touched the tips of her fingers. "Ilse would not want me to owe you too much. I told her about us after Covent Garden."

So Ilse knew that Stefan had chosen her. And yet Madeleine still spared no expense to win Stefan's approval: inviting him to the Tour d'Argent restaurant, pawning her own necklace. What a fool she was making of herself.

"I will let you walk back to your hotel," Madeleine said. "I'm going the other way. Cable me as soon as you reach America. Write to the opera house, not my home address. Henri didn't suspect a thing all these years. He doesn't need to start now."

Ten

June 1940

Ten days after insisting that Weygand would save France, Madeleine tottered into the living room of her mansion in Neuilly, her eyes heavy with sleep, and turned on Radio Paris. The flower beds were blooming under the cloudless sky. It was a day to sing Turandot at La Scala and bask in a record-breaking number of curtain calls.

"The government left for Tours during the night," the announcer said, his words muddled by the heavy vibrato in his voice.

Madeleine fell backward onto the sofa. French officials couldn't possibly have fled. They could not have abandoned their citizens. Was that not treacherous?

The Moreaus' maid, Rose, carried Madeleine's breakfast tray out of the kitchen.

"Paris will not be defended," the announcer said.

Rose shoved the tray on top of a sideboard before she could drop it.

"Henri!" Madeleine called out toward the stairwell.

"He went to the opera house," Rose said.

On a day like this?

Madeleine phoned his office, but he did not pick up. What was he doing at the Paris Opera to begin with? Her head throbbed. They were running out of time.

Madeleine turned toward Rose. "Get our suitcases out of the attic."

She scrambled up the marble staircase, along the gallery crammed with paintings in gilded frames, loosening the belt of her nightgown while she dashed past Henri's study—full of his papers—and into their bedroom, which would have been cluttered with her clothes if Rose didn't spend considerable amounts of her time putting order in Madeleine's wake. Pictures of Henri and Madeleine in performance hung on the walls and the dresser, next to a couple of Madeleine alone, plus one of a young Henri conducting the Royal Concertgebouw in Amsterdam.

Madeleine ran her hand across her favorite dresses in the walk-in closet and decided on a bright-orange silk gown with golden embroidery. The long-brimmed matching hat would protect her from the sun. Where had Rose hung the scarf that went with it? Madeleine was determined to stand out in her exit from Paris, as if it were a performance. But was she even thinking of the right things? Perhaps the shock from the defeat was clouding her judgment. If the house was ransacked, what should she take with her?

Madeleine gathered the pictures of Henri and her brother on her dresser—Alexandre as a little boy in his Sunday clothes, in a round hat, holding a wooden horse, and then accompanying Madeleine and their mother through the Bois de Boulogne—their mother smiling, her hair pulled back in a bun, in a long dress flouncing around her wrists. Oh, their mother smiling.

If the French Army wasn't going to defend Paris, the war was lost. Madeleine's brother had died for nothing.

She grabbed her jewelry box and her most expensive Lucien Lelong dress before rushing back downstairs. The government's cowardice enraged her. Perhaps she should head for Philadelphia, even without a contract. If the *Boches* in power knew she had made up excuses to get out of her contract at Bayreuth, her name would appear high on their list of people who needed to be taught their place. Better not to stick around to find out if it did.

Madeleine stuffed her belongings into the suitcase that Rose had brought and slammed it shut. Tires crunched on the gravel at long last. Madeleine stormed onto the driveway.

"Paris is going to fall," she said before Henri could lower his car window. "We have to leave."

Henri stepped out of the Peugeot and raised an eyebrow at Madeleine's dress, which was too sophisticated to be worn before the evening. But he seemed to understand why she was wearing it.

"The national road is packed," he said. "Even coming back here took me almost an hour."

The circles under Henri's eyes had darkened with every setback from the French Army, despite journalists' upbeat talk in *Le temps*. From a Clark Gable look-alike he had morphed into Douglas Fairbanks after the demise of the silent movies—a man on a downward slope, perhaps soon an also-ran. Madeleine hated seeing him like this.

Gustave lifted a cardboard box full of music scores out of the trunk and carried it into the mansion.

"I picked up a few things at the opera house," Henri said.

He led Gustave into the dining room, Madeleine on their heels. From the box he pulled out papers and mementos, pictures of himself with local celebrities, his favorite baton, framed reviews of his conducting—his career summarized in a handful of baubles that would vanish in smoke if the *Boches* decided to set fire to Paris. At the bottom of the box were the items he had picked first: the pictures and reviews on Madeleine's dresser, a couple of framed photographs, a pile of scores she had annotated.

"How did you know to go just now?" Madeleine asked.

"Emile called before he left for Normandy. You were too"—Henri hesitated—"tired to hear the phone ring." She had drunk a bottle of Pinot Noir the night before, distraught about Stefan and perhaps about the war, if she cared to admit it.

"You knew that the *Boches* were coming and you scampered to the opera house instead of waking me up?" Madeleine's voice rose.

"To tell you what? They won't be here for one or two more days."

"To tell me to pack," Madeleine almost shouted. "We could've been the first to leave."

Henri piled his collection of scores onto the end table by the armchair. "We're not going."

This was not the time to make jokes.

"I won't abandon my orchestra," Henri said. "The Germans would strip me of the directorship."

"You can conduct elsewhere," Madeleine said.

Henri picked up a photograph of himself on the podium—*Rigoletto*, Madeleine recognized at once—and dusted off the frame with his sleeve. "It would've helped if you'd sung at Bayreuth, but I won't supply them with more reasons to rob me of everything I've worked for."

Madeleine took the pictures of her brother and placed them in the suitcase with great care. "Everyone is leaving, you said so yourself. If they're all getting out of town, what do they know that we don't?"

"Lemmings have a very small brain," Henri said.

Madeleine almost laughed, despite the circumstances.

"The Germans invaded Austria and Czechoslovakia without bloodshed," Henri said.

Germans occupying Paris: that seemed as preposterous as Rossini rewriting the end of *Barber of Seville* so that Rosina married Bartolo.

"I'd rather not see for myself whether they'll stay on their best behavior or not," Madeleine said.

"But it'll matter not to flee," Henri said. "They'll remember who they see first. We'll remain at the top of the opera world for years, if we play our cards well."

The buzz in Madeleine's veins tempered her urge to break every glass, vase, and plate in the house, belting out Tosca's final aria after the guards had executed her lover Cavaradossi. Groveling at the *Nazis'* feet? She was ready to hit a high E right there, and maybe upgrade it to a high F on the fly.

Henri sat down at the piano. "We'll wait for them. We'll smile. You'll sing sixteen bars of Wagner, and they'll be under your spell."

Madeleine grabbed her suitcase with both hands. The handle weighed heavily in her palms.

"Wherever you think you're going, you're not taking the car," Henri said without looking at her.

"I'll walk until I reach Marseilles, then," Madeleine said.

"You won't venture five kilometers out of town before you turn around."

She would prove him wrong. The sunlight threw a large rectangle on the Persian rug, showing off its colors. She could bring that memory with her to America, since she couldn't take the Steinway.

"Hitler's troops will demand to be entertained," Henri said while he annotated the score. "Do you imagine they'll watch ballet? And they don't speak a word of French, so they'll stay away from theater. No, opera will be perfect for them."

Madeleine saw his point. This annoyed her even more than if he had been thoughtless, because he knew how to tempt her.

"Lots of Strauss and Wagner," Henri said. "Maybe some Italian works too. You'd shine in all of them. What's possessing you that you want to give your power away?"

Madeleine shifted her grip on the suitcase. She had packed too much in it.

"If the Met wanted you, they would've invited you after you sang Isolde at Covent Garden," Henri said without looking at her. The same thought had crossed Madeleine's mind. "Now, let's go over the mad scene."

Madeleine closed her eyes, just to see, when she opened them again, if time had rewound back to the previous day: France's soldiers fighting for their country, victory perhaps difficult but still possible, Henri caring only about music and not about politics.

Henri began to play the piano. Every note of music injured Madeleine's ears.

"I will not entertain the *Boches*," Madeleine said.

She lugged her suitcase to the front door and down the driveway. At the mailbox, she stopped to adjust her grip. Henri stood on the threshold, observing her. He had crossed his arms, like a headmaster annoyed at his star pupil.

Madeleine's gaze drifted to the house behind him. For decades it had rooted her amid her travels, the demand of performances, the constant whirlwind of fellow performers waltzing into and out of her career—faces that blurred in her mind, names she hadn't bothered to learn. In that home, she had practiced all her roles, so that when she stepped onstage, her voice would elicit pure awe.

Then she said a silent goodbye to Henri. She should have left him after Alexandre died at the front while he spent the war out of harm's way. Instead, she had spent twenty-four years resenting him for his cowardice.

Madeleine adjusted the hat on her head and marched down her driveway, onto the street. A neighbor was locking the gate to his house, a suitcase on either side of him. Behind him, his wife and two children cried. The man nodded at Madeleine—a silent encouragement, perhaps, a reassurance that they were doing the right thing. Madeleine reminded herself to raise her chin and pull her shoulder blades back, to keep away the tears. She should not let the future scare her. She would begin a new life in the United States.

The man and his family walked toward the boulevard d'Argenson, slowed down by their luggage. Madeleine had no idea how to leave town by foot, so she followed them. Her suitcase kept bouncing against the side of her leg, bruising her. A couple scurried out of their house, dressed in haste, the man's face unshaved, the woman's hair uncombed. They had piled all the belongings they could carry into their arms, but items were already falling down, and they couldn't pick them up without dropping everything else. No one talked—there was nothing to say about the misfortune they shared. The only noises were the shuffle of feet, the cries of children, and most annoyingly, the chirp of sparrows in the poplar trees. Birds sang their song as if nothing momentous were happening today at all. The words to Dido's lament, in *Dido and Aeneas*, popped into Madeleine's mind.

She squinted when she caught sight of the boulevard ahead. It took her a second to realize she was looking at throngs of people, all headed in the same direction, fleeing the Nazis together. Their slow march reminded Madeleine of lava flowing down the slope of a volcano. But as a schoolgirl, Madeleine had learned that the Mount Pelée volcano eruption of 1902—the deadliest eruption ever in a French territory—had killed twenty-nine thousand on the Martinique island because villagers outside the city of Saint-Pierre, seeing the ash clouds, had believed it would be safer to take refuge in the city. Saint-Pierre had been almost completely destroyed. Peasants would have had a greater chance of survival if they had run the other way. Should Madeleine even follow the crowd? She couldn't even see her neighbor anymore in the throng.

Around her, infants bounced in their mothers' arms. A father, trudging forward without a jacket, hunched under the weight of large sacks he had filled with whatever belongings he had managed to grab. Children stumbled along, crying for toys they had forgotten at home. Babies wailed in the heat. A grandfather pushed a wheelbarrow containing a chest of silverware. Madeleine mused about Stefan—had he walked to the train station in Vienna with Ilse, had he taken a car to the border, had he felt the same gloom that surrounded her now, or had he hoped he would be safe in France and the worst for him was over? Perhaps she would ask him in a letter, after he had reached the United States and his ordeal was over.

Madeleine looked at the people around her again. All shuffled toward the Bois de Boulogne and the beltway. From there, the road to Orléans. An elderly woman in a lemon-yellow dress tottered forward before she collapsed on the pavement. The crowd stepped around her without slowing down. Some even walked across her body as if it were a tree limb fallen in a storm. Madeleine, who had not gone to church in twenty years, made the sign of the cross and looked away. What a shame, to leave a dead body uncovered. But Madeleine would have risked getting trampled if she had stopped. Her feet were hurting and her suitcase was not becoming lighter. Perhaps she would have to throw items into the sewer.

The group was inching forward at an exceedingly slow pace. The German tanks would soon catch up with them if they did not accelerate. Madeleine thought again of the Mount Pelée eruption and the villagers hurrying to their deaths when they believed they were escaping to safety.

Someone touched her sleeve. It was Henri. She hadn't expected to see him—she had been walking for about half an hour now, although she had barely covered five hundred meters. She hadn't expected such relief either.

Henri shrugged at her surprise. "Your hat is hard to miss." He lit a cigarette, he who rarely smoked because Madeleine disapproved of it. "The Germans know they can't run the whole country by themselves. Don't miss your chance again."

Madeleine grabbed the cigarette from his hand, took a long drag out of spite, and handed it back to him. She coughed. She had never enjoyed smoking to begin with.

"The musicians need you," Henri said, and took a drag from the cigarette.

Madeleine hesitated.

Henri grabbed her suitcase. She pulled on the handle, but he held fast while Madeleine tugged hard on it. At last, Madeleine let go of the handle and knocked the cigarette out of his hand. An elderly man behind them picked it up and stuck it between his lips.

Madeleine and Henri glanced at each other.

"Let's keep control of the opera house," Henri said.

Eleven

Gray-green Magirus trucks with those ugly swastikas painted on their side rumbled through the gates of the German embassy, a tarp covering the metal arches over the truck beds. The Nazis sure hadn't wasted any time in spreading over town like an infestation of rats. On the corner of the rue de Lille, Yvonne adjusted the veil on her hat, like an actress preparing for a performance. Didn't she look prim and proper in that costume of hers? Housewives from the sixteenth arrondissement didn't dress any better. She'd daubed her cheeks with rouge to hide her pallor. The previous day, she'd received a letter from the War Ministry: Jules had become a prisoner of war. She'd placed about twenty phone calls, but the dotards who pretended to be in charge had no clue where her son was.

Yvonne trudged to the gate on weak legs. The whole street was empty except for a German car at the intersection with the boulevard Raspail. She was trying to decide what to say, but she wasn't thinking straight. She just wanted to see her son again. She wasn't sure of how to go about that. She wasn't sure of anything.

She'd found her way back to the capital with the first wave of Parisians, all of them chastened by the futility of their escape after becoming stranded on the road to Orléans. Exhaustion had prevented them from walking farther. Yvonne had slept in the fields because the inns brimmed with patrons paying seven times the going rate for a cot in a hallway. As far as she knew, no one had stayed behind in Paris except invalids confined to their home and retirees who'd rather die at home than on a country road. But now that the Germans hadn't pillaged Paris, Yvonne hoped they'd help her find her son.

The guard by the gate, barely out of his teens, waved his rifle at her so that she would step back.

"I need to speak to an officer," Yvonne said in German.

The soldier looked surprised that she spoke his language. "If you don't have an appointment, you can't go in."

Yvonne hesitated about what to say next, but the soldier was blocking her way, and she needed to find Jules.

"I was the star of the Bayreuth opera festival last year," Yvonne finally said. "Winifred Wagner herself adored my singing."

"Who?" the soldier asked. "Move along."

A wave of panic rose in Yvonne's chest. She needed to find Jules. Every day counted. What if his hands were irreparably damaged in that prisoner-of-war camp? His career would be ruined if she couldn't intercede in his favor. Worse, he could be beaten and tortured. She needed to make the soldier step aside and let her pass. She could only think of one way to impress him.

"Herr Hitler called me an enchantress at the Bayreuth festival," Yvonne said, cringing when she heard herself say the name of the man she despised.

The soldier looked unconvinced. "Everybody pretends to be friends with our Führer these days. Your people still went to war with ours, though."

Yvonne's little speech wouldn't be enough. She wished it'd been, but she'd always known she was likely to be held at the gate. She'd taken the photograph with her, after all.

Yvonne took a deep breath and, hand trembling, held out the picture where she sat with Adolf Hitler. She felt excruciating shame for using it, but she wanted to find Jules more than she wanted to save her pride. How ironic that this was the only advantage she'd ever had in life.

The soldier's eyes darted from the photograph to her face and back to the photograph.

Yvonne steadied her hand. Perhaps that picture could serve a better purpose than separating her from her son.

A Grosser Mercedes roared down the rue de Lille and pulled to the checkpoint. Small swastika flags fluttered over its front bumper. Its windows were half rolled down. Yvonne stepped out of the car's path, the picture still in hand. She could only see the officer's chest from where she stood. An Iron Cross dangled around his neck. He was holding a sheaf of papers that he'd pulled out of a large envelope.

The officer leaned toward the picture and then looked straight at her. "Madame Chevallier! What a pleasure to see you again."

Yvonne had met the officer at Winifred's party following her first performance in Bayreuth. He'd chatted with her when everyone else was engrossed in conversations with politicians, socialites, and industry magnates. What was his name again? Yvonne had left the party right after Hitler told the story about *Rienzi*. She'd been so upset about having to sit at Hitler's feet that she'd scurried away without saying goodbye, never expecting to see the officer again. But a year later he still remembered her name when she didn't remember his.

The officer gestured at her to join him in the car. "Tell me what brings you here."

Yvonne left plenty of space between them on the back seat. She tucked the awful picture into her purse while the car rolled through the embassy gates. The officer held an envelope addressed to one Hans-Hermann, the last name covered by the papers he'd been reading. Yes, Hans-Hermann. Yvonne remembered now.

"Hans, my son is a prisoner of war," she said.

He gave her a long look. Yvonne guessed he was doing the math in his head.

"I had him very young," Yvonne said. She didn't add he'd volunteered, although she would've had to have a son at fifteen for him to be drafted now. Better that Hans-Hermann think less of her than have him realize Jules had chosen to go to war against his compatriots.

"I'll ask my colleagues in the war department about him," Hans-Hermann said.

The chauffeur pulled over in front of the German embassy. The Hôtel de Beauharnais, it'd once been called. It'd served as a private mansion for a wealthy nobleman in an earlier century. Yvonne wasn't surprised the Nazis had appropriated it. She'd heard they'd grabbed for themselves all the luxury hotels in Paris. A soldier was carrying inside a painting that looked to Yvonne like a Vermeer. Employees at the Louvre had sent the museum's holdings out of town before the Nazis occupied the city, but many art dealers hadn't safeguarded their stock in time.

"Wait," Hans-Hermann said, when Yvonne reached for the door handle. He got out of the car and walked around the trunk to open Yvonne's door for her. No one had ever held a door open for Yvonne, not even Paul. That just wasn't done where they came from. They'd been too busy trying to survive to have manners. Yvonne was more touched than she wanted to admit.

"Also, I'm looking for work," she said.

"Don't tell me you've given up on your singing," Hans-Hermann said. "That'd be criminal, with the voice you have."

"I haven't gotten cast in recent months."

"Those dimwits can't tell a pearl when they have it right in front of them," Hans-Hermann said.

It was nice having someone agree with her on that, although she wished that person had been French.

Tall white columns framed the entrance, which stood under an Egyptian-like portico with a long flight of stairs. Yvonne and Hans-Hermann entered the palace. Hans-Hermann paid no attention to his surroundings, while Yvonne did her best not to stare at the mantelpiece in green marble and gilt bronze, the Italian mosaics, the chandeliers dripping with crystal. This had been the house of a real person? She could see why the French Revolution had come about. Officers in gray-green uniforms strode up and down the marble staircase, looking busy and proud that they were restoring Germany's honor after its defeat two decades earlier. But they hadn't even gone to the front; what did they have to be proud about?

Yvonne caught her image in a full-length mirror under the stairs. How pitiful she looked in the middle of such grandeur, her hairstyle mediocre, her clothes plain. Yet she needed to get Jules released.

"I could sing for the officers here, if you'd like," Yvonne said. "There won't be much entertainment for them in Paris if they don't speak French."

"You deserve a bigger stage," Hans-Hermann said. "The Paris Opera, nothing less."

That name, the Paris Opera, exerted the same pull on Yvonne as it had when she was an understudy. She yearned to work there again, as a principal this time, instead of earning a pittance as a store clerk in a music store and singing in a church choir. Emile had refused to hire her back because of that shameful photograph. Hans-Hermann wielded enough power to open doors for her, if he cared. Yvonne could tell because his uniform bore golden insignia pinned in the middle of the silver shoulder strap. That was the first thing she'd bothered learning about the occupiers: how to read from their uniforms who had the highest rank. But she doubted she'd be the only one eager to extract favors from Germans.

Hans-Hermann offered his arm to Yvonne at the bottom of the grand staircase. "Let me introduce you to one of my subordinates. He'll get you as many engagements here as you wish. As for the Paris Opera, what if we devised a strategy over dinner?"

Yvonne clutched his arm with both hands, and with it her one chance of success.

"The Ritz, six o'clock?" Hans-Hermann said. "I'll send my car to pick you up."

"I'll meet you there." Yvonne smiled, but she wouldn't let her neighbors find out that she mingled with the enemy.

Hans-Hermann's face closed like a book slammed shut.

"I'll be in that neighborhood for my voice lessons," Yvonne said without losing her smile.

Doubt lingered in Hans-Hermann's eyes.

"I'm rehearsing Sieglinde in *Die Walküre*," Yvonne said. "Maybe I can sing it for you sometime."

❧

Yvonne emerged from the metro station at the corner of the rue des Capucines and rue de la Paix and had to pause to collect herself. She hadn't been to that part of Paris in years and it felt like she'd stepped into a different world. Place Vendôme was lined with jewelry stores and salons of haute couture behind round arches and Corinthian pilasters. In the middle of the square, a bronze column marked Napolèon's victory at Austerlitz. A row of German cars idled in front of the Ritz hotel. Yvonne had expected it, because the Nazis had made the hotel their headquarters, yet the sight was jarring. The unavoidable swastika hung over the entrance. Would the Germans ever stop hanging swastika banners everywhere, like dogs peeing against every tree?

Yvonne crossed the street toward the hotel and promptly twisted her foot in the gutter. She fell, scratching her gloves against the sidewalk. How could she be so clumsy the one time she had to impress a dinner guest? She took off her gloves and rearranged her hat on top of her head. Hans-Hermann wouldn't look at her hands, she told herself. She shouldn't lose her composure now.

She wore a gray dress with white trim, slightly austere, elegant enough for a formal occasion as long as she hid the stain on her sleeve under a bracelet. In the subway, an old man in overalls had spat on the ground when she'd exited the metro car. Her pretty dress poked under her rain jacket, and the only Parisians going out for dinner these days were those who thrived under the new regime, sympathizers, opportunists. Yvonne never would've described herself as a sympathizer, but she did see an opportunity.

The Ritz's lobby, packed with gilded frames and crystal chandeliers over the mandatory marble floors, was overrun with Nazi officers chatting in German. Yvonne searched in vain for Hans-Hermann and, clutching her purse, ventured forward among the adversaries of France. She couldn't afford to show any contempt for them. Her son's release depended on it. She sat down on the edge of a plush armchair. How would confident heroines sit?

Busboys pushed carts and dragged luggage around her. One of them cast her a dark glance. It must be obvious that she was visiting a *Boche*. She could imagine the names he was calling her silently—traitor, whore, harlot—and stared down at her feet. After years of use, her white stilettos had turned gray near the soles and their straps were worn, but they matched the trim of her dress. A pair of black polished dress shoes stopped near Yvonne's stilettos, so close that their tips almost touched. Yvonne looked up, already smiling.

"My humble abode," Hans-Hermann said in French. "The restaurant is behind those columns."

The maître d' rushed toward them when they entered the dining room and took Yvonne's rain jacket. When she'd pulled her dress out of her closet, it'd seemed suitably modest and respectful of the catastrophe that'd struck France, but now it embarrassed her. Such opulence around her, and she was in such drab clothing. No one else in the room had made that mistake. The restaurant brimmed with German officers in uniforms and a handful of civilians, the men in business suits, the women in backless gowns, laughing and clinking glasses over feasts worthy of a royal family. Yvonne wouldn't get what she sought looking plain.

The maître d' led Hans-Hermann and Yvonne to a table in the back. By the window, a short man whose stomach was rippling out of his pants was eating beef roulade. Hans-Hermann made the Nazi salute when he walked past him and the man made the salute back without bothering to stand, as if Hans-Hermann didn't deserve his full effort.

The Nazi officer winked at him. "Always the first one to find out where the pretty ones are," he said in German, unaware that Yvonne understood him. His small eyes reminded her of a pig's.

"This is Yvonne Chevallier, the opera singer," Hans-Hermann said. "She sang at Bayreuth last year. The Führer swears by her."

The Nazi officer nodded appreciatively. His gaze lingered on Yvonne's chest. "Introduce me," he said.

Kriminaldirektor Klaus Koegel, his name was. *Kriminaldirektor* sounded like a title in the German secret police. Yvonne took a good look at the man and his thick, square face pockmarked by narrow eyes. Gestapo, naturally. She'd heard terrible things about those men. She gripped Hans-Hermann's arm but couldn't bring herself to say she needed to sit down. The men might conclude she had some reason to reproach herself, beside her distaste for the Nazi regime. Stage Yvonne wouldn't make a mistake like that.

Klaus waved his fork at Hans-Hermann. "You dug a quality one too," he said in German. "You'll go far in life, Hans boy." He planted the fork into his beef roulade. "And get that list we talked about on my desk by tomorrow, pretty blonde in your bed or not. In fact, maybe I should take care of the pretty blonde while you take care of the list."

Yvonne let her gaze wander around the dining room, her face still, as if she had no clue what he'd just said.

"You'll have it tomorrow morning," Hans-Hermann said sharply.

"Now, don't be peeved, Hans boy. It's not my fault all the officers' girls end up in my arms." Klaus jabbed a thick finger in the air. "Talk with the consulates, not just the embassies. Especially in Marseilles. Make sure they stall when they receive visa requests."

"I've done that already," Hans-Hermann said, sounding annoyed.

"Do more of it. It should be right up your alley, shouldn't it? You like artists. Maybe you can keep a painting or a manuscript when you arrest them." Klaus's ugly smile returned. "I really don't think you'll have time for your lady."

Hans-Hermann nudged Yvonne away. He gave her the best side of the table, so that she could admire the dining room and its patrons while Hans-Hermann faced the back wall lined with mirrors. The maître d' pushed Yvonne's chair back a second too late when she sat down. She landed on the hard edge and struggled not to fall onto the floor. But maybe she'd sat down too quickly. Maybe it was her fault. The maître d', all smiles, handed her the menu.

Yvonne's eyes watered when she read the names of the entrées. Rumors swirled that rationing would officially start in October, but restaurants that catered only to the victors, because of their prices, must've long been hoarding food. Yvonne had never known such delicious meals even existed. Melon gazpacho with dried breast duck. Langoustine roasted with citrus, oyster mushrooms with pistachio. Crabmeat with marinated radish and corralled velvet. Red snapper with grilled trombolino zucchini. Rabbit from Burgundy with mustard, confit shoulder, and roasted rack. At the Ritz it looked like the good times were there to stay. Perhaps it wasn't a coincidence the restaurant was full of Nazi officers.

Yvonne had no clue how to behave in a situation like this. The smell of a roasted rack of lamb and mussels dripping with sauvignon blanc sauce drifted from her neighbors' plates. Before she'd lost her job at the opera house, Yvonne hadn't known pangs of hunger could grow so intense.

She asked Hans-Hermann what he'd recommend, to flatter him. In truth, she was so famished she could've eaten anything.

"The lady will have the red snapper," Hans-Hermann told the maître d'. "For me, the rabbit. We'll share the best bottle of Bordeaux you have in the cellar."

It amazed Yvonne that the Ritz management hadn't smashed every single good bottle of wine they had against the walls before the Nazis marched into Paris.

For a moment she thought she recognized her manager Raymond at the other end of the restaurant. It took her a minute to realize she was wrong. She should've been relieved—nobody she knew was watching her compromise herself—but to her surprise, she felt a tinge of disappointment. She would've wanted Raymond to see how quickly she was making allies, eating at the Ritz with the victors. She would've wanted Madeleine to witness her change of fortune too. They'd take her seriously from now on.

Hans-Hermann arranged his napkin on his lap. "I thought about looking you up when I learned I was being transferred to Paris, but I wasn't sure you'd care to see me, since you left the party in Bayreuth without saying goodbye."

"I was feeling sick," Yvonne said, her voice steady. That wasn't a lie. She'd been feeling sick all right, sitting that close to Hitler.

A waiter brought them a bottle of 1928 Château Margaux. He made a show of presenting it to Hans-Hermann, uncorking it, pouring him a sip, waiting while Hans-Hermann swiveled the wine in his glass and sniffed it. Yvonne found such theatrics pretentious. But she made herself look dazzled.

"It smells like cedar and tobacco and the woods of Saxony after the rain," Hans-Hermann said. And, after the waiter had poured each of them a glass and left the bottle on the table, "Can you tell I don't know what I'm talking about? I usually stick to Hofbräu beer."

Yvonne clicked her glass against his. "If you ever decide to leave the military, you're destined for a brilliant acting career."

She drank a long sip of Château Margaux, to give herself courage, but the taste distracted her. She was used to cheap wines that tingled on her palate. Drinking expensive wine was a revelation, a bit like her first trip to the Paris Opera. Madeleine Moreau was singing Leïla in Georges Bizet's *Pearl Fishers*. Until then, Yvonne had admired the sopranos of the Dijon Opera. She'd never believed they were excellent—they wouldn't have stayed in Dijon otherwise—but she'd assumed they were good because she'd never heard anything better. Madeleine had disabused her in her very first minute onstage. Yvonne immediately wanted more of that wine. She'd waited for finer things long enough.

"So what is it you do in Paris exactly?" she asked Hans-Hermann.

"I was sent in to supervise the review committee in the culture department." Hans-Hermann's casual tone told Yvonne he cared about his new role a lot. "My staff reads manuscripts of books to be published, scripts of plays to be staged. You get the idea."

He oversaw the censorship office. Yvonne had never had a conversation with someone so powerful. She had to play her cards well before other Parisians tried to ingratiate themselves with him.

Yvonne pointed to Klaus. He was now wolfing down a large portion of tarte tatin surmounted by an enormous scoop of vanilla ice cream. "How's that related to consulates?"

"Oh, something I got pulled into," Hans-Hermann said. "On occasion, to stay in your colleagues' good graces, you have to help them with their pet projects." Hans-Hermann waved his hand in the air. His wedding band caught the light of the chandeliers. Yvonne hadn't noticed it in Bayreuth. But married or not, he was the only person she knew who could help Jules.

"What he's after is not urgent," Hans-Hermann said. "We've just come to town. We can waste a bit of time looking for people and not finding them."

Yvonne waited for him to say more.

"Artists who fled the regime," Hans-Hermann said. "Some of my superiors want to ship them back east, if we locate them. They set a bad example when they left."

Yvonne wished he hadn't taken any part in that. But it must've been Klaus's idea, not his. After a moment, she pulled herself together and returned in character. Stage Yvonne liked maybe not all Germans, but at least the one in front of her. Otherwise, Jules would waste away for years in a prisoner-of-war camp.

The waiter placed their dishes on the table very ceremoniously, as if the cooks had braved the elements that same morning to fish the red snapper out of the Atlantic Ocean and chase the rabbit through the fields of eastern France. At home, Yvonne ate beans and carrots out of tin cans. She admired the fish, the vegetables, everything perfectly presented on the plate. How happy—genuinely happy—she felt to be sitting in front of such food. When she looked up, Klaus was eyeing her from his table.

"That friend of yours is staring at me," Yvonne said.

"He's not my friend," Hans-Hermann said, exactly as she'd hoped. He tasted a piece of rabbit. "Let's plan your return to the Paris Opera. When would you like to sing?"

"Tomorrow," Yvonne said, only half joking.

"So, the season premiere," Hans-Hermann said.

Yvonne must've made a face, because he added, "I never promise something I can't deliver."

❧

"I'll fetch my chauffeur," Hans-Hermann said after they'd finished their meal.

But the neighbors would think Yvonne was sleeping with a *Boche* if she returned home in a Nazi car. She had her pride.

"I don't want to be an inconvenience," she said. "Your chauffeur has to rest."

"You're not going to take the subway by yourself at this hour."

His tone admitted no dissent. Hopefully everyone in Yvonne's building would be sound asleep by the time Hans-Hermann's car pulled over by the front door.

The chauffeur was barely older than Jules, the son of a general maybe, somebody whose family enjoyed enough connections to let him ferry German officers through Paris instead of guarding prisoners in camps near Mannheim or Baden-Baden. Yvonne had never sat in a vehicle that looked so expensive. It was worthy of generals and movie stars. She'd expected Hans-Hermann to send her home in his sedan while he stayed at the Ritz, but instead he sat down next to her. Yvonne fought her impulse to press herself against the armrest. Stage Yvonne welcomed the companionship. She needed him to put in a good word for Jules.

Parisians on the sidewalk glimpsed the Grosser Mercedes as it zoomed by. Yvonne didn't get a good look at them—her compatriots were already in the rearview mirror, their silent judgment a thing of the past. The speed of the car sickened her. It wouldn't help her case if she vomited all over the leather upholstery.

"Rolf," Hans-Hermann said to his chauffeur, "if my car has as much as a scratch when we go to the garage tonight, you're walking home to Frankfurt."

Rolf slowed down. The contents of Yvonne's dinner settled in her stomach.

"Do you think my son could be freed in time to see my debut?" Yvonne asked.

"I told you I'd ask my colleagues." Hans-Hermann sounded irritated. "I work for the culture department, not the War Ministry."

Who'd help Yvonne if Hans-Hermann lost interest in her? She had to be more careful.

They reached the working-class tenements of the tenth arrondissement, where Yvonne lived. Hans-Hermann eyed the buildings around him: the peeling paint, the moss on the awnings, the boarded-up windows. Yvonne wished he'd drunk too much to notice.

"You deserve so much better," Hans-Hermann said.

Yvonne was really beginning to like him.

Hans-Hermann escorted her to the front door and made a little bow over her hand to say goodbye. Yvonne's insides stirred when he took her fingers. She hadn't expected to feel anything for him except a vague satisfaction that he'd selected her, among all the women in Paris, to have dinner with.

"You'd better start rehearsing," Hans-Hermann said.

Twelve

The Moreaus' car pulled in front of the opera house. Yet another swastika flapped from its roof. The banners had spread to all the public buildings within two days of the defeat, like a measles epidemic in an elementary school. Madeleine blamed groveling, spineless Vichy officials for disfiguring the city so fast. But the only thing she could do now was to shield her eyes. Storefronts remained closed on the Place de l'Opéra, their owners still away after the exodus, except for a restaurant at the corner of the rue Auber that was packed with Nazi officers lounging under the parasols. The sky did not show a single cloud. How scandalous that the *Boches* could enjoy such magnificent weather in the city the French had lost.

"Just the idea of coming here every day makes me want to hold a high G for thirty seconds straight," Madeleine said.

"You can warm up your voice as you see fit," Henri said.

A group of German soldiers peered through a storefront's shutters. An older man who was waiting at the crosswalk nodded when they passed him. The soldiers nodded back and offered to carry his groceries across the street for him. They displayed enough manners for Parisians to conclude that they shouldn't fear the occupiers if they followed orders. Madeleine could not get her eyes off the older man, who was so glad at the soldiers' courtesy. Nazi soldiers deserved no gratitude.

"Hopefully, de Gaulle will have sent this circus packing by next year," Madeleine said. "Two years at most."

She had been in attendance, anonymous in the crowd, when Hitler had reviewed his troops on the Champs-Élysées the previous month. While the Nazis had marched in goose step down the avenue, bystanders had held back tears and repeated the words they had heard on the forbidden BBC: de Gaulle would keep fighting until France won.

Henri tapped his fingers against the armrest. "De Gaulle is a deluded man. We lost the war. Better to admit it than stay stuck in the past." He put his hand over Madeleine's. "We're going to walk in, and you're going to tell Emile you'll sing all the roles you've been cast in, and all the roles he sees fit in whatever other operas he decides to show now that the Germans occupy Paris."

"We could move to Lyons or Marseilles. There'd be plenty of work for us over there." The Free Zone looked more appealing to Madeleine by the day.

"As if the Germans would let us cross the demarcation line," Henri said. "We have too high a profile here."

"What about a world tour, then?" Madeleine said. "The United States is still neutral."

Henri squeezed her fingers. "They'll see through our transparent little attempt to get away from them. They won't grant us exit visas. But if we cooperate and prove ourselves agreeable to the Germans now, they may allow us a trip in a few years."

That sounded like an eternity.

"Let's do our best work this season, here, now, with Emile, who's trying hard to deal with the situation he has."

Madeleine squeezed Henri's hand back. "He has to beg me first. I will not work in these conditions and not be implored for it."

"I'll make sure to tell him that, then," Henri said matter-of-factly.

"And even then, I'm not convinced I'll be able to do it."

Henri looked more closely at her. "Did you have a bottle of champagne for breakfast?"

"I wish I had," Madeleine said.

"Why can't you see how serious the situation is, then? We're too famous not to draw attention on ourselves if we disappear. Besides, you and I both know you'd lose your mind in three days if you sat at home while someone else sang in your place."

He smiled at her, trying to cajole her into compliance.

Singing for the Nazis in her birth city—that would require untold strength from Madeleine. They'd invaded her country. They'd keep French politicians under their heel, begging for mercy. All pretense of civility was gone. The Germans were only bloodthirsty middlemen, eager to destroy educated people. Yet it terrified her that her public might forget her within weeks if she did not sing. Who would she be, then?

"Why should anyone else but we decide what is high culture in Paris?" Henri asked. "We won't keep our power in this town if you don't sing, and if we don't, all the people you ignored or demeaned or aggravated during your years on the stage will come out of the woodshed and stab us in the back."

Madeleine stepped out of the car. "Your eloquence is a marvel."

☙ ❧

Inside the opera house, Madeleine deplored that Emile had not swapped the gilded mirror frames for plain ones nor removed the rococo lamp fixtures. The *Boches* did not deserve any of this. Maybe they'd steal it.

Henri offered her his arm at the bottom of the stairs. "Whatever gets thrown your way, you can handle it."

If only Madeleine could share his optimism.

The building was ghastly silent. The director for *Lucia di Lammermoor* should have been preparing the first rehearsal while the seamstresses labored over the costumes for the premiere, but no excitement ran through the building before the new season. The staff had not returned to their desks. The corridors remained quiet. Madeleine's high heels echoed on the spiral staircase while she climbed the steps toward the cupola with Henri, heading for Emile's office. In the antechamber, the typewriter of his secretary Denise lay covered, untouched since the exodus. The door to Emile's office had been left ajar.

A small, round-faced man scribbled down notes at a large cherry-wood desk covered with piles of papers. A deep crease ran across his forehead. All the opera singers in Paris feared him because he could break their career between lunch and dinner—all except Madeleine, who earned him so much money that he always agreed to her whims.

Cigarette smoke lingered in the air. "So you didn't stay in Normandy," Madeleine said, trying not to grimace at the smell.

Emile started. His ink pen left a long line across the page.

"Did I scare you?" Madeleine asked.

Emile checked the time on the Bulova clock. "I only expected Henri. What were you saying?" He gathered his papers.

"That you didn't stay in Normandy."

"They would've put a German at the helm if I hadn't come back. I couldn't allow it."

"We didn't even leave Paris," Henri said. His voice brimmed with pride. For him, this small gesture counted as courage. He settled into one of the armchairs facing Emile's desk. "In the end, there was no looting at all."

"They'll loot us all right, just not in the obvious way," Emile said. And then, pointing at Madeleine, "You should've warned me she'd be here."

"Why wouldn't she come along?" Henri said. "She wasn't going to let us decide the new season by ourselves. When you told me to come, I thought you meant for me to bring her as well."

Madeleine perched herself on the other chair. She couldn't ask right away about her mail, in case Henri became suspicious, but surely Stefan had written her from America by now.

Henri dug his elbows into the armrests. "So, *Lucia.*"

"We have to pick something else," Emile said. "The censors prefer a German opera."

Censors—Madeleine loathed that title. As if they deserved to pass judgment on Donizetti.

"The repertoire doesn't lack German works," Henri said carefully.

"We can also roll over and play the good puppies in front of our new masters." Madeleine tapped her foot against Emile's desk. "Let's start with something in French, but totally unrelated to the times, so they can't find a reason to censor it."

Both *Les Troyens* and *Samson and Delilah* provided grand spectacles ripe with plot twists thanks to the inspiring female heroine. They would be excellent vehicles for her.

"The Germans will forbid it outright, and they'll never forget we tried to pull it off," Emile said. "We might show French operas later, but not to start."

Madeleine would not have scowled more if he had suggested that Giacomo Meyerbeer outshone Richard Wagner. "They'll trample us if we don't prove we have some spine."

"They'll make life very difficult for certain people here if we can't convince them to look the other way. We need to stay on good terms with them." Emile paused. "Please, Madeleine."

Certain people—surely the payroll of the opera house included Jewish employees. But what had happened in Germany would not be repeated here.

"The Vichy government won't pass anything remotely like the Nuremberg laws," Madeleine said. "They won't allow their citizens to be treated that way."

"You can't seriously believe it. You're not that foolish." Emile looked at the clock again.

"If you're going to be unpleasant, I'd rather pick up my mail than listen to you. Just tell me what opera you've decided on when I return. I'll sing anything." Madeleine stood up.

Smoothly done, she told herself.

"Denise isn't back in Paris, so all the letters are in a box on her desk," Emile said.

Madeleine rummaged through the pile of mail in front of the covered typewriter. There, at last, she snatched an envelope that bore Stefan's handwriting. The letter had been posted from Marseille the previous week—before he had boarded the ship, then. She tore the envelope open.

"You lack manners this morning," Henri said from Emile's office.

Madeleine dismissed the reproach in his voice. He could not possibly know about the affair. She had covered her tracks, and in any case, the cheating had ended years earlier. From the envelope she retrieved a sheet of paper, pulled from a notebook. *We are still waiting for our visas,* the letter said in small, measured handwriting. *Embassy employees have*

taken our money, but no progress has been made on our cases. Can you help?
Stefan had listed a hotel in Marseilles as his return address.

A chill went up Madeleine's spine. The fear moved to her shoulders.
She reread the letter. It was dangerous for Stefan to be stuck in Marseilles. The Germans would surely try to arrest any high-profile resi-
dent of their territories who had fled the Third Reich, and Stefan, for
those Nazis who knew opera, would be high-profile indeed. Madeleine
shoved the letter into her purse and returned to Emile's office. Henri's
gaze lingered on her. Maybe she seemed a little pale. She made herself
smile. Stefan would be thrown into jail if the Germans laid hands on
him, but they hadn't found him yet.

"We already have the sets for *Magic Flute*," Emile said to Henri when
Madeleine entered. "That'd be the easiest solution." Mozart, a composer
Madeleine did not care for. And there was no role for her in that opera.
She didn't have the range for the Queen of the Night and hadn't sung
Pamina in decades.

"Too lighthearted," Madeleine said. "We can't ignore the tragedy
that has befallen France."

She had to intercede on Stefan's behalf to the US ambassador. That
would get Stefan his visa. She had met William Bullitt once at a Bastille Day celebration and viewed him as a good man. He enjoyed min-
gling with influential Parisians and had attempted to persuade her that
the United States was more than a country of cowboys. But Madeleine
would wield no influence whatsoever with him if she did not sing at the
opera house.

"Let's open with Wagner," Madeleine said. "*Tristan und Isolde*."

Henri looked at her as if she had grown two heads. Isolde was one
of her signature roles. Hadn't she been insisting a moment ago that she
would refuse to sing until properly implored?

"The defeat broke my heart, but I am a professional," Madeleine
said, as if she read Henri's mind. "I will fulfill my duty. My art
demands it."

"I'd have to check that the Germans agree." Emile rearranged his
papers. "Your behavior at Bayreuth didn't win you any friends. But we

should talk about it later. I've got people coming. Will you stick around for a bit?"

Madeleine began to laugh, until she realized he wasn't joking. Before the war, he wouldn't have made her wait one minute.

Emile opened a box of Cuban cigars. He had never smoked them in front of Madeleine. In fact, she hadn't known him to like cigars. He was nervous about something.

"Whatever you decide to open the season with, we'll help you with it," Henri said. "No one sells tickets like the two of us."

Emile eyed Madeleine, as if to check that she agreed with Henri, and then hungrily took a puff of cigar. "I'll keep that in mind. Now, if you'll excuse me, I need to prepare for my next meeting."

Madeleine plucked his cigar from his hand and threw it into the wastebasket. "What's more important than deciding on the opera season?"

Emile fished the cigar out before it set fire to the papers he had discarded. "I didn't say my next meeting wasn't about that."

Footsteps drew nearer in the corridor. Military boots—Madeleine had sung in enough *Fidelio*s to recognize the thud of their soles against the tiles. High heels hurried in a sharp clatter alongside the boots.

"My dear Madeleine," Emile said, "you must decide right now that you will refrain from throwing heavy objects at anyone's head, especially mine."

A German officer appeared in the doorframe, towering over the room. A red-and-white cross dangled from his collar. Yvonne—Yvonne!—clung to his arm in a Chanel dress she could not afford.

Madeleine reined in her surprised and reacted before Yvonne did. "Yvonne dear, you should introduce us to your friend."

Only bystanders who had not interacted with Madeleine could have mistaken her tone for friendliness. The others would catch the implication in her voice: Yvonne was sleeping with an occupier.

"Hans, I mean Generalleutnant Hans-Hermann von Moderling," Yvonne said, her head high, "this is Emile Jouhaud, the general manager of the Paris Opera. Henri Moreau, who conducts the Opera Orchestra.

And his wife, Madeleine, who was scheduled to sing Isolde in Bayreuth, until life decided otherwise."

"I am delighted that our paths intersect at last," Hans-Hermann said to Madeleine. He spoke French slowly but flawlessly. "It is such a pity you had to leave Germany so quickly last summer. Wagner did not skip town any faster when he was fleeing his creditors." He held her gaze.

"I was disappointed I had to withdraw but am glad we finally meet," Madeleine said evenly. "And what do you do in our beautiful city?"

"I head the cultural office," Hans-Hermann said.

Madeleine laughed a throaty laugh. Henri called it her fake laugh, because she only used it when she was playing a role, but she could command it at will. "Let me guess. You decide which shows go on." Yvonne had chosen her ally well.

"My direct reports decide that sort of thing, but it is indeed part of my office's responsibilities," Hans-Hermann said.

He ambled to the armchair that Madeleine was sitting in, close to Emile's desk. Yvonne strolled alongside him.

"Madeleine was just leaving," Emile said.

Yvonne installed herself on the sofa against the wall. "Oh, why doesn't she stay? This way we'll all be on the same page."

Madeleine hugged her purse as if she needed it to keep herself warm. Stefan's letter rustled against her hand. Emile saying that she was leaving, Yvonne encouraging her to stay: that could mean only one thing. But Stefan would never obtain a visa for the United States if Madeleine was shoved out of the limelight. She pressed her heels into the rug, counted to three. The fear subsided just enough for her to stay calm. She had to be smart, or Stefan would soon be in jail.

"It seems that you have not cast Yvonne here as often as her voice would warrant," Hans-Hermann said to Emile.

"We're certainly open to casting her more often in the future," Emile said.

"In the present," Hans-Hermann said. "The season premiere."

Madeleine had opened every season at the Paris Opera for the past fifteen years.

"If that's what you want," Henri said, "but few singers, even experienced ones, can handle the pressure of the season opener."

"She handled the pressure fine in Germany," Hans-Hermann said. Not only for the premiere, but for the second performance as well. Yvonne had shone in the little time she'd had before Marta's arrival. "Now, Herr Jouhaud, I heard Frau Chevallier sing in Germany, and it is a grave slight toward the good people of Paris not to let them hear her sing."

"Scheduling—" Emile said. The word came out as a pathetic mumble.

"They have to hear her as Isolde as soon as possible," Hans-Hermann said.

How had Yvonne won over that Nazi officer so quickly? Madeleine imagined her walking through Pigalle—Paris's red-light district—offering her services to any Grosser Mercedes rolling past her. She needed money, after all.

Emile and Henri glanced at each other. Madeleine could tell from the looks on their faces that Emile was about to offer that little striver the role for the season premiere and Henri would not object. But Isolde was Madeleine's favorite role. She would impress Bullitt with it, and then he would rush to Stefan's aid.

"I suppose she can sing it," Madeleine said. "She had fine reviews in that. Besides, it'd be difficult for her to learn something new in a few weeks. She can be our one-trick pony."

Emile slammed shut one of the drawers in his desk.

"I know plenty of roles," Yvonne said.

"We don't doubt that," Henri said, "but I'm not sure if many German soldiers are in the right mind to watch a love story at the moment. If our Madame Chevallier feels up to the task, though, an opera with more action and characters, more entertainment, would certainly hold the attention of the troops."

The silence stretched until Hans-Hermann said, "Go on."

"There are several choices. *Die Walküre*?"

Henri could really be brilliant when Madeleine needed him. Wagner's opera had ruined the voice of many an inexperienced singer anxious to prove herself. Yvonne did not have the training to pull it off, but she wouldn't dare admit it in front of her *Boche*.

"Yvonne would make the perfect Sieglinde," Madeleine said.

"You want to sing Brünnhilde," Yvonne said, referring to the leading female role. "I won't let you upstage me."

"That wasn't my intention," Madeleine said, although it had been. "You can sing Brünnhilde, and anyone of your choosing can sing Sieglinde." Yvonne would ruin her voice even faster if she sang the leading role.

Yvonne tugged on her necklace of pearls. Hans-Hermann must have bought it for her, just like the Chanel dress. Madeleine enjoyed watching her distress. There was no way in the world that Yvonne was ready to take on the role of Brünnhilde. But she would not say so to Hans-Hermann.

"So, Brünnhilde for me," Yvonne said.

"And the opera house should be reopened as early as possible," Madeleine said. "There are so few options for entertainment in the summer. Those poor German soldiers must be getting dreadfully bored. Everything in Paris is closed before mid-August, but what about the fourth week?"

She looked straight at Yvonne. The season would then begin one full month before its typical start. This would give Yvonne little time to prepare. Yvonne wedged her fingernails between two pearls of the necklace. Her eyelids fluttered. She seemed to no longer be in the same place as they were. One month early—that was daunting.

With a snap, the string of the necklace broke. The pearls tumbled onto the ground, rolling under the furniture, scattering all over the room. Hans-Hermann's eyes narrowed into slits. Yvonne turned as pale as a corpse.

Madeleine hadn't expected to feel sorry for her, but Hans-Hermann looked like he could have slapped her.

Taking pity on Yvonne, Madeleine kneeled onto the rug. "The same thing happened to me last week. You'd think jewelers would invest in better quality for their products." She picked up pearls from the floor.

They were real pearls; she could tell from the touch, scratchy and uneven. That necklace should have cost a fortune. Madeleine would bet Hans-Hermann hadn't paid a tenth of what it was worth.

"We'll never find them all," Yvonne said, crestfallen.

"No one will clean this office until we have," Madeleine said, and looked at Emile.

"Naturally," Emile said.

Henri picked up two pearls without leaving his chair and handed them to Yvonne. Her face was crimson.

"I'll give you the name of our jeweler to repair it," Madeleine said.

"He'll do it for free," Henri said. "I had an argument with him about a necklace of ours where the chain broke, and now the necklace is lost. He's eager to get back in our good graces."

Madeleine collected the pearls and handed them to Yvonne. "I think that's it."

It took some time while Hans-Hermann counted them. "Sixty-eight," he finally said. "That matches what the store clerk said."

Yvonne couldn't have made a bigger smile if she had been told she had won a recording contract with Deutsche Grammophon. She beamed at Madeleine. Before she could say thank you, Madeleine jabbed Emile's calendar with a blood red fingernail. "What about August twenty-fourth?"

"Staging *Die Walküre* on such short notice is complicated," Emile said.

"Let's pick a smaller opera," Hans-Hermann said. "Something with only one soprano role." It would go to Yvonne and not Madeleine.

Henri thought about it for a minute. "What about *Parsifal*?" he finally said.

Madeleine pressed her hand against her purse, over the spot where Stefan's letter was. *Parsifal* was Alexandre's favorite opera—she viewed that as a good omen. The part of Kundry would rid her of Yvonne just fine. The little harlot would try to sing it and fail, and Madeleine would sweep in and save the day. William Bullitt would be amazed.

The role of Kundry fascinated Madeleine almost as much as Isolde did—a witch who struggled under the spell of an evil sorcerer but also saved the hero Parsifal, a score that required tackling fiendishly difficult notes and staggering interval leaps to convey the inner torment of the female protagonist. Yvonne would never make a credible Kundry. She looked too naïve, she lacked the inner fire, and she did not have the technique.

"We have everything we need to show that opera tomorrow," Emile said. "Can the orchestra be ready in time?"

"Naturally," Henri said.

"But is the role big enough for Yvonne?" Hans-Hermann said.

"The number of notes isn't what matters," Madeleine said. "Only the difficulty."

Yvonne smoothed her dress over her knees, as if she were saying a quick prayer, before she looked up. "I'll do it, but Charles-Antoine must be hired as my accompanist. Guillaume will sing Parsifal. Henri will conduct. And, of course, Madeleine will be my understudy."

Henri sat straight and then smiled.

Thirteen

Yvonne ran up the coiling staircase of the opera house that led to the rehearsal room as Hans-Hermann followed behind her. She wished he hadn't accompanied her for the first rehearsal of *Parsifal*, to let her enjoy the illusion that she'd been cast as Kundry on her own merits. But what mattered was that she'd sing, didn't it? And then she'd earn praise for her singing, and her acting, and spectators would never know she'd hitched her star to a Nazi. She turned to Hans-Hermann in the stairs and, when their gaze met, gave him her brightest smile. The night before, he'd boasted of arresting in Orléans a family of Jewish German actors who'd decided to hide in the provinces instead of trying to make it out of France, and had been denounced by the son of the woman who was sheltering them. That woman had been taken in with them. When Hans-Hermann talked about her, he kept saying that one could not commit such acts and expect no consequence. Yvonne had to dig her fingernails into her palm to avoid asking if he referred to the Nazis persecuting people on the basis of their religion and stealing everything they owned. She didn't care to see the inside of a prison cell, nor the inside of a gun barrel.

Thankfully, Hans-Hermann headed for Emile's office instead of climbing the last flight of stairs with her. He held a list of names. It was one page long, with one name per line. Yvonne had spied it in the Grosser Mercedes. The names were French, and the top three were circled in red. She could think of only one explanation for Hans-Hermann bringing a list of French names to Emile, and she didn't like it. Writing the list was apparently the reason he'd picked her up late, although perhaps he'd made her late on purpose. She'd kept asking when Jules would be released from the camp, because no matter how much attention she gave the Nazi, she wasn't getting any closer to her goal. She knew she shouldn't have—one of these days he'd likely have her jailed—but she had to get her son home.

The rest of the cast was waiting for Yvonne when she rushed in. What a mistake on her part. Madeleine would've strolled in as if everyone else deserved to be kept waiting. Charles-Antoine had already taken his post at the Steinway. Henri, seated at a large wooden table near the window with a view of the avenue de l'Opéra, flipped through his papers, sleeves rolled up because of the summer heat. He was slightly disheveled, as if he could spend his effort either on mastering the score of *Parsifal* or on polishing his appearance but not both. He looked up and nodded when Yvonne closed the door, but the rest of the cast members didn't greet her. As a matter of fact, they behaved as if they hadn't noticed her coming in. What had Henri told them about that meeting Hans-Hermann had attended? Perhaps he'd encouraged them to make her fail.

"Vichy was dreadfully tedious," Guillaume said, in the loud voice of boors who hoped the whole room would hear them while they pretended to talk only to the person in front of them. He'd hidden from the war in a government job thanks to his wife's connections. "You can't understand life in the provinces until you've spent a week there. Some days, life was so dull I wished I'd gone to the front."

Imbecile. Cowards like Guillaume deserved so much more than Jules to rot in a prisoner-of-war camp.

Yvonne crossed the room toward the music stand. Hans-Hermann had told her the matter with Jules would be resolved shortly, but that'd been weeks ago and anything had yet to happen. She was beginning to doubt he had any plan to bring him home.

Two other singers had gathered near the large window over the square: a bass Yvonne recognized from a previous production of *Fidelio* and the baritone who had sung Cesare Angelotti in *Tosca*, now the wounded ruler Amfortas. It was a good cast, full of opera veterans. They'd help her shine onstage, and if she didn't, would take the attention away from her. She opened her score.

"Let's begin, now that we're all here," Henri said. Was his tone reproachful, or was Yvonne imagining things? She had pushed aside Madeleine, after all.

Guillaume claimed the music stand next to Yvonne's but ignored her. Having been Madeleine's pet, perhaps he felt loyalty to his previous partner. The other singers kept talking to each other. Yvonne felt like an invisible wall was separating her from the cast. Her mouth felt dry. Her hand shook when she took out a pencil to write notes on the score. She hadn't expected such nervousness: it was only a rehearsal. But it was the first one; she had to make a good impression. Her sense of isolation scared her. The other singers had already dismissed her as a musician. Yes, Henri must've told them about her Nazi friend.

Henri gave Charles-Antoine the signal.

"Gurnemanz" sang, followed by the knights and squires. They were marking the notes, not pushing their voices for the first day. When Yvonne's turn came, she sang with her full voice, to impress them, but she strained to reach the top notes. The room was too hot, the atmosphere too somber, the enmity of her colleagues too intense. She'd planned to win her castmates over by singing Kundry with an emotion that eluded Madeleine, but the more she tried to push through, the more her voice fell short. A colossal failure.

Hans-Hermann stepped into the doorframe, sheet of paper in hand. At the sight of him, Yvonne pulled every single note out of her lungs as if she were crawling over broken glass. If she disappointed him, she'd return to being an also-ran.

Just when Yvonne's voice was improving, Charles-Antoine played the wrong bar.

Henri signaled to stop and gestured to Hans-Hermann. "You can come in, if you fancy it," he said.

If only Hans-Hermann hadn't joined them so early—not before she'd had a chance to impress her colleagues with her artistry, and that was a long way from happening. They'd all think she was using Hans-Hermann to obtain roles she didn't deserve, when he'd admired her so at Bayreuth.

"I have this for you." Hans-Hermann gave Henri the sheet of paper. Yvonne recognized the list of French names from the car.

"Your general manager agrees it is correct," Hans-Hermann said.

Henri looked at the paper, but his eyes did not move down the page.

"Those employees will need to be replaced," Hans-Hermann said. If he'd wanted to show Yvonne he didn't care about embarrassing her in front of her colleagues, he couldn't have picked a more effective way.

There was a moment of silence. The singers pressed their lips into thin lines, but Hans-Hermann didn't read the names aloud, and neither did Henri. That was a relief. But perhaps that was what the Nazis wanted: it was harder to fight for people when one didn't know their names.

Henri kept the obliging expression on his face. "Not too many musicians qualify to become principal double bass or"—he consulted the paper—"associate principal cello here."

"People come, people go," Hans-Hermann said. "Surely you have handled departures before."

Charles-Antoine folded his hands on his lap.

"It takes time to find the right musicians for this orchestra," Henri said. "I doubt I can identify suitable replacements before winter."

"You won't have a choice," Hans-Hermann said. "In about a month, a new law will forbid certain people from working in the public service. Take care of this before the season begins. Musicians need enough rehearsal time."

Charles-Antoine pored over the score as if he'd glimpsed a secret in the music that he'd been unaware of.

"I'll expect the list of new musicians from you in two weeks," Hans-Hermann said. His voice betrayed no emotion. Yvonne was seeing a side of him she hadn't witnessed before, but she'd expected it. She'd stop seeing him as soon as Jules returned.

Henri said nothing.

"You may have to make changes in the cast too." Hans-Hermann's gaze lingered on the man singing Amfortas, who had thick eyebrows and curly dark hair.

Amfortas pulled the little cross he wore around his neck from under his shirt. He was Catholic.

Henri filed the piece of paper away, avoiding the gaze of his colleagues. Madeleine would've thrown a fit if she'd been in the room, Madeleine who'd fled Bayreuth and carried the pictures of her dead brother on every trip and was now, the rumor went, learning needlepoint at home while newcomers starred in the roles that should've been hers. Yvonne hadn't expected to miss her rival, but she did. Only Madeleine and her histrionics might have delayed the Jewish musicians' fate. Yvonne felt small and useless.

"Let's start again, from the beginning," Henri said, eyes down.

Charles-Antoine played the piano.

Yvonne waited for her cue. Was there really nothing she could do, or was she making excuses? She only had her voice and her good looks as an asset, and that hadn't even managed to free Jules.

Finally, it was her turn. She sight-read the score. After a few bars, her glance drifted to Hans-Hermann. He was scowling at her. She'd get herself in trouble if she didn't sing better. Real trouble.

Yvonne collected herself and imagined herself as Kundry stumbling in the forest, exhausted after a long gallop on her horse, in a mad dash to bring King Amfortas a vial of balsam for a wound that wouldn't heal. Hans-Hermann looked distinctly more pleased now. Yvonne infused her notes with hope that her potion would soothe the king and shame that she'd served as his enemy's puppet—shame that she was still subjected to the evil magician's curse, that his dark arts would compel her to do his bidding if he summoned her again. Her anguished voice ricocheted onto the walls of the rehearsal room and soared to a thunder. Henri forgot to mark the beat.

Charles-Antoine played a series of wrong notes and ruined the moment.

Hans-Hermann marched out, the scowl back on his lips.

"I seem to recall much praise about you," Henri said to Charles-Antoine. "I'm not sure if it was as warranted as I wanted to believe." He sounded dismayed rather than angry.

"I shouldn't have come," Charles-Antoine said. "You'll have to find yourself another rehearsal pianist soon anyway."

Yvonne dropped her pencil. Wouldn't he have mentioned observing Rosh Hashanah or Yom Kippur in all the years he had taught her if he had been a Jew?

"I don't go to synagogue, but I doubt Yvonne's friend cares about such details," Charles-Antoine said.

Henri looked at Yvonne as if she'd set a trap for him and he'd fallen into it.

"I didn't know," Yvonne said.

Surely, Henri would run afoul of the Germans if they learned he'd hired a Jewish musician after their arrival. But wouldn't Yvonne too? She'd imposed Charles-Antoine, after all.

Charles-Antoine closed his score.

"Naturally you'll stay," Yvonne said. "I'll never learn the role in time without you."

She knew she was a rare trophy for Hans-Hermann. None of the other pretty Frenchwomen who dined with Nazis at the Ritz had done anything to distinguish themselves on their intellectual merits. If she held firm, Hans-Hermann would make an exception for her teacher. That, if nothing else, would earn her the grudging respect of her colleagues.

"Let's start from the top, now that our German friend is gone," Henri said.

Charles-Antoine played the score again, this time without mistake. Yvonne's singing improved immediately. Here and there she forced her voice, because she tried so hard to mesmerize her audiences, but she had a real chance at spinning her web around the *Boches* on opening day.

"I can hear why they liked you so much at Bayreuth," Henri said when she was done.

Yvonne hadn't expected him to compliment her. She'd taken the role away from Madeleine, after all. In that moment she'd have agreed to ten-hour rehearsals just to hear a shred of praise from the conductor again.

They went over "Ich sah das Kind" next. Yvonne hadn't prepared for it, but Henri seemed to enjoy what he heard. She accepted all of his suggestions like a castaway who'd been dragging herself through the desert and at last reached a pool of water. She had no one else in her corner.

"When you sing, I detect nuances in the score I've never noticed before," Henri said.

Yvonne could've sung for him forever. It'd only taken a handful of compliments, like crumbs thrown to a hungry dog who then follows a passerby for kilometers. She knew she should be more discerning, but she didn't want to disappoint him, now that he'd said all those nice things about her.

"Is there time for extra rehearsals before the premiere?" she said. "I want the performance to be perfect."

"I'll make time," Henri said.

The other singers glanced at each other.

"It'd help if Madeleine could attend," Yvonne said. "She sang Kundry to great acclaim a few years back. It was a production with—what was his name?—Stefan Kreismann in the title role."

A shadow came over Henri's face. "I'll ask."

After a moment, he relaxed. "Why, indeed, we should involve Madeleine in our success. You should come to our house. What about Wednesday?"

❦

Madeleine's house looked like a castle between the chestnut trees. Yvonne couldn't stop admiring it. Turrets bracketed the main structure of large white stones. It had a mythical status in Yvonne's mind. Madeleine often hinted at the parties she hosted there, dropping names of politicians and industry magnates, the Parisian high society that she mingled with instead of socializing with other singers—people who, in her world, didn't count for anything at all. Yvonne knew that included her. She didn't bother looking offended. She didn't have the energy for that. She'd never hosted a party, lavish or otherwise, except on Jules's birthday when he was a child, and even he couldn't remember it.

Yvonne walked up the path to the front door in a long cotton dress and a wide-brimmed hat that flounced around the rim. She'd tried to look like a Neuilly socialite visiting a friend, but as she neared the front door, it occurred to her that both Henri and Madeleine knew she was only a harlot with a powerful German friend who could open any door for her, even if she didn't deserve it. They'd laugh about her behind her back. The neighborhood, so peaceful, seemed located in a foreign country. In Yvonne's neighborhood, construction workers shouted at each other all day long amid the din of hammers and saws. Here, tree leaves rustled in a soft breeze. Birds chirped. Wealthy people would know what kind of birds they were, their gardener would've told them, but there was no one to tell Yvonne. Sparrows, she decided. She envied Madeleine for living amid such tranquility.

Through the large bay windows, Yvonne spied on the goings-on inside the house. Madeleine was seated at the dining room table, finishing her breakfast. Her red silk night robe—worth six months of Yvonne's salary, at least—could've passed for a kimono in *Madame Butterfly*. Henri, standing, was arguing with her. Presumably, Madeleine didn't welcome Yvonne's arrival. It pleased Yvonne, in an odd way, that she'd finally needled the star into a reaction to her existence. Forcing the former grande dame of the Paris Opera to listen while Yvonne prepared for the premiere seemed like a wonderful way to pass the time.

Yvonne rang the brass doorbell. A maid opened the door, her face marked with deep wrinkles and her gray hair pulled into a bun. Behind her, a chandelier dangled from the high ceiling—a cathedral ceiling, Yvonne thought it was called, and if it wasn't, well, that was the name she'd picked for it. A marble staircase coiled along the wall. It led to a gallery adorned with paintings and a reading nook on the second floor.

"Are you coming in?" Rose asked, rather sharply.

Under the staircase, a mirror hung in a gold frame over a table with a granite top. This house reeked of money. Yvonne was losing her confidence by the second.

Henri was waiting for her in the living room. Madeleine chewed on a bit of croissant, perhaps so that she didn't have to greet Yvonne. The country was preparing for rationing, but it hadn't come into effect yet, and people were hoarding as much as they could afford.

"Would you like a glass of water?" Henri said.

Yvonne shook her head—she didn't want to be a bother—and them immediately regretted it.

Madeleine had drawn her eyebrows in pencil and put kohl around her eyes, but if she'd believed Yvonne should be treated with respect, she wouldn't have worn a night robe that late in the morning.

"Let's get started, then," Henri said.

Yvonne smiled at him. Madeleine could try to antagonize her, but she wouldn't be the one stepping onstage at the premiere.

The Steinway was positioned in the shade against the wall. Surely Madeleine rehearsed comfortably there. Her high notes wouldn't echo against the walls and make her head throb, the way Yvonne's did when she tried to practice at home. On the mantelpiece, photographs of Madeleine and Henri in performance reminded their guests they stood in the proximity of greatness. Yvonne would've picked other pictures of Madeleine's—something where she'd have looked more fierce even if it meant she'd look less pretty. A recording of Franck and Debussy sonatas lay on the Victrola. Yvonne guessed Madeleine didn't listen to opera. She wouldn't tolerate hearing a soprano who wasn't her.

Henri sat down at the piano. "My dear Kundry, we shall begin." He looked friendly, as if he had Yvonne's best interests at heart. But they all pursued their own agenda, Henri, Madeleine, Emile, Raymond. Yvonne had her own agenda too.

Madeleine finished her croissant and held up her glass of water as if to say, *Once you've made a disaster of things, I'm ready to toast your mediocrity.*

They started with the "Grausamer" piece. That was Kundry's signature aria in the second act, where she recounted for Parsifal the curse Klingsor had placed on her, condemning her to immortality until a man resisted her charms.

Yvonne struggled with the first few notes. She felt like a fraud in the brand-new dress Hans-Hermann had bought for her, wearing a costume and playing make-believe, never the beloved star she'd dreamt to become. She forced the notes, but Madeleine's wealth made her self-conscious.

"This is close to perfect," Henri said.

His lie stung Yvonne even more than criticism. He wanted to either ingratiate himself with Yvonne or annoy Madeleine mightily. Yvonne wasn't much more than a doll to him, and a Nazi was pulling the strings. Perhaps she possessed the raw qualities for success, but she didn't have the nerves.

Yvonne fell off a note.

"Thank goodness you're getting the extra practice," Madeleine said.

"You're thinking too much about how to sing correctly and not enough about what you're singing," Henri said to Yvonne. "That's unlike you. Even my wife tried to act more like you after she read the reviews of your Isolde at Bayreuth."

Madeleine slammed her glass of water against the table.

"Think about what the character feels," Henri said.

"So much thinking," Madeleine said with fake gaiety. "Let's stop thinking altogether. About singing, about the mess the country is in. No more thinking allowed in this house!"

"The country is not in a mess," Henri said. "What are you trying to achieve, making such comments in front of her? Do you want her to tell her officer? He'll report us."

Yvonne's cheeks burned. She wouldn't have told.

Madeleine signaled to Rose that she should take her breakfast away. "That would certainly show the kind of person she is, denouncing her compatriots to further her career."

"I haven't denounced anybody," Yvonne said.

"But you would, if that served you," Madeleine said.

Madeleine rose and sashayed toward the sideboard in her kimono and plucked a silver box overflowing with cards and envelopes. When she returned to the dining room table, she sat in the exact spot that would distract Yvonne the most.

Henri played the piano with one hand and waved the other hand in the air, counting the beats. For a couple of bars, Yvonne recovered that free, tempestuous way she'd sung Tosca at the Conservatory of Music, and then the magic vanished. She was good yet forgettable. Maybe if she blocked Madeleine from her view, she could focus on the music. What a mistake to venture into the lion's den.

Madeleine scribbled addresses on a stack of envelopes with the same speed she signed autographs. "I can't wait for the season premiere. It'll be such joy to watch you make a fool of yourself."

Henri turned red. "If you'd like to get thrown in jail, I can lock you in the garage and bring you tap water." He glanced at Yvonne. "Please don't let her bother you. She's not in her right mind today. The heat, perhaps."

Yvonne tried not to look bothered. "If she didn't think I was going to shine at the premiere, she wouldn't lob all those snide remarks at me."

Madeleine laughed.

"Someone should find another pastime beside sulking and taking on airs," Henri said without looking at his wife.

He pointed at a bar in Yvonne's score. "If you fear you're going to run out of breath, then of course you can pause here. But you should've gotten a breath over there, so you don't really need one again."

"What about you two respect the score?" Madeleine asked while working on her stack of envelopes. She wrote more slowly now.

"Uproarious that you of all people would say that," Henri said.

Yvonne heard nothing special in her singing when they repeated the aria. Was she being too harsh on herself? But the energy always shifted in the room when she sang her best. In front of Madeleine and Henri, she sang as competently as hundreds of sopranos wasting away in the provinces, yet not better. Hans-Hermann would replace her. She loathed herself.

"Everyone in the audience will be rooting for you on opening day," Henri said. "Who doesn't hope to witness the consecration of a new star?"

Madeleine threw the box of greeting cards at his head, but he swatted it down just in time. Yvonne picked a card up from the floor. The Moreaus were throwing a party the following Saturday. A party during the Occupation: how nice it must feel to wallow in money. But that also meant all the interesting people who didn't have big bank accounts would be there, and some interesting people who did would be too.

Henri stuffed the cards back in the box. "The ebbs and flows of fame have always fascinated Parisians. Opening day will be the event of the season."

Madeleine strode out and slammed the door.

Henri played the piano again. Yvonne relaxed, now that Madeleine had left. Could this room turn into Klingsor's domain? Could she become Kundry through a feat of her imagination?

She'd better. It wasn't like she had a backup plan.

She negotiated a difficult transition with panache and held the high notes easily. It was as if a cork had popped. One moment she struggled to follow the score, and the next her voice rose without effort. The notes burst out of her mouth, precise and perfect and bewitching. Henri couldn't keep his eyes off Yvonne while he moved his fingers along the keyboard.

Madeleine opened the door to the living-room and, shuffling her feet, sat down again in front of her envelopes.

Yvonne finished the aria.

"We should make sure we have enough salts in the house on opening night," Henri said. "The ladies are going to faint."

"Her German officer will feel provoked if you keep praising her," Madeleine said.

"He should be proud of the gem he found," Henri said.

He looked at Yvonne a second too long, right in front of Madeleine.

Fourteen

Henri tapped a spoon on the rim of his glass. His and Madeleine's guests had gathered in the living room in sequined evening gowns and starched tuxedos, everyone enthralled by the plates of cold cuts and champagne that he, like a magician, had summoned out of thin air and at considerable expense on the black market to impress his audience. Madeleine, standing by the buffet in a red silk dress, willed her face to look at peace. She had received another letter from Stefan. *Our visas have not arrived*, he had written in his small, measured handwriting. *Our situation is becoming more precarious by the day.* He and Ilse had been stuck in Marseilles for over a month. Madeleine had failed him by not securing his exit papers. What was the point of having the money to buy Veuve Clicquot champagne by the case if one could not use it to secure a man's freedom? He must have known she would feel that way; otherwise he would not have written. But she had not given up yet. There was a reason she was throwing this party, with these guests. Henri was not aware of it.

The US ambassador William Bullitt was listening to the president of the Citroën factories describe his impressions of New York City in excruciating detail despite his bad English. Bullitt's long face surmounted by a large forehead gave him an intelligent air. He looked like he spent his life reading memos and dictating policy briefs. Madeleine had fretted that he would not accept her invitation, but in the end, he had proved very willing to mingle with the French high society: members of the Parliament's National Assembly, actors from the Comédie-Française, novelists who had won the Goncourt Prize, editors in chief of important periodicals. She was biding her time before telling him about Stefan. The French government insisted that the Germans would not interfere with life in the Free Zone, south of Lyons—they had required it as part of the armistice—but Madeleine did not believe that the *Boches* would keep their word. Sooner or later, they would order the French police to collect refugees of interest, or they would invade the Free Zone outright.

Henri tapped on the rim of his glass again, more forcefully. Madeleine knew what he would say and took a quick sip of Veuve Clicquot before she heard him say it.

"To celebrate us coming together," Henri said, "I'd like to ask my dear wife to sing a few musical excerpts."

He did not say *to help me maintain my control over the Paris Opera Orchestra, now that my dear wife has been dethroned*, but Madeleine knew he thought as much, because he had told her so. They'd had many arguments about it. Madeleine was not used to losing her power, and Henri obsessed over losing his. It amazed her that Henri was now the more successful of the two, when he owed her his career. The lavishness of the party showed he still had friends in high places—French or German friends, Madeleine could not guess, but friends with extensive connections to the black market and the clout not to be bothered about them. Her marriage was on the rocks, but she could not afford losing him now. The party was the perfect opportunity for her to prove that she still sang better than Yvonne, that Yvonne's rise was due only to the company she kept.

The guests shouted to Madeleine to please sing, as if she had not already made up her mind. Henri had selected them for their connections to power: industry magnates, politicians, people who were regularly mentioned in the newspapers just like he and Madeleine were. Neither Henri nor Madeleine cared about their guests' musical education if they had the clout and the money to help realize whatever project the Moreaus had for the Paris Opera.

When her audience had pleaded with her enough, Madeleine put down her flute of champagne and took her spot by the piano. She doubted that her guests could truly appreciate her singing—how many of them had even studied music theory when they were little, understood the extraordinary feats her voice was capable of?—but she would not give another performance for many more weeks and she was determined to make this crowd love her, if the connoisseurs were not available.

Madeleine sang Elektra, her notes sharp and her technique flawless. She had chosen that aria because Elektra stood up for her dead father after everyone else had told her to capitulate. Instead, Elektra waited for her brother to come and avenge the family, even when trusted confidants argued that she had lost her mind, and she was proven right. Madeleine suspected that her audience did not care for such nuances, but how could William Bullitt decline her request after her voice had mesmerized and stunned and awed him?

The doorbell rang while she sang. The maid, Rose, wiped her hands on her uniform and stepped out of the room. Madeleine kept singing, the pain of Elektra obvious. She tried to act a little more; spectators seemed to enjoy that. Madeleine had reached the halfway point of her aria when Yvonne, whom she most definitely had not invited to the party, stepped into the room in the latest Elsa Schiaparelli gown embroidered with flowers in metal, leaning on her Nazi officer's arm.

A high D squeaked in Madeleine's throat, but she kept going, pretending not to sense that the atmosphere had shifted now that a German in uniform had joined the gathering. Her audience stiffened—the industry magnate who had traveled to New York, an heir from the family who owned the naval shipyards in Nantes, even Bullitt, who stood in her house on behalf of the United States. Yvonne's officer could point a finger at any of them and announce that they were going to prison, never to be seen again. Madeleine had wanted to hold the party in defiance of the new regime, but she realized now it was only highlighting how much everyone feared those men, herself included, sweating abundantly over her forehead and down the back of her pretty dress.

Madeleine raised her hand to the ceiling and held the last note. Her guests did not dare breathe when the music dissolved into the air, as if they feared ruining the magic. Only when Madeleine lowered her arm did they greet her performance with resounding applause. They had to mean it, didn't they? They weren't just clapping because they stood in her home. Madeleine had missed the sounds of success in that long, dreary summer after the French defeat. Even Yvonne appeared to clap, although it seemed to Madeleine that she did not strike her gloved hands hard enough to make any noise. Madeleine nodded at William Bullitt as if she had sung only for him. He applauded with the others, but without haste, and stopped almost immediately. Hans-Hermann was already striding toward him, Yvonne in tow. That little opportunist.

Of all the people in the room, Henri seemed the least surprised by this arrival. It occurred to Madeleine that perhaps Yvonne had not come unannounced; perhaps Henri had invited her to the party.

"Here is the sole ambassador of a major nation who stayed in Paris during the exodus," Hans-Hermann said to Yvonne about Bullitt, within Madeleine's earshot. He had not greeted Madeleine, although she was the hostess. "We found him right there at the embassy when our troops entered instead of hunkering in Tours with the others. How does it feel to be the only diplomat who isn't a coward?"

"I didn't think about it in terms of cowardice or courage," Bullitt said. "For me it went without saying." He bowed over Yvonne's hand. "I've heard extraordinary praise about your Isolde at Bayreuth. I can't wait to hear you at the season premiere."

His voice was even, perhaps a little cold, but as a diplomat he owed it to his country to remain levelheaded. "Extraordinary praise": those were words—about Yvonne—he had to mean. The evening was not going according to Madeleine's plan.

Yvonne tugged on her long evening gloves, which were blue like sapphire. Hans-Hermann nudged her. Her eyes drifted to Madeleine and then back to Bullitt. "Would you like me to sing now?"

"That would be such a treat," Bullitt said.

The party was careening toward disaster, as far as Madeleine was concerned. Yet if Bullitt wanted Yvonne to sing, Madeleine could hardly interfere.

"Sing us the piece you've been practicing," Hans-Hermann said.

Yvonne planted herself by the Steinway piano, a little closer to Henri than Madeleine had been. The room quieted down. Madeleine retreated toward the buffet. Yvonne, singing in her living room! And she herself forced to pretend at welcoming her so her guests wouldn't intuit that the little bit of power she still clung to had just dissipated into the air. Gazes shifted from Hans-Hermann to Madeleine to Yvonne to Hans-Hermann again. Madeleine pasted a smile on her face. At last, Yvonne gave Henri the signal.

Her voice threw a spell on the crowd from the first notes of the "Grausamer" aria. Guests with empty plates did not deposit them onto a tray. Others who had filled their glasses with wine did not take a sip. Those who had been admiring photographs of Henri and Madeleine did not give them another glance. They all listened, entranced.

Madeleine kept an eye on the clock. The aria was about six minutes long. She couldn't wait for it to be over—this humiliation in her own house.

The crowd clapped mightily when Yvonne was done—a thunder of applause raining down over the little striver, louder, it seemed, than the applause they had greeted Madeleine with. Did they mean it? Or were they trying to ingratiate themselves with Yvonne's officer, or simply to save their skin? They could hardly boo her in front of her *Boche*, even if they wanted to. Someone asked Yvonne what else she would star in that season. Yvonne basked in the compliments, standing on Madeleine's rug in Madeleine's living room next to Madeleine's husband. Bullitt nodded approvingly at that opportunist, although he had taken a few steps toward the front door while no one was looking. Madeleine would have to make the best of it, then.

Hans-Hermann joined Yvonne and chatted amiably with Bullitt about Franklin Delano Roosevelt's nomination for a third term as US president. Yvonne left to get a drink of water.

Madeleine, flute of champagne in hand, cornered her near the Steinway. "I would've hired you to entertain my guests for the evening if I'd known how much you cared about singing in my house."

"Henri said I could come. He said I could bring Hans too." Madeleine had a hard time imagining that her husband would invite a Nazi into their house. She must have looked unconvinced, because Yvonne quietly added, "I asked him if we could come. The Germans won't release my son if I don't matter in Paris. I can't wait to sing until the season premiere. I knew Hans would love to hear me sing in your house."

Hans-Hermann and Bullitt were still talking, but now Henri had joined them. Yvonne lowered her voice. "Hans doesn't like you, because of Bayreuth."

Madeleine wrapped her arms around herself, flute of champagne still in hand. It had seemed such a noble idea at the time—the star refusing to sing for Hitler, even if she had not publicized it that way—and now she had a target painted on her back. But that was not why she was talking to Yvonne. She had to keep her wits.

"I wonder what that son of yours will think of your new friend when he returns," Madeleine said.

Yvonne's knuckles turned white around her glass. She kept her eyes on Hans-Hermann, who was now talking in the corner with the president of the Citroën factories. Bullitt had drifted away.

"It's not like I can find the Free French in the phone book," Yvonne said in a low voice.

So her conscience was bothering her after all.

"I'm not talking about those," Madeleine said with a benevolent smile. One would have thought she was an abbess correcting a novitiate. "But maybe you could help get, say, a few refugees out of France. Surely that'd please your son, don't you think? After all, I hear he volunteered for the war."

Yvonne gave her a long look. Madeleine was tempted to tell her that she talked too much to the seamstresses and the wigmakers at the opera house.

"A Jewish friend of mine is stuck in Marseilles," Madeleine said. "He needs a visa to the United States. He has applied for one, but his application languishes in the bowels of the American consulate. You could make the US ambassador remedy this in a heartbeat, though. He seems quite taken with your singing."

Yvonne was drinking in her every word, but at the mention of Bullitt she blinked hard, as if this was too much to ask.

"My friend is one of the best tenors working today," Madeleine said. She could not let Yvonne lose her nerve now. "Stefan Kreismann. Maybe one day you'll sing with him. No one can surpass his Tristan."

Yvonne cocked her head to the side. Bullitt now stood with Henri near the Steinway. Hans-Hermann was taking long, slow steps through the room, hands clasped behind his back, peering at every artifact on Madeleine's shelves, as if he was looking for evidence he could hold against her later, signs she opposed Germany and would sabotage the Third Reich any way possible.

"Then you can tell your son you're only socializing with the Germans to save innocent people," Madeleine said. "Even just one. It'll make a difference for that one."

Yvonne exhaled sharply and walked in a straight line toward Bullitt, fast enough that she couldn't lose her nerve and turn around without making a fool of herself.

Bullitt waved his cigarette high in the air when he noticed her striding toward him. "I may have to attend every single performance of yours this season, Madame Chevallier. Your voice has no equal."

Envy swept over Madeleine when she heard his praise, and then she decided it was beside the point. Stefan needed his visa. She would listen to politicians lavish compliments on Yvonne for seven days and seven nights if that helped resolve Stefan's situation.

Yvonne accompanied Bullitt on the terrace, walking past Henri. He was asking Hans-Hermann asinine questions about his military career, and Hans-Hermann was answering with a single word for each. Madeleine followed on Yvonne's heels, as if the living room were suffocating. It was a balmy evening, cool under the stars. How Madeleine wished that the visa had been issued already. Stefan would be on his way to Philadelphia; Bullitt would take pride in having contributed to his escape from a Europe gone mad.

"I'd love your advice on a personal matter." Yvonne smiled brightly at Bullitt. "A dear friend of mine is stranded in Marseilles, waiting for a visa to the United States."

Madeleine watched the expression on Bullitt's face change from curiosity to dismay. How many Parisians had been asking him to help friends of theirs? He could not secure visas for everyone.

"Not only is he a good friend, but he's the best tenor of his generation," Yvonne said. She must have noticed Bullitt's expression as well. "His name is Stefan Kreismann. It'd mean so much if you could put in a good word. I'm sure people in the United States would be enthralled by his singing."

Bullitt clearly had never heard of Stefan. He shrugged a little, as if to say that it was not his fault, but his hands were tied.

"Unfortunately, my orders are clear," Bullitt said. "The United States is to remain neutral in the conflict. The Germans will win, and we won't issue visas to refugees they plan to arrest. That would only jeopardize the relationship between the two countries."

He looked at Yvonne less amicably, now that she had attempted to obtain a favor from him, and returned inside. Yvonne seemed crestfallen that she had failed. That son of hers might never forgive her now. Madeleine tried not to let her disappointment cloud her thinking. What next? She had to devise another plan.

Hans-Hermann, finding Yvonne on the patio, pulled her toward the exit. "We still have to drop by that party at the Ritz. I'll get demoted to reviewing crossword puzzles in *Paris-soir* if I don't show up."

Yvonne hesitated, as if she wanted to plead her case with Bullitt one more time, but Madeleine could see there was no point. He had said no without any possibility of a reversal. Hans-Hermann wrapped his arm around Yvonne's shoulders and led her out without looking at the other guests.

The tires of the Grosser Mercedes squealed when the sedan turned around on the driveway, adorned with its ominous Nazi flags over the front bumpers. Two beams of light swept the living room like blades of knives cutting across Madeleine's face. She was only noticing now, at the scope of her relief, how terrified she had been as long as Hans-Hermann stood in the room.

Bullitt lit up a Gauloise, one elbow against the mantelpiece. The smoke curled toward the chandelier. Henri fetched him an ashtray before Madeleine could.

"What did Yvonne talk to you about?" Henri asked Bullitt. "She seemed dejected when she left."

For a moment, Bullitt did not speak, too absorbed in admiring the rings of smoke rising from his cigarette toward the ceiling.

"She hoped I'd help an opera singer get a visa to the United States," he said after a while. "Someone stuck in Marseilles. Regrettably, I can't interfere."

If only Henri would leave it at that.

"Who was it?" Henri asked.

Bullitt tapped his cigarette against the ashtray. "One Stefan Kreismann. Does the name ring a bell? I'm not an opera connoisseur."

Madeleine gulped down her Veuve Clicquot so fast that the champagne tickled her nostrils. She could not pass up this chance. "He's one of the greatest singers the world has ever heard," she said with authority.

Henri glared at her.

"Nothing I can do, I'm afraid," Bullitt said.

He crossed the room toward an American art collector and his wife who were still trying to ship two of their Matisses and one Picasso across the Atlantic. Things would have become so simple if he had decided to throw his weight behind Stefan.

"How does Yvonne even know Stefan is in Marseilles?" Henri asked.

Madeleine swept the air with the back of her hands in a gesture that meant *Your guess is as good as mine.*

Henri brought his face an inch closer to hers. "Stefan asked you to help, didn't he? And you're so desperate to save him that you enlisted Yvonne, in my own house, in front of my own guests."

His gaze bored through her.

"I wouldn't ask Yvonne for a hand if my life depended on it," Madeleine said, and turned and walked away.

❦

Two days later, Hans-Hermann opened wide the door to an apartment on the quay Voltaire and stepped aside to let Yvonne enter. It was in the seventh arrondissement, a neighborhood of *hôtels particuliers*, art galleries, and small upscale restaurants where patrons looked like they were busy striking deals in the shadow of the École des Beaux-Arts. He'd told Yvonne they were going to visit apartments to find something more suitable for her than the dump she lived in. Suitable—yes indeed. In the living room, a grand piano gleamed over the hardwood floors. *Steinway and Sons* was written on the side. She had to read that twice. It was hard to focus on anything else after that. A novel had been left open on the couch, as if the owners had had to leave in a rush but would return soon. On the windowsill, a plant hadn't been watered in weeks. Through the windows, the dark waters of the Seine lapped against the pillars of the Pont du Carrousel. The roof of the Louvre peeked over the lush trees of the Tuileries Gardens. Yvonne suspected the closets were still full of the previous owners' clothes. The rightful owners. And she could guess why they had fled.

"I can't afford this," Yvonne said. "People buy castles in the Loire Valley for the money this apartment is worth."

"It won't cost you a thing." Hans-Hermann sounded reproachful. "If you don't want it, someone else will take it."

His tone made her shiver. There was always a hidden cost to gifts, and although she had not slept with him yet, she could guess he would expect to after she owed him such a gorgeous apartment. He had been good to her, but she didn't like the idea of being bought. Would he even respect her if she caved in, or would he treat her like an object among the many he owned? She knew him so little, and until then she'd only seen of him the facade he wanted to show: pleasant, cultivated. It dawned on her that maybe it was all an act. To him maybe she was just a puppet, and he was pulling the strings.

If he'd decided he wanted the stolen apartment for her, then she didn't have a say in the matter. There was still time to break up with him and disappear into the French countryside. He'd find himself another girlfriend. But she was nobody without him. She needed to stay in his good graces until Jules returned from the prisoner-of-war camp.

"It's so unexpected," Yvonne said. She looked at the belongings of the people who used to live there and thought she couldn't eat at their table, sit on their couch, sleep in their bed. This apartment wasn't hers to keep. But Hans-Hermann hadn't asked her once if she liked it or not. For him, the answer seemed evident. Yvonne tried to remember the friendly smile he'd had at Bayreuth.

"I had to fend off three of Goering's associates just to be first in line for this," Hans-Hermann said.

So the owners had fled Paris and the Nazis had confiscated their home. Yvonne couldn't say yes to that. But she couldn't say no to Hans-Hermann either. He'd never forgive her. French people had been shot for less insubordination than that.

Hans-Hermann lifted the piano lid. "Can you imagine, letting Goering's pigs have this? They couldn't play 'Für Elise' if their life depended on it. Here, sing me something."

Yvonne sat down at the piano, but she didn't dare place her fingers on the keys.

"Sing," Hans-Hermann said coldly.

Yvonne sang what she always sang on such occasions, "Sempre Libera" in *Tosca*.

"It doesn't sound the same when it's on a Steinway, does it?" he said when she was done.

Yvonne nodded. She didn't know what to say.

"How can you be so ungrateful when I went out of my way to find you a gift?" Hans-Hermann said.

If he were to shoot her right there, Yvonne thought, it might be weeks before anyone found her body. Or maybe he'd dump her body into the Seine and give the apartment to his new girlfriend, and Jules would never know what had happened to her. She hadn't told anyone where she was going.

"I'm in shock, that's all," Yvonne said.

"So when should I tell the movers to bring your things here?"

Yvonne paced the floor, trying to collect herself and think of an excuse to stall.

"Your son will be glad to practice on such a piano when he returns," Hans-Hermann said.

"Is there a date for that?" Yvonne asked. She would leave Hans-Hermann as soon as Jules was released. Settle down in a small village where she knew no one and Hans-Hermann wouldn't find her. She had many faults, but she wasn't a thief.

"Soon enough," Hans-Hermann said. His eyes were cold and his tone colder.

"You've been saying that for weeks," Yvonne said. "It's hard for me to concentrate in rehearsals when I'm so worried about him." Jules would have been in Paris by now if Hans-Hermann had put in a good word, even if he'd walked all the way from Germany.

"I head the cultural office," Hans-Hermann said. "I'm not in charge of the prisoners of war. I already find myself lucky that generals take my phone calls."

"If you can't get him released, just say so," Yvonne said. This was her last recourse for making him keep his word—suggesting he was unimportant. "I understand you can't do wonders. It's kind of you to throw me crumbs."

Hans-Hermann pressed the middle C key on the piano, although he probably didn't know it was middle C. "This is more than a crumb."

"Are you going to bring my son back or not?" Yvonne said in a small, timid voice, so that Hans-Hermann wouldn't shoot her.

A shadow crossed his face. "You'll have neither this nor your son if you don't wise up." And, more softly: "You deserve this piano. You deserve this apartment."

Yvonne picked up the book the owners had left behind. It was a collector's edition of the novel *Man's Fate* by André Malraux. Yvonne

had heard about Malraux but not about the book. She placed the
novel back on the shelves where she saw a gap between hardcovers. She
knew she had too much at stake—her job, her son, her life—to oppose
Hans-Hermann.

"I'll move here as soon as my son comes back," Yvonne said.

"He'll be back ten days from today," Hans-Hermann said. "But
you're moving in now."

He took Yvonne by the hand—she didn't want him to touch her
but couldn't withdraw her hand—and led her through the kitchen, tiny
but well equipped with wooden cabinets and a small gas oven, then the
bathroom, still full of hairbrushes and makeup products, and another
room used as an office, brimming with papers. Yvonne said she found
everything charming. That was so plainly the reaction Hans-Hermann
expected from her, but the thought of moving into this apartment hor-
rified her. Hans-Hermann showed her a room with a small window
that could serve as Jules's bedroom. Here, the desk. There, the bed.
Jules would like it if he didn't find out where it came from. But he was
a smart boy—he'd figure it out. Across the narrow corridor, the master bedroom, overlooking the inner courtyard, featured a large bed in
chestnut wood, a watercolor of a seascape, and nightstands surmounted
by austere reading lamps.

Yvonne knew what would happen as soon as she saw the bed. She
didn't flinch when Hans-Hermann kissed her. She'd already stood up
to him once that afternoon, about Jules, and he was unlikely to take
kindly to another rebuttal. His hands found their way under her dress.
She smiled and pulled him onto the bed.

ᥫᥭ

Jules's dirty French uniform looked glued to his skin when he
stepped out of the Gare de l'Est on the Monday before the season
premiere. The afternoon was unseasonably cold. Yvonne wished
she'd brought a cardigan with her. Parisians hurried about in jackets and long-sleeved dresses. Under their arms, newspapers blared
headlines about the Battle of Britain, where German dive-bombers

had attacked radar stations off the coastline of Kent. Jules slung his duffel bag over his shoulder and traipsed along the platform. He'd lost weight around his face. Yvonne hoped the war hadn't changed him more than that.

Jules stopped when he noticed her running toward him. Yvonne gave him such a big hug he almost fell backward. He barely hugged her back.

"You shouldn't have gotten favors for me," Jules said.

"You couldn't stay there until the end of the war. Your career would've been ruined."

"What career?" Jules said.

Yvonne shoved a paper bag into his hands. Thankfully, they looked neither broken nor bruised. "Here, have something to eat." She remembered how much he'd enjoyed Paul's pastries on the day he'd left for training.

Jules didn't open the bag. "I loathed leaving the others behind. We should've all gotten out together. Those *Arbeitskommandos* will give me nightmares for years."

"Your friends will get out eventually," Yvonne said. She opened the bag for him. A whiff of warm chocolate croissant wafted into the air.

"I thought Paris was under rationing," Jules said.

It was. Yvonne was tempted to bite into the croissant—she hadn't eaten any in so long—but instead she held it out him. "How did the Germans treat you?"

"Oh, just grand. We had tea and petits fours every day."

"Really?" Yvonne said, hopeful.

"Jesus, no, Mother. What do you expect? We were on work detail." Jules still didn't take the croissant, so Yvonne held it high until he relented. Other travelers were staring at them. If Jules hadn't taken the croissant, somebody might have grabbed it. Paris was still getting used to the rationing. "The *Boches* made us work in the fields. The guards weren't friendly, but they only pushed us around when we didn't reach our numbers." He licked his fingers after he finished the chocolate croissant.

A swastika banner hung from the outsized clock in the arrival hall. Jules made a large circle around it, as if going under the banner would bring him bad luck.

"Those are all over Paris," Yvonne said. "You'd better get used to them."

An elderly woman tried to sell them wilting flowers, but she kept staring at Jules. A Frenchman in uniform had become an unusual sight: most troops lingered in German camps. She must've wondered what he was doing there. Jules hurried along. A railway man in blue overalls elbowed him in the ribs when he walked by. His bag fell to the ground.

Jules grabbed Yvonne's arm so that she wouldn't chase the man. "He knows Frenchmen don't come back early unless they have friends in high places, and anyone in high places at the moment isn't a friend of France."

"The war is lost," Yvonne said. "He should make his peace with it."

Jules glanced at her but didn't reply. Instead, he strode toward the exit.

Yvonne trotted to catch up with him. "You'll have to start preparing for the entrance exam of the Conservatory right away if you want to have a chance this year." Would Jules enroll in the Paris Conservatory if she skipped town? Would he care enough about his career to continue studying if she was away, and would Hans-Hermann care enough about her to cause problems for the son when he couldn't find the mother? But perhaps Jules could enter one of the regional conservatories of music and transfer back to Paris after a year, when Hans-Hermann had forgotten about her.

"I hope the guys in my platoon don't get pneumonia." Jules swung the exit door wide open and stopped to take in the sights of the capital: its dirty sidewalks, its panhandlers, its empty storefronts. What did he notice first? At least he was back. There would be time for talking later.

Winds from the north pushed clouds across the sky. In front of the newsstand, two businessmen in well-pressed suits took bets on when the stock exchange would reopen. A line of bicycle cabs stretched where the taxis used to wait. The roadway remained empty; few Parisians had driven since gas was rationed. To Yvonne, this didn't even look like Paris. Jules took a step toward the Métro entrance.

"We're taking a bicycle cab," Yvonne said.

The men behind the handlebars looked old and scrawny, like work-horses that might tumble over if they took one more step forward. Jules acted as if he hadn't seen them.

Yvonne pulled on his arm. "I'm the lead soprano at the Paris Opera now. I'm not taking the Métro." She pointed at the first man in the line of bicycle cabs. "I'll give him a good tip if you come along."

The man nodded at Jules to accept.

Yvonne settled in the cab and smoothed her dress. Jules sighed but sat down next to her.

"Quay Voltaire," Yvonne said to the rickshaw driver. And to Jules: "We moved, and we'll most certainly move again soon."

The driver struggled to gain speed toward the boulevard de Magenta. One of the bicycle wheels squeaked. Parisians plodded on the sidewalks, hats pulled low on their foreheads. The storefronts looked drab and empty. The hard wooden chairs of the rickshaw hurt Yvonne's back, but this wasn't the right occasion to use Hans-Hermann's car.

Jules tapped his bag with the heel of his boot. "Lead soprano, uh? What happened to Madeleine Moreau?"

"She's still there, but I sing better."

"Sounds like you made friends with the *Boches* and she didn't."

Had she already lost the love of her son? They weren't even home yet.

The driver avoided a bicycle by an inch at the intersection with the rue de Richelieu. The other rider yelled at him. The rickshaw driver pedaled faster.

"The opera house needed a fresher voice," Yvonne said, although if that'd been true, Emile wouldn't have picked her.

Jules buried his face in his hands.

They spent the rest of the trip in silence, until the bicycle cab pulled up in front of Yvonne's apartment building.

"Did you inherit money while I was gone?" Jules said.

"I'm looking after another singer's apartment," Yvonne said. "She was cast into an opera out of town. It'll only be a couple of weeks. Then we'll move again."

She'd begun looking at the map of France, searching for locations where Hans-Hermann wouldn't find her. But if she sang, he'd hear about it sooner or later. So she kept being drawn to only one city, and it wasn't for its operas—Le Havre, the harbor where ships bound for the United States left from. Surely there were consulates in that town. She could sing there, and if Hans-Hermann found her, she'd get a visa for America—if not the United States, then Chile or Argentina. But youngsters who volunteered for a war didn't sail away from it, and she didn't know if she could bear to leave Jules behind.

Yvonne led Jules inside the building, past the concierge's quarters and the mailboxes all the way to the small open-cage elevator with its intricate metalwork. She placed one hand on Jules's arm when they reached the top-floor landing so that he wouldn't sprint down the stairwell when she gave him the news. "There's someone inside. He helped you get freed. Be nice to him. He can help your friends too, if you thank him enough." She didn't add *Maybe we won't have to put up with him so long* in case Hans-Hermann could hear through the door.

Jules leaned back on his heels. Yvonne watched his expression change as he realized what exactly she'd just told him. She unlocked the door.

Hans-Hermann put the *Völkischer Beobachter* down on the table and stood up from the armchair. He'd moved into the apartment at the same time Yvonne had, although he kept his suite at the Ritz hotel to please his higher-ups. Sometimes Yvonne thought he'd found the apartment for himself but used her as a decoy. The German authorities, it seemed, didn't approve of expropriating French residents without the proper paperwork.

"Here's the valorous son who signed up for the army when he could've stayed in bed," he said, looking impressed, although that same morning he'd argued to Yvonne that Jules should move in with his father so that they'd keep the apartment to themselves.

Yvonne nudged Jules forward. He gave Hans-Hermann a limp handshake, then examined the many books on the shelves. "Your friends certainly have different literary tastes than you," he said to Yvonne, his tone heavy with meaning.

Yvonne forced herself to laugh. "With my schedule, I don't have any literary taste at all. I don't even have time to read." She pretended to smile right until she walked into the kitchen, where she rummaged through the fridge while trying to eavesdrop on Jules's conversation with Hans-Hermann, but there was only silence. She took out the roast beef Hans-Hermann had bought, laid it out, then returned to the living room, hoping to impress Jules with her feast. It would've been impossible to get so much food if Hans-Hermann hadn't helped, out of self-interest. Jules was still standing in front of the bookshelves, as if it were a matter of critical importance that he read every book title. Yvonne could tell from the expression on Hans-Hermann's face that he was beginning to feel offended, and she worried his anger might boil too fast for her to do anything about it.

"Jules is a big reader," she said. "Literature and music: those were the two subjects he was good at in school."

She served Jules first and then Hans-Hermann. In the meantime, Hans-Hermann opened a bottle of Bordeaux. Yvonne felt relieved, knowing she'd avoided an argument.

"Maybe there's a concert you can attend this weekend," Yvonne said to Jules. "Or you can start preparing for the audition. At least select what you'll play for the judges." The more Jules stared at his plate, the more Yvonne spoke an avalanche of words. "My advice for you is to choose pieces by famous artists, but not what made their name. For instance, some of the lesser-played Chopin nocturnes. Or an overlooked Beethoven piano sonata, like the Sonata No. 4 or the No. 28. Don't you like the No. 28?"

Jules nibbled his food, head down. Finally, he pushed his chair back. "I'm not hungry. It must be the train ride."

"Your room is at the end of the corridor, if you'd like to rest," Yvonne said.

Jules shuffled out of the living room and down the hall. If only Yvonne had had more time to explain the situation to him.

Hans-Hermann drank his wine. "He'll get used to us eventually. In due time he may even become one of the regime's best friends, if he wants any career in Paris."

Fifteen

August 1940

A row of German cars waited to pull over in front of the opera house. At the front of the line, officers in dress uniforms, showing off their embroidered collars and as many medals as they could muster, lent their arms to ladies in designer gowns, their necklines daring, the trains sprawled on the steps behind them. Through the window of the Peugeot inching its way in traffic, Madeleine glanced at the billboard where her name should have been.

"We're still early," she said to Henri. "We can drive around the block one more time. Paris is so pretty this time of year."

Henri, dressed in his conductor's suit, held the score of *Parsifal* on his lap. Soon he would stand in the limelight. Madeleine envied him. Aside from the party at her house, she had not received applause in 107 days. The end of the summer, when the opera house stood dark, always aroused gloom in her; she was like an alcoholic in withdrawal, scheming how to procure her next drink. But in normal times she could have counted the days until her next performance and convinced herself that audiences would soon shower her with acclaim. This summer she didn't know when—if—she would stand onstage again.

"Or we can go in," Henri said. "I need to concentrate before the performance."

The car rolled to a stop in front of the main entrance. Henri stepped out next to the *Cantata* sculpture, reached inside the Peugeot, and dragged Madeleine out. She wore a black dress with a cashmere shawl, also black, and only a touch of eyeliner as makeup, along with her signature red lipstick: the great Madeleine Moreau, in mourning because the Germans had occupied Paris. Back at home in Neuilly it had suited her dramatic flair, but now she looked old and past her prime amid an exuberance of colorful ladies' gowns, an ocean of silk in orange, yellow, and baby blue, and rivers of pearls and cascades of diamonds. What was Stefan doing at this very minute? She had sent him a note at the hotel behind the Marseilles Opera that he had listed as his return address, telling him she would help, but it would take time. Since Bullitt had refused to grant him a visa, she would have to find a forger. She had no clue how to do that, but she would figure something out. She was certain she would.

Guests laughed and waved at newcomers stepping out of elegant Mercedes. Madeleine was tempted to yell at them—France had lost, what were they so happy about?—perhaps because she had drunk two glasses of champagne by herself while Henri was getting ready, to give herself courage, and then a half bottle more because the Occupation angered her so; or because Stefan was stuck in a country that no longer welcomed him; or because Henri was conducting while Yvonne sang; or perhaps, just perhaps, because only a few drops had remained in the bottle when she hid it in the sideboard.

Henri dragged her toward the steps leading to the entrance, between the bronze busts of Haydn and Pergolesi, around a group of operago-ers exchanging pleasantries in the breeze. The men spoke in guttural sounds that irked Madeleine; the women replied in perfect French that exasperated her even further. Surely Alexandre was rolling over in his tomb.

Inside, Henri waved at someone in the crowd. Madeleine took pains not to notice the whispers and the finger-pointing around her. Snippets of conversation drifted to her ears. Why would she not sing if she was well enough to accompany Henri to the premiere? Perhaps guests would suspect she had been shoved aside through no fault of her own. Yvonne was sleeping with a *Nazi*, for heaven's sake.

Henri tugged Madeleine along to the boxes, where she would sit. Yvonne had given her the best seat in the house, the middle seat in the front row of the center box. Madeleine could not even hide behind other spectators.

They made their way past the statues of torchbearers and up the grand staircase. Madeleine was not accustomed to entering the opera house via the main door. She had forgotten the opulence of the lobby, its marble columns and painted ceilings. It seemed almost indecent that the foyer still awed and dazzled now that it teemed with Nazis. She stumbled on a step, grabbed the banister, pulled herself up before stopping abruptly at the top of the stairs: Yvonne's officer was holding court under one of the ornate frescoes by Paul-Jacques-Aimé Baudry. Around him, half a dozen people in civilian clothes assented to his every word. They looked ready to prostrate themselves at his feet. Madeleine graced them with a look of withering contempt, which they did not notice.

"How spineless they all are," Henri said in a whisper. "Sycophants."

Madeleine realized he had been looking at the same group of people.

"Mollusks," she said, and they exchanged a smile.

They had to be French, since the Germans wore uniforms. Madeleine recognized Robert Brasillach, the anti-Semitic editor in chief of *Je suis partout*, easy to spot with his round glasses and his hair parted to the side. He regularly published the names and addresses of Jews in hiding. Madeleine bumped into another guest while she was staring at Brasillach. That man disgusted her so. She clung tighter to Henri's arm. Champagne and revulsion did not make a happy mix. Not far from Brasillach, Georges Suarez, who led the newspaper *Aujourd'hui*, was munching on petits fours. Suarez also penned editorials against the Jews. Now he nodded thoughtfully at Yvonne's friend. Repulsive.

"Who invited them?" Madeleine asked.

Henri did not know. But someone had wanted them there.

Madeleine stormed into the box, hoping to hide from the other attendees while Henri was off to the orchestra pit. She was disappointed to find a young man already seated. He was reading a book in the first row, right next to her seat. His buzz cut reminded her of soldiers, but he was not in uniform. Instead, a business suit hung loosely over his shoulders. He closed his book when Madeleine sat down. How odd to bring a book to the opera. Then Madeleine pressed her hands against the velvet-covered edge of the box and forgot about the young man.

Most of the parterre remained empty except for a woman alone in the second row, attired in black lace, and a family of five in their Sunday clothes. A little boy bounced on his seat while two girls with bows in their hair pointed out features of the auditorium to each other—the red velvet of the seats, the gilding of the decorations, the hand-painted ceiling so high above their heads. Everybody else lingered outside in the grand foyer, chatting and joking as if a war were not raging on, even after France had admitted defeat. Just the previous night, after the air-raid sirens had woken Madeleine, she had sworn she had seen between the clouds the faint shadow of British bombers headed for ammunition factories in the east of France, although Henri insisted that her imagination had played tricks on her. She hoped so hard that the Brits would put an end to this madness.

Cardboard trees rose from the dark on the stage. A castle was painted on a tarp that covered the back wall. A cot had been pushed stage right, for King Amfortas to rest on. Madeleine analyzed lines of sight and then decided she would have triumphed on that stage if Yvonne had not stolen the role from her.

"You're Madeleine Moreau," the young man said.

Madeleine was pleased that he had recognized her.

"I'm Jules Chevallier," he said. "My mother talks a lot about you."

Madeleine had not known that Yvonne's son had been released.

"She told me you left Bayreuth right before the premiere," Jules said. "It took courage, I'm sure."

Courage—that was what Alexandre had displayed at Verdun. What Madeleine had shown in Bayreuth was closer to foolishness, but she was still proud she had behaved the way she had. But she did not contradict the boy. She didn't even know if he meant what he said, or if he was just trying to ingratiate himself with her.

Madeleine perched herself on the edge of her seat. She shouldn't have drunk so much. She had hoped to doze off during the performance, to be spared listening to Yvonne, but now she needed her wits.

"What do you know about me in Bayreuth, exactly?" she asked.

"You left, and my mother met her beau," Jules said.

"Hans," Madeleine said, slowly tearing a small corner of the program between her fingertips.

"Hans-Hermann. Only Yvonne calls him Hans, and"—Jules winked—"I don't think you want to resemble her."

Madeleine laughed despite herself.

"He gifted her an apartment at quay Voltaire," Jules said. "View of the Seine River, the Louvre Museum, even a Steinway piano in the living room."

That got Madeleine's attention.

"All that stolen from a Jewish family, naturally," he said.

"Naturally," Madeleine said, although she was stunned. She had pegged Yvonne for a striver and an opportunist but not for a thief—yet, clearly, her beau wouldn't have found her a fancy apartment in a wealthy part of town if she hadn't asked him to do it. It unsettled her, that she had misjudged Yvonne so.

"Can't wait until the Germans lose the war and my mother gets her judgment day," Jules said.

He waited for Madeleine to speak, but she was not going to trust anyone who had Yvonne's blood in his veins. She browsed through the program as if she had never read Guillaume's biography before.

"You had a certain expression on your face, just a moment ago," Jules said.

Madeleine didn't know what he was talking about.

"I see the same expressions on passersby when I walk down the street," Jules said. "You all think I shouldn't be back, that the only reason I got back early is that I'm friends with the *Boches*."

"I know your mother has connections. I don't think you do."

"I'd be the first one to shoot them if it didn't mean they'd murder dozens of Frenchmen for every one of their own grazed by a bullet."

"Think of your hands," Madeleine said. "Aren't you a pianist?"

"My mother wants me to be a pianist. But whatever France needs at the moment, it's not more people playing Chopin."

Madeleine liked him.

"You certainly don't take after your mother," she said. Perhaps Jules was putting on a show for her benefit. She would find out soon enough.

The light of the chandeliers flickered in the gallery around the boxes. The performance would begin soon. Operagoers strolled into the two-thousand-seat auditorium. German officers led the way, followed by clusters of Parisians who hoped to develop relationships with the new rulers, between comments on Wagner and *Parsifal*. Honest French citizens would have sat in the nosebleed seats of the family circle, where no Nazi would have ventured. But Madeleine did not find herself in the nosebleed section either. Spectators would most likely reach the wrong conclusion about her support of the regime. Yvonne sure knew how to get under her skin.

Footsteps drew near the box. Madeleine glanced behind her. Hans-Hermann hunched forward to avoid bumping his forehead against the top of the doorframe. Another German officer, so short that he barely reached Hans-Hermann's shoulder, followed him. His eyes were small and narrow like a pig's, his stomach so large that he couldn't possibly see his feet.

"Klaus, this is Madeleine Moreau, the previous leading lady of the Paris Opera," Hans-Hermann said. "Frau Moreau, Kriminaldirektor Klaus Koegel."

At the word *previous*, Madeleine was tempted to roll her eyes, yet she kept her poise. What a transparent attempt at annoying her, but she did not say it out loud. No doubt Yvonne was just a pawn to him, a trophy. She would get discarded eventually. Then Madeleine would become the queen of the opera house again.

Klaus bowed over Madeleine's hand. The remnants of her dinner, soaked in champagne, moved into her throat.

"How kind of you to give your spot to Hans's woman," Klaus said.

They were both trying to provoke her—Madeleine wasn't even sure what they were after. But she was certain they had been briefed about Bayreuth, and they had a score to settle. She pasted a smile on her face and decided to look vain and dumb.

Hans-Hermann made himself comfortable next to Madeleine. She shifted her weight to the opposite side and, for good measure, waved at Emile and his wife, who had just entered the neighboring box. Emile nodded, but his wife pretended not to see her. Madeleine did not look forward to spending four hours contorted on a seat to remain as far from Hans-Hermann as possible. Thank goodness for the two intermissions. She would need a lot more alcohol than she had already imbibed to survive the performance.

The lights dimmed, and a burst of applause greeted Henri's entrance into the orchestra pit. How dashing he was in his conductor's suit. He bowed to the audience before turning to face the orchestra. Madeleine felt like she was looking at a stranger, a man who simply resembled her husband. Henri never conducted the orchestra when she did not appear in the cast. Yet here he was, glancing at his violinists, his cellists, his trumpeters, checking that every musician was ready to begin. The crowd grew quiet. Shadows moved onstage. Henri raised his baton.

Madeleine had not listened to her husband make music in years. Naturally, she had heard the orchestra from the stage, but she did not remember when she had last paid attention to Henri's artistry, his interpretation of the score, the unique sound he drew out of his musicians. This evening he conveyed Wagner's themes of agony and redemption with as much panache as Arturo Toscanini or Wilhelm Furtwängler. Perhaps Madeleine's absence freed him to fully express himself. She had not expected such a discovery. Had she been holding him back?

About twenty minutes into the performance, the choristers playing the Grail knights pointed together at the back of the audience. *Look who is riding toward us! Her horse's mane is flying wildly!* The knight Gurnemanz peered alongside them. *What, Kundry is back!*

Madeleine tensed on her seat. The music took on a new urgency as the singers recounted Kundry's progress toward them. Soon, Yvonne would make her entrance. Madeleine remembered her own case of nerves on performance nights. The stagehands used to place a bucket in the wings in case she needed to throw up. She wished she could go back to those evenings.

At last, Yvonne stormed onto the stage in a dress dyed a shade of blue as deep as the sky at night. Her disheveled hair cascaded over her shoulders. She threw herself onto the ground and handed Gurnemanz a potion to soothe his wounded king. Madeleine disagreed with her writhing at Gurnemanz's feet, but Yvonne's emoting seemed to fascinate the audience, as if Amfortas might heal in front of their eyes thanks to Yvonne's powers alone. Her notes were centered on pitch, the top ones rising effortlessly over the orchestra, the transitions between vocal registers negotiated without a hint of rubato. Then for several minutes Yvonne's Kundry had no spoken part, thrashing about when Madeleine used to remain motionless on the floor, and to Madeleine's dismay, her portrayal of the sorceress kept the audience spellbound. At long last, a stuffed swan, pierced with an arrow, fluttered over Yvonne's head and crashed onto the stage. Guillaume bounded out of the wings as Parsifal, bow in hand.

Henri conducted as if he were possessed, sweeping the air with his baton toward the violinists on the left and the basses on the right. He seemed to believe that the orchestra would not achieve the sound Wagner had heard in his head if he did not cajole them with the movements of his hand. Yvonne sat up on the floor and eyed Guillaume. The libretto called for her to sing again. Madeleine always struggled with her high notes when she didn't stand on her feet, chest open and chin high, but Yvonne on the ground acquitted herself brilliantly of the task. Every note sounded effortless, a miracle of perfection repeated again and again. Like a sorceress, she had erased any sign of her technique, although she must have kept the beginning of a yawn on her lips as she had been taught in school, relaxed her tongue against the floor of her mouth, kept her breathing consistent and imagined her throat so wide open that, in Charles-Antoine's favorite saying, an egg could have glided down without touching the sides. Hans-Hermann leaned forward, his arms pressed against the edge of the balcony. Even Jules could not look away from his mother. Goose bumps crept up Madeleine's arm.

Yvonne's Kundry finally stalked out, pretending to disappear between cardboard bushes, not to return until the second act. Madeleine clung to her belief that nothing should distract from a singer's voice—no flailing of the arms, no throwing of oneself on the floor. Yet she sensed that Yvonne's performance had etched itself in the public's mind.

❧

Hundreds of Third Reich officers stamped their boots against the hardwood floors when Yvonne emerged from the wings for the curtain call. Klaus and Hans-Hermann hollered "Brava!" above the din. Madeleine had hoped that Yvonne would humiliate herself—miss notes, forget lines, or otherwise prove that she did not deserve her moment in the limelight—but the audience clearly adored her singing. Envy consumed Madeleine. She had mouthed the role of Kundry behind her fan throughout the performance, her resentment growing with each bar of music. Jealousy was a new feeling for her. It burned in her with an intensity she had not known herself capable of.

Yvonne ventured backstage and led Henri out onto the planks. The crowd roared. Yvonne and Henri stood next to each other, exhausted but smiling. The entire cast held hands while they bowed. Anger rippled through Madeleine when Henri squeezed Yvonne's fingers. She had never realized before that he did not need Madeleine to give his best.

Carnations rained over Yvonne. She gathered up the flowers one by one. It seemed she would not leave the stage until the clapping had waned, and the audience showed no interest in letting the applause dwindle, although the embroidered stage curtain slowly descended behind the singers. Yvonne bowed and bowed again. Finally, Henri pulled her back behind the curtain.

Klaus tapped the leg of Madeleine's chair with his foot. "What pity you not sang onstage," he said in broken French. "You is the one with real talent."

Madeleine stood up to leave. She had almost reached the door to the box—from there, the lobby with its golden gildings, towering sculptures, and marble staircases, the main doors opening on the grand foyer, the terrace, and then fresh air—when someone pulled her back.

"Surely you'd like to go and congratulate Yvonne now," Hans-Hermann said.

❧

Madeleine peered inside the dressing room that used to be hers. Jules looked over her shoulder. Madeleine had grabbed his arm when Hans-Hermann pushed her forward, although he did not seem eager to be there. Hans-Hermann and Klaus stood behind them, as if to close their escape route. Yvonne, seated in front of the dresser, was taking off her makeup. Tucked in the frame of the mirror, a small photograph showed Jules a few years younger, maybe fifteen, his hair combed and parted to the side. Piles of books about Wagner sat on the shelves. Yvonne most likely never opened them, but they would impress visitors.

Henri was heaping superlatives on Yvonne. "This is going to be the talk of Paris. People will camp overnight in front of the box office to buy a ticket." Had he ever been that proud of Madeleine?

The room overflowed with bouquets of roses—red, red and pink, red and white, red and yellow, pink and white—and a single bouquet of red tulips, pushed to the side. There were more flowers than when Madeleine sang, but most of them must have been bought by Yvonne's Nazi. Yvonne had changed into a blue velvet dress with silver metal embroidery on the sleeves—a Jeanne Lanvin dress, surely another present from her *Boche*. She stared at her reflection in the mirror while Henri talked, as if she couldn't quite believe the evening had really happened. Henri's fingers brushed up against the back of the chair, pulled away, returned again.

"You were astounding, stupendous, magnificent," Henri said to Yvonne.

It was as if Yvonne had bewitched him.

"An enchantress," Madeleine said from the open door, remembering what Hitler had called Yvonne in Bayreuth.

Behind her, Jules exhaled sharply.

Yvonne gave her a long look, but waved at them both to come in.

Jules stayed in the hallway. "I'll see you at the reception. You're busy now."

"Don't be silly," Yvonne said. "How did you like the performance?"

Jules did not answer. Madeleine relished the growing distress on Yvonne's face—the corners of her mouth sagging, her incessant blinking.

Yvonne waited for Jules to say something and then turned to Madeleine, as if the question had been aimed at her.

"It's hard for me to judge," Madeleine said. "I only attend my own performances, and I watch those from the stage." She laughed her fake laugh.

Henri pressed his hands against the back of Yvonne's chair, so close the tips of his fingers touched her shoulders. "Your singing was sublime."

He reminded Madeleine of a groveling little dog, begging for a treat. How could he be impressed by Yvonne when he had never showered Madeleine with so many compliments since their marriage? Was it all an act to please her Nazi, or did he mean it? It scared Madeleine most of all that he might mean it.

Military boots came closer down the hallway. A moment later, Hans-Hermann marched into the room, followed by that short man with the face of a pig.

"A triumph," Hans-Hermann said to Yvonne. "Everyone in the audience is raving about you. *Where did she come from?* they keep asking. *Why haven't we heard her before?*"

Yvonne gave him an exhausted smile while she finished applying a fresh coat of makeup. Everybody who wanted to show they mattered in the social order would attend the reception, even those who found opera utterly boring: politicians, socialites, industry magnates, foreign dignitaries. Henri had retreated to a corner of the room, far away from Hans-Hermann and Klaus. At least he had not completely fallen over into their camp yet.

William Bullitt arrived with a bouquet of flowers. Madeleine had never seen him at the opera before.

"How you humanize Kundry!" Bullitt said. "When you were onstage, the audience only had eyes for you."

Madeleine hoped that Bullitt did not mean it.

His smile vanished when he noticed Klaus. "Kriminaldirektor Koegel, your men are never again to pretend that they are Americans in order to pull off an operation," he said in French.

"His French is rudimentary at best," Hans-Hermann said of Klaus, but did not repeat Bullitt's words in German.

Madeleine translated instead. Bullitt nodded his thanks at her.

"I don't have to remind you that Marseilles is off-limits for your men," Bullitt said to Klaus, again in French. "It is particularly reprehensible that your people used the good name of the United States to reel in refugees."

Madeleine translated again. Yvonne pushed hairpins into her *chignon-banane*, listening. Bullitt's bouquet lay in front of her, but there was no vase to put it in.

"They never said they were Americans," Klaus said in German. "There was no need to tell you anything."

Madeleine translated that too.

"But you insisted you had a message from the consulate, didn't you?" Bullitt said. "You told that poor man and his wife that their visas were ready for pickup."

A sense of foreboding enveloped Madeleine. She must have become pale, because Henri glared at her. At last, she remembered to translate. Yvonne dabbed her cheeks with rouge and reached for her tube of lipstick, her eyes going from the reflection of Bullitt to Klaus to Madeleine in the mirror.

"I'm not familiar with details," Klaus said with a cold smile. A man of his rank tasked underlings to worry about those things.

"Whom did you arrest?" Madeleine asked in the mediocre German she had learned through diction classes, forcing her voice to remain steady but not quite succeeding.

"Someone told us Stefan Kreismann's whereabouts," Klaus said offhandedly, as if the whole matter were extremely boring. "We didn't let him flee this time."

Yvonne dropped her lipstick. In the mirror, Madeleine's face turned white as a corpse.

"My dear Madame Chevallier, I wish I had listened to you and granted him his visa," Bullitt said.

Madeleine collapsed onto a chair. She would have collapsed onto the floor if the chair had not been right behind her. Perhaps one part of her brain was still striving to keep her safe, when the rest had already shut down at the news.

"Did you know about this?" Yvonne asked Hans-Hermann.

"It was out of my hands," Hans-Hermann said.

Henri grabbed Madeleine's arm and lifted her up. "Make an effort," he hissed between his teeth. "You're embarrassing me." To Yvonne he said, "We'll let you get ready now."

Jules left behind Henri and Madeleine, resolutely ignoring his mother. In the distance, a cane hammered the floor.

At the end of the hallway, Charles-Antoine carried a bouquet of orchids toward Madeleine's—no, Yvonne's—dressing room.

"I'd stay away if I were you," Madeleine said in a voice so feeble she could barely hear herself.

Charles-Antoine took one look at her and stopped. Henri pulled her along, but Madeleine dug her weight into her heels. Jules held her elbow, against Henri's will.

"The Germans arrested Stefan Kreismann in Marseille," Madeleine said to Charles-Antoine. The words stunned even her when she said them aloud. Stefan, arrested. How horrifying. How wasteful.

Charles-Antoine lowered his bouquet. The orchids pointed toward the floor.

"It so happens I need a rehearsal pianist," Madeleine said.

"We can't hire a Jew," Henri said.

"Of course we can," Madeleine said, in the same tone she would have taken if he had suggested days were not twenty-four hours long. They had enough money to make any trouble go away, as long as they weren't obvious about it.

Henri pressed his lips tightly together. He obviously did not share her optimism but did not say more.

"Surely there's something you could use me for?" Jules asked Madeleine. Either Yvonne wanted her son to spy on her rival, or he truly loathed his mother for her new friends.

Did she want to find out?

Perhaps not, but she was getting bored by herself, and she could use an assistant for company.

"I can certainly find suitable tasks for you," Madeleine said.

Henri shook his head.

"He'll be my assistant, not yours," Madeleine said without glancing at him.

The door to Yvonne's dressing room opened. Yvonne and Hans-Hermann strode out toward the reception area, where French collaborators eager to enrich themselves would hobnob with German officers who pretended not to despise them. Hans-Hermann looked pleased with himself. Yvonne kept her face devoid of any expression. Walking at a snail's pace, her hand resting on Hans-Hermann's arm, she resembled a woman condemned to death, who marked every step in those last few moments as she headed to the scaffold. Madeleine pressed herself against the wall to let them pass, her arm around Jules's elbow.

Henri curled his hand into a fist and rubbed its side against the wallpaper while he stared at his lead singer and her German beau. For a moment, he did nothing else. Then he followed Yvonne and Hans-Hermann toward the din of voices ready to celebrate the new star.

Yvonne took off her high heels and her earrings in the apartment on the quay Voltaire. The building was quiet. Everyone was sound asleep, apparently. She groped her way down the corridor. Hans-Hermann had had heavy curtains installed to meet the nighttime blackout rules, but he still didn't let her use the ceiling lights, even after he'd put in blue lightbulbs, only the small lamp on the side table. She had to reach it before she could turn it on. At last, the lamp cast long blue shadows over the room.

"We should push the table closer to the wall," Hans-Hermann said. "Those shadows across the curtains are too big."

Yvonne didn't reply. She'd learned that when he said "we should," it meant he'd get it done the next day, whether she agreed to it or not. She sat down on the sofa and put her feet up on the ottoman. "It was a great party. Thank you for making it possible." Hans-Hermann had arranged for all the food and beverages, although Yvonne didn't believe the money had come from his personal account.

Truth be told, operagoers had enjoyed the party more than Yvonne. The news that Kreismann had been arrested in Marseilles had ruined her joy at making her debut in Paris. It terrified her that Hans-Hermann had let the arrest happen. What else was he capable of? She'd convinced herself he wouldn't get involved in such matters—he'd focus on manuscripts and scripts of plays—but clearly she'd been deluding herself, and now Hans-Hermann was little more than a stranger who was living with her and could order her arrested if he didn't like the way she talked to him.

Hans-Hermann unfastened the top button of his uniform. "We should decide what you want to sing in next."

"*Tristan und Isolde*," Yvonne said. "I only wish I could get a Tristan of Stefan Kreismann's caliber. Guillaume will look like a little boy in his father's clothes in that role."

"People are rarely as irreplaceable as they think," Hans-Hermann said. Was the remark also directed at her?

Yvonne still had the idea of leaving him. She could pack a suitcase, take the train to Le Havre. She even had looked at the timetable at the Saint-Lazare train station and scribbled down the timetables in her notebook so that Hans-Hermann wouldn't find the paper schedule if he went through her things. She could sing under a stage name or return to being a store clerk. But she couldn't use Raymond as manager then, and clerks made a pittance. Her life would become difficult. She needed to save money, just one more week.

Hans-Hermann sat down in the armchair opposite hers. "You did good tonight. Everybody looked impressed."

"I tried," Yvonne said. She snuggled into the sofa cushions. Maybe she'd fall asleep there. It'd been a long evening.

"What do you think about Emile?" Hans-Hermann asked out of the blue.

"He's a good man," Yvonne said.

"There's a rumor going around that he kept Jewish musicians on the payroll, although they don't perform in public anymore."

It felt like iced water ran through Yvonne's veins. She forced herself not to move on the couch so she wouldn't arouse Hans-Hermann's suspicions, but now she was wide awake.

"He wouldn't take such a risk," Yvonne said, although of course he would, if he had any sense of duty. "I've never known him to be friendly toward the Jews."

"The anonymous letter I received was very specific. I bet it's his accountant, or his secretary."

"People say all kinds of lies when they're jealous. Emile wouldn't do anything to lose the directorship of the opera house." She said it in a tone that accepted no doubt, no dissent.

"I'll find out what's what eventually," Hans-Hermann said. "His wife is highly susceptible to power and uniforms. She'll tell me."

Yvonne didn't like the hint in his voice. "There won't be anything to tell you," she said curtly. "I'm going to bed now."

She made her way through the dark corridor and turned on another blue light and got ready for bed bathed in blue. Better that than having the British bombers select the building as a target. She feigned sleep when Hans-Herman joined her. She waited until she heard him snore. Then she went through the pockets of his coat—nothing. After a moment's hesitation, she took his briefcase. She wasn't supposed to know the code, but she'd made a mental note of it one day when she'd seen him open it. He'd let his guard down only once out of the hundreds of times he'd carried that suitcase around. It said something about him, that he distrusted her. But there was nothing in the briefcase either. She put it back where she had found it and sat down on the sofa, feeling powerless. The blue light gave the room an odd atmosphere.

"What are you doing?" Hans-Hermann asked from the door.

Yvonne started. "I had a nightmare," she said, glad that the room was too dark for him to see her cheeks turn red. "It helps me to have light on, and I didn't want to wake you up. Maybe I'll doze off here." Two minutes earlier he would've caught her holding his open briefcase. She buried her hands under her thighs so he wouldn't see them shake.

"You're not going to sleep on the couch when you have a real bed," Hans-Hermann said. He fetched her some water in the kitchen.

Yvonne dutifully headed back to the bedroom. No need to aggravate him now. She'd tell Emile about the musicians. He'd deny it, but at least he'd be warned. And maybe he'd get a different accountant, if he trusted his secretary. Whether that would make any difference was out of Yvonne's hands.

Part Three

Sixteen

Two years later
July 1942

Madeleine sang Sieglinde's aria in the first act of *Die Walküre* as if she were in front of a crowd waiting to shower applause on her, not standing in Charles-Antoine's apartment on the boulevard Malesherbes. Sieglinde was telling the wounded hero, Siegmund, that a stranger had stuck a sword in a nearby tree on the day she had been forced to marry her abusive husband. No one had been able to pull the sword out. Madeleine spread her arms wide and paced the floor, mindful of how much audiences adored Yvonne's sweeping gestures. She did not have quite the right voice for Sieglinde, but Yvonne had claimed Brünnhilde for herself. Madeleine had considered refusing the role, mindful of the slight; by then, though, she had been off the stage for two years. She was desperate to sing at the Paris Opera one more time before her voice deteriorated to the point where it became noticeable to spectators.

Would they even recognize her? She had lost weight because of the rationing. Henri had once brought back home sugar and eggs and meat and bread, all scarce items, courtesy of Hans-Hermann—a gift to Henri "for helping Yvonne shine onstage"—but Madeleine had refused to owe the Nazis anything. Instead, she had directed Rose and Gustave to eat her portion and take any leftovers to their relatives.

At the dining room table, Jules nodded as if Madeleine deserved an award. He had been a good assistant ever since Madeleine hired him and claimed he remained in awe of her artistry. To show him her

189

gratitude—he did not have to do any of that—she had promised to introduce him to a renowned piano teacher she was friends with so he could continue his training.

Sieglinde's aria filled Madeleine with cautious optimism about her career, despite the challenges. Her vocal cords did not feel stiff. She did not have to push more air out of her lungs to produce her high notes—a trick she had relied on more as she aged. When Charles-Antoine accompanied her, Madeleine would have sworn that her voice remained as supple as in her student days. Maybe she could keep working for a while longer. She appreciated the distraction from the anguish that the Nazis had brought about. The Soviet Union and the United States had entered the war against Germany, but the Third Reich was holding its ground. Madeleine's hopes for an Axis defeat had been dashed twice, first in June 1941 and then in May 1942. Stalin's troops should have crushed Hitler's, angered at his betrayal of the nonaggression agreement. Then the Americans had attacked in North Africa, so far away it seemed they would never set foot in France. The countries that were supposed to save France had entered the war, and yet the fight was still raging on. The Nazis had burnt down the Czech village of Lidice after one of their officers had been assassinated. Churchill had faced a motion of censure in the House of Commons because of the heavy British losses in North Africa. Madeleine sang to drown her sorrow and waited for better days.

Someone banged on the front door. The three knocks would have woken up a dead man. Charles-Antoine stopped playing, and Madeleine silenced herself. They all looked at each other, but it was too late to pretend the apartment was empty.

Jules went to the door. Police officers wearing the French flag on their armband shoved him aside.

"Charles-Antoine Monnier?" one of the police officers asked.

Charles-Antoine nodded. Roundups had become common, but he had never been targeted before. In December, the police had arrested French Jews from the upper classes: lawyers, professors, businessmen. They had not been heard from since. Henri had opposed Charles-Antoine's rehearsing with Madeleine at their home because he

feared that sooner or later the Nazis would reproach them for employ-
ing a Jew. He wasn't wrong, but Madeleine would not distance herself
from her former teacher, especially now. So Jules accompanied Madeleine to her lessons in Henri's car—Henri's only concession to Madeleine's well-being, and then only because Jules had asked him to, Jules
who had fought for France. Madeleine did not ask where the gasoline,
in shortage all over Paris, was coming from.

Two policemen lifted Charles-Antoine from the piano bench.

"Show your elders some respect," Madeleine said.

"My elders ain't Jews," the younger policeman said. And to
Charles-Antoine: "Hurry up."

Jules wedged himself between the two of them. "French people
betraying their compatriots. Are you proud of yourselves? Such valor!
Such courage!"

The man didn't even bother answering Jules. "We can leave now if
you don't plan on packing anything," he said to Charles-Antoine.

Charles-Antoine reached for his cane. His hands shook. Madeleine
leaned against the piano to steady herself. She had only seen one other
roundup: when Gustave was driving her up the boulevard des Italiens,
she'd seen *Boches* gathering men near the Richelieu-Drouot metro station and pushing them into vans. They did so whenever there had been
an attack on a Nazi officer, from a rock thrown into a Grosser Mercedes
to someone firing a direct shot. The fact that they picked Parisians at
random for execution was supposed to be a deterrent. Morale in Paris
had never been lower.

"Let me help you," Madeleine said to Charles-Antoine. What
awaited him—a prison cell, a bed in an internment camp? Or simply
an annoying interview at police headquarters before a young captain
dismissed him with a snap of his fingers?

She opened Charles-Antoine's closet by the front door for him. In it
hung a long row of jackets, each with a yellow star sewn onto the front.
The Germans had required the star at the end of May. She had seen him
wear those jackets before, yet she could not get used to that ugly star, as
if Jews were cattle that should be branded to be recognized from afar.

Madeleine had never expected the Vichy government to acquiesce to the Nazis' demands. A yellow star—the Germans could force their own Jewish citizens to wear it, but she had believed France to be a country of intelligent people. It still enraged her that she had been proved so wrong.

"You should arrest thieves and robbers instead," Jules said to the policemen. "People who corrupt France. Everyone in the Vichy government."

"Shut up or we're taking you too," the younger policeman said.

Madeleine retrieved a suitcase behind rain boots and summer shoes. "Here, help me," she told Jules.

"That drawing," Charles-Antoine said in a small voice, pointing at a piece of art on the wall.

Jules plucked a charcoal drawing of a teenage girl from its hook and wrapped it in a towel.

"That was my wife when she was younger," Charles-Antoine said. "She drew it herself, quite a few years ago."

"Where is she?" the older policeman asked. "She has to come."

"She's dead," Charles-Antoine said. "I am glad she cannot see the shame you're bringing on our country."

His colleague waved the butt of his rifle at him. "You gonna get one of those in your teeth if you don't hurry up."

"The stomach," his superior said. "How many times do I have to tell you? The stomach, not the teeth." And to Madeleine: "If the old man isn't ready in five minutes, we're dragging him out without any suitcase at all."

Madeleine dashed into Charles-Antoine's bedroom. On the nightstand, reading glasses had been left next to a copy of Arnold Schoenberg's *Theory of Harmony*. The Schoenberg book would have to stay behind, but she shouldn't forget the glasses. Madeleine scooped up an armful of clothes, summer shirts and cotton pants with sweaters and jackets for the cooler nights. Surely France would be up in arms about this roundup. It was one thing to shove foreigners into police vans, but

French citizens treated that way! Public pressure would force the Germans to reverse course. Jules helped Madeleine fold the garments.

"I'm gonna count down from twenty," the younger policeman said, "and if he ain't ready when I get to zero—"

Madeleine shut the suitcase and handed it to Charles-Antoine.

The policemen shoved Charles-Antoine toward the front door. His cane slid onto the floor. He dropped the suitcase and fell onto the ground.

The younger policeman kicked Charles-Antoine in the shin. "If we were *Boches*, we'd finish you off right here."

Jules lent Charles-Antoine a hand to get up. His eyes were blazing with fury. "Why aren't you taking me?" he taunted the policemen. "I'm Jewish too."

"He . . . he doesn't mean that," Madeleine said.

The older policeman took Jules by the elbow. "If he says he's Jewish, we'll assume he is."

"Do you believe everything people tell you?" Charles-Antoine asked, dusting himself off.

"No one is dumb enough to pretend they're Jewish when they're not," the policeman said.

He led Jules out. His colleague escorted Charles-Antoine. Madeleine ran behind them into the street. Jules strode with his chin high, but Charles-Antoine looked frail and slumped. Henri's Peugeot was parked by a fire hydrant. Gustave folded the newspaper and threw it on the passenger seat, surprised that the lesson had ended so early. The policemen shoved their prisoners into the back of a van. An entire family was already huddled inside, the parents and four children, including a babe wailing in his mother's arms. The fear in their eyes alarmed Madeleine. What had they been told?

"You're making a mistake," Madeleine said to the older policeman. He climbed onto the back of the van without glancing at her. She grabbed his arm. "The French minister for cultural affairs will hear about this. I'm Madeleine Moreau, for Christ's sake! I demand that you tell me where you're going." She hadn't known that her voice became very shrill when she was terrified.

The policeman looked at her expensive dress. "The Vél d'Hiv," he said.

⌒〜⌒

Gustave drove Madeleine to the quay Voltaire. Which building was Yvonne's again? Jules had mentioned it to her, but she had forgotten the exact number. Did the social climber live above the art gallery or next to it?

"Pull over," Madeleine said.

She stumbled out of the Peugeot and squinted over the names of the residents by the first doorbell, and then the second one. It was getting dark. Dread gnawed at her. It was her fault that Jules had been in the room with her and Charles-Antoine. Hopefully he wouldn't get himself shot.

A car rounded the corner of the rue Bonaparte. The swastika flags mounted on its front bumper drew bigger until the Grosser Mercedes stopped two doors down from Madeleine. Yvonne got out; she had wrapped a stole over her dress. She walked slowly, as if she had spent too much time on her feet. Hans-Hermann remained on the back seat.

Yvonne shrieked when Madeleine stepped out of the shadows.

"Jules has been arrested," Madeleine said. "He said he was Jewish when the police came to take Charles-Antoine."

Yvonne opened her mouth, but no sound came out. Already Hans-Hermann was getting out of the Mercedes.

"Haven't you heard?" Madeleine said to Yvonne. "There's a roundup going on."

This seemed to wake Yvonne up. "What's that roundup Madeleine is talking about?" she asked Hans-Hermann.

"You'd have to ask the French police," he said. They would never do anything without Nazis' orders for it, but there was no point in Madeleine saying the obvious out loud.

"They're rounding up Jews," Madeleine said.

"You must tell them to free Jules. He was taken by mistake."

"They wouldn't have taken him if he hadn't given them a reason to," Hans-Hermann said.

"But he's not Jewish," Yvonne said.

"I have other things to do besides saving that boy again." Hans-Hermann marched back to the Grosser Mercedes. His driver, Rolf, put the sedan in drive. The tires squealed when he maneuvered the turn onto the bridge.

"We have to go and see the police chief," Madeleine said. "Let's take my car."

Gustave drove quickly through the deserted streets. Police headquarters was on the other bank of the Seine, on the quay de Gesvres, a stone's throw behind the Châtelet square. Madeleine and Yvonne did not talk on the way. Yvonne picked at the strap of her Louis Vuitton bag. She looked incapable of having coherent thoughts, let alone plotting strategy. Madeleine stared ahead at the boulevard du Palais stretching in front of them and then at the courthouse on the left behind the iron gates. She had not expected Jules to show such courage in solidarity. That impressed her—inspired her, even.

The car came to a stop in front of a gray, nondescript building behind the Théâtre Sarah-Bernhardt. *Préfecture de Police* loomed in large letters over walls punctuated by barred windows. Even the front door was painted gray.

Madeleine dashed inside with Yvonne on her heels. Two men in overalls nodded off in the waiting room, a small space crammed with wooden chairs and, by the door, a trash can overflowing with garbage. An elderly lady in a veiled hat knitted at furious speed. In the main room, a policeman typed a report as if he weren't keeping anyone waiting.

Madeleine marched toward him. "The senior officer on duty, now."

The policeman directed her toward the captain's office with a nonchalant gesture. A man wearing a pencil moustache put a newspaper aside when Madeleine entered. It was open at the crossword puzzle. Yvonne stepped next to Madeleine.

"I am Madeleine Moreau, and this is Yvonne Chevallier, of the Paris Opera house," Madeleine said in her opera singer voice that could project all the way through the auditorium. "My colleague's son was arrested in the latest roundup by mistake. It goes without saying that we expect him released immediately."

The captain chewed on a piece of tobacco. "It's going to take days before we know who we hauled in. Do you have any idea how many people we locked up?"

Madeleine did not have the time to play guessing games.

"Give me a number," the captain said.

Madeleine picked a number at random, leaning toward the high side to please him. "One thousand." That would fill the parterre of the Paris Opera.

The captain puffed out his chest. "Nine thousand!" He seemed proud, as if he had personally handcuffed every single one of them. But that number could not be true. That would have been madness. "And tomorrow we're going back to grab the ones we didn't get today."

"Should we go to the Vélodrome d'Hiver, then?" Madeleine asked. "My colleague's son needs to be freed."

The captain looked surprised that she knew about the Vél d'Hiv. "No one is leaving that place without the proper paperwork," he said.

Yvonne clutched Madeleine's arm. It was not the right time for her to faint.

"We could get your entire family tickets to the opera," Madeleine said. "What about *Magic Flute*? That always pleases children."

The captain smoothed his moustache with his index finger, mulling things over.

"Your superior will be green with envy when he finds out," Madeleine said.

"Can we sit close to the stage?" the captain said after a while. "My kids like to see actors' faces."

"The best spot," Madeleine said, although that was not true. "Now how do we get Madame Chevallier's son out?"

"The order to free him would have to come from the Germans," the captain said. "The Gestapo planned the whole thing. To them we're just the hired help."

❧

Yvonne and Madeleine hastened back to the Peugeot.

"Avenue Foch," Madeleine said to Gustave.

Gestapo headquarters was at number eighty-four, in a wealthy neighborhood of Paris crisscrossed by tree-lined avenues full of historic mansions with high ceilings.

"I was going to leave him," Yvonne said out of the blue without looking at Madeleine. "Hans-Hermann. I was going to tell Jules tonight, take the train to Le Havre tomorrow morning, and disappear. Hans-Hermann is powerful, but he isn't the Gestapo either. He wouldn't have looked for me. July was a good time to do it. Nothing's happening at the opera house."

"You can still do it," Madeleine said.

Yvonne glanced out the window. "Either we get Jules released and I have to keep a closer eye on him so he doesn't get himself in trouble again, or we don't get him released and I have to keep asking for his release."

Gustave slowed down when the Gestapo building came into view, right before the avenue ended at Porte Dauphine. He made a full stop at the intersection with the rue Pergolèse. The street was eerily quiet. Not even a single elderly man walked a poodle. The silence was ominous rather than peaceful.

"It'll bring me bad luck if I get closer," Gustave said.

Yvonne rushed out toward the iron gates and the swastika flag flapping over rows of equally spaced windows bracketed by elaborate stonework and forged-steel railings. Madeleine strode behind her, careful not to race. With those goons, it was best not to seem too eager, nor too desperate.

Yvonne was already pleading with the Gestapo officer at the front desk when Madeleine pushed through the doors of the building. The top of the officer's hair was parted in the middle and the bottom shaved off with a razor. A lamp covered by a green shade drew a circle of light over an empty cup of coffee and papers stacked in a neat pile. Next to the lamp, a small statue of a bear, the emblem of Berlin, raised its front paws in the air. The room reeked of cigarettes.

"Go and talk to the French police," the officer said to Yvonne.

"They sent us here. My son got taken by mistake."

"We don't make mistakes," the officer said.

"But he's not Jewish," Yvonne said.

"Then why was he taken?"

"I don't know," Yvonne said. "I wasn't there."

"But you know he was taken," the officer said.

Yvonne clicked her tongue. "Generalleutnant Hans-Hermann von Moderling would want you to release him."

The officer pulled a cigarette from his pack of Eckstein. "If he did, he would've let me know."

Yvonne began to shake but steadied herself against the German officer's desk. The officer stared at Yvonne's hands pressed against his property, glared at her, reached for a ruler, looked at her fingers again. Madeleine pulled Yvonne to the side.

"Whom should I talk to about this?" Yvonne asked. Her voice was trembling.

The officer pushed the phone toward her. "Anyone you'd like, but I doubt you'll succeed." He blew a ring of smoke into her face.

Yvonne asked the operator to connect her to the German embassy. The officer eyed her with faint amusement.

"I'm Yvonne Chevallier of the Paris Opera," Yvonne said. "I need to talk to the ambassador."

The person at the other end of the line said something that Madeleine did not catch.

"I'll leave a message if he's not available, but if you tell him it's me, he'll come to the phone. He attends all my performances."

She tugged on the phone cord. Madeleine's apprehension grew.

"My son was arrested in the Vél d'Hiv roundup by mistake," Yvonne said. And after a moment, "The ambassador will hear about this." Her voice was less assured now, as if she were trying to convince herself.

She hung up. Madeleine would be willing to bet that the employee wouldn't pass along Yvonne's message, or if he did, only to make fun of Yvonne's temerity.

The officer gestured toward the exit just as the doors leading to the street flew wide open. A group of Nazi soldiers hauled French prisoners in—their faces already swollen from the punches, noses broken, lips split. Yvonne covered her mouth with her hand.

Behind the soldiers, an officer with a piglike face stepped toward Yvonne and Madeleine. He looked familiar, but Madeleine could not place him.

"Frau Chevallier!" the officer said. "What happy surprise."

"Kriminaldirektor Koegel, I need your help," Yvonne said, suddenly hopeful.

Madeleine recognized him now. He had attended the reopening of the opera house when Yvonne starred in *Parsifal*. He had also engineered Stefan's arrest. Madeleine had yet to receive news from Stefan in the labor camp east where he had been transferred. Germany, Poland—Madeleine wasn't sure where. It would be like the *Boches* not to allow prisoners to send letters.

"Let's chat in my office," Klaus said to Yvonne in German. He blocked Madeleine's path when she tried to follow them up the spiral staircase and switched to his poor French. "We need you not, Frau Moreau. Go home now."

❧

Klaus ushered Yvonne inside his office on the second floor and closed the door. The room had hardwood floors, white walls with trim, and twelve-foot ceilings. In the air lingered the smell of fresh lacquer. A daybed was propped against the back wall.

Klaus plucked a bottle out of a drawer and poured himself a shot of Jägermeister. "A drink, my dear Frau Chevallier? Tell me what worries you so."

When he told her this in German, Yvonne felt like she belonged to a club of powerful people—the ones who understood him—and her satisfaction worried her most, because she absolutely hated Klaus.

He hunched forward as he spoke. Maybe he'd learned his manners from watching movies featuring doctors at their patients' bedside, although it made him appear even shorter.

Yvonne sank into a leather armchair. "My son and my former teacher got caught in the Vél d'Hiv roundup."

Klaus downed the shot and poured her one in another glass. "The police are under strict orders to only take Jews."

"My teacher's contributions to music—"

"If he is a Jew, then it is normal he was taken. Orders are orders." Klaus clicked his glass against hers. "Now what about your son? Is his father Jewish?"

"He was in the wrong place at the wrong time," Yvonne said. "The policemen got carried away. You can't let them keep him if he's not Jewish."

Klaus gulped down his drink without any comment.

"My former husband and I come from generations of Catholics," Yvonne said. "Jules was baptized when he was an infant and confirmed when he was twelve."

"So why did the police arrest him?"

"He might've let them believe he was Jewish too," Yvonne said.

Klaus eyed her over the rim of his glass, then he finished his drink. "Quite a son you have, Frau Chevallier. These people are the reason France lost the war, and he's on their side."

Yvonne stayed quiet.

"You should hope my men knock some sense into the son of yours. As a matter of fact, you should encourage us. Otherwise, he'll do worse, and then he'll be shot."

Yvonne's teeth chattered. "The boy doesn't care about politics. He dreams of becoming the next Alfred Cortot. That's a famous French pianist."

Klaus pushed his empty glass against the ashtray. A small British flag was painted at the bottom. He got up from his chair and sat down on the armchair next to Yvonne's. "Frau Chevallier, I'll help you, but I hope you understand you're very lucky."

He placed his hand on her knee. Yvonne started. Of course. What had she expected? She didn't have anything else to bargain with.

"Now, I certainly don't want to make you do something you don't want to do," Klaus said. "If I make you uncomfortable, just say so. We Germans know how to treat our women. And perhaps your son prefers being in jail."

He slid his hand under her dress. His fingers felt like worms crawling on Yvonne's garter and then her skin.

"Now, you can tell me to stop or you can take off your clothes. I will let you decide. Your son chose to get arrested, after all."

For a moment, Yvonne didn't move. Then she slid out of her dress as if someone else was controlling her hands.

"Everything," Klaus said.

Yvonne took off her slip and stood naked in front of him, avoiding his gaze.

Klaus prodded her breasts as if they were udders on a piece of cattle. "I'm not forcing you, Frau Chevallier. You can walk out of this room if you choose. On the other hand, if you find it so important to get your son out of jail, you could lie down on the couch over there. But again, only if you are so inclined."

Yvonne lay down on the daybed and stared at the ceiling. An ink stain was splattered near the chandelier.

Klaus knelt between her legs. "I'm going to make you hit a high note or two, my dear."

⌒⌒

Klaus pulled up his pants after he rolled off her and checked his watch. "I have an appointment in five minutes. You'd better hurry out."

Yvonne slid off the couch. Her hands trembled as she put her clothes back on. She was distracted by the urge to rub raw every part of her body that Klaus had touched.

"You don't expect me to help you get dressed, now, do you?" Klaus said.

"When will my son be freed?" Yvonne asked without looking at him.

"I suppose you'll have to wait a few days and see if I'm a man of my word. It'll be a surprise!" Klaus laughed.

Yvonne's legs weakened under her. After all this, she still hadn't secured Jules's release.

Klaus shoved Yvonne into the hallway. An officer strode around her as if she were a piece of furniture forgotten in the middle of the corridor. She stood there and, after a long moment, turned toward the stairs about twenty feet away. She only had to put one foot in front of the other, but the air pressed against her chest, preventing her from moving. At last, she took a tiny step forward. She'd walked like that onstage the previous year, for the mad scene in *Lucia*. If she told herself she was playing a role, then she could take another step forward amid the German officers, and another. She reached the landing and, grabbing the guardrail, resisted the temptation to throw herself down the stairs. Instead, she began the long walk home, Klaus's smell still on her.

Seventeen

The following Monday, Madeleine stepped out of her car onto the rue de Grenelle and, clutching the basket full of victuals that she had bought on the black market, crossed the street toward the Vélodrome d'Hiver. It was a squat, sprawling building that stretched an entire city block down the rue Nélaton. Madeleine had never attended a race at the indoor cycle track, nor a boxing game, nor a circus performance, any of which could attract twenty thousand customers. In fact, she did not remember ever venturing into this working-class neighborhood in the fifteenth arrondissement. The Eiffel Tower loomed over the skyline on the other side of the avenue de Suffren. A German banner stretched along the platform on the tower's second floor: *Deutschland siegt auf allen Fronten*. Germany wins on all fronts. What a disgrace.

Gustave called out from the Peugeot. "You're certain you don't want me to go with you?"

"Someone needs to ring the alarm if I don't come out," Madeleine said.

"You could choose not to go in."

"I'm not a coward like that husband of mine," Madeleine said, although she wouldn't have minded having at least Yvonne by her side. But she had not been able to reach Yvonne since they had rushed to the Gestapo together. Yvonne had canceled all her rehearsals for the week. Apparently, she had fallen ill.

A French police officer was guarding the entrance to the *vélodrome*. He spat out tobacco when Madeleine drew near in her red travel suit and a matching hat. Her attire guaranteed that she would impress the guards and draw the attention of the prisoners if she managed to sneak inside. She couldn't think of another way to find Jules and Charles-Antoine. That morning's newspapers whispered, in tiny paragraphs buried on page six or eight, that ten thousand French Jews had been rounded up over the past few days. Instead of splashing the astounding news on its front page, *Paris-soir* had picked for its lead story the forthcoming holiday of five hundred schoolchildren. They would camp in the woods outside Fontainebleau, courtesy of the newspaper, which was sponsoring the trip. Below the fold, two articles described the recent German attack of a city named Stalingrad on the Volga River. Stalin was rumored to have left Moscow to advise the troops himself. The Nazis insisted they were about to win the war.

"I am delivering a care package for two of the prisoners," Madeleine said to the policeman.

"What do you think this is, a social club?"

"Your supervisor approved of my coming."

"And who'd that be?"

Madeleine pulled out a one-hundred-franc bill from her purse. She had told Henri she needed money for a new dress. "The man I talked to on the phone said he'd allow it if you all got rewarded for your troubles." She kept the bill between two fingers, at eye level. "He's expecting me inside anytime now, with a reward for him too." It took all her self-discipline for her voice not to tremble. She had no idea how any of this was going to turn out, except that Jules and Charles-Antoine surely had had no food since they had been taken, and they needed to eat.

The policeman plucked the one-hundred-franc bill from her hand. "What's in the basket?"

Madeleine lifted the tablecloth that she had covered buttered slices of the *pain de campagne* with. "The bread's two days old, but that's better than nothing."

The policeman lifted the loaf of bread.

"I'm not sure how old the butter is," Madeleine said. "It has a bit of a smell."

The policeman hesitated.

"You can take a bite if you want, but you may get very sick," Madeleine said.

The man put the loaf back into the basket and waved at her to move along. The one-hundred-franc bill made a rustling noise in his palm.

"So what does that supervisor of yours look like?" Madeleine asked.

"He walks with his hands behind his back and barks at whoever comes near. A real sweetheart." The policeman was already peering toward the end of the street, indifferent to Madeleine now that he had decided she could enter.

Inside the velodrome, the air felt stale in the summer heat. Curtains were drawn over the ticket windows on the side. A long corridor led to double doors that Madeleine assumed hid the racing track. Another policeman was guarding those doors. A second policeman was talking to him, slightly hunched forward, his hands clasped behind his back. The officer, then. Madeleine pressed herself against the ticket windows, out of his sight. She counted to fifty and looked again. The officer had disappeared, leaving only the policeman behind.

Madeleine retrieved another one-hundred-franc bill while she strode toward that man. "Another bill just like it awaits you if I find who I'm looking for."

The officer gave her a long look and then shoved the bill in his pocket. For a moment he did not move. Madeleine worried he would shake his head and say that the prisoners weren't allowed visitors. But he stepped aside. Could things be so simple for someone who had money to spend?

"You might regret it when you smell the stench," the policeman said.

Madeleine opened the doors onto a dark stone corridor, policeman in tow. The smell of piss and shit overwhelmed her. She covered her nose. A yellow puddle had pooled in a corner.

"The toilets clogged on the second day," the policeman said. "They're doing their business everywhere. Do you still want to come in?"

Madeleine tried not to gag. "But aren't janitors cleaning the toilets?"

"None of them cares to clean the Jews' piss," the policeman said.

He nodded at his colleague standing guard and opened the door to the velodrome. Madeleine dropped the basket onto her feet when she saw the scene, picked it up before it could roll away from her. About two-thirds of the seats were occupied. Thirteen thousand people was her best guess—a number even higher than what newspapers had reported. Babies wailed. Tears glistened on children's cheeks. Adults were slumped in their seats, their one suitcase next to them. She had known there would be a lot of people from the newspapers, but she had not realized how it would look like once she got there. The world had gone insane.

Madeleine in her red travel suit, carrying her basket, must have looked like an apparition. And how would she find Jules and Charles-Antoine?

"Is there an order, perhaps, to how these people are seated?" Madeleine asked the policeman.

He laughed.

"I have money for you if you help me find who I'm looking for," Madeleine said.

"Come back tomorrow when we line up the first ones to go to the trains," the policeman said. "We'll do roll calls for those we're shipping out. It's going to take some time before they're all gone, though."

"Gone where?" Madeleine asked.

"Drancy first, and then somewhere east. It'll take a week to get them all outa here, easy. If you come back every morning—"

"Who's going first?" Madeleine asked, her terror mounting.

"I don't decide those things," the policeman said.

Madeleine held out another one-hundred-franc bill. "Call out the names of Jules Chevallier and Charles-Antoine Monnier."

The policeman tucked the money into his breast pocket. "Call them out yourselves. I've helped you enough." He strode back to the door. "We're changing shifts in fifteen minutes. If you're not back outside by then, you'll get locked up with them. I won't try to find you if you're running late."

Madeleine tottered into the velodrome. Its sheer size awed her, and the shock of discovering so many prisoners was not helping her think straight. She stumbled along the outer circle, peering down at the prisoners in case she recognized a cane with a silver pommel or a blond-haired teenager. When that failed, she wobbled down the stairs and positioned herself toward the front, near the best seats close to the racers, scrutinizing faces. Perhaps Charles-Antoine and Jules would notice her. She sure attracted attention in that bright red suit of hers.

She scrutinized face after face, walking faster. Her despair mounted.

The prisoners stared at her with pity, as if she had been arrested with them and had lost her mind from the strain.

Was it possible that Madeleine had succeeded in entering the Vél d'Hiv and now would not find her two friends? She couldn't check thousands of faces by herself. Jules and Charles-Antoine had to notice her. Madeleine meandered one last time through the stadium. Her basket bounced against her chest. She had not been able to help Stefan, and now she had located neither Charles-Antoine nor Jules. How useless she felt.

"Madeleine!" a voice called out.

Jules waved at her from the second tier of seats. Charles-Antoine was leaning on his cane. He had aged five years since Madeleine had last seen him, but his eyes perked up when he recognized her in the crowd.

"I brought you this." Madeleine showed off the loaf of bread and, under a second tablecloth that had seemed to cover the bottom of the basket, Brie cheese and *saucisson*.

"Christmas in July," Jules said.

"I'm not sure how fresh it is, but I had a piece and didn't get sick."

Madeleine felt other internees' hungry gaze on her while she emptied the basket. She wished she had brought food for all of them. What had civilization become? These were French citizens. More than that. These were people.

Charles-Antoine handed a slice of bread and one of *saucisson* to the young boy seated nearest from him. The boy wolfed the food down and mumbled thank-you while he was still chewing.

"What are the papers saying about the roundup?" Jules asked.

"They're barely spending any ink on it. I contacted journalists, but the ones I know are art critics. No one dares write about what

happened." Madeleine turned toward Jules. "Your mother and I are trying to get you released."

"I don't want to get released," Jules said.

Charles-Antoine shook his head. "Your talent is better used
elsewhere."

"How can I live with myself after what I've seen?"

"There's no point in you following me wherever they're sending us
Jews," Charles-Antoine said. "Enough lives are being destroyed here.
You have so much to look forward to."

"Surely you don't expect me to play the piano at times like this,"
Jules said.

"I can think of plenty of things you can do besides playing the piano
if you make it back outside," Charles-Antoine said.

Jules leaned back in his seat. "They won't release me anyway."

"I have to leave before the shift change," Madeleine said. "Don't lose
hope. I'm doing all I can."

She wanted to say more, but Jules cut her off. "A new soldier just
showed up. They're changing crews. Hurry out."

Madeleine raced to the exit. A policeman she had not seen before
greeted her at the top of the stairs.

"Where the heck do you think you're going?" he asked.

"I'm a friend of your colleague's," Madeleine said. "He's expecting
me out now. I was just settling a personal matter."

The policeman scoffed. "That's one dumb escape attempt for sure."

Madeleine plucked out her wad of one-hundred-franc bills from her
purse. "I wouldn't have so much money if I were a prisoner, would I?
You would've confiscated it. Here. My treat." She slapped a bill into his
palm.

"You must've hidden the money in your suitcase while you were
packing, then. Step back."

"Check my name on your list of prisoners." Madeleine willed her
voice to stay even.

"Stop wasting my time and get back to your seat," the policeman
said.

The door opened behind him.

"Oh, the crazy lady has returned," a voice said. "I guess she didn't want to get shipped to Drancy after all."

The policeman who had stood guard outside was leaning against the wall, eyeing the money in Madeleine's hand.

"You can't possibly have let her in," the second policeman said. "You'll get fired if the captain finds out."

The first policeman reached forward and grabbed the money in Madeleine's hand. "No one will know as long as you don't tell them." He gave the other policeman a bill from the wad.

"Give me all her money or I'll report you," the second policeman said.

Madeleine dashed toward the exit while they argued. She didn't even have time to ask what price would buy Jules's and Charles-Antoine's escape from the Vél d'Hiv.

At last, she swung the front door open. She raced past the guard and, fearing that the policemen would pursue her, threw herself into the back of Henri's car. Gustave started the engine. Madeleine shook uncontrollably. She had never felt so much shame—at the French police for arresting their fellow citizens, at herself for not being able to get them out despite her renown. She wished she had wielded enough influence to alter the course of history, but in the end, her voice counted for nothing.

❧

On the last Sunday afternoon in July, Yvonne stepped into the German Institute on Hans-Hermann's arm, scheduled to give a recital for the Nazis. She was careful to keep a smile pasted on her face, showing gratitude for the opportunity she'd been given. At least Hans-Hermann didn't require her to heap abject praise at him or grovel at his feet, but she would've done it if he'd ordered her, just to avoid being shot in the head. Hans-Hermann fumed about leaflets that'd been dropped in public places all over Paris, as if Yvonne cared. Apparently, the leaflets exhorted the French to keep fighting, just like General de Gaulle had said in his radio speech in June 1940. Yvonne barely listened to him. It'd been a week since Jules and Charles-Antoine had been arrested, and she'd yet to receive any news about their fate.

The institute was located on the avenue d'Iéna in the sixteenth arrondissement, a stone's throw from the Jardins du Trocadéro. Every building on the street exuded old money and understated elegance except for this one, ruined by the swastika that hung over its front door. Hans-Hermann nodded at someone who must be the institute's director. The man stood with Henri next to a painting of a contemplative figure in a frock coat, silhouetted against an expansive sky: Caspar David Friedrich, the master of Romanticism, from those happier days before the Fritzes had become bloodthirsty warmongers.

Only a few steps away, a larger-than-life picture of Adolf Hitler hung high on the chimney. Yvonne made sure not to clench her teeth in case Hans-Hermann was keeping an eye on her. Guests milled about in the institute's reading room before the concert, chatting happily about the news from the eastern front. The Battle of Voronezh had ended in Axis victory. Nazi officers strutted around as if their tanks were already filled with the petroleum of the Maikop and Baku oil fields. Parisians in well-tailored clothes, their faces ugly with greed, congratulated them with the eagerness of opportunists aiming at a share of the spoils. Yvonne wished she were anywhere else. She placed her scores on the music stand in front of the chimney, careful not to look at Hitler's portrait. She'd prepared a program of Strauss and Wagner, and at the last minute she'd added Marguerite's aria in *Faust*. All the programs had to be reprinted, but the employee in the basement of the opera house, where Emile kept a press, had been happy to indulge her. He must've known she was the girlfriend of a German officer. Henri would accompany her at the piano. He seemed happier to entertain the *Boches* than she was. More content, at least. She hadn't told him she felt she was not only Marguerite, doomed by her love, but also Faust, who sells his soul to the devil.

Madeleine stood in a corner by the wall, in a plain black dress meant not to draw attention to its owner. She held a coupe of

Taittinger champagne without drinking from it. In the middle of the room, Emile and his wife exchanged pleasantries with a Generaloberst from the Wehrmacht. His braided gold shoulder boards with three silver pips gleamed under the light. Yvonne had learned how to figure out the rank of each officer from his uniform. Emile's wife leaned so much on the officer's arm while she laughed that she looked like she was married to him and not Emile. Yvonne winced. Emile must be so embarrassed. Catherine, that rival of Yvonne's from her days at the Conservatory, strutted into the room in a pillbox hat. Yvonne hadn't known she'd come, but she wasn't surprised. Anybody who wanted to benefit from the Occupation was in the room. Her husband was following her, shaking hands. The few other men in the room wearing business suits rather than uniforms had to be French. Yvonne recognized two of them from pictures in the newspaper. They grinned just as much as they had during the Bastille Day reception with Prime Minister Édouard Daladier and President Albert Lebrun, except now they were socializing with the Nazis.

Klaus was nowhere in sight. What did it mean that he hadn't arrived? Would he free Jules, or would he not show up, letting Yvonne hope and then become crestfallen at the cruel joke he'd pulled on her? She glanced through the large window whenever a car pulled up but was disappointed every time.

At last, shortly before three o'clock, a Grosser Mercedes pulled over by the sidewalk. Klaus pushed himself out, hindered by his weight, and then reached inside and dragged Jules out. Yvonne clutched the sides of the music stand so she wouldn't jump forward to greet her son. That would've given the attendees something else to gossip about. Better not to draw attention.

Jules hobbled into the German Institute. Klaus followed on his heels. Jules looked like he'd been wearing the same clothes for days, but his face showed no bruises, and his hands weren't bandaged. He'd hurt his right leg, though, maybe his knee. Yvonne slapped a sweet, indifferent smile on her lips, pretending to have seen him at home that very morning, feigning to be only glad he'd arrived at her concert on time.

"How did you get him freed?" Hans-Hermann asked Klaus in German.

Klaus stuffed a handful of toasts heaped with caviar into his mouth. He made Hans-Hermann wait while he chewed. "Your girl has very convincing arguments," he said after a while. "I'm glad she used them on me."

Hans-Hermann stared at him. He couldn't have missed the hint in what Klaus had said.

How lucky for Yvonne that Jules didn't understand German. Trapped between Klaus and Hans-Hermann, he sized up the plates of amuse-gueules before his gaze returned to the Gestapo man. "What about Charles-Antoine? We got separated after the transfer to Drancy."

Klaus licked his fingers. "By now I expect him to arrive in Auschwitz," he said in slow and heavily accented French. "Fresh air of labor camp in Poland will do wonder for his health."

"He's not suited for labor," Yvonne said.

"We'll see if our men decide same when he gets there," Klaus said. He placed his fat hand on Yvonne's back. She willed herself not to step away from him.

Jules saw Klaus's hand and stalked to the back of the room.

Hans-Hermann squeezed Yvonne's forearm. She couldn't meet his gaze.

"She did exactly what you think she did," Klaus said in German. "Unsurprisingly, I won the comparison hands down."

The vein on Hans-Hermann's neck throbbed. Yvonne should've felt sorry for him, but he wasn't a much better person than Klaus. He'd just been glad to have a pretty woman on his arm.

"Of course, we'll keep the apartment," Klaus said. "And the car. Your chauffeur is better than mine, and the car more recent."

Hans-Hermann stood still for several seconds, nostrils flaring. Then he turned on his heels and slammed the front door behind him.

Henri indicated to Yvonne it was time for the concert to start. She took her spot by the piano, afraid her legs would give out from under her. Could she make Klaus lose interest in her and torment someone else? Jules lingered by the exit, behind the last row of seats. He looked so sick it would've been easy to believe he had a terminal disease. Madeleine joined him.

The conversations quieted down. Yvonne gave Henri his cue. At least, at the opera house the auditorium was dark when she stepped onstage so she didn't have to look at a sea of gray-green uniforms. The sight now made her skin crawl. But if she kept her eyes on the back wall of the German Institute, she could forget whom she was singing to.

Jules stared at all the paintings around him—anywhere but at Yvonne—while Yvonne electrified the audience with her rendition of Brünnhilde, *die Marschallin*, and *Faust*'s Marguerite. Now that her son was safe, she could express her desolation at her own fate. Klaus nodded, like someone who'd just bought a racehorse and received proof at the first race he'd purchased the right one.

After taking a sip of water, Yvonne sang "Mild und leise" from *Tristan und Isolde* and "Ho-jo-to-ho" from *Die Walküre*. Audience members surrounded her when the applause died down. A group of Nazi officers elbowed a lady wearing small, round glasses and a gentleman with a top hat who'd been gushing to Yvonne about her performance out of the way. Almost hidden from Yvonne by the throng of her admirers, Jules said something to Madeleine. She took a good look at him, lips half-open. Well-wishers crowded Yvonne's field of vision. For a moment, she lost sight of her son. Klaus planted himself by Yvonne's side and nodded thanks as if the compliments were aimed at him. When Yvonne got another glimpse of Jules, Madeleine was whispering something to him and sliding her ruby bracelet off her wrist. After a pause, she slipped it into Jules's palm.

A wave of fury overwhelmed Yvonne. She'd barely managed to get Jules released—and now she was stuck with a Gestapo man—but Madeleine was already agitating to get him in trouble. To whom would Yvonne beg for mercy if Jules was arrested another time?

When Yvonne looked again, Madeleine was standing alone. Yvonne's anger simmered into a slow-burning fire. Perhaps Jules had wandered into the next room to check the artwork or find a plate of food. Yvonne forced herself to laugh with the guests. They'd seen her in *Tristan und Isolde*, they said, when the Berlin Staatsoper had traveled to Paris the previous year and she'd reprised her role opposite Max Lorenz. Other admirers had bought tickets for the upcoming season opener. Yvonne as Brünnhilde! They couldn't wait.

Finally, everyone who'd sought to praise Yvonne had done so, but Jules still hadn't returned. The hired help was piling dirty tablecloths. The institute director brought out one last tray of food for the artists. Henri chewed on a toast of caviar while the director pontificated about the recital. Madeleine headed to the coat check.

Yvonne caught up with her. "Where's Jules?"

"He left," Madeleine said.

"What did you ask him to do? I saw you give him your bracelet."

Madeleine glanced at Henri, but he was too far away to overhear. "I didn't ask him anything. He needs money for where he's going."

What did she mean, where he was going?

"He's going to join the Free French," Madeleine said under her breath. "Gone, now."

One second Yvonne was standing, and the next she was slumped on a chair and Madeleine was waving a fan into her face. Klaus had taken advantage of the commotion to eat more caviar. The institute director handed Yvonne a glass of water. Yvonne didn't want water but took the glass nonetheless because everyone was staring at her.

"The heat," she said.

She repeated Madeleine's words in her mind. Even with the United States and the Soviet Union at war against Germany, the Allied chances of victory remained nil, as far as she could tell. The Germans had routed the Soviets at Kharkov. They'd also burnt the town of Lidice after Czech paratroopers had murdered SS Reinhard Heydrich. They would crush the Free French, and Jules with them.

Klaus, having eaten all the remaining toast, strolled toward Yvonne as if he had all the time in the world.

"Where is your precious son?" He grabbed her by the elbow and wiped his fingers on her sleeve.

Yvonne dabbed her forehead with a handkerchief. She couldn't lose her wits now, or she'd be dead. "He left. I told him to go find another place to live. I'm tired of his antics."

"Wise choice," Klaus said.

He wrapped his arm around Yvonne's waist. Every inch of his skin touching hers through his clothes felt like a red-hot poker scarring her. Yvonne stared straight ahead, toward the Grosser Mercedes blocking traffic on the avenue d'Iéna. What would her neighbors on the quay Voltaire think when they saw her with yet another German officer? But then, what they'd think was the least of her problems. What Klaus would do if he became angry with her—if he learned she'd lied, or he found out about Jules going to the Free French—terrified her. The Gestapo man pushed her forward.

Klaus smirked when Yvonne scooted inside the car. She was trapped now. He pressed his disgusting little fingers on her knee before Rolf, seemingly unfazed by Hans-Hermann's change in fortune, turned on the ignition. Yvonne clenched her teeth. By the time they'd reached Pont Alexandre III, extravagant in its art-nouveau style replete with cherubs and winged horses, Klaus had moved his hand under Yvonne's dress and up her thigh. She dug her fingernails into the armrest, shocked he wouldn't even wait until they were alone. She still wouldn't look at him. He said something in German that sounded like a taunt. It was barely a ten-minute drive along the quays, but it felt longer than a bad production of the entire *Ring* cycle. When they reached Yvonne's building, Klaus stepped out from his side of the car as if nothing had happened. Yvonne pulled her dress down, her knees shaking. They waited for the elevator cab in silence. Klaus glanced left and right, his thumbs hooked in his belt, looking pleased by his new residence. At last, the elevator cab hoisted them to the top floor.

Klaus whistled when he stepped into the apartment. "Hans has good taste."

"I'll check that Jules really is gone," Yvonne said.

In his room, a shirt was thrown over the back of a chair. Shoes were scattered around the bed. It seemed Jules could return at any moment. But the duffel bag he'd brought back from the war was missing, as were a handful of clothes. On the bookshelves, a gap had been left where Paul's first collection of poems had been filed. Paul had autographed it for him when Jules was a boy. Yvonne's heart broke into tiny pieces.

"If he's gone, he didn't bother packing his things with him," Klaus said behind her.

"He's gone all right." Yvonne refused to let him into Jules's room. "Would you like something to drink?"

Klaus tapped her on her buttocks. "I could use nightcap before I make you sing." He laughed at his own wit. "I bet Hans keep bottle of Jägermeister somewhere."

"I'm afraid I only have red wine, but it's the best vintage," Yvonne said.

In the kitchen, she grabbed the bottle of cheap Merlot she used to prepare beef stews and returned to the living room with two full glasses of wine. Klaus was inspecting the bookshelves. Why did he bother? Yvonne was sure he couldn't distinguish a Goncourt Prize winner from a romance novelist. She put *Götterdämmerung* on the Victrola. Rosa Ponselle belted out "Starke Scheite schichtet mir dort." She was good, but Yvonne sang better.

Klaus took a sip of wine and smacked his lips together. "Best vintage, uh?" he said after a while.

Yvonne nodded feebly, sensing a trap.

Klaus inspected the label on the bottle. "Cooking wine. Think I couldn't tell?"

"It was the best wine we drank at home when I was a girl," Yvonne lied. "My mother always said it was—"

"Spare me your drivel," Klaus said. He placed a cigarette between his teeth, pulled out his lighter, lit the cigarette, took a puff. Perhaps he wouldn't get any angrier than that.

Yvonne motioned toward the Victrola, but he grabbed her by the elbow and twisted her arm behind her back. She knew better than to shriek or to let him see it was painful.

"Don't you ever lie to my face again," Klaus said. He inhaled sharply with the cigarette still dangling from his lips and, while the tip was glowing red, took it between his index and forefinger and crushed it against Yvonne's forearm. Yvonne recoiled, but he held her fast. At first, she was too stunned to shriek, and then she realized she shouldn't shriek no matter what, because he would never stop tormenting her if she didn't hold strong now.

She started counting in her head, slowly, while he kept pressing the cigarette against her arm. After she reached eight, Klaus let go of her. "You'd better come up with a good excuse for this scar when you wear short-sleeved dresses for your concerts," he said.

Yvonne forced herself not to look at the wound, although she wanted to run to the kitchen and put some ice on it.

"It's always good to have a distinguishing feature," Klaus said. "This way if someone finds you at the bottom of a dumpster, they'll have a greater chance of identifying you."

Such foresight, Yvonne wanted to scoff, but kept her mouth shut.

Klaus took a long gulp of the cooking wine without even pouring it into a glass.

"You should go on tour all over France. Be an example for your people. They've got to see good things happen to those who cooperate with us."

Yvonne's fingers were cold enough that the pain in her shoulder decreased a little when she pressed them against her burn. "Only what happens in Paris matters," she said. She had no interest in becoming the face of collaboration with the Nazis.

Ponselle negotiated a difficult passage with brio. Klaus didn't seem to hear the music.

"Aren't your parents in Dijon?" he asked.

A shiver went down Yvonne's spine. Gestapo men kept themselves well informed for one reason only.

"I don't get along with them," Yvonne said.

Maybe he also knew her parents had refused to travel to Paris since the Occupation had begun, even after she'd sent them tickets to hear her sing. Her father claimed the pharmacy kept him too busy and he couldn't spare her mother, who worked behind the counter. Yvonne had a good idea of what they'd think of Klaus.

"You can sing for them anyway," Klaus said.

Yvonne refilled her glass with wine. "I'm needed here." She didn't like the turn the conversation was taking.

"Only a few performances. We'll send you to Lille, Nantes, Strasbourg. And Dijon, naturally. People will work with us after they see the good we did to your career." He kissed her on the neck. "I'll make you sing right here. Give you the extra practice."

Klaus unbuttoned her dress while the record played on the Victrola. Yvonne stared at the bookshelves, ready to pretend he wasn't about to crawl on top of her.

"Look at me," Klaus said sharply.

A wave of blind anger washed over Yvonne, because he wouldn't let her ignore him. "I'm only going to Dijon if Charles-Antoine is released," she said while he pushed his weight against her. "I'll cover myself with ridicule if he's not there to help me practice. I'll return in triumph or not at all."

"It's too late for him," Klaus said. They were lying naked on the couch now. He rubbed his hairy chest against her breasts. Yvonne tried not to squirm.

"Then I won't sing," she said.

Klaus brought his face closer to her so that she didn't see anything but his sweaty forehead and the big pores on his nose while he was enjoying himself. "I suggest you do what you're told."

Eighteen

December 1942

The brakes of the Grosser Mercedes squealed when the car pulled over in front of the Grand Hôtel La Cloche in Dijon, scraping its tires against the curb before coming to a halt in front of a snowbank. The five-story stone building at the edge of the historic district exuded—what was the word?—respectability in a Haussmann style worthy of Paris: rows of long rectangular windows, wrought-iron railings in front of each balcony, a mansard roof, decorative moldings. The lamps between the hotel windows would've lit the outside of the hotel from top to bottom if the war hadn't imposed a blackout over the city. The city hadn't changed at all since Yvonne had been there last, and she couldn't even remember when that was. A trio of swastika banners flapped over the building's entrance. Straight ahead, past the arch of Porte Guillaume, the rue de la Liberté stretched over cobblestones to the Grand Théâtre, where Yvonne would sing the following day. She wished she'd come back to Dijon under different circumstances, but she'd had no say in the matter.

Klaus bolted out of the car.

"What idiot hits the curb in a car of mine?" His breath made little circles in front of his mouth when he talked. He inspected the damage to the hubcaps and, opening the driver's door, smacked Rolf across the face. "Don't drive fast if you don't know how to do it," he said in German. "Don't drive at all! Get a job as janitor at the embassy when you return to Paris! That'd be a better match for your skills."

He pulled Rolf out of the Grosser Mercedes and took the keys away from him. "You're taking the train back. Or you can hitchhike. Whatever you prefer. I'll get a new chauffeur. No one who scratches my car remains in my service."

Everyone on the street was glancing at them now, trying not to stare. Yvonne buttoned up her coat and pulled on her gloves. She always felt safer when she put layers of clothes between her and Klaus. She couldn't bring herself to look at him directly in case that'd provoke his latest outburst, of which he'd had many, but she cast a side glance at Rolf. At least he wasn't a French boy, wondering if he could take the subway or if he'd be caught in a roundup to avenge one Nazi officer who'd been grazed with a bullet and get executed the next morning with twenty other innocent men.

Rolf shivered in the snow, humiliated in front of the passersby. He didn't even look nineteen anymore. He looked like he'd enlisted underage, a German version of Jules but one indulged by a prominent father who'd used his connections to keep him out of harm's way.

"You must've been a race car driver in a previous life to have made us arrive on time," Yvonne said to Rolf while Klaus, apoplectic, inspected the damage. "And race car drivers damage their car every so often."

The expression on Rolf's face softened. They'd left Paris late because Klaus had stayed at the Gestapo headquarters long past their planned departure time. Yvonne suspected he'd interrogated prisoners. He'd been in a foul mood for weeks because the Battle of Stalingrad wasn't going well. Soviet troops had encircled the Sixth Army back in November, and after the Axis defeat in North Africa and the scuttling of the French fleet in Toulon to avoid falling into the hands of the Germans, a lot depended on the Soviet front. Klaus hungered for mass arrests that would show the Third Reich's grip on Paris. To obtain arrests, he needed confessions.

The Grosser Mercedes had turned onto the quay Voltaire at five o'clock. Klaus had told Rolf, "The dinner in Dijon starts at seven." It was normally a two-and-a-half-hour drive, closer to three this time of year, because snow in the east made the roads slippery. But the highway had been empty due to the rationing of gasoline, and Rolf had kept his foot pressed on the accelerator the whole time. The faster he drove, the happier Klaus seemed, until Rolf scraped the hubcaps against the curb.

The Peugeot that had followed the Mercedes all the way from Paris stopped behind them. Madeleine got out first, a little wobbly on her feet after the high-speed drive. Henri came out next, looking green.

"Good thing the performance isn't until tomorrow afternoon," Madeleine said. "It'll take the whole night for my stomach to get out of my throat."

A billboard caught Yvonne's attention. *Yvonne Chevallier in Die Walküre—sold out!* She smiled.

"They should've made your name even bigger," Klaus said.

Madeleine strolled by the billboard, where her name appeared fifth, her head resolutely turned the other way, as if she hadn't noticed the slight. Instead, she scowled at the line of small shops by the hotel and said to Yvonne, "I can understand why you left."

She climbed the steps to the front door in a bright-red gown and matching stilettos that were completely out of place for the season but guaranteed that everyone would notice her from a hundred yards away. An elderly couple on the threshold stepped aside to let her pass.

Yvonne felt a tug in her heart. Here they were, her parents, standing awkwardly a few feet away from her, waiting to enter the hotel in her hometown where a reception would be given in her honor: a short man who'd lost twenty pounds despite the extra ration cards Yvonne had secured for him (to whom had he given them? or had he thrown them away?) and a tall, blonde woman with a wrinkled face but the bearing of a dancer, wearing the Marie-Louise Bruyère dress Yvonne had sent her. And Yvonne, in front of them, looking like a movie star, but with a Grosser Mercedes and a Nazi officer right in her back.

Yvonne expected her mother, Janine, to give her a hug, but instead, Janine gave her a quick peck on the cheek and smiled the same smile she used to give her great-aunt when she came to visit: the corners of her mouth moved up but her eyes remained cold.

Her father, Christian, gave her a nod in lieu of a hello. He'd been the more forgiving of the two when Yvonne had fallen pregnant with Jules out of wedlock, but now he didn't say a word, didn't look impressed by his daughter at all. He looked like he pitied her, in fact, and he didn't even know Jules had left her to join the Free French. Yvonne had hoped to return to her hometown in triumph, but now she was embarrassed it'd only been possible because she'd hitched her star to the Nazis. No one knew she had any talent at all. No one knew either that her arms and shoulders were covered with cigarette burns. Once, Klaus had placed the cigarette too close to her hair, and a strand had withered and crackled under the heat. Yet to save Jules, Yvonne would've done it all again in a heartbeat.

Ladies in evening gowns from many seasons ago—fabric had become rationed early on when Germans had settled in—and bedecked in family jewels strolled past on the arms of their tuxedoed husbands. They strove mightily to outshine each other and yet looked hopelessly provincial in their dowdy dresses. These were the women Yvonne had spent years hoping to impress.

Christian looked behind Yvonne's shoulder. "Didn't Jules come with you?"

"He had urgent things to do for school," Yvonne said, uneasy about the lie that had been dragging on for months. She hadn't written her parents with the news because she'd been concerned the Germans might be opening her mail, and now plenty of them were within earshot, so she couldn't be truthful either.

"He never writes us," Christian said. "Quite a grandson we have."

They went inside. The small chandeliers and plain mirrors of the Grand Hôtel La Cloche were quaint compared to those in the Ritz in Paris, but the abundance of roses, tulips, and lilies in the lobby, far out of season, drew attention away from the surroundings.

Guests admired the view of the snow-covered Darcy gardens when they trickled into the hotel ballroom. Yvonne wished she could've admired it with them. She felt scared all the time now when Klaus was nearby, even when she'd put enough ointment on her shoulders that the recent cigarette burns didn't sting. She could tell from Klaus's behavior that Hitler was furious he hadn't won the war yet. Klaus was furious when Hitler was furious, and that meant nothing good for her.

The dinner attendees strolled by round tables ornamented with enormous winter bouquets of orchids and carnations, each set up for eight dinner guests. Yvonne realized the bouquets were enormous because she was being treated as a special guest. Silverware for a five-course meal gleamed under the light. Five, not three—had she become the star of Dijon? She so hungered for compliments from French people, but especially from those in her hometown. A chamber orchestra played the piano rendition of *Tannhäuser*'s overture in the corner. It was such a pleasing sight. Yvonne hadn't expected to be so moved, but tears were coming to her eyes.

She found her name next to the mayor's at the lead table, front and center. Her parents had been assigned seats on the other side of the same table. This was notable. Dijon's high society consisted of about sixty families, who always ran into each other and ensured no one else was admitted into the inner circle, and Christian and Janine hadn't made the cut. But now Yvonne's gown and pearl necklace outshone those of the most pretentious matrons examining place cards in the ballroom. And this evening, Christian and Janine were seated at the mayor's table.

Next to Klaus's empty chair, two men in Gestapo uniforms, one higher ranking than the other, were talking to each other in low voices. Yvonne guessed one was the head of the Gestapo in Dijon and the other one his underling. She wasn't sure where Klaus had gone and didn't care to find out. He could skip the dinner as far as she was concerned. Between the Gestapo officers and her parents, a tall man who wore steel-rimmed glasses introduced himself as the presiding judge of the local tribunal, then introduced his wife. Yvonne's parents looked awed by the company around them, although none of the wealthy people made conversation with them.

At the next table, Madeleine gestured to the waiter to bring her a bottle of Burgundy. Her neighbor was probably boring her. All the people from Dijon looked dull to Yvonne, and most likely even more so to Madeleine. That would make Madeleine want to drink.

Klaus arrived at last. The anger on his face barely faded when the two Gestapo officers, jumping to their feet, threw their arms up in the air to greet him. Grand guignols, all of them, but Yvonne made sure not to laugh. Klaus sat down, acknowledged Yvonne, scanned the room (was Yvonne imagining things, or did his gaze linger on Henri and Madeleine?), and then waved at the waiter. "Do you have beer? It's going to be a long evening."

Already the mayor was stepping to the podium. "Today we are gathered to honor one of our own, the great Yvonne Chevallier, who has had such a distinguished career at the Paris Opera and inspired so many little girls here in Dijon."

The last bit was an obvious lie, but Yvonne didn't mind her parents hearing it.

The mayor held up a velvet cushion. A key gleamed in the middle. "Therefore, it is our great pleasure to give Madame Chevallier the key to our city."

Yvonne's parents gasped. She hadn't warned them, preferring the gift to be a surprise. Did they remember as vividly as she did their neighbors' slights when Jules was born? Attendees applauded a long time, whether they liked Yvonne and her family or not. It was part of a performance, Yvonne guessed. But to her, the clapping was balm to an old wound. She pushed back her chair and strutted toward the podium for her acceptance speech, looking happy and carefree and definitely not caring about her former neighbors' approval.

Yvonne talked about the voice teachers she'd had as a girl in Dijon, all of them now retired and most of them dead, except for one, Marie-Joséphine, who cried in the back, and about the success those teachers had made possible for her later on. She talked about growing up in the city and how it'd helped her stay focused on her craft. She left out all the reasons why she'd wanted to escape, but in the end she didn't lie: the foundations she'd laid in Dijon had helped her succeed in Paris. The way she said it, everyone in the audience felt they'd played a role in her career.

When Yvonne returned to the table, she handed her father the cushion with the key. Christian held it as if it were made of glass. Janine stroked it, her mouth round with astonishment. They were working-class people who'd come from nothing. They wouldn't get invited to a dinner with the mayor a second time. Yvonne held herself as if she were receiving much-overdue respect from the room, although she wasn't sure she did. Maybe the mayor just wanted to ingratiate himself with Klaus.

The meal stretched on for two hours, most of which Klaus spent in conversation with his Gestapo colleagues. Yvonne felt sick from the sheer amount of perfume the judge's wife was wearing, but she stayed on her chair for as long as Klaus talked to the other Nazi men. No one dared leave before them, until Madeleine yawned and found her way to the door. She could get away with gestures like this. Yvonne surely couldn't. Klaus finished off his wine in one gulp and finally gave her the signal to head upstairs. Yvonne kissed her parents good-night.

"I'll see you tomorrow at the performance," she said.

"We're not sure we'll be able to make it," her father said. "Quite a few people fell ill during the last snowstorm, and they all need medication. If we can fill all the orders in the morning, then we'll come."

Yvonne tried to hide her disappointment, but she must not have done a good job at it, because Janine said, "We'll make an effort."

Yvonne nodded and hurried to catch up with Klaus.

He walked slowly to the elevator, as if he were determined to give every guest one last chance to watch them before they retired for the night: the ugly, fat, short Gestapo man who could condemn anyone to death in a second and, on his arm, the French soprano, beautiful and famous, who'd serve as his trophy until he tired of her. They made their way upstairs. The click of the door to the presidential suite closing behind them was as sharp as the safety being removed on a Luger pistol. Yvonne sensed the danger immediately.

"Now, where is the son of yours?" Klaus said from behind her. But Jules's whereabouts couldn't be what preoccupied him so. "Clearly, he isn't living in Dijon like you said, and you must've heard of him by now. Sons don't abandon their mother."

Yvonne pressed herself against the flowery wallpaper. "He hasn't spoken to me in months."

"I question the wisdom of you lying to me so openly," Klaus said, and lit up a cigarette. He gave Yvonne a long, cold stare. If it hadn't been her son they were talking about, Yvonne would've told him everything on the spot to avoid another scar. They were becoming difficult to hide.

"I assumed he'd returned to Dijon, but for all I know, he might still be in Paris," Yvonne said.

"Living on what money?"

"Maybe he gives piano lessons." Yvonne slid along the wall away from Klaus. "Maybe he unloads trucks at the Halles market. It's a mystery to me."

"Just my luck, picking the Frenchwoman with the traitor son." Klaus shoved her onto the sitting chair and slapped her so hard Yvonne felt her neck might snap. Even when he laid hands on her, his actions showed razor-sharp focus, as if he'd decided beforehand the number of blows he'd administer and was counting them as he went.

Yvonne whimpered.

"The apple never falls far from the tree," Klaus said. "Maybe you're a traitor like him."

"When have I cared about politics?" Yvonne said, slumped on the chair. She tried to get up, but Klaus pushed her against the sideboard in the nonchalant way others discarded trash bags into dumpsters.

"I should've had him shipped east," Klaus said. "I won't make that mistake twice." Between his index and forefinger, the ash of the cigarette was growing perilously long.

Yvonne coughed. "He won't give you any reason to arrest him again," she said.

Klaus wrapped his hand around her throat and squeezed tightly. "He pretended to be a Jew, and now he's disappeared. Maybe I should send your parents east until I find him."

Yvonne flailed her arms to defend herself with the vase full of flowers, just out of her reach, but only managed to knock it off the table. It shattered on the floor, spilling water and flowers all over the rug.

"I'll teach you to lie to me," Klaus said. The ash scattered on Yvonne's cheek. The tip of the cigarette glowed when Klaus inhaled. It was only an inch away from Yvonne's face. What makeup could even hide such a scar? Yvonne struggled harder to free herself, but that only made Klaus smile and aim his cigarette more pointedly at her cheekbone. Not her face, Lord, not her face.

Yvonne screamed all her hatred of him in one long, guttural sound.

The suite door swung open and a figure stepped in. Madeleine didn't even blink at the sight of Klaus holding a lit cigarette up to Yvonne's face, tip facing her.

"Henri has urgent questions about Brünnhilde's aria in the second act," Madeleine said.

Klaus stared at Madeleine incredulously.

"It is very important for Henri," Madeleine said. "He was hoping that Yvonne would clarify a few things for him. May I borrow her for a minute?"

At last Klaus lowered his cigarette. "My dear Frau Moreau, you and I will have a word when we are back in Paris." He made a steady smile at Madeleine, so cold it felt threatening. Madeleine, struggling not to lose her wit now, took Yvonne by the hand and pulled her out of the room, her eyes on Klaus the whole time, as if staring at the enemy would keep him at bay.

She brought Yvonne to her own room next door. Henri was not there.

"He's having drinks at the hotel bar with some of the town notables," Madeleine said. "They're trying to convince him to conduct the Dijon Orchestra next season. He'll never agree to it, but he likes that they're fawning over him."

Yvonne sat down on the sitting chair, an exact replica of the one in the presidential suite, although Madeleine's room was smaller and the decorations less expensive. She touched her throat. "Do you have ice?"

Madeleine brought her ice cubes. "Hopefully he'll fall asleep soon."

"Not a chance," Yvonne said. "I just hope he'll be in a better mood when I return." She checked her face and seemed relieved Klaus hadn't injured her.

"Why does he want to talk to me?" Madeleine asked.

"He says odd things sometimes. He likes to throw people off. I wouldn't read too much into it."

"He seems a bit unhinged," Madeleine said.

Yvonne nodded. "I can't say I like him much."

Madeleine hesitated, then took her chance. "You'd do so much for France if you shared what he does with people who can take action about it." She spoke in a low voice, probably so she could argue that Yvonne had misheard her if her suggestion got her into trouble.

Yvonne had thought the same thing before. "I've looked through his pockets, but whatever he brings home stays locked in his satchel, and he never makes phone calls when I'm nearby," she finally said. "He didn't reach the rank he's at by being naïve."

"If he didn't take you seriously, he wouldn't be so cautious around you," Madeleine said.

That seemed to please Yvonne. Then she collected herself, dropped the melting ice cubes in the sink, and returned to the presidential suite where Klaus was waiting for her.

❦

Applause roared through the Grand Théâtre when Yvonne, exhausted after the five-hour-long performance, stumbled out of the wings for the curtain calls. The auditorium seated six hundred spectators, but they made the noise of six thousand, hollering "Brava!" and clapping so hard it sounded like the walls were crumbling down. Yvonne shielded her eyes from the spotlights and peered into the darkness in front of her. Was the audience giving her a standing ovation? Her knees felt weak. She hadn't expected her triumph in Dijon to move her so. She raised her hand at the center box, where her parents sat next to Klaus. She also saluted the left- and right-hand boxes, where faded gold fixtures glittered in the light from the stage; and the parterre, where management had added wooden chairs next to the threadbare velvet seats to accommodate more attendees; and the dress circle; and the family circle; and the boxes again; and yet the applause didn't dwindle. Another wave of "Brava!" erupted, followed by a couple of "Bravi!" Madeleine had just joined her onstage. Yvonne hadn't expected the people of Dijon to have learned how to conjugate the feminine and plural forms of "Bravo!" in her absence. Madeleine and Yvonne bowed side by side. The clamor that erupted threatened to bring down the chandeliers.

A dark-haired woman about twenty-five years of age, in a buttoned-up dress with flouncy sleeves, brought out bouquets of roses for the artists. She smiled brightly at Yvonne when she handed her the flowers, baring her gums. The rest of the cast lined up on the edge of the stage: Siegmund and Siegfried and Hunding and Wotan and Fricka and Gerhilde and Orlinde and Waltraute and five more Valkyries, saluting in unison. Yvonne fetched Henri out of the wings. They all bowed one more time, sharing the pride of this performance they'd taken part in. Yvonne wished the moment would never end.

At last, the stage manager lowered the curtain. The cast's smiles vanished when the gold tassels touched the ground. Madeleine clasped her bouquet of flowers and trotted out while the rest of the group spilled into the wings.

Henri wiped his forehead with his silk handkerchief. "They sure have better taste than I expected before coming here."

Yvonne returned to her dressing room, a small, dark space the size of Raymond's desk, barely big enough for her to stretch her arms without touching the walls. How fiercely she'd hoped to sing in the Grand Théâtre when she was young, and how tiny and drab the building appeared now. The staffer who'd offered her the flowers burst in with half a dozen more bouquets, reading the names on the cards that accompanied them while Yvonne changed for the reception behind a folding screen. On the tiny cards, the mayor, the chairman of the chamber of commerce, the presiding judge of the court of appeals all enthused at her success. She'd save the cards for her parents.

Yvonne clasped a pearl necklace around her neck, hesitated in adding a silk scarf, decided it'd needlessly cover the pearls. From her dressing room, the foyer was only a few moments' walk away. Madeleine, brandishing a glass of Louis Roederer champagne, was already holding court at the center of the room. She even seemed willing to revise her opinion of France outside the capital and consider the possibility that one might find here, on occasion, opera amateurs just as thoughtful as the ones in Paris. Then the well-wishers rushed to greet Yvonne, and Madeleine looked as if no word in the entire French language would accurately describe the contempt she felt for the provinces. This made Yvonne smile.

The little ladies of Dijon showered Yvonne with praise, blurting out words like "entranced" and "mesmerized." They repeated them at will although they might not have understood one thing about the performance. Yvonne's parents huddled with another couple near the bust of local opera composer Jean-Philippe Rameau. So they'd come after all. Yvonne smiled to herself. Only when she drew closer did she recognize Paul, who appeared sullen and withdrawn. The woman standing next to him in a plain woolen dress must be his second wife, Elisabeth. She looked mousy, bland. Of her Yvonne only knew that she taught at the Lycée Carnot like Paul, but mathematics instead of French.

When they noticed her walking toward them, Elisabeth and Paul, without even exchanging a glance, pressed themselves against each other, as if it were of the utmost importance to show a united front to the enemy. Yvonne smiled harder, but not as hard as Elisabeth now. Christian looked behind his shoulder and gulped down his drink when he recognized his daughter.

"What a spell you cast over the audience," Elisabeth said. "I never thought opera could keep me on the edge of my seat for so long."

Something behind Yvonne caught Elisabeth's attention. Paul leaned closer. Yvonne braced herself for what'd come next.

Klaus wrapped his arm around her waist. "She was stupendous, wasn't she? My little opera star."

That was what he liked to call her when he was having his way with her. Yvonne forced herself to stay still.

Paul couldn't take his eyes off Klaus's hand. Yvonne had told her parents a German officer would accompany her to Dijon, but she hadn't warned Paul, since she hadn't known he'd attend her performance.

Then, as quickly as Klaus had arrived, he let go of Yvonne and crossed the foyer to talk with the other Nazi officers. Paul handed his flute of champagne, still about full, to a waiter picking up empty glasses and took a wide step toward the exit.

Yvonne pulled him back. "Jules told the police he was Jewish during the Vél d'Hiv. He would've been sent east if Klaus hadn't intervened."

"First he volunteers for the war, then he pretends he's Jewish, and now he's joined the Free French," Paul said. "Don't you see the link with the company you keep?"

Christian and Janine gasped at the same time. This wasn't the way Yvonne had expected them to find out. How did Paul know? Jules must've written him when he'd left, in case he didn't come back.

"Do you realize what you've done?" Paul asked Yvonne. His voice cracked like a whip. "You can't up this one, short of sleeping with Hitler."

Yvonne dropped her glass, spilling champagne over her dress. She dabbed the stain with a napkin to no avail.

"I'll go and fetch my scarf," she said, relieved to have an excuse to flee Paul's anger.

She hurried down to the side door that led backstage and barged into her dressing room, which was fragrant with roses of all colors. The young woman who'd brought her the flowers was drawing a large *V* sign on the mirror with her lipstick. V for victory, and it was unlikely she meant it for the *Boches*.

Yvonne stopped on her heels. The woman jumped back.

Military boots echoed in the hallway. Klaus must've noticed Yvonne running out of the party. She grabbed her scarf from the back of the chair, dragged the staffer out of the room, and shut the door.

"How many times do I have to tell you I need water for those roses?" she asked in a shrill voice. "Hurry. We're leaving for Paris soon, and I want to bring them home."

The young woman, looking paler than Rigoletto after realizing he'd caused his daughter's death, nodded twice and turned 180 degrees on her toes.

Yvonne tied the scarf around her shoulders, hiding the champagne stain just as Klaus reached her side. "I don't know why her incompetence surprises me. It's Dijon, after all. If people here had any brains, they'd move to Paris." She nudged him away from her dressing room. "I'm glad I left this town. I had too much ambition for it."

She was careful to keep her face turned away from him so he wouldn't notice her shock after seeing the Allies' *V* painted in lipstick across her mirror—a warning of her future comeuppance, no doubt, once the Nazis lost. The young woman had smiled at her so warmly when she'd handed her the flowers onstage.

Yvonne and Klaus strode down the corridor in silence. Klaus had made a profession out of interrogating suspects. Surely he could guess something was on Yvonne's mind.

"Who spills champagne on such an expensive dress?" Klaus finally said. He'd paid for that dress.

Yvonne dabbed her scarf over the champagne stain to placate him, hoping it wouldn't stain the fabric.

"You're such a klutz," Klaus said, although he sounded less agitated now. Yvonne hoped everything would be fine. "But audiences adore your voice. Sing in Berlin."

For a moment, Yvonne was at a loss for words. What a death blow that'd be on her reputation, or whatever was left of it. "They'll prefer a German singer," she said.

"On the contrary. It'll be excellent for morale. We'll have you visit military bases too. You're the person our troops need."

Klaus held the door to the foyer open for her. Peals of laughter were rising from the reception. Patrons swarmed around Yvonne to congratulate her. At last, Yvonne remembered to look grateful. The little ladies elbowing each other to shake her hand smiled so broadly Yvonne could see their bottom teeth.

She talked to each of them, pretending not to know they loathed her just like the young woman did. But their smiles were fake; that was obvious to her. They didn't respect her any more than when she'd been a young mother seventeen years old.

Against the wall, Rolf was eating petits fours.

"What are you still doing here?" Klaus said to him in German. "Do you think the reception is for dimwits like you? You should be walking your way back to Paris."

Rolf stared at him and, rather than arguing, shuffled toward the exit, but not before grabbing another handful of hors d'oeuvres. Soon Klaus was distracted by the Gestapo officers surrounding him, all eager to chat with the high-ranking officer who had come from Paris.

Yvonne caught up with Rolf. "Do you have money for train fare?" she asked in German.

He did not.

Yvonne unrolled a couple of bills from her purse. "You'll have a better trip back to Paris than I will."

Rolf counted the money, his eyes wide, then said quickly without looking at her, "The boss found out about the Résistance cell at the opera house."

What Résistance cell?

"He knows the leaflets are printed on the press in the basement," Rolf said. "The ones we've been finding in public spaces all over town."

Hans-Hermann had mentioned those flyers once before, at the German Institute.

"The man he arrested this morning talked easily, after the boss pulled his fingernails," Rolf said. "He'll arrest the others himself when he's back in Paris on Monday. Frau Moreau too."

"What about her?" Yvonne asked. Madeleine was much too selfish to risk her career for honor and freedom.

"She's been distributing the flyers all over Paris," Rolf said.

Yvonne inhaled sharply. She needed a moment to take that in. Madeleine, so different from what she'd always assumed, so much more honorable too.

"Printing and distributing," Rolf said. "And she's the one who came up with the idea of going through our officers' coat pockets during performances. At least that's what the man said."

"Which man?" Yvonne asked.

Rolf moved a little closer to the exit. Nothing good would happen if Klaus realized he was still there.

"He sang in the season premiere the first year we were here. The king, I think."

An icy cold spread through Yvonne's arms. She knew exactly who he was talking about. "Amfortas."

"Aiding Résistance efforts—that's a capital offense," Rolf said. "She won't even make it to the camps. The boss will finish her off at headquarters. Well, I'd better hightail it out of here."

He touched his cap with the hand that held Yvonne's money for the train fare and bounded out of the room. A circle of well-wishers drew closer to Yvonne after he vanished. Everyone wanted to ingratiate themselves with the star, even if they despised her. She tried to think about what to do next while she exchanged polite words with sycophants. It wasn't her problem that Madeleine had gotten herself in trouble. She didn't have to help.

But Madeleine hadn't had to help her either, the previous evening at the hotel.

Yvonne gestured to Madeleine that she needed a word. She made it look like she meant to introduce her to her parents. Madeleine sighed but came closer.

"Remember that man who sang Cesare Angelotti in *Tosca* a few years back, and Amfortas in *Parsifal*?" Yvonne said.

Madeleine raised an eyebrow. She hadn't expected that question, right then, in Dijon.

"He got arrested and told Klaus you distributed flyers you helped print in the basement of the opera house," Yvonne said. "Also, something about going through officers' coats during performances."

Madeleine cocked her head to the side and blinked, and pinched her lips, and when she failed to speak after a full thirty seconds, Yvonne thought, *Lord Almighty, she's guilty of everything.*

"People have been lying about me since the beginning of time," Madeleine said at last, although the blood was rapidly draining from her face. "This is only someone's latest attempt at settling scores because I became more famous than them. Or perhaps I had an unkind word during rehearsal that they never forgave me for. Yes, I remember now. I didn't like how he sang Amfortas last time and told him so."

"I was Kundry in that production," Yvonne said. There was no other female role in *Parsifal*.

"Did I say Amfortas? Slip of the tongue. I meant Angelotti. We had strong words about the church scene in *Tosca*." Madeleine stood even straighter than usual. "Anyway, what you've heard are lies."

She waded through the crowd, unaware she didn't know how to act. Yvonne wondered how she'd escape Klaus.

❧

Klaus's car was stranded in the snowy ditch when Madeleine and Henri came across it on the way back from Dijon. Yvonne stood by the side of the roadway, bundled in her coat and scarf, stomping her feet to keep herself warm.

"Pull over," Madeleine said to Gustave.

Klaus revved up the engine to get the Mercedes back on the road. Its wheels spun, but the car did not move an inch.

Yvonne took refuge in the Peugeot. Gustave cranked up the heat.

"Go and help him," Madeleine said. She tried to sound casual, so that it wouldn't be obvious how scared she was of Klaus.

To Madeleine's surprise, Henri followed Gustave out of the car.

"He's not even injured," Yvonne said about Klaus, the disappointment in her voice obvious. "Just mad. The car has a big dent in the front bumper."

Gustave and Henri pushed the Mercedes toward the road while Klaus remained behind the steering wheel. Gustave didn't push very hard, but Henri gave it his best effort, his face red with exertion. Madeleine's gaze kept returning to Klaus. She had never expected the man who had sung Amfortas to get caught. It had seemed simple enough and not really dangerous to print those leaflets and leave them in public spaces when no one was looking. Perhaps also futile, but Madeleine had been glad to take action. How much had Klaus tortured "Amfortas" before he admitted the bit about the coat check, which had indeed been Madeleine's idea? She had been proud of doing it, and she remained proud despite her fear, but the officers had never left valuable information in their pockets.

Someone must have seen Amfortas and denounced him. He had been too brazen. That was how Madeleine had learned what he was doing, after all. She had stumbled onto him printing the leaflets when she had gone to the opera house's basement after hours to mimeograph the program of her next home recital. Dumb of him not to lock the door, even if he thought he was alone in the building. Maybe he had made a mistake again, and this time it had turned deadly. Madeleine couldn't imagine that Klaus would have let him live.

"Let's go and push the car with them," Madeleine said.

Yvonne, still in the pretty dress she had worn at the reception and holding her flowers, looked at her as if she had lost her mind.

"He won't forgive you if you stay in the car by yourself," Madeleine said. "We have to make a show of trying to help him."

Their shoes crunched in the fresh snow. Madeleine's toes felt numb almost immediately, but she still took her spot by the bumper and pretended to push. Henri was trying hardest of all.

A truck full of German soldiers pulled over to help them. The highest-ranking officer gave the Mercedes a long look.

"A dog jumped in front of the car," Madeleine said.

At the steering wheel, Klaus looked pleased by her version of events, although the snow showed no paw prints at all.

The officer directed his men to go help Gustave and Henri. "We can't let the ladies freeze," he said.

Madeleine and Yvonne returned to the Peugeot while Klaus revved the engine. The men grunted around the bumper. The car moved about a foot out of the ditch. Klaus looked noticeably happier.

"He's a sadistic bloodhound, but he does have one weakness," Yvonne said, her eyes on Klaus. "You saw that yesterday, no?"

She touched her throat, where Klaus's fingers had left slight bruises.

"He likes to beat his woman up?" Madeleine said.

"He can't stand the idea of looking bad."

Right away, Madeleine saw an opportunity.

The soldiers pushed the Mercedes back down onto the road, hollering congratulations at each other.

Madeleine rolled down the car window, ignoring the biting cold, and gestured to get the officer's attention. "Could we borrow one of your drivers for the Kriminaldirektor? His regular chauffeur is sick."

A young man volunteered to drive Klaus. He was perhaps twenty-five, a little chubby, with the most Aryan blue eyes and blond hair. Klaus got out of the driver's seat for him. He tapped on Madeleine's car window instead of getting right back into his own car.

"We still must talk, Frau Moreau. Tomorrow morning, ten o'clock? Let me know when you arrive at avenue Foch."

Madeleine pushed her back into the car seat. Her hands felt ice cold. No sound came out when she opened her mouth, so she nodded.

Yvonne joined Klaus in the Mercedes. Gustave and Henri returned to the Peugeot.

"If he doesn't love us after this," Henri said, blowing on his hands.

Madeleine could have thrown up right into the snow. "Wait to put the car in gear until they're gone," she said to Gustave. "He'll want to be first." She didn't recognize her own voice. That was what terror sounded like.

"Why does he want to talk to you?" Henri asked.

"Your guess is as good as mine," Madeleine said. And, after a moment, "I'll go and see Emile after dinner."

⁓

Emile lit up a cigarette in his study, amid books in haphazard piles. Madeleine had never met anyone who liked to read as much as he. For her, books were to be used as decoration. Recordings—that was how she judged people. The smell of the cigarette bothered her, but she was glad Emile had agreed to see her when she rang him.

"Those Jewish musicians who lost their job when the Germans came into power, what happened to them?" Madeleine asked.

"It's better if you don't ask."

"But do you know how to find them? Are they safe out of the country, or are they here?"

Emile eyed her over the curls of cigarette smoke. "What difference does it make?"

Madeleine took it to mean they were in hiding. If they had been safe elsewhere, Emile would have said so. She retrieved a small pouch from her purse and dropped its contents on the desk: a gold bracelet, a pair of diamond earrings, two pearl necklaces—jewelry Henri had given her years earlier and hopefully had forgotten about. That was what she had returned to Neuilly to fetch, under the pretense of having dinner at home before going out again.

"Sell this and use the money to help them," Madeleine said. "Maybe have an auction at Drouot. Give the money to the musicians in person. The *Boches* won't guess who it's for."

Emile stared at the pearls as if they were amber-hot coals, impossible to touch without inflicting third-degree burns on oneself. "They could figure it out."

"They're too convinced of their own superiority," Madeleine said.

"One of the musicians could get caught. He might talk. I courted trouble enough when I kept them on the payroll until the Vél d'Hiv."

Madeleine had not known that.

"How do you think they survived so long?" Emile asked. "But I had to stop after the roundup. It became too dangerous."

"So they need money now," Madeleine said.

A key jingled in the lock of the front door. Then high heels clattered down the hallway.

"That's my wife coming back from cheating on me with a general from the Wehrmacht," Emile said without any emotion.

They listened in silence while closet doors opened and closed.

"Then you really need to get even," Madeleine said. She pushed her jewelry closer to him. "I'd sell them myself, but it'd attract attention."

Emile took the earrings and the pearls in his palm as if weighing them. On the other side of the door, his wife hummed a happy tune to herself. Emile dropped the jewels into his breast pocket.

"I have a house in Normandy," Madeleine said. "Send them over there. They can say they're the new housekeepers." Her mother wouldn't tell. "Catholic eight generations through, just doing me a favor."

⁊⸻⁊

The guard let Madeleine into a small, dark room in the basement of Gestapo headquarters. It had a long table, lit by a lightbulb hanging from a cord, and two chairs on either side. Klaus occupied one of them. Madeleine sat down on the other. The cement floor was marked with dark stains. Blood, probably. Madeleine did not look at those stains for long for fear she would lose her composure. Her stomach was tied in knots. She kept her hands under the table so that Klaus would not see them shake. Her mouth was dry. She used the old opera trick of biting the insides of her cheeks to create saliva. The guard stationed himself by the door. In the distance, someone screamed. Madeleine pressed the heels of her shoes hard into the ground. She had expected screams in the building, but it wasn't the same as actually hearing them. She could not make a mistake now.

Klaus browsed through his notes. "My dear Frau Moreau, someone has been saying troubling things about you."

"I've been dealing with calumnies my whole career," Madeleine said.

Her voice sounded assured enough. It was a bit higher than normal, but Klaus hadn't talked to her enough before to notice that. She had the voice of someone whose conscience was clear, didn't she? That morning she had made sure to look the part too, applying a thick coat of foundation and dusting her cheeks with rouge, ready for the performance of her career. It was not the real Madeleine sitting in front of Klaus. The real Madeleine would have been racked with anguish, or about to say something she would regret. But the fake Madeleine was innocent and determined to convince Klaus of it.

"Those things they're saying aren't related to your career," Klaus said. "Rather, they're about your other activities."

He gave her an even look.

But unless he had a picture of Madeleine dropping off flyers, he couldn't prove a thing. If "Amfortas" had denounced her by that time, Klaus would have handcuffed her immediately. Or would he? He had wanted his girlfriend to shine in *Die Walküre*. That required the performance to be a success. Which, in turn, required Madeleine to sing Sieglinde in Dijon.

"You mean, like helping a fellow tenor go to Marseilles? He needed fresh air. Paris was bad for him."

"Your activities in the basement of the opera house, and throughout Paris."

Madeleine provided Klaus with her best frown. "What do you think I'd do in the basement of the opera house? I spend most of my time at home, practicing for a record I hope to make with Pathé. Ariadne in *Ariadne auf Naxos*, Senta in *The Flying Dutchman*, and Isolde." She hoped the list of names would bore Klaus and dull his interrogation skills.

Klaus did not say a word. Maybe he guessed what she was doing. She was pushing her luck. But the fake Madeleine stayed on the Nazis' good side.

"I'm too busy to bother with anything besides opera," Madeleine said.

Klaus let a moment pass and then lined photographs in front of her, methodically, the way card dealers laid cards on a casino table. At first, Madeleine didn't understand what she was looking at. Then she recognized a swollen face caked in blood. Her stomach twisted. It was the man who had sung Amfortas. In her mind she had known he was dead from the moment Yvonne had warned her, but she had not expected the *Boches* to take pictures of his corpse. He had suffered a slow and agonizing death. She had known that too, but there was a difference between knowing something and seeing the proof.

"He was in so much pain at the end he begged us to shoot him," Klaus said. "We said we would if he told us who worked with him."

Madeleine kept her eyes on a corner of the pictures—not the body itself but a patch of the floor that had not been splattered with blood—so that she could remain calm.

"He gave your name," Klaus said.

She wished she had her red fan from Ceylon so she could snap it open. "And doing what? Clearly, he said the most outrageous things to see if you'd believe him."

"After a certain level of pain, the brain is no longer capable of telling lies," Klaus said. "He said you were distributing flyers with him, trying to set the population against us. He also said you instructed the girl at the coat check of the opera house to go through the pockets of our men's uniforms."

"I don't even know who the girl at the coat check is," Madeleine said. "It'd be beneath me to strike a conversation with her. I know my place in the social order in Paris." This was exactly why she had done it, to the girl's astonishment.

Klaus removed the pictures, so she had no choice but to raise her gaze to his.

"The girl at the coat check confirmed it," Klaus said.

Madeleine felt like she was about to urinate on herself. But she had not seen the girl at the coat check in two months—the girl had been there for the first month of the season and then had disappeared, and her colleague, who didn't know about the scheme, had said life in Paris had become too hard for her and she had gone home to the provinces.

"Lies," Madeleine said. She stared straight at Klaus.

Klaus made a little noise, like a grumble.

Madeleine, sensing she had gained an advantage, pointed at the pictures Klaus held. "I'm barely on speaking terms with my colleagues, that man included. And you think that out of the blue, I would ally with a stranger to do things I don't even agree with? I can't stand the Brits, for heaven's sake, and the Yankees even less. Shame on them for never inviting me to the Met."

Klaus stared at her. Finally, he gathered his papers. "Make yourself comfortable. You're going to be here a while."

"I am famous all over France, Kriminaldirektor Koegel. Every newspaper will cover my wrongful detention if you keep me here. Do you really want my fellow citizens to organize demonstrations in my favor?" Madeleine leaned her elbows on the table and stared at Klaus. She was playing her last card now. "There'll be pictures in the paper. Many people will question your judgment. Frankly, with the reputation of a diva that I have, you'll look laughable all the way to Berlin for even believing I could care about anything but myself!" She added a little crooked smile to her performance. "Herr Goebbels himself will call you to ask what got into you for you to commit such an egregious mistake. Years from now, this will be used as a case study of how to ruin a perfectly distinguished Gestapo career."

Madeleine pushed back her chair. The guard blocked the door.

Klaus's upper lip twitched. He eyed Madeleine without a word, like a poker player trying to determine whether his adversary held a royal flush or not. Madeleine waited. Adrenaline coursed her veins after her little speech. She worried that she would make a mistake in the excitement of the moment.

Klaus still couldn't decide. Madeleine could tell from his eyes that he didn't believe Amfortas could have lied, but he also didn't believe Madeleine would behave like a street peddler.

Madeleine stood up. "Now if you'll excuse me, I have a rehearsal to attend."

Klaus nodded at the guard that he could let Madeleine go. "For now," he said.

Nineteen

November 1943

Yvonne came out of the wings at the Berliner Staatsoper to thunderous applause. By now she knew the role of Isolde as if she were her doppelgänger, but she'd been anguished nonetheless that she'd fail. Traveling to Germany's capital had unsettled her—all those soldiers and civilians striding through the streets as if Germany would rule over the world for centuries to come. And then, to add to her distress, the Royal Air Force had bombed Berlin a few days before the performances, when Yvonne was already in Berlin. Not just flown over it, not just triggered the air raid sirens, but actually dropped bombs over it, causing explosions that shattered windows and fires that could be seen and smelled from a kilometer away. It'd never bombed Paris, although it'd bombed factories in the suburbs. The rumor was that no pilot wanted to be responsible for destroying the French capital's history. The RAF didn't have such qualms about Berlin. Thankfully, the bombing had occurred far from the Staatsoper, and Yvonne had focused on rehearsing with Herbert von Karajan and Max Lorenz.

The cast members lined up at the edge of the stage and saluted the center boxes, where Joseph Goebbels—Hitler's Reich minister of propaganda—Klaus, and other Nazis sat. Yvonne took care not to stand out, and that meant bowing as low as her fellow singers, although everyone in the audience knew her as the Frenchwoman. Every time she stood up, she glanced left and right to see what smile the other performers had pasted on their face and made sure to imitate them exactly: not more enthusiastic than them and not less. If Klaus decided she'd disrespected Goebbels in the curtain calls, he was sure to dig yet another cigarette butt into her arm, next to where her smallpox vaccine mark was. Yvonne had stopped wearing sleeveless dresses.

She smiled and bowed, bowed and smiled, determined to keep herself out of trouble. The auditorium wasn't nearly as memorable as the one at the Paris Opera. Cream and brown colors abounded rather than gold and scarlet red. Hitler hadn't come, thank goodness. He'd attend the next day's performance instead. Yvonne would've liked to think his absence had helped her sing well, but she feared Goebbels even more than Hitler, because Hitler had scant time to think about artists amid a world war, whereas they played a central role in Goebbels's propaganda.

A loud whirring noise startled Yvonne—was it another air raid?— until she realized a stagehand had just turned a fan on now that the performance was over. Max nudged Yvonne. She remembered she should fetch conductor Herbert von Karajan from the wings. The clapping grew into a roar. What did Henri and Madeleine think of the performance? Yvonne wondered. Klaus had "invited" Madeleine to come along on the trip as Yvonne's understudy, and he'd made sure the program listed her name as such, although typically lead singers' possible replacements weren't mentioned. Henri had accompanied Madeleine. On the plane— Yvonne's first trip by air—he'd looked far more delighted to be visiting the capital of the Third Reich than either of the two women, but maybe he was just playing a role.

Onstage, the curtain slowly descended in front of the performers. Yvonne kept the smile on her face until the curtain touched the ground and the performers dropped each other's hands. She couldn't wait to return to Paris. What a pity she had to sing at military bases with Klaus first while the Moreaus headed back to France, but it'd delay her by less than a week. She tripped over a prop when she stepped into the wings. The RAF's reaching Berlin had unsettled her. At least she'd be home by the time the next raid came about. Surely two attacks on such a prized target as Berlin wouldn't happen within days of each other.

At the reception, the Germans all talked with one another and no one paid Yvonne any attention. At the other end of the foyer, full of the same creams and browns as the auditorium, Madeleine sulked while Henri talked to Karajan, his hands moving fast, probably paying his respects like an obsequious pupil.

Yvonne didn't want to make conversation with Madeleine. She would've looked like she was begging for her praise. Instead, she ate a petit four by herself and reminisced over the Bayreuth festival she'd attended before the war. No Hans-Hermann to distract her this time. Perhaps it would've been best if he'd never talked to her, but it was too late to have regrets. One more petit four, and then straight to bed. The hotel they were all staying at, the Hotel Royal, was only a short walk down the long Unter den Linden avenue. Yvonne liked the hotel enough. Management had given her the room farthest from the elevator, as she'd requested, and the food was tolerable for a German establishment. If only Hitler hadn't announced he'd attend.

A balding man with round spectacles and a worn maroon worn suit approached Yvonne.

"Stupendous. Epoch making." He spoke French with a slight accent, but that accent wasn't German. "I have to admit, I hadn't expected you to come here."

Yvonne made a polite smile. "Why not?"

"My dear lady, the rumors about the camps are becoming quite insistent."

Yvonne's eyes narrowed. Who was this man? Everyone around her was chatting in German, indifferent to her and this stranger. At the other end of the grand foyer, Klaus was conferring with other Gestapo officers. He was probably boasting about the number of Frenchmen he'd killed. Yvonne was glad he had his back turned to her.

Yvonne tried to keep a lighthearted expression on her face but lowered her voice. "You mean the relocation camps?"

The man pushed his spectacles up his nose. "You know they're extermination camps. You've had eleven months to instruct yourself."

Yvonne had no idea what had happened eleven months earlier, but his tone made her shiver.

"Don't tell me you haven't heard about the declaration by the United Nations back in December," the man said, his eyes narrow, his distaste obvious.

Yvonne remembered it now. The Polish government-in-exile had sounded the alarm. The members of the United Nations had issued a joint declaration condemning the mass murder of the Jews.

"It's hard to know what to believe," Yvonne said. "Civilized people don't put each other in gas camps."

"So you've decided to play the dumb blonde to shirk your moral responsibility?" The balding man laughed. "Let me tell you, nothing short of running away as fast as you can will do the trick."

He kept smiling at her, as if they were exchanging pleasantries, but moved closer to her. "You can't be that oblivious to the turmoil around you, can you? You can't be that stupid."

"Germany censors the news we get in Paris," Yvonne said in a weak voice.

"It's mass murder on a scale we've never heard of. The able-bodied are worked to death. The infirm are left to die of exposure and starvation or are massacred in group executions. When you show your face here, everyone thinks you approve of it."

Yvonne said nothing for a long moment. Around her and this mysterious man, guests continued to sip champagne and chat amicably. Every so often, someone laughed. Yet, having seen Klaus up close, she knew he was capable of all the man was saying and more.

A waiter presented them with a tray of appetizers. Yvonne waved him away as if he were a fly circling the desserts.

"The Allies' statement was published on the first page of the *New York Times*," the man said.

Yvonne heard a veiled reproach in his voice. "Don't you worry it may be propaganda, trying to drag more countries into the war?" she said.

"Many other newspapers published it too," he said.

Yvonne was running out of excuses. Her cheeks turned hot. "Who are you?"

"A friend of Count Raczynski—the man who wrote the note to the western governments, alerting them. But let me guess. You've never heard of him."

Yvonne didn't dare admit it.

"Convenient, isn't it?" The man looked at her with contempt. His mouth kept smiling, though. If Klaus observed them from afar, he'd conclude she was chatting with a boring well-wisher.

"You didn't try very hard to inform yourself, did you? I suppose that smiling for photographs with your new friends took up all your time. But looking away now is the same as supporting mass extermination."

Yvonne almost dropped her glass.

"I'll leave you to enjoy the company of the murderers now," the man said. "Just hope you won't be the one murdered in the next phase of their madness."

He vanished in the crowd before Yvonne could ask him more about the Jews' fate.

～

That night, Yvonne could sleep only in fits. The man's words echoed in her head. *Massacred in group executions*, but also *looking away now is the same as supporting mass extermination* and *you didn't try very hard to inform yourself, did you?* Klaus was snoring beside her. All those innocent people. Observers would assume she'd known all along and hadn't cared. But perhaps she hadn't cared to know, and that was as much an indictment as the other way around.

The radiator in her hotel room hissed. Yvonne turned around in bed and covered her ears with a blanket so she wouldn't hear Klaus.

She hadn't believed death camps existed—internment camps, she could believe, but not death camps. She'd known about the Vél d'Hiv roundup, of course, about Jews being dragged out of their apartments in Paris and sent east. Jules had no longer needed her protection once he'd joined the Free French, so she couldn't pretend she'd remained silent for his safety. Was she so sure Klaus would've tracked her in Le Havre and retaliated for trying to escape him? She could've left a note saying she was going to put rocks in her pockets and throw herself into the Seine River. He wouldn't have dredged the river. And even if he'd sent divers in—he was capable of gestures like that—by the time he'd realized she hadn't drowned, no one who'd been on the train to Le Havre would've remembered seeing her. She had no family over there. Its only appeal was the ships to the United States, but Marseilles was also a port, and its opera was better. He would've looked for her in Marseilles, not in Le Havre.

Yvonne looked at the pot of water she'd put on the radiator to humidify the air. She realized now that she'd lived the past few years wrong, and somewhere along the way she'd missed the last exit out of the hell she'd walked into. How dimwitted for her to let this happen. How contemptible. She'd thought she could walk a fine line between right and wrong, becoming a public figure in occupied Paris and socializing with unsavory characters, but there was no excuse for associating with mass murderers. She hated herself for her cluelessness.

She racked her brain. When had she gone wrong? Was it right after Jules had left to join the Free French? Yes, it probably was. She should've fled Paris too. She'd missed her chance. Months later, here she was in Berlin singing for the Nazis, and the Nazis were committing crimes against humanity.

Did people around her know—did Emile? Did Raymond? Did they look at her and think she didn't give a damn about Jews like Charles-Antoine who'd been so kind to her? Who else at the opera house knew? Who had acted on that knowledge? Who had tried to save some of their Jewish colleagues, or helped Résistance members while Yvonne was eating at the Ritz hotel?

Yvonne would never get over the contempt she felt for herself, she was sure.

She turned in bed all night long. At dawn, she decided she couldn't change the past, but she could behave honorably in the present. She wouldn't sing for Hitler, now that she knew about the extermination camps. There'd be a couple of difficult hours, but if she held firm, she'd get her one moment of moral courage. It wouldn't make up for not leaving Paris earlier, but it was better than nothing. She rehearsed what she'd tell Klaus, imagined what he'd reply, rehearsed her answers to that. The hardest part was the first few words.

Klaus finally woke up.

"I seem to have a sore throat this morning," Yvonne said in a whisper, propped up against a pillow, trying to make her voice sound strangled.

Klaus pushed himself up on his elbow. He looked at her with his eyes half-open as if to ask why in the world did she think he cared about her sore throat, but then he remembered where they were.

"You have to sing for Hitler," Klaus said.

"Maybe I just need some hot tea." Yvonne, talking slowly, pretended that uttering each word hurt her throat more.

"How dumb of you to fall sick now," Klaus said, his voice rising in anger. "Half my classmates at the military academy are coming to see you tonight with their spouses. Do you think we'll keep you around if you can't sing? You were nothing before we came along, and you'll be nothing again."

Yvonne called room service for a big kettle of tea. She was tempted to find herself cured so he wouldn't get mad at her. But she couldn't waver now.

Klaus got dressed and went down to get breakfast, not offering to bring her anything, slamming the door as he left.

Yvonne didn't mind, happy to put some distance between the two of them. When the tea came, she found her resolve again and threw it into the bathroom sink. She couldn't take her mind off from the death camps, and she was in no state to sing for Nazi officers. Let Madeleine deal with the Germans and their insanity. Let her have her picture taken with Hitler. But Yvonne had to tell Madeleine so she could warm her voice properly. If a Frenchwoman gave a bad performance at the Staatsoper, the Nazis might believe she was provoking them.

Yvonne called the front desk and gave the clerk a message for Madeleine. Then she positioned her empty cup of tea on the nightstand as if she'd drunk it, lay down in bed, and stared at the ceiling, ruminating about the camps. What could still be done?

Madeleine knocked on her door ten minutes later. Yvonne opened it in her bathrobe and returned to bed without as much as a greeting. Every few seconds, she tried to sniff.

Madeleine planted herself in the middle of the room. "You're doing this on purpose, aren't you?"

"It's not about getting even," Yvonne said in a small voice, but under Madeleine's glare she stopped pretending to be sick. "A man at the reception yesterday told me about the extermination camps."

Madeleine stared at her, aghast. "Don't tell me you didn't know. There are plenty of hints in the press."

"I thought it was propaganda to set public opinion against the Axis."

Madeleine pressed her fingers against her temples as if she couldn't fathom the sheer stupidity of this comment. "The Germans are very proud of their camps—of their efficiency in killing people on a massive scale."

Yvonne, lying in bed, closed her eyes for a second.

"If you ask nicely, perhaps they'll give you a tour of one of their facilities," Madeleine said. "I'm not sure if there's any extermination camp nearby—I think those are in Poland—but there are labor camps for sure over here and prisoners die all the same, except it's of typhus or starvation."

"I can't sing knowing this is going on," Yvonne said. "What would I look like?"

"The same you've been looking like for about a year now."

"But I really didn't kn—"

"That doesn't matter," Madeleine said.

Yvonne groaned and folded her arms over her face, covering her eyes.

"I can sing if you're sick," Madeleine said. "But your Gestapo man will say you embarrassed him in front of Hitler, and then he'll make you pay. I'd rather not bring you back to Paris in a casket."

Yvonne moved her arms away from her face and looked at Madeleine. Madeleine looked back at her. There weren't too many ways for Yvonne to save herself now. "Oh God," she said. "God, God, God, God."

"I doubt He's going to answer you on that one," Madeleine said.

❧

Yvonne had until the half-hour call to decide if she'd sing or not. She could still back out of it, pretending illness. Spectators arrived in a steady stream of tuxedos and colorful gowns. Grosser Mercedes lined up in front of the Staatsoper. The buzz of conversations drifted to Yvonne's dressing room, a spare room that looked like storage space with a desk surmounted by a mirror and a dozen lightbulbs. The wooden boards creaked under her feet when she sat in costume at the dresser to do her makeup. A loud "Sieg heil!" resounded through the building. Yvonne's hand slid on her face, leaving a streak of eyeliner up to her temple. She rubbed the side of her arms until the urge to retch into the wastebasket had faded, and fixed her makeup. She tried a few of Isolde's main phrases, unsure if she could bring herself to hit high notes after she'd compromised herself so. The result scared her. She'd never sounded worse.

Madeleine poked her head into the room. She took one look at Yvonne and said, "All right then. But since you've sung for Hitler before, everyone will believe you're sick. You'll get in trouble with your beau and no glory whatsoever for trying to take a stand."

"I have to save myself somehow," Yvonne said in such a whisper she could've been talking to herself.

Madeleine tapped her gently on the shoulder. "We got past the point where you could save yourself a while back."

Yvonne remained still. Madeleine waited.

"Half an hour to curtain," someone bellowed in the hallway. "Chevallier, you didn't sign in."

Madeleine looked at her.

Finally, Yvonne covered Madeleine's hand on her shoulder with hers. "Then I suppose it no longer matters if I sing well or not." She got up and waved at the stage manager in the corridor. "Do you have a pen?"

❧

Klaus and Yvonne stayed a few more days in Berlin after Yvonne's last performance. They'd planned to leave for Bavaria the morning of November 23. The suitcases were packed, the travel clothes set out. Her Isolde had been well received—Hitler was on record in the *Berliner Zeitung* praising her—but what a relief for Yvonne to put Berlin behind her.

She woke up during the night to the walls shaking and windows breaking. Explosions in the background made her ears hurt. She remembered to open her mouth wide to save her eardrums. She couldn't sing if she became deaf. But she couldn't sing if the building collapsed over her either.

She knew right away what was happening. The Brits were bombing Berlin again, and this time not a distant neighborhood but right in the center of town—the Unter den Linden avenue.

Klaus, swearing, dusted pieces of glass off his undershirt and crouched under the desk. Yvonne lay down in the tub. She thought of Jules. She truly hadn't believed that Berlin could be bombed while she was there. Previous raids had been mostly a taunt from the Royal Air Force, sure to enrage Hitler and his goons. Maybe she would die that night. And what would her obituary say? *French soprano killed in Berlin bombing a few days after singing Isolde for the Nazis.* No one in France would rush to her funeral.

After what felt like a very long time, the planes finally left. The electricity had been cut, but fires outside, amid the smoke and the dust raised by the bombings, provided enough glow that it wasn't too difficult to move about. Yvonne groped her way to the bedroom.

Klaus, hands on the windowsill, was yelling expletives to the sky, as if the RAF pilots could hear him. He looked pale. He looked, in fact, as if the great torturer of Paris had never had his life in danger before. Yvonne glanced at herself in a piece of broken mirror. She looked less pale than him.

He quickly put on his uniform. Yvonne slid into a dress and followed him outside. She started coughing as soon as she reached the hotel lobby. The crumbled buildings cast odd shapes in front of the fires. The French embassy had been hit, as had the British embassy. The Staatsoper had been spared, for now, but it looked like a lot of the city had been turned into smoking ruins. How many civilians dead? How many homeless?

"They want total war? They will get it!" Klaus said. His eyes were crazed. "We will avenge this! Scorched earth! No mercy!"

Madeleine and Henri stumbled out of the hotel. Madeleine was wrapped in a blanket. She seemed quite pleased by this turn of events, now that she'd survived it. To her, it likely meant Great Britain would never stop until Germany had been defeated. Henri ran his hand into his hair again and again, trying to make sense of what he was seeing, and not apparently managing to.

Amid the rubble, someone was snapping photographs of the damage.

"You're going to write an op-ed for the French papers," Klaus said to Yvonne. His eyes were less crazed than before, and his voice was lower. "Brits and Yankees are barbarians. France must do everything it can to help Germany win the war."

But Yvonne had no interest in writing that. It'd sound like she was trying to excuse the side that'd created extermination camps.

"Someone will already have published their own account by the time we return to Paris."

"We'll send it from here. You'll read it into phone. They'll stop the presses to publish it, I guarantee it."

"I wouldn't find the right words," Yvonne said. "I'm a mediocre writer on a good day."

Klaus took his gun out of his holster and stared at her.

"Tell me in German what you want me to write, and I'll translate it," Yvonne said shakily.

Klaus put his gun back into the holster. "And when you are back in Paris, you'll give interviews about what you saw here. Innocent people asleep, dead! Destruction caused by snakes!" He waved his hand at the raging fires and the mountains of billowing smoke. "Thousands will have been killed, and probably more than one thousand made homeless. France must support Germany to the very end!"

Yvonne's heart sank. If she did this—and she could hardly choose not to, unless she wanted a bullet in her head—she'd become the face of collaboration between France and Germany at the very moment when more people guessed that Germany had sunk into evil. The world—and she with it—was doomed if the Nazis won. But she was doomed if the Allies won, because they'd hold her time with Klaus against her. There was no hope for her at all. Maybe there never had been.

Part Four

Twenty

A thick column of smoke rose over Gestapo headquarters in the avenue Foch. Yvonne ran through empty streets. The exterior of the buildings hadn't changed from the previous week, the previous month, but now the Germans had lost the war. Yvonne had anticipated that outcome since the Nazi defeat at Stalingrad, but until the end she'd worried the Germans might turn the situation around. The joy of France winning was mixed with the fear of what'd happen to her next. Her neighbors at the quay Voltaire, who'd greeted her with smiles throughout the Occupation, now slammed their doors shut when they glimpsed her in the hallway, except for the concierge, who hissed at her instead.

Yvonne's German tour in the fall of 1943 had met remarkable success. She had enraptured Nazi soldiers from Bavaria to Schleswig-Holstein, as well as every Third Reich official in Berlin. The newspapers had covered her performances with the adoration usually reserved for Marlene Dietrich, marveling that Yvonne looked more like a Teutonic princess than her German colleagues. Hitler's Germany had adopted her. She wasn't proud of it.

To Yvonne's surprise, despite the white smoke above the building, when she reached Gestapo headquarters, no flames shot from the windows. Instead, the fire tore through a pile of documents as high as a child in the inner courtyard. Klaus, sleeves rolled up, his shirt sticky in the back, dropped manila folders into the blaze.

"My little opera star," he said when he noticed her. "I expected you not here. Came you to help? You better hurry up."

Klaus dropped more documents into the flames. The fire engulfed the papers within seconds. He wiped his brow. "I could have do great things in life if luck be on my side."

A couple of choice words crossed Yvonne's mind, but she decided against uttering any of them. "I'm looking for files you have," she said. "On people I know."

"Are you trying to save your skin?" Klaus asked. "Silly woman." Yvonne recognized the gruff voice he'd lately been using with all his underlings—his new chauffeur who shuttled him between the German embassy and Gestapo headquarters, the assistant in charge of bringing him reports from the field, the subordinate who'd tracked him down to the Moulin Rouge cabaret to inform him that General Friedrich Paulus had surrendered what remained of his army.

Klaus emptied one last box into the fire. "You be lucky if they hang you not," Klaus said, going back inside.

Yvonne, following him, stumbled over the threshold.

"I just want a folder or two," Yvonne said.

Klaus climbed up the spiral staircase without glancing at her and paused on the landing of the top floor. "That will help you not."

"That's not why I'm here," Yvonne said.

"I leave France if I am you," Klaus said. "Opera is in Buenos Aires."

"I just want—"

"Allies see camps when they liberate cities in east," Klaus said. "Once news public, you pay for what we did. Waste not time with pieces of paper."

"My life isn't in Argentina," Yvonne said. She hurried behind Klaus into the archives room. A metal drawer had been left open. Klaus kicked it shut and opened the next one. The initial of the last name was written neatly on the outside. *M.*

There was nothing under Monnier, so Charles-Antoine hadn't been denounced.

Yvonne, peering over the rows of manila folders, checked the other labels until she pulled out the folder that bore Madeleine's name.

"I take the file of husband if I am you," Klaus said. "Lot more in that one." He lobbed Henri's folder toward Yvonne. The file was as thick as the collected librettos of Richard Wagner.

Yvonne pored over Henri's name on the cover. She dreaded opening the folder. Something so thick—either he'd been denounced multiple times by many people, although she'd never seen him do anything against the *Boches*, or he'd done the denouncing himself.

"Take or burn it, but stay not there like flowerpot." Klaus stacked piles of papers into his arms.

Yvonne opened the folder. She riffled through reports filed by Gestapo men—accounts of Henri's behavior at dinner parties, comments he'd made, guests he best got along with. Then a name leapt at her: Stefan Kreismann. Oh, yes, the tenor whom Madeleine had exhorted her to help. Yvonne struggled to make sense of the words in front of her. According to the report, Henri had written to Klaus that Stefan Kreismann, star singer of the Vienna State Opera who'd fled Austria after the Anschluss, was hiding in Marseilles while he waited for a visa to flee to the United States. Henri had included the address of a hotel in the Vieux-Port where he believed Stefan was staying. He'd found it on the back of a letter but didn't know if it was still valid. Yvonne's hands shook. The more she tried to collect herself, the more she trembled. At the bottom of the page, a handwritten note: the Gestapo had located Stefan Kreismann based on the information Henri had provided and shipped him to Auschwitz.

Auschwitz. That was where the Nazis had sent Charles-Antoine after the Vél d'Hiv.

Klaus glanced at the letter about Stefan over Yvonne's shoulder and grabbed one last stack of papers before heading downstairs. "That man is lucky if he come back from the camp."

"What about Charles-Antoine?"

"He was old," Klaus said.

"What does that even mean?" Yvonne asked.

"Old people not do well in extermination camps," Klaus said.

Yvonne took in the news. Her teacher, in a gas chamber. "You murderer," she said between her teeth.

Klaus slapped her. A piece of paper fluttered from the folders he was carrying—a memo on the letterhead of the Renault factories.

"Pick it up," Klaus said.

"You pick it up, if you care about it so much," Yvonne said, rubbing her cheek. *Murderer, murderer!* She said in her mind. Charles-Antoine, dead.

Klaus stroked his Walther pistol in the holster around his belt. "I'll pretend I didn't hear that, unless the paper is still on floor when I count to five."

Yvonne knew she was beaten. She picked up the paper and held it out for him, her lips pressed thin, until Klaus grabbed it, and then she shoved Henri's file into her leather bag. Better not to give Klaus an excuse to shoot her while the Free French were drawing near. What an ill-timed death that would be.

"Be angry if you like, but de Gaulle and his men will come after you all same," Klaus said.

They'll come after you first, Yvonne thought.

She followed Klaus down the stairs, careful to stay far away from him in case he did decide to use that pistol on her. Klaus looked at her when he reached the courtyard, which was thick with smoke. What was left to say? Yvonne had been his toy, and yet she wasn't broken. She bolted onto the street. Behind her, fire crackled as new papers were added to the blaze. The pavement was blisteringly hot from the August heat. Yvonne shielded her eyes from the sunshine and dashed forward, staying close to the stone walls.

At the intersection with the rue Pergolèse, two French soldiers about Jules's age, in battle fatigues caked with dust, aimed their rifles at her.

Yvonne raised her hands. "There's a Gestapo officer at eighty-four avenue Foch, probably on the top floor. He'll shoot you if you turn onto the avenue, but the back alley will lead you right past the Hungarian embassy, and from there you can get into the building through the side door."

The soldiers nodded without a word. They reached the alley and lengthened their stride, like leopards on the prowl. Yvonne lingered on the corner after they'd disappeared out of her sight. Her hands were clammy. Finally, a single gunshot. If Klaus had shot first, one of the soldiers would've shot back. Yvonne allowed herself a tiny smile and darted through the deserted streets.

❧

Gustave maneuvered the Moreaus' car around the throngs of French citizens kissing and dancing on the Champs-Élysées. Henri and Madeleine were silent in the back seat. On the radio, the announcer repeated every few minutes that the tanks of General Leclerc had rolled into Paris and were nearing the Place du Châtelet. Closer to city hall, the Germans who hadn't fled had shot at civilians from the rooftops, but the street fighting had become rarer now that French soldiers had forced them back. Despite the danger, Parisians ventured outside to witness the liberation of their city.

Madeleine drummed her fingers against the armrest while the car inched along the avenue de l'Opéra. She wore a red dress with a white-and-blue scarf and had planted a rosette in her hair. The blue, white, and red ribbons Rose had tied around the side-view mirrors of the Peugeot fluttered along the car. No one could fail to recognize the colors of the French flag. What a pity Henri looked so shell-shocked by the Germans' defeat.

The swastika that had hung from the roof of the opera house lay in a pile of ashes at the center of the square. Madeleine wished that Stefan had shared this moment with her. Hopefully she could convince him to settle in Paris after he was released from the camp—she refused to imagine he might not have survived. Vienna would stir too many memories in him, though—his neighbors feting him as a famous tenor before the Anschluss and then shunning him, settling into his house after he had fled, wearing his clothes and eating his food while he struggled in poverty.

Gustave pulled over at the artists' entrance. He opened Madeleine's door before retrieving a large case of Perrier-Jouët champagne from the trunk, which he gave to Henri.

Madeleine strode down the familiar hallways of the Paris Opera. Gilded mirrors and lamp fixtures from the previous century still bracketed black and white tiles. It seemed impossible that Nazis had ever roamed through the corridors. She cast a glance behind her: Henri was stumbling under the weight of the case of champagne, his face as pale as his shirt. Madeleine was tempted to slap him so that he wouldn't look so guilty. Of course, the many receptions he had attended with the *Boches*, while the rest of Paris had suffered under rationing, would be held against him. Madeleine herself wished she had done so much more for the side that had been right all along, besides distributing leaflets and offering her house as a refuge in Normandy.

Voices sang in the distance, the staff of the opera house gathering on the main stage. Employees were belting out "La Marseillaise" on the wooden planks of the performance hall, having grabbed all the French flags in the props department. A musty odor floated around them. They had been in storage for four years. A young seamstress from the costume's shop wrapped herself in the largest flag, far more imposing than Madeleine's tricolor outfit. She scowled when she noticed Henri and, lifting her chin, made a show of slowly looking away. Henri placed the case onto the desk where Tatyana wrote her letter in *Eugene Onegin* and uncorked a bottle of Perrier-Jouët. Employees gathered in a loose circle around him. They were careful not to draw too close, but the *Libération* of Paris did warrant a toast of champagne. Henri poured generous servings to everyone within arm's reach, his forced smile getting bigger with every coworker he greeted who refused to smile at him.

The bass who had sung Titurel in the 1940 production of *Parsifal* plucked another bottle of champagne from the case after Henri emptied the first one.

"I wouldn't stick around if I were you," Titurel said to Henri as he popped the Perrier-Jouët open. "People are settling scores with anyone who was close to the *Boches*. You're in their line of sight, as you should be."

Titurel filled the glasses around him with a generosity that gave away the fact that he had not paid for any of this and did not worry about the drinks running out.

Henri hesitated.

"Go home," Madeleine said. "I'll call the house when I need a ride back."

Henri still did not move. He saw the risk as well as Madeleine did, she was sure: if he did not quickly change the opinion of singers and staff about him, he would be shoved off the stage for good. But now was not the time to protest the way his colleagues were treating him. Finally, he strode toward the exit, as if he had forgotten something in the car.

"Have you seen Emile?" Madeleine asked, holding out a glass to be filled with champagne.

Titurel threw yet another empty bottle of Perrier-Jouët into a wastebasket. "He fled for Toulouse. His wife had an affair with a Nazi general during the war. The Free French shave the heads of such women."

Madeleine felt sorry for Emile. He had been good to her. But she had no time to wallow in pity. "Who's replacing him?"

Titurel pointed at a man who towered over the crowd from his six-foot-two-inch frame and clasped the hands of anyone passing by. Georges de Véricourt, Emile's second-in-command. Before the war he had stayed in Emile's shadow, constantly agreeing with him and never offering an original thought. Now he controlled the opera house.

Madeleine headed toward Georges like an ocean liner crossing the Atlantic. "What is the first role you can cast me in?" Her voice rose toward a high C. She could never disguise her goals when she had set her heart on something.

Georges slapped a musician on the back, grinning, but looked noticeably less pleased when his eyes met Madeleine's. "France wants younger singers now. And not wives of conductors who socialized with the Nazis."

"You were all too happy to have connections with the *Boches* thanks to Henri," Madeleine said. "My brother died in the Great War. Have a bit of respect."

Georges left his flute of champagne on a table from the scene at the inn in *Carmen*. "That is long past. My brother was shot last year. The *Boches* murdered two of my wife's cousins in the spring. When their bodies were found, it took dental records to identify them. And my nephew, killed in April—tortured first, then electrocuted. What were you doing while Hitler's men exterminated him?"

"I let Jewish musicians in hiding use my house in Normandy," Madeleine said. She wouldn't even mention distributing leaflets. That seemed so futile in comparison to what others had accomplished.

"But if they'd gotten caught, you would've said they'd broken into your home and you had no idea they were there," Georges said.

"My mother was in the house with them. They lived in the house-keeper's quarters."

"So your mother helped them," George said smugly.

Madeleine wasn't going to argue. "I also tried to help Stefan Kreis-mann leave for the United States. You can ask him once he's released. Better yet, you can hire him. Emile agreed to cast him as Edgardo in *Lucia* before the war." Georges would never check the precise role with Emile. Madeleine could allow herself a few embroideries if they bene-fited Stefan's career. "Naturally, I'll have the title role."

"Haven't you heard?" Georges asked. "Stefan Kreismann is dead. Some labor camp out in Poland. Typhus, I think."

Madeleine tilted her head. The words could not be real. Stefan could not be dead.

"A friend at the Vienna State Opera told me," Georges said. "I'm not sure how he found out. It happened a while ago."

Madeleine slumped into one of the chairs used in *Carmen*'s second act. She felt numb, as if her ability to have any emotions again had just vanished into the ground.

A girl not older than eighteen raised her fist in the image of Liberty on the barricades of 1830 in the painting by Eugène Delacroix. "To the French troops!"

"To the French troops!" the others yelled back.

Stagehands struck up "La Marseillaise" again. The crowd joined in, Georges along with them. Madeleine opened her mouth to sing the French anthem, but no sound came out.

⌒

The knock on Yvonne's door startled her. It was a quick rap, almost subdued, so it couldn't be the Free French, who would've banged. Yvonne shoved Henri's folder back in her suitcase and pushed her suitcase into her closet, under her blue Schiaparelli gown, which was worn out now and missing sequins but still her favorite dress. Her dismay at what she'd read about Henri in the Gestapo file hadn't diminished—Henri, who'd shared such keen insights into Wagner's music, capable of disgracing himself so.

Every day Yvonne considered fleeing to Dijon, and every day she talked herself out of it—she'd already inflicted enough shame on her parents. But even if she didn't leave, she owned a few things she hoped to save from her neighbors' pillaging. She locked the suitcase.

Whoever stood outside the door knocked again. It must be Hélène, Yvonne's one remaining friend. She ran errands for Yvonne while her neighbors believed she'd fled Paris. Yvonne hurried out of her bedroom, trying not to bump into the furniture. The shutters in the living room were drawn, although it was the middle of the afternoon, both to keep the August heat out and to ensure Yvonne wouldn't be seen from the street.

"I wasn't expecting you to bring company," she said to Hélène after opening the front door.

She stepped aside to let Henri in. His temples had turned gray. More wrinkles stretched across his forehead. Yvonne remembered Kundry's "Grausamer" aria, her joy at singing under his conductorship. And yet this same man had denounced Stefan Kreismann. She plastered a smile on her lips.

Henri tripped against the side table, where the phone had been ringing off the hook earlier in the day. The apartment must seem very dark to a visitor just coming in. In the small space between the shutters, the sun shone brightly in a cloudless sky.

Hélène followed Henri inside. Her salt-and-pepper hair was pulled up into a headmistress's bun. The large pair of glasses perched on her nose gave her an austere look, which she cultivated to intimidate Raymond's clients. Her dress showed wear at the collar.

"He wouldn't take no for an answer," Hélène said. "I tried to warn you, but you didn't pick up your phone."

Yvonne locked the door. The dead bolt wouldn't keep the Free French out, but it'd at least dissuade her neighbors from storming in. She worried about vigilante justice as much as the punishment doled out by de Gaulle's soldiers.

Hélène handed Yvonne a brown paper bag. "Here are all the groceries I could get. I'll keep looking."

Yvonne peered inside: one potato, one carrot, and something that might've been wilted spinach. She pressed the bag against her chest. "Thank you. I doubt I'll have much longer to wait before the Free French show up."

She'd enjoyed too much fame during the Occupation, been photographed with Klaus too often, for them not to find their way to her.

Henri strode into the living room. The piano caught his attention first—a Steinway. He nodded appreciatively, although he must've known that the piano was not Yvonne's. Then he ventured near the bookshelves. His face remained expressionless as he read the titles on the books' spines. Yvonne wished she could've talked intelligently about Malraux and Gide and any Goncourt Prize winner, but only opera mattered to her. She'd added a few items of her own here and there—opera scores, pictures of her triumph at Bayreuth—but she'd also kept every single object that'd belonged to her predecessors. In fact, she'd convinced herself that moving their belongings would bring her endless bad luck.

"Why didn't you leave?" Henri asked without looking at her.

"To go where? Better to stay here and get the matter over with." Yvonne liked how decisive she sounded, even if she was only pretending.

On the coffee table lay the previous day's edition of *Le Parisien libéré*, which had published its first issue only a week earlier. Newspapers under Nazi control during the war had ceased operations. They'd never have regained the trust of the public. Hélène had bought the paper for Yvonne because of a picture on the front page, above the fold. It showed women in tears, their heads shaved, huddled in the back of an army truck while they were paraded in front of jeering bystanders.

"The matter, as you call it, might not be taken care of in one fell swoop," Henri said.

Such comments annoyed Yvonne. "Why did you want to see me?" It was a surprise that he, of all people, had crossed Paris to talk to her.

Henri placed his hat on the table. Beads of sweat pearled at the roots of his hair in the sweltering heat of August. He wiped them off with his silk handkerchief. "I wanted to talk to you about the season after next. Of course, for now you'll have to keep a low profile. But in two years, you should be able to return to the stage."

Yvonne placed the bag of groceries on her dining table. The fires the Germans had set before fleeing east had barely stopped smoldering. "You didn't come all the way here to chat about opera."

"You'd be perfect in *Turandot*," Henri said.

Hélène stepped toward the door. "I'll see myself out if you don't need me."

"Wait," Yvonne said. "Who knows when we'll have a chance to get together next." She turned toward Henri. "What is it you're after?"

Henri tapped his index finger on the picture of the women with their heads shaved. "Surely you're aware it's not going to end at that."

"I've been telling her the same thing, but she refuses to listen," Hélène said.

Henri plucked a small model of the Brandenburg Gate from the shelves. It had been a gift from Herbert von Karajan after Yvonne won over the crowds at the Staatsoper. For a moment he admired the four horses drawing the chariot led by the Roman goddess of victory on top of the templelike gate. Then he seemed to remember where he was.

"We have some disagreeable months ahead of us," Henri said. "Months, not years, if we keep our wits together."

Yvonne placed the model of the Brandenburg Gate back on the shelves. "And what would I have to do for that?"

"Did Klaus Koegel ever talk about me?" Henri asked.

Yvonne wouldn't use her trump card now. "He said you conducted Wagner better than the most talented German conductors."

Klaus couldn't have named a single German conductor if the fate of the Third Reich had depended on it, not even Wilhelm Furtwängler, but Henri looked as pleased as a child on Christmas Day.

"I conduct Wagner better than anyone in Europe, and you'll be the one onstage when I do so again," Henri said. "It's important not to make waves now, do you understand?"

Yvonne waited for him to say more.

"No one will admit to attending the parties at the German Institute or the Ritz," Henri said, gripping her arm. "They'd out themselves as collaborators. So the Free French will ask you the questions others refuse to answer. You're one of the few French people—the only person, perhaps—who saw everything that happened over there. You'll decide whom to bring down with you and whom to save."

Yvonne freed herself from Henri's grip. She knew what he wanted now.

"There are pictures," she said.

"Naturally. I had to attend social events related to my musical directorship. The Nazis happened to come. I didn't seek them out." Henri brought his face within inches of hers. How ugly he looked when he was scared. "The Free French will believe you if you insist I was never there willingly. Say that I always supported de Gaulle's men, long before anyone else threw in their lot with them. There'll be steady work for you when things calm down, I promise."

Yvonne stared at him. Where was the man she had once admired for his musicianship? Now he just looked small and despicable.

"I'm going to go now," Hélène said.

"Can you wait?" Yvonne asked. "I need to ask you something."

She turned toward Henri. "You have no intention of helping me out. You just want to buy yourself time."

Henri pressed her fingers between his, like a drowning man clutching a lifesaving raft. "Oh, I want to help you out plenty, Yvonne dear. It pains me to see the trouble you're in. We both know your career would've followed a very different trajectory if Madeleine hadn't interfered."

Yvonne tried to free herself, but Henri wouldn't let her.

"You don't even decide who gets cast now," Yvonne said. "And you won't decide two years from now."

"There's only one way to find out," Henri said. "You'll need work when you come out of prison."

Prison?

Henri was hurting her hand now. "You were wined and dined while Paris suffered from rationing. You were the face of collaboration after your trip to Germany. You can't possibly expect to get off with a slap on the wrist. Naturally, you'll be tried for treason. But I'll help you if you help me."

"You're hurting me," Yvonne said, because he was crushing her fingers. Even if he wielded enough influence to pull her back onto the stage some years from now, would he keep his word? She was tired of powerful men using her. She wasn't even that sure she wanted to sing again. She had once very much wanted to sing, and here was the result.

She escorted Henri to the front door. He pressed his foot against the frame so Yvonne wouldn't shut the door in his face.

"The new government will freeze your assets," Henri said. "You won't have any money for a lawyer. Do you really believe that a public defender will lift a finger for you? You'll get raked over hot coals for the company you kept during the war. Be smart."

Yvonne leaned the door against his shoe until he retreated into the hallway. She turned the dead bolt and returned to the living room, flustered by his talk of prison.

"Do you know a good lawyer?" she asked Hélène.

Hélène put the book she'd been browsing through back in its place on the shelves. "Raymond knows everyone who matters in Paris. I'll go through his address book and pretend the request's coming from him."

Yvonne realized she was shaking. She hadn't expected to go to prison. She'd expected the Free French to humiliate her and kick her out of the apartment, but she'd convinced herself they'd focus on bringing black marketeers to justice, and Parisians who'd sent their compatriots to their death. Prison—that was a different beast.

"Whoever I find, how are you going to pay him?" Hélène asked.

Yvonne showed Hélène her bedroom, down the dark corridor. In front of her closet lay the two suitcases where she'd piled her belongings, one open and one closed. The closed and locked one contained the Gestapo folder about Henri, along with some mementos she wanted to save. She didn't tell Hélène any of that. Dozens of evening gowns in a multitude of colors and fabrics still hung in the closet.

"Here, pick any dress," Yvonne said. "That lawyer will want his wife to look pretty. And take some for yourself too."

Hélène's finger glided over the sleeve of one of Yvonne's evening gowns, barely stroking the velvet, as if the dress would evaporate if she rubbed it too strongly.

"Klaus got those dresses for me, and I doubt he paid for any of them," Yvonne said. "Let's put his loot to good use."

Hélène pressed the top of the gown against her chest and stretched the sleeves over her arms. She'd look like a queen in that gown. Yvonne had never seen such a childlike smile. She folded the dress that Hélène had selected into the other suitcase and piled two more dresses on top of it, for the lawyer. At the last moment she added one more dress for Hélène, most suitable for luncheons.

"I'll try to find you a good lawyer, but whether he'll want to represent you is up to him," Hélène said.

At last Yvonne picked up the suitcase that contained the Gestapo folder. "Would you mind safeguarding this? It mostly has newspaper cutouts about my performances, opera programs, silly memories of my fame, but they mean a lot to me."

Hélène took the suitcase from her hands. She seemed to care a lot more about the new dresses.

A squeal of brakes tore through the afternoon quiet. Yvonne peered through the window. Soldiers were spilling out of an army truck. Their armbands bore the Lorraine cross, emblem of the Free French—two horizontal marks, the one on top smaller than the one at the bottom, and a vertical line cutting through both. They rushed into the building.

Yvonne rubbed the side of her arms despite the heat. They'd found her fast.

"Stay here," she said to Hélène. "I'll go and open the door for them."

Yvonne waited in silence by the half-open door as footsteps came nearer. She couldn't feel anything—a sure sign she was scared. She supposed it was better than indulging in a fit of crying, although maybe tears would've pacified the soldiers. At last, the Free French reached her floor. The soldier in the lead bounded toward her. A scar crossed his eyebrow. He brandished a long straight razor.

"Yvonne Chevallier? You know why we're here."

He grabbed her by the arm and pulled her out of her apartment, toward the lobby and the street, where his comrades stood ready to jeer at Yvonne while they shaved her head.

Twenty-One

The doorbell rang. Henri put down his glass of cognac and looked at Madeleine. Did it mean anything that it was the bell and not a rough knock on the door? The French doors were open onto the terrace, and whoever it was could easily walk around the house and enter through the garden. It was a beautiful morning in early September, not too hot yet, made more delightful by the *Libération* of Paris two weeks earlier. Every house was flying a French flag from a window or across the doorstep.

"Maybe we should close the doors," Henri said.

"If they want to find you, they'll do it eventually." Madeleine sat down at the piano and played a Chopin etude, just to see how the person at the door would react. She wasn't as good a pianist as she was a singer, but she was still better than most pianists in Paris, although she was out of practice.

Henri shook his head. He had aged in the past few months, and even more so since the tanks of General Leclerc had rolled into the city—his face had become puffy, his jawline slacking, and he had lost hair on top of his head. Madeleine had gained weight too since she had learned of Stefan's death, and now she found little energy for anything besides reading about the latest developments of the war in the newspapers. British troops had liberated Brussels, and then Antwerp, Ghent, Liège. The Belgian government in exile had just returned from London. Charles de Gaulle had formed the Provisional Government of the French Republic. War was still raging on the Eastern Front, but an Allied victory seemed likely. Madeleine never grew tired of reading about her side's victories.

The bell rang again.

"A polite visitor," Madeleine said. "Rose!"

Rose hurried from the kitchen to the front door. During the Occupation she'd shuffled her feet and kept her head down, but now there was a distinct spring in her step, and sometimes Madeleine heard her laugh to herself. Madeleine liked having her around. She wished she had the same enthusiasm. The war was over, but Stefan's life was over too.

Rose came back a moment later. "It's a young man in uniform."

"Alone?" Henri asked.

Rose nodded. "He says your tempo for the Chopin piece is a bit slow."

Madeleine jumped up so fast her chair toppled behind her and ran to the door, not wanting to believe it before she'd seen for herself.

Jules laughed at her surprise and then her delight. "Figured I'd check on you," he said. His face was thinner than before, his hair shorter. No one would have pegged him for a pianist.

Madeleine took his hands in hers. "It's you, it's really you!"

She couldn't help checking on his hands. The skin was rough and callused, but he had no obvious injury to his fingers.

"Come in, what do you want to eat? Rose, make him the best lunch he's ever eaten!" Madeleine said.

Rose laughed—there was still no end in sight to the rationing—but she was already peering into the pantry and making a menu.

"Passing through or staying a while?" Henri asked, as if he cared.

"Staying a while, hopefully. I only arrived this morning."

Rose was already putting a plate in front of Jules, a glass of water.

"Get us a bottle of Bordeaux from the cellar," Henri told her. Wine was rationed like other staples, but a good friend of Henri's owned a vineyard. "If we don't celebrate for something like this, when will we?"

"To a quick end to the war," Jules said after Henri had uncorked the bottle. Rose had found a slice of ham and mashed potatoes for him.

Madeleine caught the dismay in Henri's eyes, although it lasted only a second before he composed himself.

"Sometime in 1945, maybe 1946 at the latest," Henri said. "Those Japanese are fierce."

To Madeleine he sounded like he wouldn't have minded postponing the inevitable. She wished he'd barricade himself in a wing of the house and never come out when she was around.

"Where are you going to sleep?" she asked Jules. And, when he shrugged, she said, "Stay with us, there's plenty of room. We have two guest rooms we never use, and of course, my piano is yours, if you'd like to practice."

"Maybe once the war is over," Jules said. "Until then—"

"But Charles-Antoine often said—" Madeleine stopped when she noticed how that name pained Jules. "The roundup wasn't your fault, and you have too much talent to let it go to waste."

"After I've had a chance to rest," Jules said, in a tone that meant never. But he would not remain with the Free French forever. Madeleine was already making plans for him in her head.

"Here, do you want to listen to the radio?" Madeleine asked. "You can sit in Henri's lounge chair. Radio Paris was shut down at the *Libération*—such a Nazi mouthpiece—but there are still stations with good music."

She turned the radio knob until she found a symphony—Ernest Chausson, Symphony in B-flat Major. Jules sat down. He looked incongruous in that fancy chair, wearing his tired dusty uniform. Madeleine grabbed a pile of papers that had been on the coffee table to make room for the glass of wine. A red stamp on an envelope caught her attention. Second notice, the stamp said.

"What's this?" She waved the envelope at Henri.

"A bill I've forgotten to pay, probably." He didn't meet her gaze.

Madeleine looked at the return address. "Hotel Meurice."

"The Free French headquarters," Jules said.

"I won't let myself be intimidated by some low-ranking official plucked from the provinces," Henri said.

Madeleine ripped the envelope open and pulled out a sheet of paper. "The Free French have been summoning you?"

"They want to chat with me, along with a lot of people," Henri said. He pointed at Jules. "I bet they want to chat with his mother a lot more than they want to chat with me."

Jules almost toppled over his glass of wine with the back of his hand.

"Have you seen her yet?" Madeleine asked.

Jules's fingers shook around the stem. It seemed prescient of Madeleine not to have pronounced Yvonne's name.

"He only arrived this morning," Henri said.

Madeleine hadn't felt happiness since she'd learned of Stefan's death, and yet when she looked at Jules, she couldn't help but marvel at the fact that he'd come to check on her before his own mother.

"Even if I'd been in Paris for months, I wouldn't have paid her a visit," Jules said. "I want nothing to do with her. What an opportunist she's been, a traitor even. As far as I'm concerned, she might as well be dead."

Henri went upstairs.

⟡

Gustave drove past Tiffany on the rue de la Paix, the Ritz on Place Vendôme—empty at long last of the Nazis who had infested it for four years—and the Ladurée shop on the rue de Castiglione, which sold the best macarons in all of Paris. Elegant arches lined the rue de Rivoli toward the Meurice hotel, where Gustave would drop off Henri and Madeleine. They were quiet in the back seat. Henri held the summons from the Free French in his hand. The Germans had requisitioned the Meurice for the head of the Kommandantur and his staff when they had occupied Paris, so the Free French had claimed it for themselves as soon as they set foot on the Right Bank. It was located right next to the Angelina teahouse, in front of the Tuileries Gardens. Cars with French flags painted on their sides idled by the entrance. Madeleine stumbled out of the car, unsteady on her feet. Henri looked even more frightened than she did. The butler in his white-and-blue uniform held the door open for them, in front of a mosaic on the sidewalk displaying a big *M*. Under other circumstances Madeleine would have bantered that surely the *M* referred to her and not the hotel, but she was in no mood for joking.

Inside the Meurice, men in khaki uniforms hustled about on black and white marble tiles. Porcelain columns supported clusters of small lamps topped by amber lampshades. The hotel, decorated in a late Louis XVI style known for its clean lines and smooth colors, brimmed with tasteful, expensive material that would have pleased Marie-Antoinette. It had hosted King Alfonso XIII after his ouster from Spain, and later the Prince of Wales as well as monarchs from Italy, Belgium, and Denmark. The head of the Kommandantur had enjoyed a high opinion of himself.

The lawyer already stood in the lobby. Madeleine thought his name was Clément, although she hadn't paid much attention to Henri's lawyer before. He wore a goatee and glasses over a Balenciaga suit. If Madeleine had imagined the costume for the notaries in *Don Pasquale*, she would have come up with the same attire. It bothered her when people dressed to play a part. Conventional thinking would not help her and Henri out of the trouble they were in.

The summons demanded that they present themselves at the Emerald Suite on the fifth floor. Madeleine's heels dug into the thick carpet outside the elevator. The door to the suite had been left ajar. Madeleine entered without knocking, before Henri or Clément could hold her back. Cardboard boxes were lined along walls painted a pale yellow. Windows framed by drapes in silk velvet opened on the rue de Rivoli. In the back of the room, behind a walnut desk decorated with bronze ornaments, a small, wiry officer wearing one star on his shoulder boards and a small tag that said SOUCHAL browsed through stacks of folders. He looked up when Madeleine entered with Clément and Henri behind her. From his expression, Madeleine knew at once that she should have knocked.

"Monsieur and Madame Moreau," Souchal said. "We're honored."

The sarcasm in his voice irked Madeleine, although she was pleased that he had recognized them.

"My clients came as soon as their schedules allowed," Clément said. He knew about the second notice for the summons. "They're in high demand."

"From the Germans or the French?" Souchal asked, then reached for a folder at the edge of his desk without waiting for the answer. "Sit down."

Madeleine and Henri settled on plush yellow armchairs. Clément dragged forward a chair that had been pushed against the wall.

Souchal opened the folder. "Quite some company you kept during the war."

"My clients fulfilled their contractual obligations," Clément said. "It's not up to them to decide who sits in the audience."

"Brisk business for you now, I'm sure," Souchal said.

"Madame Moreau in particular was rarely seen onstage during the Occupation," Clément said, without commenting on the slight. "Sieglinde in *Die Walküre* was her only role, back in 1942. Yvonne Chevallier sang Brünnhilde. That was a transparent attempt by Madame Chevallier to force a comparison with her, and by all accounts Madame Moreau filled France with pride." He inched his armchair forward. "For someone of her stature, staying away from the opera house to the extent she did sent the message loud and clear that she didn't approve of the Nazis. She sacrificed some of the best years of her career to take a stand."

"People stay away from the limelight for all kinds of reasons," Souchal said. "Maybe she found another pastime more to her liking."

Madeleine dug her fingernails into the upholstery, enough to leave a scratch on the fabric. "What would it have been?" He could not understand how much she yearned for her audience's applause.

"You sang a leading role in an opera by Hitler's favorite composer in the middle of the Occupation," Souchal said. "Someone who detested the new regime wouldn't have behaved like that. But my main questions are for Monsieur Moreau." He focused on Henri, who sat so pale in his chair that he looked seasick. "You led the Paris Opera Orchestra during that time. You were often seen with Yvonne Chevallier and her Nazi friends. Do you want to tell me how much you cooperated with the Third Reich now, or do you prefer that I find out some other way? I'm not going to like the extra work, let me tell you that. So you may come clean now."

"I've always supported France," Henri said in a squeaky voice. Madeleine found him pathetic.

"But you thrived during the Occupation," Souchal said. "You were in your wife's shadow before the war. Your own musicians believed your wife had imposed you as conductor because she was married to you and others could've done your job just as well. When Yvonne Chevallier found her way to the stage, though, you really got to show your worth. The two of you got along surprisingly well, didn't you, given that she stole your wife's roles? I've stopped counting the pictures of you with her and her protectors."

Souchal laid out newspaper photographs in front of Henri. Yvonne always stood between him and Hans-Hermann or him and Klaus. This dated the pictures easily: before and after 1942. Henri remained a constant in Yvonne's pictures, no matter who her companion was. Every photograph showed the two of them smiling next to each other in the grand foyer of the Paris Opera or at the German Institute, and at least one Nazi officer touching Yvonne's arm. They raised flutes of champagne at the camera as if they never drank anything else. In the pictures Yvonne leaned just a little closer to Henri than to her German officer, but the German officer held her arm. Yvonne and Henri could have been lovers if the circumstances had been different. But surely he had feared antagonizing Yvonne's Nazi friends. A coward through and through, Madeleine told herself.

"Conductors are expected to appear at receptions after their performances," Henri said. "Antagonizing the Germans would have been pointless. And anyone can take a picture with me."

"Maybe not so many times," Souchal said.

Madeleine was glad to hear him say it.

"Yvonne pulled me along," Henri said. "She refused to be the only French person in the photographs. What did you expect me to tell her? We were told to obey her every whim. I just played the role she wanted me to play."

Souchal gave him an even look and waited for Henri to tell him more.

"The reopening of the opera house this coming year will be spectacular," Henri said. "I've prepared the whole schedule already. *Manon* as the season opener, then *Carmen*. *Samson and Delilah* after Christmas and *Les Huguenots* around Easter. Jewels of the French repertoire to celebrate our victory over the Axis."

"I didn't mean to have you talk about music," Souchal said.

"That's all I know," Henri said.

Souchal scoffed at Henri's obvious attempt to pretend he was indifferent to politics.

"Collaborators who held important roles during the Occupation shouldn't stay in their functions now that Paris is free."

"I only did my job," Henri said, sounding annoyed. He took a deep breath and slowed his voice. "If you're here talking to us, I assume you've already arrested Yvonne. She's a far bigger fish."

Madeleine placed her hand on his arm. He should not get Yvonne in trouble to save himself.

"We shave the head of women like that," Souchal said, his voice neutral. "But we keep our prisons for scum who robbed their compatriots, enriched themselves at the expense of innocent people, or denounced their neighbors."

He looked pointedly at Henri, who drummed his fingers against the armrest. "That's a little rich to let her roam free, after she went to Germany in 1942 and 1943 and sang for the Nazis," Henri said. "I did my duty in front of my fellow Parisians. I'd never have agreed to go to Berlin." He opened his briefcase and placed articles he had cut out from the *Berliner Tageszeitung* on Souchal's desk. It reported that the bigwigs of the Third Reich had heaped dithyrambic praise on Yvonne. "Nineteen forty-two, imagine! They were already rounding up folks at *métro* stations and shooting them dead whenever someone pulled a hair from a *Boche*'s head. No one could still pretend the Germans were cultivated little angels at that point. There's no excuse for what she did."

Madeleine leaned toward the side of the armchair farthest from Henri, as if a stench were emanating from him. "Yvonne's officer decided she'd sing in Germany," she said. "She went where he sent her. She had no choice in these matters."

"What my client means," Clément said, "is that she witnessed a wide range of behaviors during the Occupation, and while even that of Yvonne Chevallier can be explained in part by some mitigating circumstances, her own and that of her husband are irreproachable."

"You have to make an example out of Yvonne, not us," Henri said.

Madeleine took a long look at him. Was this the same man who had complimented Yvonne on her singing until he had used all the positive adjectives in the French language? Had he so little spine that he would throw Yvonne to the wolves to escape justice's wrath?

"She was already made an example," Madeleine said. "Have you seen her since the Free French shaved her hair? Her head was wrapped in a scarf when she came to the opera house to collect her last paycheck. She looked frightful."

"She was the face of collaboration," Henri said. "What did she expect?"

"She was doomed the moment the *Boches* took an interest in her," Madeleine said, her voice rising. "It must be bad enough for her to be branded a traitor when her own son fought with the Free French."

"Her own son who now wants nothing to do with her," Henri said.

"What makes you so sure?" Souchal asked.

Madeleine answered first. "He showed up at our doorstep a few days after Paris was liberated. He lives with us for now."

Henri leaned back in his armchair, looking smug. "Ask him whom to throw in jail."

Twenty-Two

February 1945

A guard led Yvonne into the courtroom. She looked older than her forty-one years in a shapeless gray prison uniform. Her hair had grown back. It was no longer obvious she'd had her head shaved, although she felt an invisible brand on her forehead. The official charge against her was treason, for singing Isolde in Berlin in late 1942 and then Brünnhilde in 1943 for the *Ring* cycle. Hitler had attended multiple times, to Yvonne's surprise but to no one else's, thankfully ignoring Yvonne and talking to his generals instead—jubilant after the victory in Kharkov, tense after the setbacks in Stalingrad, enraged once the Soviets had vanquished the German Sixth Army, but always insisting he'd win the war. Yvonne wished he'd never come.

Her lawyer, Sylvestre, was waiting for her at the defendant's table. He hunched in his chair in a cheap suit frayed at the wrists. Yvonne didn't know if he was good—if he even usually handled criminal cases—but Hélène hadn't found anyone else willing to represent her. Maybe he appreciated Yvonne's singing or maybe he liked Schiaparelli dresses for his wife. It didn't matter, as long as he got Yvonne out of jail. The dark cell, the damp air, the gibes of her cellmate, the guards who yelled all the time—everything about prison repulsed her. Some days she mouthed arias in her favorite operas from dawn to dusk as if it could prevent her from losing her mind. At other times she repeated the mad scene in *Lucia di Lammermoor* for hours on end, until her cellmate turned toward the wall and sang lullabies at the top of her lungs. Perhaps thanks to Sylvestre, Yvonne would be sentenced to time served, nothing else.

Spectators bundled in layers of coats and woolen scarves packed the courtroom. Paris was facing its harshest winter in years. The driver of the jail van taking Yvonne to her trial had marveled at the ice covering the Seine. Inside the courtroom, the air was so cold that Yvonne's breath made little clouds in front of her mouth.

The guard unfastened the handcuffs around Yvonne's wrists. The audience jeered.

"Nazi whore!" a woman yelled in the back.

"We should gas you too," a man shouted from the side.

The crowd lined the rows of wooden seats, hostile and menacing. Yvonne looked down at her feet. She wondered how often Klaus had given the order to send prisoners to Auschwitz or Treblinka, knowing full well what would happen to them there. She wondered, too, if staying with him until the *Libération* had made her complicit, if she shouldn't have grabbed a kitchen knife in the middle of the night and dug it into his throat, although she'd have had only a couple of hours to vanish before his goons rushed onto her trail.

She'd always postponed the moment to make a decision, and then when the Allied victory had become more and more certain, she'd focused on surviving one more day and waiting for the Free French, and then the decision had been made for her: she hadn't needed to stab Klaus nor put herself at risk. Now she regretted it.

"Let's burn her at the stake—that's all she deserves," a woman said behind Yvonne's back.

"Let's quarter her in front of city hall, if we can find horses for it."

The crowd murmured its approval. Attendees shook the wooden barriers that separated Yvonne from them. Would they lunge at her during the trial? She couldn't count on the guards to protect her if spectators decided to take her punishment into their own hands.

A woman in a faded red travel suit pushed her way through clusters of other attendees. Madeleine had shown up late, as always. Yvonne had never seen such gloom in her eyes. She doubted it was because of the trial.

"Don't stare," Sylvestre said.

A gentleman in the first row gave up his seat for Madeleine. "She was a colleague of yours, wasn't she, Madame Moreau? Here, I'll sit a few rows back."

Madeleine perched herself on the edge of the seat, not even looking satisfied that strangers still recognized her in public. Her gaze met Yvonne's. She looked appalled.

Behind Madeleine, spectators leaned forward, their faces tense with disgust at the person on trial. Concerned citizens, they would've called themselves. Honest French men and women who hoped to see justice rendered. Yvonne recognized a handful who'd frequented the German Institute with assiduity, gorging themselves on champagne and caviar and laughing at the bons mots of Nazi officers.

Jules wasn't there.

The four jurors who'd decide Yvonne's fate entered through a side door, stern and freshly shaven. They were all men, a young man Jules's age and three in their forties, their hands callused and their suits threadbare, working-class men uninclined to forgive Frenchwomen who'd cavorted with the Germans. Yvonne dreaded going to prison for years.

The new French administration had prosecuted public figures much more famous than her, traitors like Robert Brasillach, who'd published the hiding places of Jews in his newspaper. Brasillach had been condemned to death—a straightforward affair; the jury had deliberated for only twenty minutes—and now Yvonne sat in the same accused box.

"Send the trollop to the guillotine!" someone shouted.

Yvonne hadn't expected support from the crowd, but its hostility frightened her. Would the judge keep her in prison if the gallery opposed her release?

Sylvestre took a newspaper from his briefcase and shoved it across the table toward her. It was that morning's edition of the Communist journal *L'Humanité*. "I take it you haven't seen the headlines yet."

"Nazi camp of Birkenau," the headline began. Under it, pictures of men who stared at the camera behind barbed wire, so frail they looked like skeletons covered with skin. "A gigantic factory where death was manufactured," the headline continued.

In a heap, the naked corpses.

Yvonne dropped the newspaper to the ground and had to pick it up. She'd never tried to imagine what the extermination camps looked like. Those eyes in the pictures. The bones protruding under the flesh. She grabbed Sylvestre's arm. He pulled his arm away, looking distinctly unhappy to have taken on her case.

Sylvestre turned the newspaper facedown to hide the photographs. "Surely you understand what it means for you. Your friend was involved in this."

"He wasn't my friend," Yvonne said. "More like my tormentor."

She'd rummaged through Klaus's pockets at night, browsed through his letters, even snatched the key to his briefcase and peered through his notebooks while he slept, but he must've seen through her little scheme because she'd never found anything that could've helped the Free French, if she'd ever known how to reach them.

A woman spat at Yvonne from behind, the saliva sliding down her neck.

Yvonne wiped the spit off with her handkerchief, aware that everyone in the courtroom was looking at her. She was careful not to betray any emotion in case that set off more rancor, more invective, and perhaps a volley of objects thrown at her.

The judge stepped into the room in a long black robe like Don Curzio's costume in *The Marriage of Figaro*. Everyone rose to their feet. The court secretary asked Yvonne to stand up. She stated her name for the record. Yes, she understood the charges against her. Treason—it was what it sounded like. Betrayal of her country, disgrace, and dishonor.

Sylvestre had warned her the presiding judge might question her at length, as he was entitled to do in that part of the trial. But the judge showed no curiosity about Yvonne. His face was stonelike except for a glimmer of disdain in his eyes. Surely by now he'd listened to the testimonies of dozens of Frenchwomen in Yvonne's situation.

Next it was time for the prosecutor, a tall man with hollow cheeks who bore a definite resemblance to an undertaker, to call witnesses for his side. He shuffled through his papers. "First to speak is Jules Chevallier."

The blood drained from Yvonne's face. She hadn't seen Jules since that Sunday afternoon at the German Institute almost three years earlier when he'd been released from the Vél d'Hiv and disappeared to join the Free French. The door to the antechamber opened.

Military service had added muscle to Jules's arms. He seemed neither afraid nor embarrassed to testify against his mother. Instead, he displayed the easy stride of someone conscious of the importance of the moment and proud of doing the right thing for France. He kept his eyes on the judge while he crossed the room and, once on the witness stand, squarely faced the prosecutor. Not once did he make eye contact with Yvonne.

"Her first *Boche* gave her an apartment he stole from a Jewish family," Jules said. "She paraded with the second one at the German Institute. I'm sure you've seen the pictures. Those parties made the most decadent years of the Roman Empire look like Lent service in a Catholic nunnery."

Yvonne's cheeks burnt. The crowd hissed, rightfully so. Yvonne would've hissed too, if she'd sat among the spectators. Hunched in the press box, the journalists scribbled down every word Jules said. Why shouldn't they? He'd fought the war on de Gaulle's side. The aura of victory floated around him. Yvonne had tarnished France's honor.

Jules retreated to a wooden bench next to the box after his testimony. Yvonne expected the judge to give Sylvestre the floor, but the prosecutor didn't sit down.

"Calling Henri Moreau to the stand," he said with a smug smile.

Henri strode into the room, wearing a crisp business suit. The old resemblance to Clark Gable had returned, now that the war had ended. The audience fell silent. During the Occupation, newspapers had printed many pictures of him socializing with Nazis at the opera house. Parisians doubted his loyalty to France now, but they were eager to hear his statement about Yvonne more than they cared about his views of the Germans. Yvonne heard behind her the distinct sound of a fan snapped open.

The prosecutor paced the space between his table and the witness stand. "You worked extensively with the defendant during the war. Tell us what your experience was like."

"She got roles she wasn't qualified for," Henri said without hesitation, "and then we all had to help her so that her lover wouldn't get mad at us because she was so mediocre."

Yvonne tensed on her seat. Whatever she was, mediocre was not it.

Henri needed a moment to compose himself. "In this business, a few seasons are an eternity. Some singers will never enjoy the career they deserve because they were kept off the stage in those critical years." He spoke with a passion he'd never displayed off the podium. The calumnies hung in the air, inscribed into the court transcript for posterity.

"Did Madame Chevallier perhaps help some of the Jewish musicians employed at the opera house after the new laws threw them into the street?" the prosecutor asked.

Henri shook his head. "Believe me, I asked. She kept saying that nothing could be done. Who was she kidding? She could've used her authority to save many people." That was such an egregious lie. "Instead, she denounced an honest man."

What was he talking about? Yvonne had never denounced anyone.

Henri pressed his hands against the guardrail surrounding the witness's stand. "She threw to the wolves an Austrian tenor who was waiting in Marseilles for his visa to the United States. Stefan Kreismann, one of the greatest tenors of our generation, an artist of incredible musicianship, was sacrificed to Yvonne Chevallier's runaway ambition so that she'd stay in her *Boche*'s good graces. Can you seriously consider not giving the maximum to someone with such moral depravity?"

Yvonne glanced at Sylvestre and shook her head no, but Sylvestre didn't appear inclined to ever look at her again. She snatched Henri's Gestapo folder from under his notes. "Did you ever read this?"

Sylvestre avoided her gaze, as if to say she should consider herself lucky he'd shown up at her trial. Yvonne opened the folder and gave him the papers to read.

Henri was peering at the audience while he gauged the effect of his speech. The crowd murmured. He'd won them over.

Sylvestre scanned the documents as fast as he could. He clenched his fists, wrinkling the paper, when he reached the bottom of the last page.

The judge cleared his throat. "Does the lawyer for the defense desire to cross-examine the witness?"

For a moment it looked like Sylvestre wouldn't cross-examine Henri, but at last he pushed back his chair. "Monsieur Moreau," he said, "is the Austrian tenor you were talking about the same Stefan Kreismann who used to be your wife Madeleine's lover?"

The murmurs in the crowd stopped.

Henri's face turned red. "That's irrelevant."

Sylvestre brandished Henri's letter. "The same Stefan Kreismann you denounced to the Gestapo after learning that your wife Madeleine was trying to enlist the help of the American ambassador William Bullitt for his escape to the United States?" His voice boomed through the courtroom. A moment ago, Sylvestre had believed Henri, but now he'd realized his mistake.

Yvonne glanced over her shoulder. Madeleine kept her eyes on Henri, her forearms pressed against the wooden barrier that separated the crowd from the defendant and her lawyer, red fan dangling from her hand, so still that she resembled one of the statues on the roof of the Paris Opera. Behind her, the crowd elbowed each other and whispered.

Henri tried to scoff. "Accusing me of the crime I've just told the court your client committed—your theatrics are transparent."

Sylvestre held the letter high in the air, first toward Henri and then toward the crowd. "This is the letter you sent the Gestapo telling them where to find Monsieur Kreismann. It angered you that your wife had had an affair with him. You weren't supposed to know about it. In fact, you thought it was over after Monsieur Kreismann refused to leave his wife for yours, but when your wife begged the US ambassador to help him, you worried that the affair had never stopped, didn't you? And that eminent dignitaries like Monsieur Bullitt, whom you had hoped to impress, would understand she'd cheated on you."

The crowd shifted uneasily on their seats.

"You have more imagination than the best librettist, but that letter was forged," Henri said.

"This is only one of many damaging documents in your file," Sylvestre said.

Drops of sweat ran down Henri's temples, although the spectators in the room were still wearing their coats. "That only means the forgery is very good," he said.

"Is it a forgery," Sylvestre asked, "that you denounced one of the singers at the opera house for running a clandestine press at the opera house? You sent that singer to his death in the Gestapo basement."

In the back rows, a woman had to be carried out while the rest of the spectators waited for Henri's answer.

Yvonne glanced at Madeleine, who looked like she could've moved to New Zealand and not yet found herself far enough from Henri. The other spectators might doubt Yvonne, but Madeleine believed her.

"I haven't denounced anybody, and I don't know who has been using my name to destroy my colleagues, but my conscience is clean," Henri said.

"Your conscience is as clean as bedsheets in a brothel," Sylvestre said, brandishing the letter for the jury.

Someone in the back clapped their hand against the wooden bench.

"The defendant's lawyer can sit down if he is not going to ask any questions," the judge said.

Sylvestre held his hand up. He needed a moment more. "My client attempted to help Monsieur Kreismann at your wife's request, Monsieur Moreau, and when you found out, the prospect of your associates learning that your wife had cheated on you set you on a path of destruction. Now two men are dead: Monsieur Kreismann died in Auschwitz and Monsieur Truchet—the man who operated the press—at the hands of Gestapo officers here in Paris. Does that erase the humiliation of the affair, Monsieur Moreau?"

"Monsieur Moreau is not on trial here," the prosecutor said.

"He should be," Sylvestre said.

"Yvonne was jealous of my wife," Henri said.

"She didn't denounce your colleagues," Sylvestre said. "You did."

The dismay in the crowd grew.

Sylvestre raised the piece of paper higher. "My client isn't the traitor here. You are the one who betrayed your country, Monsieur Moreau."

At last, he sat down next to Yvonne. Henri stumbled out of the witness box and onto the bench next to Jules. Jules slid away from him.

"The accused will answer questions now," the judge said.

Sylvestre nudged Yvonne forward. It took her a moment to realize the judge was talking about her.

The prosecutor paced the floor in front of him, like a tiger ready to pounce. "Did you have an affair with Generalleutnant Hans-Hermann von Moderling?"

"Yes," Yvonne said. Her voice sounded strangled.

"Did you have an affair with Kriminaldirektor Klaus Koegel?"

"I didn't have much say in the matter."

"This is a yes-or-no question," the prosecutor said.

"Yes," Yvonne said.

"Quite a busy social schedule you had."

The crowd guffawed. For the spectators, it was a welcome moment of comic relief after the past few tense minutes. Yvonne sustained the prosecutor's gaze.

"Did you go to Germany in 1942 to sing *Tristan und Isolde*, first at the Berliner Staatsoper and then at military bases throughout the Third Reich?" the prosecutor asked.

"Again, I didn't have—"

"Madame Chevallier," the judge said, "if you keep answering yes-or-no questions by anything else than yes or no, you will be held in contempt of the court."

"Yes," Yvonne said.

"Did you publish an op-ed in *Paris-soir* following the bombing in Berlin, exhorting the French to be in solidarity with the Nazis against the Allies and deploring the German casualties and the damage—Nazis who, as I assume we all know by now, relentlessly exterminated millions of Jews?"

There was no point in explaining that Klaus's gun had been pointed at her head. "Yes," Yvonne said.

The crowd hissed again.

"At your return from Germany, did the newspaper *Le Temps* run an article on you, calling you, as a compliment, 'The face of collaboration'?"

Yvonne hadn't wanted to do it, but Klaus had decided it'd happen. Résistance efforts were intensifying all over Paris, and he wanted to show Parisians what a good example looked like. "Yes," she said.

The prosecutor raised his arms to the ceiling. "National dishonor is too weak a term to describe your behavior. We should deprive you of your citizenship. You don't deserve to call yourself French." He returned to his seat, his questioning of Yvonne finished.

Sylvestre stood up again. Yvonne shook her head no—she didn't want to talk any further. She didn't want him to make excuses for her, not after she'd seen the pictures at Birkenau.

Sylvestre then pleaded for her in vehement terms. Yvonne watched him pace the floor in front of her, waving his arms, but couldn't bring herself to listen to his words. It seemed so pointless: the energy in the crowd remained as hostile as before.

The jury took only a few minutes to deliberate. The four men filed back into the room without acknowledging Yvonne's presence.

"Guilty," the foreman said.

The judge looked down while he mulled things over.

"I sentence you to three years in jail," he finally said, and banged his gavel.

If the judge believed she'd denounced anyone, he should have condemned her to more, and if he believed she was innocent, he should've released her on the spot. Yvonne's consternation overwhelmed her. She'd hoped so much the judge would allow her to leave prison the same day, despite the odds.

Sylvestre gathered his belongings. Henri's folder still lay on the desk in front of him.

Madeleine, lurking behind them, snatched the folder before Sylvestre had a chance to stop her. She blinked repeatedly while she read. A prison guard snapped handcuffs around Yvonne's wrists. Already the spectators angled for better seats. Another trial would start soon. By the side door, Yvonne took one last look at Madeleine. Madeleine dumped the folder back into Sylvestre's arms and headed for the exit.

"Madeleine," Henri said when she strode past him.

Madeleine hastened by like Queen Marie-Antoinette riding in her carriage, indifferent to the clamor of the peasants.

The guard pulled Yvonne away. The gray corridors of the courthouse appeared to have gained a new brightness now that she knew she was returning to a damp cell in prison. Outside, the van was idling by the curb. Yvonne filled her lungs with fresh air. She would've stood on the sidewalk longer, enjoying her last minutes of freedom, but the guard pushed her into the van and slammed the door.

❧

Madeleine returned to her house with Jules but without Henri. Rose looked at her when she stepped in, seeming surprised not to see Henri, since they had all left the house together that morning, and then her gaze met Gustave's as he walked behind Madeleine. Rose did not ask any questions after that.

Madeleine took off her coat and gloves. "You may take the day off, Gustave," she said. "We won't need the car for the rest of the day."

"But Monsieur—"

"Monsieur can walk home."

Madeleine placed all the pictures of Henri facedown on the mantelpiece.

The phone rang. Madeleine barely registered it, but Jules did.

"Journalists have been calling," Rose said.

"Madeleine," Jules said.

"Give me a moment," Madeleine said. "I can't talk to the press just now."

Henri had sent two men to their death—what could she have to say about that? Of course, Stefan's death, and the role Henri had played in it, was agonizing. At least Madeleine could tell herself that perhaps Henri had been taken over by a fit of jealousy; perhaps he hadn't been thinking clearly when he sent the letter. Denouncing "Amfortas," though, was only a cold-blooded calculation to ingratiate himself with the Nazis.

"Get my husband's best suits into suitcases—cardboard boxes if you don't have anything else," Madeleine told Rose. "He'll be donating them to the Red Cross. Frenchmen returning from prisoner-of-war camps will appreciate his generosity, I'm sure."

She gestured at Jules. "And please pick a suit for yourself. Pianists always need good suits for their concerts."

❧

Henri had barely stepped into the house when the phone rang again. Madeleine moved her eyes but not her face to look at Henri. Sharing that man's bed again was impossible.

"People have been pushed off trains for less than what you did," Jules said. He was sitting across the phone from Madeleine.

"You're young," Henri said. "You don't understand the world." He opened the bottle of cognac.

Madeleine let the phone ring four times before she picked up. She listened to the person on the other end of the line and then hung up but scribbled something on a notepad. Jules read it sideways and made a mark on the back of a music score.

Henri glanced at Rose.

"Journalists," Rose said. "Madame writes down which newspaper it is. I think the young man is keeping a tally."

"That's ridiculous," Henri said. "Madeleine—"

"I don't speak to murderers," Madeleine said, her voice flat. She wasn't even trying to make it so. She had lost her ability to feel anything.

"I wish you'd sent Gustave back to fetch me at the courthouse," Henri said nonetheless. "I had to find a taxi—in this weather."

The phone rang again. This time Madeleine slammed the receiver down right after picking it up. "I wonder if Stefan got to leave for Auschwitz in a taxi."

"He was bound to be arrested," Henri said. "It's not my fault he was Jewish."

Madeleine snapped her fingers at Rose. "We'll be filling more boxes with Monsieur's personal effects. And please have Gustave check the attic for something that could serve as a sleeping bag or a tent for the garden."

"You're not serious," Henri said. "It's freezing."

Rose scurried upstairs. She came back with a cardboard box filled to the brim with men's clothes.

"Have you lost your mind?" Henri asked.

By then, the phone was already ringing again.

"The newspapers have been calling for hours, asking for my comments," Madeleine said. "I'm married to someone who sent two men to their death; what do I have to say about it?"

"They would've been arrested sooner or later," Henri said. "Who knows if it's even my letter that sent them east, or someone else's?"

The sun was setting early that time of year, and the living room had become dark. Henri turned on the lights. "The Germans' rules were clear. Those men broke the rules. They can't have been that surprised at their fate."

The phone rang. Madeleine picked up, listened for a moment. Then she articulated slowly into the receiver, her voice ice cold: "My husband wants you to know he thinks the people he denounced to the Gestapo can't have been that surprised at their fate. Please print it as is. Would you like me to repeat? Maestro Henri Moreau wants you to know he thinks the people he denounced to the Gestapo can't have been that surprised at their fate, because they broke the Nazis' rules and those rules were clear."

She hung up. Under the lamp, she could better see her reflection in the mirrors in the room. Her face was smudged with eyeliner and mascara, although she would never admit she had cried.

The phone rang almost immediately.

"My goodness, unplug that thing," Henri said.

Madeleine was developing a migraine from the incessant ringing, but she would not unplug the phone. "The journalists are asking good questions. I like listening to them, and sometimes I even know how to answer."

"You really should calm down," Henri said. "If we hadn't been married for so many years, I would—"

At that moment, Madeleine knew exactly what she would do, although it scared her. There weren't too many reasons to divorce according to the law: adultery, and she was the one who had done that; conviction of a serious crime, and he had not been convicted; and finally, cruelty. Yes, cruelty would work, given the circumstances. Any judge would agree with her. If she found a good lawyer, she might even keep most of their assets, because Henri would be keen on avoiding the publicity.

"Our marriage has come to an end," Madeleine said to Henri, and felt a bigger relief than she had in years.

Twenty-Three

Three years later
February 1948

Yvonne had braced herself for the moment she'd see the opera house again, and yet she forgot to exit the city bus when it pulled over near the century-old palace. The familiar gilded statues of Harmony and Poetry and the bronze bust of Beethoven entranced her. Parisians milled in front of the marble columns, next to billboards that didn't bear her name. She pressed her palm against the bus window. Was it nostalgia that twisted her stomach? Regret? A burning wish she'd known fame under different circumstances and her career hadn't come to an abrupt halt? Or simply the ache of realizing that a new generation of sopranos were now singing roles she'd hoped to make hers?

The bus jerked forward, and Yvonne jumped to her feet. The driver swore but let her out. On the sidewalk, she adjusted the black hat on top of her head. Her blonde hair had grown back to her shoulders and was now tied up into a perfect *chignon-banane*. She strode past announcements of upcoming performances. Henri's name jumped out at her. His career had sputtered in the year after the trial but regained momentum ever since. Parisians wanted to focus on rebuilding after the war, and the authorities had dropped all charges.

Yvonne crossed the street toward the artists' entrance, on the side of the Galeries Lafayette. Her hand shook when she pulled the door open. Would she ever step back onstage again? That dream had helped her stay sane in prison—three years of sharing a cell with a madwoman who had stabbed her neighbor to death in a robbery attempt. Every day Yvonne had recited an opera in her head, *Tosca*, *Bohème*. Sylvestre brought her scores every so often. Two years into her jail sentence she'd rehearsed her first Wagner arias since her arrest, but always in French, and never Isolde. That role reminded her of Bayreuth and Berlin—her past glory and her biggest shame. In prison she'd received no news of Jules, but Paul, whom she'd begged to write once a year about their son, insisted he was doing well. He'd graduated from the Paris Conservatory of Music the previous June. Paul hinted that he might abandon a career as a pianist to join a humanitarian organization, but also that powerful protectors believed a world that'd witnessed Nazism still benefited from his music. Yvonne had to read that sentence twice. She so wished she'd been able to hear Jules play.

She breezed past the security guard with the nonchalance of a long-time employee who expected the guard to let them through, if he bothered to look up from his newspaper. Her high heels echoed on the tiles. The same full-length mirror that she'd hurried past every day during the Occupation still hung against the back wall in a tarnished gilded frame. The handrail that Hans-Hermann had touched, and Klaus, and dozens of Nazi officers, stretched along the spiral staircase. One day Yvonne had been preparing for the 1944–1945 season at the opera house and the next day she'd vanished, yet the Paris Opera hadn't changed at all. The Opera's memory of her had been expunged without effort, like a page torn seamlessly from a novel, so that only the most attentive observer would muse over her absence.

On the top floor, seated in front of the director's office, the secretary folded her hands over the appointment book when Yvonne wandered in and refused to let her know whether Georges de Véricourt could spare a few minutes. Denise had worked for Emile during the war. Yvonne used to sashay past her desk on her way to discuss her next roles. Now Denise crouched over her papers, ready to drag Yvonne out if she took one more step. Two men were already waiting, seated in chairs lined against the walls, under photographs of recent productions. The older man looked like a manager and the younger man a singer. A baritone,

Yvonne decided, although she couldn't know without hearing him sing. They sipped from cups of coffee and ate tiny biscuits that Denise had placed on the saucer. Yvonne's stomach growled.

"I told you on the phone, Monsieur de Véricourt is busy," Denise said. "You shouldn't have come."

Yvonne lamented that Emile hadn't kept his job. He, and not Henri, had programmed French operas alongside German ones, treated his staff fairly, and refused to grovel at the *Boches'* feet. Sylvestre had even explained that he'd kept Jewish musicians on the payroll until the Vél d'Hiv, although they'd been forbidden to play in public. Yet because his wife had had an affair with a Nazi, his career hadn't survived the purges at the *Libération*. Yvonne remembered very little of Georges's behavior during the war except that he'd always agreed with Emile.

Denise stood up to prevent Yvonne from reaching Georges's door. Two male voices drifted from his office.

"I only need a minute," Yvonne said. "I'll sing eight bars for him and I'll leave."

"He doesn't have a minute," Denise said. "Not for you, anyway."

Yvonne perched herself on the edge of a chair, handbag on her lap. "If he doesn't want to see me, he should tell me in person."

"Does it really matter if he throws you out himself?" Denise asked without showing any interest in the answer.

"Yes, it does," Yvonne said.

Denise slid a sheet of paper in her typewriter. "You're going to be here a while."

Yvonne and the two other visitors rose to their feet when Georges flung open the door to his office. He was so tall his head grazed the doorframe.

"*Aida* in two years, then, and *Turandot* the year after that," he said to the short bespectacled man who accompanied him. "We can't afford both the same season, no matter what our star says."

Georges wore a silk tie and a gray suit of the best fabric, a definite upgrade to his wardrobe since his days as Emile's right-hand man. What had changed the most about him was his stride. He marched forward now like a man who expected the Red Sea to part in front of him to let him pass.

Yvonne blocked Georges's way.

At first he didn't recognize her, and when he did, he smoothed his silk tie with his thumb instead of greeting her. "They certainly release the worst criminals these days." He stepped around Yvonne and accompanied the bespectacled man to the door. "Your client has got to commit to *Aida* now. Make sure she understands that."

Yvonne extended her arm when he turned around. He didn't shake her hand. Instead he signed a piece of paper that Denise held out for him.

"I still sing better than anyone on your roster," Yvonne said.

Georges peered at the appointment book on Denise's desk. He tapped on a name. "Move him to four o'clock. I don't think I'll be back in time."

Denise handed him a folder and pointed at the two seated men. They were next.

"I didn't denounce Stefan Kreismann," Yvonne said. "Henri did."

Georges tucked the folder under his arm. "Stefan Kreismann isn't the problem. Your serial Nazi lovers are. Your singing for Hitler is. Don't come here again."

How to make him understand that she couldn't pinpoint the moment where she'd made the wrong choice, short of not going to Bayreuth in 1939? That would've meant never singing onstage, never sharing her talent with the world. Georges was right to be mad at her, and yet she cherished the memories of the applause.

"Madeleine took my side, didn't she?" Yvonne asked. "That's why she no longer sings when Henri conducts." Madeleine's face at the end of the trial, when she had deciphered Henri's signature at the bottom of the letter, was etched in Yvonne's mind.

"Madeleine stopped singing altogether," Georges said. "She had no interest in it after Stefan Kreismann's death. You may have heard that she divorced Henri."

Good for her.

"Yet you're letting him conduct the orchestra when he caused a man's death," she said.

Georges strode to his office door without looking at Yvonne. "You're bitter that your time in the limelight was so short. Out, now."

He disappeared into his office. The baritone and his manager didn't even acknowledge Yvonne when they followed him inside. Denise smirked, that little mouse with glasses.

Yvonne stepped back until she felt the doorknob pressing against her spine, then slunk outside. So, no Paris Opera for her ever again. Maybe she could sing in Lyons or Brussels under her maiden name. She hurried down the spiral staircase to the first floor. She shouldn't lose faith, although Raymond had dumped her from his roster. He refused to deal with the backlash when—not if—a rival of Yvonne's reminded the public that French courts had once found her guilty of betraying her country. She couldn't blame him. She couldn't blame anyone but herself.

Outside, a newsboy shouted the headlines of the afternoon papers. The wind was blowing hard, chasing an empty paper bag in front of the Galeries Lafayette. Yvonne tottered along the side of the opera house, past the main entrance, across the street. Ladies enjoyed a cup of tea by the bay windows of the restaurant on the corner. A gentleman in a tailored suit of the best fabric stepped out of a cab. Behind him, the butler of the five-star Opéra hotel hoisted the man's suitcases out of the trunk. Yvonne pressed her hand against the stone wall of the hotel. What would she do if she couldn't sing again?

Someone was playing Johann Sebastian Bach in the hotel lobby, the music drifting through the revolving door. Yvonne had often listened to Bach as a teenager in Dijon: his partitas, his cantatas, and of course the Brandenburg Concertos. She pushed the hotel door open.

The pianist, his back turned to the glass doors, played under an outsize crystal chandelier. A linen suit hung loosely on his shoulders—a summer suit, out of season. He'd slid a wooden cane under the piano bench. Large mirrors multiplied his likeness tenfold. Yvonne hovered near an armchair among travelers in expensive outfits. Two read the *International Herald Tribune*, one scribbled notes in a pocketbook. A lady wrote a missive in large, round letters, like a schoolgirl. They paid the Bach partitas no attention, didn't seem even to appreciate their difficulty. Near the soloist, on the edge of the gleaming Érard piano, a cap placed upside down for tips lay empty except for one five-franc coin.

Yvonne's gaze drifted back to the musician. She stood to his side now and could glimpse his face. She always enjoyed watching performers play.

It was Charles-Antoine.

She had to sit down. He wore his gray hair cropped short and his cheeks had hollowed, but it was Charles-Antoine all the same.

After she'd collected herself, she stumbled toward him across the marble tiles. Charles-Antoine, alive! He glanced at her when she came near. One second he was swinging left and right on the bench along with the music, and the next his eyes blazed with such rage that Yvonne didn't come closer. She waited until he finished his piece.

"I hadn't dared hope you—" Yvonne said at last.

Charles-Antoine raised his hands from the keyboard. He didn't say a word when he looked at her.

A pretty brunette in a fur coat dropped him a coin and sashayed away as if she expected the other patrons to break into cheers at her generosity. Her high heels clattered through the lobby and onto the sidewalk. How insulting for Charles-Antoine's talent to be rewarded with so little.

The silence dragged on. The front-desk clerk scowled at Yvonne. His eyes looked large behind his round glasses, like a fish's. But the hotel guests, engrossed in their conversations and their readings, appeared oblivious that the pianist had stopped playing.

Charles-Antoine flipped the page of the score to the next partita.

"I know I didn't do enough," Yvonne said.

Charles-Antoine pressed his fingers on the keys. The music dissolved in a heap of discordant notes. A gentleman in a tweed jacket stared at him over the front page of his newspaper.

"You didn't do anything," Charles-Antoine said. "Not even speaking out. Especially not speaking out. It would have required of you an integrity that you do not possess."

Yvonne rummaged through her purse, offered Charles-Antoine a silver coin—ten francs.

Charles-Antoine swatted her arm away. "You think that all can be
forgotten because you served your time. But I saw people treated worse
than animals and dropped into mass graves. You can't just waltz in
here and hope a bit of spare change will compensate for your lack of
conscience."

Yvonne threw her coin into the cap on top of the piano anyway.
Hotel guests gazed at her. A couple dressed in the latest fashion crossed
the lobby and, noticing the attention on Yvonne, looked her up and
down, as if they'd expected to find a movie star. But no successful
actress would've worn such modest clothes. They strolled away.

Charles-Antoine shrugged but didn't fish the coin out of the cap
to give it back to Yvonne. Instead, he began to play Chopin. The piece
required rapid left hand runs at the beginning of the rondo and simulta-
neous pedal trills. For a moment, Yvonne thought he'd forgotten about
her.

"I played that piece to the camp commander the first evening I
arrived at Auschwitz," he said while giving hotel guests a performance
worthy of the most exclusive recital halls, to their absolute indifference.
"When I noticed that the guards were separating men fit for hard work
from everyone else, I told one of them I could give music lessons to
officers' children. The camp commander didn't care for the piano, but
he liked the idea of impressing his colleagues if his own kids knew Liszt
and Chopin."

A group of travelers strolled in from the street. It seemed to please
them that they stayed at a hotel where a musician played in the lobby.
Yet they didn't leave a tip.

"Why didn't you get your job back at the Conservatory?" Yvonne
asked.

"When you see what people are capable of doing to each other, you
lose interest in teaching their progeny," Charles-Antoine said.

"I want to help," Yvonne said.

Charles-Antoine lifted his hands from the keyboard. "Just go."

But only two coins glittered inside the cap left upside down on the piano, and one of them was Yvonne's. "Let me help you make money," Yvonne said. "Tosca. 'Vissi d'arte.'"

Charles-Antoine pressed his lips tightly together.

"Allow me to do this one thing for you and I'll leave," Yvonne said.

Charles-Antoine reluctantly placed his fingers on the piano keys. For a while he did not move. At last he played the first few notes of music, and Yvonne's voice rose toward the chandeliers. "*Vissi d'arte, vissi d'amore, non feci mai male ad anima viva!*" The words came to her easily, as if she'd practiced them that very morning. She reached the notes without strain. How she'd missed being Tosca, worrying about the fate of her beloved Cavaradossi. How she'd missed being anyone who wasn't herself. Heads turned.

When she was done, Yvonne held out the cap for hotel guests to fill.

"You can't do that here," the front-desk clerk said. He looked embarrassed for the patrons but not for the musicians. Yet patrons reached for their purses and wallets. The cap quickly filled up, patrons outdoing each other in leaving a big tip. Yvonne had to hold it with both hands.

Yvonne handed the cap to Charles-Antoine. The hem near the visor threatened to break from the weight of the coins. "We'll get even more if I sing in French."

Charles-Antoine ran his fingers through the coins. "Have you had news from Jules?" His voice had softened.

Yvonne became still when she heard her son's name.

"I saw a billboard on the subway," Charles-Antoine said. "He's giving a recital at Salle Pleyel next month, with a special appearance by one Madeleine Moreau."

⤳

The rustling of evening gowns in the parterre was heard all the way into the wings, thanks to the acoustics in the famous Salle Pleyel. Madeleine had learned not to let that distract her. Onstage, Jules was playing Poulenc like a god. The parterre was dark, but Madeleine, in her decades as a performer, had learned to estimate crowds from the captivated silence that emanated from the seats. She bet that the house was full except for a few seats in the nosebleed section.

Jules ended the nocturne with a flourish. Hollers resounded through the hall. The audience had showered Jules with applause the entire evening—seven short pieces before the intermission and five afterward—and after each one Jules had seemed relieved that he had won their approval, as if there had ever been any doubt. Finally, he got up from the piano bench and bowed. His success delighted Madeleine.

Jules sat back at the piano and prepared to accompany Madeleine in "Mes longs cheveux descendent" from *Pelléas et Mélisande*.

Only the first two rows in the auditorium emerged from the darkness when Madeleine took her spot in front of the Steinway. They were considered good seats for laypeople who sought to see the artists up close, or had snatched a ticket at the last minute, but unworthy of music connoisseurs. The latter would prefer huddling about ten rows back, where voice and instrumentation best blended together. Madeleine didn't normally give the spectators in the first rows any attention. Yet someone there stared at her with such intensity that she had to look. When she did, her heart stopped for a beat. Yvonne was there, next to Charles-Antoine, whom Madeleine had believed dead.

Jules, already seated at the piano, hadn't noticed Yvonne. Madeleine did not draw his attention to her. It was his big day, after all. She did not want to distract him. When she turned to give Jules the signal, she only let him see her most radiant smile.

Madeleine sang Mélisande's aria competently yet not particularly well—her voice showed signs both of age and alcohol, and she could no longer hold the notes with ease—but the crowd clapped wildly at the end, as if this were the greatest example of musicianship they had ever been privileged to hear.

Madeleine returned to the wings while Jules concluded the program with a fugue by Maurice Ravel. He played better than Alfred Cortot, better than Claudio Arrau, better than any pianist Madeleine had ever listened to. Her gaze kept drifting to Yvonne, who stared at Jules from her seat while he played. Spectators jumped to their feet after the last note. Jules bowed again and again. Yvonne herself gave him a standing ovation, but because everyone else was applauding madly, he did not notice her.

Madeleine popped onto the stage for a last curtain call and pointed at Yvonne with her eyes. Jules would not have seemed more shocked if the ghost of King Louis XIV had wandered into the audience. At last he looked again at the rest of the public, who were cheering wildly. His smile, so genuine a moment ago, now appeared forced. He strode into the wings.

"I refuse to talk to her," he said.

"But maybe you'll want to talk to Charles-Antoine," Madeleine said.

Jules leaned back on his heels, incredulous and then hopeful. Madeleine knew how much it tormented him that he had not been sent to Auschwitz when Charles-Antoine had gone. They had both assumed he'd died there, selected for the gas chambers as soon as he had stepped out of the cattle train or starved to the point of collapse on labor detail. Perhaps seeing him alive after the ordeal would alleviate some of Jules's guilt.

༄

Yvonne and Charles-Antoine had been waiting only a few minutes on the rue du Faubourg Saint-Honoré with the rest of Jules's admirers when he and Madeleine stepped out. Young women smitten by Jules's brilliance and elderly couples who gushed about his virtuosic playing crowded him. Madeleine lingered to the side, letting him enjoy the moment. Yvonne should've been standing behind Jules. They could have made music together. Now Jules was working with Madeleine.

Jules signed programs briskly, in the same illegible scribble that Madeleine used to autograph her pictures.

Near the streetlamp, Charles-Antoine observed Jules. When Madeleine saw him, she laughed a small, strangled cry that sounded like she was swallowing back tears.

Jules stopped signing programs and gingerly stepped toward Charles-Antoine. He stood in front of him without a word, resolutely avoiding Yvonne's gaze.

"I wish I'd gone with you east," Jules said. "Still kick myself for it."

"That would have been a waste of your talent," Charles-Antoine said. "I've seen too many people die in the camps to be wide-eyed about the matter."

Madeleine leaned against the stone wall, under the *Salle Pleyel* banner that stretched along the height of the building. Any mention of the camps reminded her of Stefan. What had happened to Ilse? Madeleine had no information about her.

"I can find you another job if you need one," Madeleine told Charles-Antoine after she'd collected herself. "And I am happy to lend you money."

Charles-Antoine shook his head.

"He plays the piano at the Opéra hotel," Yvonne said. "Find something better."

Jules visibly stiffened at his mother's voice.

"I am opening a music school," Madeleine said. She was still talking to Charles-Antoine. "Would you like to be my accompanist? Jules's career will keep him busy with other things."

"My heart isn't in it anymore," Charles-Antoine said.

"You won't have to teach. Just play," Madeleine said.

"You say that now, but you'll quickly lose interest in teaching," Charles-Antoine said with half a smile. "In your master classes you mostly tell students to watch you sing. Weekly lessons won't be any better. You'll get frustrated when students don't make progress. Of course I'd have to take over the teaching, and I'm too tired for it."

"I could teach for you," Yvonne said to Madeleine.

Madeleine looked at her as if the years in prison had made Yvonne lose her sense of reality.

"I can teach under my maiden name," Yvonne said quickly. "I can be your assistant. I won't even call myself a teacher, and when you get tired of instructing students, you can just sit there and I'll do all the work."

Charles-Antoine remained silent. Yvonne could tell he wasn't sure what to make of it. She couldn't blame him; she wasn't sure what to make of it herself. She'd just come up with it on the spur of the moment, but she'd never taught. Many artists became mediocre instructors, because by the time they reached the point in their career where they were considering a reconversion, their craft had become second nature for them and they couldn't explain how they made the magic happen. Why would Yvonne be different?

Jules stepped between Yvonne and Madeleine, his eyes firmly on the latter. "You'll put your own reputation at risk, helping someone like her."

Yvonne couldn't stand the sharpness in his voice. "But she'll never find someone more loyal to her school," she said.

"You could give her a chance," Charles-Antoine said in a low voice. "She may surprise you."

Madeleine looked at him with imploring eyes, as if to beg him not to make it more difficult for her to reject Yvonne's proposal. Jules was right; even Yvonne saw that. So, no Paris Opera and no teaching opera either. Her own son had turned into a stranger. There was no point in staying in Paris. She'd move to a city where no one knew her and take a job as a store clerk, selling shoes or handbags or perfume.

She turned around and strode down avenue Hoche in the cold, trying not to think about never leaving her son for good when she hadn't seen him in years but incapable of thinking about anything else. She'd lost him a long time ago, if she was honest with herself. She kept hoping he'd run after her, saying he'd spoken too harshly, but there was only silence behind her. She was completely alone now.

Ahead, the Arc de Triomphe was lit in the distance. She recognized the forged-iron sign of the *métro* station. Line 1 to Les Halles, Line 4 to Château d'Eau. Soon she'd reach Hélène's apartment. She'd pack that very night and tell her thank-you the next morning and then tell her goodbye. She didn't know what she would've done if Hélène hadn't let her live with her family while she tried to earn a living. Hélène had told her young children that Yvonne had spent many years traveling through South America and had only recently returned to France. They kept asking her questions about Buenos Aires that she didn't know how to answer. After tomorrow, she wouldn't need to worry about that.

A clattering of heels followed Yvonne. Madeleine caught up with her as they reached the *métro* station. "Maybe you can assist me for a bit," Madeleine said. "I could use someone to help me teach."

Epilogue

A teenage boy singing the tenor part in the Act I duet of *Lucia di Lammermoor* flailed his arms in front of Yvonne while he pledged himself to his beloved. Next to him, a soprano not older than twenty pretended that only death could quench her passion. They were standing in Madeleine's living room. Charles-Antoine accompanied them at the piano and Yvonne marked the tempo. In an armchair, Madeleine listened distractedly while she jotted down notes for her memoirs. Her living room itself was larger than Yvonne's new apartment near Place de la Nation, not far from the neighborhood she used to live in with Paul. Yvonne had been making enough money from her lessons to move out of Hélène's in July 1949, but nothing she could afford would ever compare to Madeleine's living quarters: a three-bedroom penthouse on rue Tronchet where Madame Moreau, as she liked to call herself, could both receive students and store the many mementos she hoarded from her glory days. The apartment was sparsely decorated. Besides large photographs of Madeleine onstage and recordings of her most famous roles on the Victrola, most of the art in the room happened at the Steinway. Madeleine had wrestled it from Henri thanks to a very capable divorce lawyer.

The students strove relentlessly to outshine each other, forging their way through the score like two bulldozers on tracks that never intersected. The tenor, Simon, had entered the Conservatory that September. The soprano, Nora, was in her second year of study. At school they were viewed as promising but not at the top of their class.

Yvonne interrupted Simon mid-aria. "Don't reach for higher notes than what's in the score. Instead, react to what Nora says. People go and see operas to feel big feelings. Focus on what you want the audience to feel when they hear you."

Simon looked displeased. "What do you think, Madame Moreau?"

Both he and Nora had started taking lessons only a few weeks earlier, and Yvonne hadn't yet had a chance to prove herself to them. Madeleine had promised that she would teach them herself once they'd improved, but she insisted Yvonne was most suited to instruct them at their current level. Madeleine stood up nonchalantly and opened the window by two inches. Yvonne had noticed she liked to keep her apartment's windows ajar in the spring, perhaps to remind her neighbors that something special was happening there. Everyone in the building must know they lived near the most famous soprano of the last fifty years.

Madeleine graced Simon with an even smile. "When you win auditions, you'll be glad you listened to Yvonne's advice." She went back to scribbling notes.

Yvonne was grateful for her support, although she wished she hadn't needed it. She signaled to Charles-Antoine to resume playing. It was Nora's turn.

"Careful with your breath," Yvonne said. "Inhale through your nose here, and here." She made marks on the girl's score.

Nora nodded, eager to follow Yvonne's advice. Her voice was lovely if her lines were short, but she struggled with breath control in longer phrases. Yet she practiced all the leading roles of the repertoire. Her technique didn't quite match her ambition, but Yvonne could work with her on that.

"Your throat will get dry if you keep doing it that way," Yvonne said.

Nora looked like she didn't know how else to breathe and was upset to have that flaw pointed out to her.

"Why don't you sing it?" Madeleine asked Yvonne without looking up.

Yvonne feared the students would recognize her if she sang. But maybe her singing would help them, and she deserved any reproach they directed at her.

Her voice rose effortlessly over the piano notes, as if she'd never left the stage of the Paris Opera. *"Veranno a te sull'aure I miei sospiri ardenti . . ."* It wasn't the same when she practiced by herself at home in front of a secondhand Érard baby grand. How she'd missed enchanting listeners in performance. A smile bloomed on her lips when she finished.

"You're Yvonne Chevallier, the collaborator," Nora said. "No one else has that voice."

"The singer who went to prison?" Simon spat out the last word. He glared at Madeleine. "You didn't tell us that."

"If you don't want her to teach you, you can get voice lessons elsewhere," Madeleine said.

It was easy for Madeleine to be magnanimous. Jules wrote her, not Yvonne, from every city he passed through on his tour, describing the public's acclaim and sending along glorious reviews from the most seasoned music critics. But at least Madeleine passed on his letters, and in those moments, Yvonne could've followed Madeleine to the most forsaken lands.

"Who's going to hire us when they hear we studied with her?" Simon asked.

"You're studying with me," Madeleine said.

Simon closed his score.

Before the war, no one would've disrespected Madeleine. Yvonne waited for her to show Simon the door.

Madeleine stood up. "Let's sing the 'Mira, o Norma' duet," she said to Yvonne. "You'll be Adalgisa. I'll be Norma."

Yvonne collected herself. She hadn't sung that duet in a long time. But Charles-Antoine was already waiting for her, fingers hovering over the keyboard. He gave her a friendly nod, apparently certain she'd remember the part once the music started. Yvonne's palms became sweaty, yet the notes flew out of her lips as soon as he began to play. In a moment she became the young priestess Adalgisa, racked with guilt because she'd seduced the father of Norma's children—Norma the high priestess of the druids, who'd taught her everything. *"Mira, o Norma,"* she began, *"ai tuoi ginocchi questi cari tuoi pargoletti!"* She was Adalgisa now, just from the look on her face and a movement of her hand. The words came out clearly, her diction precise, her voice just as silky as during the war. A sparkle lit up in Nora's eyes. Simon took a step forward as if a siren's song were calling him.

Madeleine inhaled. *"Ah! Perché la mia costanza vuoi scemar con molli affetti?"* She'd obviously practiced her scales that morning. Yvonne welcomed the challenge. She liked feeling part of something bigger than herself, creating art she could not make alone.

Nora and Simon listened spellbound. The joy of performing in public turned Madeleine's cheeks pink and filled Yvonne with delight. Yvonne grabbed Madeleine's hand. Their voices soared. They hit the last note in unison.

Outside, a passerby clapped.

Author's Note

I first learned about French soprano Germaine Lubin fifteen years ago, when I came across a photograph of her sitting at Adolf Hitler's feet. That photograph had been taken during the 1939 Bayreuth Festival in Germany, where Lubin sang Isolde and Hitler himself called her an enchantress. I asked myself how an accomplished French singer could have let herself get caught in such a compromising position when war with Germany was brewing. A similar photograph ended up playing a key role for the main protagonist in my novel.

Later, I learned more biographical details about Lubin: a star student at the Paris Conservatory of Music, already forty-nine when the war broke out, the best Wagnerian soprano of her generation, so famous for her rendition of Isolde that to this day it is possible to find recordings of it—but also someone with a complicated personal life: divorced at a young age from a poet at a time when divorces were rare, mother of a son who was sent to the front and became a prisoner of war, and the mistress of a German officer during the Paris Occupation.

Lubin met her comeuppance after the war: she was imprisoned at first and then released but forbidden to live in France for several years. She hoped to resume her career on international opera stages, but public outcry thwarted her attempts. Instead, she became a distinguished voice teacher and lived quay Voltaire, in the building where my main protagonist, to her dismay, is gifted an apartment by her Nazi lover.

Germaine Lubin would make a great character in a novel, I thought when I first learned about her.

But upon reading her memoirs, I realized that Lubin would in fact make a very mediocre one, because she—to the best of my knowledge—never expressed regret for associating with the Nazis, on the grounds that she had never denounced anybody and had only wanted to sing. Instead, she complained that her punishment after the war had curtailed her career. She was, so to speak, a flat and two-dimensional character, focused on her singing and rather indifferent to the turmoil around her, although she supposedly demanded her gardener's release after the Nazis arrested him. The gardener died in a concentration camp anyway.

While Germaine Lubin herself may not have been a suitable novel heroine, I wondered: what would make good people compromise themselves for their art, little by little, until they were irremediably associated with mass murderers? I imagined such a trajectory for my protagonist, Yvonne Chevallier. Like Germaine Lubin, she was tall and blonde, and the divorced mother of a son, but younger than Lubin when the war broke out and completely unknown. Then I assigned Lubin's approximate age and fame to the woman Yvonne hoped to surpass: the opera star Madeleine Moreau. I gave Madeleine the character arc that I wished on Germaine Lubin when she ruled over the Paris Opera.

I came across many interesting stories while I researched the book. For instance, the director of the Paris Opera, who in real life was named Jacques Rouché, did help Jewish orchestra musicians survive after new laws forced them off the payroll. In Germany, Franz von Hoesslin, who conducted the 1939 production of *Tristan und Isolde* at the Bayreuth festival, was trying to stay in the Nazis' good graces because his second wife was Jewish. Tenor Max Lorenz was a real, celebrated singer with a Jewish wife. Theirs may have been a marriage of convenience: she knew of his homosexuality. When he had to appear in court because of an affair with another man, Winifred Wagner saved his career. He sang Tristan opposite Germaine Lubin in Bayreuth in 1939, to superlative acclaim.

Later in the novel, one of my protagonists is suspected by a Gestapo officer to be distributing pro-Résistance leaflets through Paris. A French art historian named Agnès Humbert did indeed leave such leaflets in public spaces as part of a Résistance network called the Museum group. After the network members got caught, the men were executed and the women sent to Germany, where they toiled away in factories.

It is not known if Germaine Lubin ever heard of Agnès Humbert or the Museum Résistance network during the Occupation, nor if she did, what she thought of them.

Acknowledgments

I would like to thank my agent, Betsy Amster, for believing in this novel from the moment she read its opening paragraph, promptly reviewing the many revisions I sent her, offering excellent, detailed feedback every time, and helping this book find its perfect home at Alcove Press. I feel truly lucky to have her as my agent. I am also extremely grateful to my editor, Holly Ingraham, for her outstanding suggestions that have significantly improved the manuscript and her overall enthusiasm regarding this project.

Next, my sincere appreciation goes to my publicist, Angela Melamud, and the entire team at Alcove Press—especially editorial and design associate Rebecca Nelson and production and editorial assistant Thaisheemarie Fantauzzi Pérez—as well as cover designer Lynn Andreozzi, for creating a cover that perfectly captures my book, and copy editor Rachel Keith, whose sharp eye was exceptionally helpful at several points in the manuscript.

Many thanks also go to Robert Eversz, Lynn Hightower, Jane Cavolina, and Jane Rosenman for their thoughtful comments on earlier versions of this novel. I am particularly indebted to Robert Eversz, who was my first instructor at the Writers' Program at UCLA Extension, for his encouragement when I did not know if my pages could ever become a published book. I am also very grateful to the other writers I met at UCLAx, especially Darren Nebesar. More recently, I have been tremendously blessed to find a cohort of exceptional writers at the Bennington Writing Seminars.

Finally, I would like to thank my parents, who believed in me from the start.